The Boy and the Hunter

A Novel
by Jorge Luis Rojas

**Demons and Wolves,
Book 1**

For CP, MC, CZ and MP.
I'm sorry.

Part One

It had been an unusually cold spring in the town of Adler, Minnesota. Nobody could explain why, but the chilly breeze and dry air of winter didn't seem to be going away at the slightest, even though it was almost April. Adler was a small town that didn't suffer from problems like giant snowstorms or dangerously high levels of precipitation, but having such cold winds that required the wearing of scarfs at this time of the year wasn't particularly common or appreciated.

Still, the minuscule population of around 5,000 people lived a happy, calm life, away from the stress of big cities and the crime and traffic that usually came with them. There were only two high schools, of which Jefferson High School was closest to the forest right next to Adler, allowing its students to enjoy occasional hikes with their biology or natural sciences teachers, where they would go and look at the flora and fauna that gave life to the woods. With the increasingly strange cold, however, the students at Jefferson hadn't visited the forest since early October.

It was a sharp breeze that plagued Adler that year. After a dramatically abnormal fall and a very punishing winter, most of the citizens of Adler were hoping for a calm, semi-warm spring to let the seasonal stress go. Instead, they got some of the most frustrating weather conditions most citizens hadn't seen in years, making schools cancel events and trips, and limiting outside activities to walking under various layers of clothing from one place to another. The forest next to Adler – officially called the Adler Natural Conservation Preserve, though not even government officials called it that – seemed to be getting the most damage from this winter's extension, as trees hadn't had the opportunity to fully regrow their leaves after winter, nor were they cold enough to remain leafless. Seeing this, most of the taller vegetation in the forest had a leafage alike the one usually seen by the very end of the summer.

Nevertheless, the high volume of trees that had grown in the preserve had made its vegetation very dense, even without its full leafage. The very dense forest seemed to be getting darker with each day's passing, with less and less sunlight getting through its thick vegetation. The citizens of Adler knew that the forest wasn't really a dangerous place to wander during the day, but you can't never be too careful when you're alone. The forest spread for hundreds of miles, with some modern roads inside of it for people to commute to the Twin Cities, which were only an hour away on a good day.

In the past twenty or so years, there had been two of those strange cases were any danger came from the forest. One of them involved a teenage girl, Harriett Miller, who had disappeared from her parents' house without leaving any trace. After a week, the police found Harriett living in the forest, half naked, starving, and with bruises all over her arms and legs. It turned out that Harriett was in the early stages of schizophrenia, and the voices in her head made her escape to the forest, fortunately, instead of damaging herself or her family.

The other case was the famous disappearance of brothers Scott and Arthur Cormac, 9 and 11, respectively. According to their mother, they had gone out to play in the backyard and suddenly disappeared after less than a quarter of an hour. As a widow, Mrs. Cormac was suspected of double infanticide immediately after the investigation was opened, but thanks to a decent lawyer and all the witnesses he could get, Mrs. Cormac was left alone almost as fast as she was persecuted. Not two days passed when the police received a call from a citizen, reporting that he had seen two boys of around the right age running around at the edge of the forest, looking worried and hurt. Soon after, the police rescued the Cormac brothers from the hands of a couple of drug addicts that kidnapped them and were planning to ask for ransom.

Apart from those two very infamous cases, the forest and its surroundings were considered extremely peaceful, almost to the point of being boring. The only thing you could hear at night were crickets and frogs making their usual sounds, and once in a while the occasional wolf howl. All of these animals were very afraid of the unnatural lights and sounds of humans, so it was practically unheard of for wolves, snakes, or dangerous insects to be seen outside of the woods.

The roads that passed along the forest line were all well lit and properly maintained, courtesy of the excellent job from the Mayor's office, who was re-elected the previous year and had, so far, seen unanimous approval from the citizens of Adler. However, it had been years since a car accident was reported that didn't involve a mere problem with the car's battery or engine.

That's why it was extremely weird for Park Ranger Alan Maffei to get a call late at night on a Tuesday, reporting a very gruesome and strange accident on the road near Adler, about two miles away. Maffei grabbed his hat, his keys, and got out of his office and into the car, and drove to where he was ordered to.

The road was completely deserted as Maffei drove away from the town. It was a school night, of course, so parents and children were all in bed by then. The few people that would be awake at that time – namely, those in pubs or clubs – where still indoors, so there was no reason Maffei could think of for somebody to be involved in a big accident at this time at night, and in this cold.

Maffei, in his early thirties and with a clear lack of rest thanks to his newborn son, was not too excited about investigating a crash on a Tuesday night. He thought it inconvenient – even ridiculous – that somebody would crash on an empty road in the middle of the forest. Just thinking about having to get out of his car with the cold breeze of post-winter made Maffei reconsider all of his life choices up to that point.

After driving two miles without seeing anything but the empty road and the light posts that brightened it, Maffei got eyes on what seemed to be a car; it wasn't on fire, nor crashed. The blue sedan, parked right under a light post, had its emergency lights blinking on and off, so Maffei decided to park behind it and get out to investigate. As soon as he opened the door, the extreme cold breezed his nose and made him moan in pain, feeling like if his nose was slowly freezing.

With his face covered with a scarf, Maffei got out and closed the car door, flashlight in his right hand, pointing at the car. As he got closer, he grew increasingly annoyed at seeing there were no signs of a crash or an accident of any sort. Until he walked close enough to see the windshield.

Maffei gasped in surprise when he saw the broken windshield, as if the car's driver had jumped from their seat to the road through the front of the car. Maffei could see some traces of blood on the glass, but nothing to see on the floor in front of the car. The officer called on his radio.

"Dispatch, this is Officer Alan Maffei, responding to a report about a car crash outside of Adler. Over." He released the button and waited for an answer, but heard nothing. "Dispatch, this is Officer Maffei responding to an emergency report. Over." Nothing.

Maffei put down the radio and kept inspecting the windshield. There were several glass shards all over the hood, but no signs of anything else. No signs of the car hitting anything, and no marks on the road to indicate an abrupt brake.

Maffei turned nervously, swearing for his life that he heard a whisper coming from the forest behind.

"Hello? Anybody there?" No response, as he expected. He took out his gun and pointed the flashlight to the edge of the forest. There was nothing to see, not even a squirrel or a snake.

Concluding he had imagined it, Maffei turned to the car. The driver's door was locked, and the keys were still in the ignition. There were some glass shards on the driver's seat, but not as much as there were on the floor next to the pedals. Maffei walked to the front of the car and tried to see if he could get his arm through the broken windshield, but it wasn't possible.

Another whisper. Maffei turned and pointed the gun. "Come out, right now," he demanded, but got no response. He heard another whisper coming from the other side of the road, so he turned again to see. Nothing. "As a member of the Police Department I order you to come out, hands in the air." Again, nothing.

Maffei walked slowly towards the edge of the forest, flashlight and gun pointing to his front. The same whispers came out of the direction he was walking to, but he couldn't make out what they where saying. As he walked, he stepped on a big glass shard in front of the car. He looked down at the piece, big enough to stab someone in the neck, even after breaking in two.

Maffei crouched and looked at the shard. There were markings of blood around the edges, and what appeared to be traces of blue clothes. He leaned closer to the shard, bringing his eyes so close to the glass that he could see his reflection.

As he got close enough to see the details of his face, he saw something else behind him. A black figure that looked like a bird, a crow. Maffei didn't have time to do anything when he felt a sudden grasp around his chest, and was instantly raised to the air and the cold breeze blinded him for the seconds to come. The shock didn't allow him to scream, and the sudden movement made him drop his gun and his flashlight at once. The cold air burnt his eyes, but he could swear there were claws grabbing him by the chest, what he was feeling around his body as he arouse into the air.

The black crow would be the last thing Officer Maffei would see before he disappeared that night.

Chapter 1
The Boy and the Hunter
George, April 3rd, early afternoon

It was at that very moment that I realized it: I had the biggest crush on Andrea Clinton. I was still skeptical about calling it a crush; that's a word that kiddies use to refer to a girl they find pretty. This was different, I thought. I guessed.

Steph said that I was a total idiot for just now realizing it, but it wasn't my fault. The only similar experience was with Mikaela Shenweller in fifth grade, and that ended up with lots of screaming and pointing and teasing. I'd say this thing with Andrea was light years ahead of that previous experience. The new mission now was to find out if she crushed me back, which I thoroughly doubted. Steph blamed my doubt on my terrible self-esteem due to my slight overweight and my past history with acne, so Andrea's opinion of me was still being evaluated.

Andrea was a very short girl, with bushy reddish brown hair and hazel eyes. As we were all 16 or 17, most girls had already developed their women bodies, and Andrea had the greatest butt in the whole year. Hands down. She was cool, too, and averagely smart; good for some things, pretty bad at math, just like me.

I thought, in general, we contrasted pretty well. It felt like a nice balance between her short stature and my slightly-above-average one. I didn't feel I needed to be fit or super toned, that she liked me in my slight chubbiness. I wished I could grow my hair like hers, but mine was all volume and no shape, unlike her perfectly kept auburn mane. Still, it's not like she made me hate myself more; instead it was more of an interesting contrast. She almost inspired me to see myself differently, which was not an easy thing to do.

#

It all started before winter break, when we were assigned as temporary chemistry lab partners when both Steph and Andrea's partner, Monica, both fell sick with the flu that week. Andrea was instructed to sit next to me in the back at my usual table, and so she did. We've known each other for years – Adler's so small it's impossible not to know every single one of your classmates and their parents – but we'd never had any kind of close relationship. She was very nice, though, and I appreciated that very much. But, unlike me, she was terrible at chem lab, so it was a full class period of me trying to explain to her what the assignment on the board said we should accomplish before the bell rang.

If there is one thing I like about this town and Jefferson High School in particular is how small the community is, in both literal and figurative senses. There is no place for cliques or douchebag jocks or goth kids; we're all shaken together into a single community, where everybody (mostly) respects each other. Not that there aren't any douchebags or mean girls, but it's not like my school is going to appear in any annual National Bullying report or whatever – those things exist, right?

Anyway. So our usual lab partners were also our usual lunch partners, and with both sick at home, we naturally just flowed together from the chem lab to the cafeteria, and sat together for lunch. That's when I realized how awesome Andrea really was. I think that was the first time the two of us sat together completely by ourselves.

"I gotta say, I really love you and Steph together," she started. I proceeded to almost choke on whatever I was eating.

"Excuse me?" I laughed. I think choking with food is one of the most unattractive things a person can do in front of another person.

"What?" she smiled. "Steph and you are together, right?"

"You mean, as in, *together* together?"

"I mean as a couple, yes. I think that's what people call it."

"Pff, no way." Would I rather sound like an 8-year-old or a 13-year-old? I'm not sure, but my tone sucked anyway. "We're just friends. Always have."

Don't get me wrong; Steph is absolutely gorgeous. Half-Korean, half-white. Big brown eyes and dark hair, petite physique and the most pinchable cheeks in the universe. Any guy who'd like to date her has to go through me first.

Though Steph has like five times more attitude than me. I don't know what I'm saying.

"Really? I could've sworn you were, like, something else. A new level of relationship."

"Oh, no. I love her to death. But she's my best friend. My sister, almost."

Andrea smiled. "That is so freaking sweet, Georgie." I almost choked again. "I hope I can find a friendship as pure as yours one day."

"Okay, first of all. Georgie?" When I moved to Adler with my mom when I was 10, somebody called me Georgie once, and it stuck with some people.

We both laughed out loud. "What? Isn't that what people call you?"

"What some people used to call me back in middle school, yeah. Half those people were dudes trying to tease me."

"Well, I like it. And I've decided I'll call you that from now on."

"You'll just arbitrarily decide that, huh?"

"Yup. You're screwed now, Georgie."

#

The day of my realization was another day that Steph stayed home sick, so I had lunch with Andrea again. It was when she was telling me about her plans for college that I got lost in her eyes as she was speaking.

"I'm pretty sure advertising is my real vocation," she said. "I watch the Super Bowl every single year with my family just to see the commercials and learn new things about how to make them."

"I think that's amazing. And, between us, I watch the Super Bowl for the commercials too."

Andrea chuckled. "Really? I thought you'd be a fan, seeing how you're always at the street games here."

"I honestly just go to those because they're too much fun. I don't know jack about football."

"Seriously? Like, nothing?"

"I mean, you throw the ball and run to the goal area, right? It's not that hard."

"You *pass* the ball, yes," she laughed. "And run to the *touchdown* area. You're doing this on purpose."

"I swear I'm not," I smiled.

Andrea took the last bite of her sandwich. She leaned to see two tables behind me, where Monica was chatting with her newest boyfriend, Miles, and his friends. They were a group of seniors who I would call the only semi-bullies in the school. They weren't even that bad, but compared to the peaceful community at Jefferson, they truly stood out as the worst of the worst.

Monica had caught an interest in Miles when we first came back from winter break, and it had derailed her instantly into what Andrea referred to as "Gone-Mon," a state of mind where Monica only thinks about her current boyfriend and leaves everybody else behind. Andrea blamed this annoying tendencies in Monica's severe daddy issues, but we weren't close enough to talk about that yet.

Still, it was uncanny how Gone-Mon and Miles complemented each other. Miles must've been 5'10" and Monica stood at only 5'2", and her dark skin and green eyes were a great fit to Miles' fairer characteristics. If Jefferson were big enough to incorporate a cheerleading team, Monica would probably be the captain, and Miles the quarterback, or something.

Andrea's facial expression changed instantly. I turned to see them too. "No message?"

"No. And I don't care if it's childish of me. I'm so pissed at her." Andrea's mom had been in the hospital for a few days a couple weeks before, and Monica hadn't even texted to say hi or wish for wellness. "Always with that damn boyfriend."

"I don't think it's childish. She's supposed to be your best friend and she wasn't there for you. I think it's justified."

Before she could reply, the bell rang, indicating lunch time was over. "I guess we'll talk about this later," she sighed. She grabbed her things and stood up. "See you later, Georgie."

"Wait!" I said, way too loudly for the situation. I stood silent for a moment, embarrassed.

"Yes?"

"Uhm, text me later, okay? We can keep talking about this if you want."

She smiled. "Will do. Thanks."

#

The one good thing about lunch being over is that my class after it was AP English. I suck at many things; numbers, sports, talking to girls. However if there is one thing I can kick ass at is writing. I can also cook a killer beef casserole and speak very good French, thank you very much. But writing and English are definitely my strong suits, and my SAT scores where very adamant in showing me just that.

I don't have friendly acquaintances in AP English, except maybe for my teacher, Mr. Larned. He allows us to call him Brandon in class. "I'm only 7 years older than you and I'm not married," he'd say, with his disguised Bronx accent. "I ain't no mister."

That day I wanted to show the class how much of a smartass I am – because that's exactly how you make friends – so I replied to Mr. Larned's signature statement. "Wouldn't you find it ironic that our AP English teacher uses the expression "ain't" on a daily basis, when speaking to his students?"

I'm sure most of my classmates expected me to get sent to the principal's office or something. I personally thought I was gonna get extra credit for being so smart. Instead, Mr. Larned just chuckled. "Now you tell me something, George McKnight," he started. I saw my classmates burying into their seats. "Do you think the inhabitants of 16th century England spoke with rhymes in the iambic pentameter?"

I wasn't sure what he was getting to. "I haven't read much about the subject. But I doubt it, sir," I answered.

"Yet, the most celebrated writer of all time represents his characters with such a style of dialogue. Why would you say Shakespeare does such a thing, George McKnight?"

I was speechless, and so were my classmates. "Maybe to give beauty to language, seeing that dialogue was almost all of what his plays would consist of."

"That's a good answer, Mr. McKnight. Now, wouldn't you say that our different cultural backgrounds make us all an interesting class?" My classmates were awestruck. I looked at the girl who sits next to me, Jaina, and saw she was avidly texting on her phone, like reporting on what was happening. "I believe you are originally from Pennsylvania, is that right?" He asked.

I nodded.

"As most of you know," he continued, looking away from me for the first time during the exchange, "the word "ain't" is commonly associated with a lesser-educated vernacular, which itself is commonly associated with the black population of this country, of which I'm part of." By this time I was honestly expecting to be called a racist in some way, which would be completely untrue. "But the word "ain't" isn't only commonly used by people of all races and social statuses, and it isn't only a popular contraction that dates to centuries ago, but it's also a staple of the average American speech that most of us use to communicate. Wouldn't you say, Mr. McKnight, that it's a little unfair to classify my speech as inappropriate, seeing that this is an advanced English class?"

I didn't know what to answer. I still wasn't sure if he was actually scolding me, humiliating me, or just giving all of us a disguised class.

"And coming back to what you said about Shakespeare. Yes, many of the things we say are simply ways of embellishing the English language on a daily basis. It's why we find it so satisfying when we hear somebody curse so loudly and sincerely, saying words that start with F and S and C that *would* actually be inappropriate for me to say right here right now," and with that, for the first time in the argument, I actually sighed of relief and chuckled, along with my classmates. "So, no, Mr. McKnight, it is not inappropriate for me to use the contraction "ain't," not only because it's merely informal and not poor grammar per se, but also because it's an expression that gives character to my speech."

After a brief silence, somebody in the back started clapping, making the rest of us start clapping as well. Mr. Larned smiled and signaled us to stop.

At least I didn't get sent to the principal's office.

Elijah, April 3rd, late afternoon

The hunter was hanging on three hours of sleep when he thought he'd finally seen something of importance. Though reluctant, he had no choice but to follow whatever it was he thought he saw, however unlikely it was for the thing to interact with anything from outside the cover of darkness the forest was sure to provide most times of the day. He would follow this thing to the end of the world, if only to end the unusual cold that had plagued the town for months too early and late. And if there was one thing he wanted to change about his current task, it was that damn cold.

For months now he'd been exploring the surrounding woods for clues about the whereabouts of these creatures he despised so much, without much success. Traveling through this Midwestern town was no easy task for him, a big city guy used to traffic and pollution and noise and chaos, just like he liked to live his daily life whenever he wasn't working. Now it was April and there were no signs of the weather getting any better, making him feel anxious and particularly frustrated with his lack of sightings.

The hunter was used to a particular way of living his life, on and off of work. He liked to keep his dark brown hair moderately long, once letting it grow past his shoulders and regretting it almost instantly. The permanent

reminders of his past assignments didn't bother him at all –
a big burn on his lower back, a missing toe, scratched
ankles and a whole collection of scars throughout his whole
body – except for a more recent one, consisting of a single
cut from the right side of his forehead to the far left side of
his jaw, courtesy of a creature he didn't like to think about,
and sometimes even forgot had existed and had had such an
important role in the aesthetic tone of his face. Elijah hated
that scar for many reasons, but mainly because he thought
it made him look ridiculous, like a character out of a
teenager's sketchbook, and he considered himself a lot
better than that.

Elijah followed what he thought was a trail left by
his prey, going from the deepest of the woods out into the
town, dangerously close to the high school grounds that
stood next to the forest. The hunter got to the edge of the
forest and didn't see anything – nor he expected to do so in
the bright light of day – so he sighed and turned back, to
look cluelessly for God knows how long. Then, out of
nowhere as he was tracing his steps back to his first lead,
he heard something. The hunter grabbed the crossbow that
was hanging from one of his shoulders and pointed it at
what he thought was an enemy of some sort. He moved
slowly towards the direction of the noise, only to see a
familiar face and feel extremely disappointed.

An abnormally big golden brown wolf was
marauding the area behind where Elijah was walking, and
probably stepped on a branch or something of sort and

made the hunter take an attack position. The wolf looked at Elijah without curiosity or much interest, but did stop what he was doing and got closer to him.

"I almost shot you," said Elijah to the wolf. "Couldn't you smell me from where you are?"

"I think age is betraying my senses," answered the wolf, with a voice as clear as any adult man's. "I caught your sense but just assumed you'd been here earlier."

The hunter put away his weapon. "I have. I've been around here for the past week looking for a lead. Any clues?"

The wolf shook his head. "I was talking to Gray about this in the morning. They seem to be hiding their scent somehow, but I have no idea how. Never seen them do something like this."

"Hiding their scent? I don't remember ever reading about something like that."

"The group may benefit from your extensive study materials, Elijah. Maybe you should look into it." The wolf turned his body away from the hunter, but turned his head to him. "Be sure to contact us if you find anything on the matter."

"Sure. Thanks, Taylor." The wolf nodded and turned his head away, and swiftly left the scene. The hunter, decisive, turned the other way and left for his hideout.

\#

Of the two residences Elijah had established in Adler, the shack was his preferred one most of the time.

Deep into the woods lied a small cabin, simple enough to look unsuspicious but not too unattended to seem abandoned. There is where Elijah would go back to rest after long days of exploration and study, or were he would run to in case of a clinical emergency after a fight.

He had some of these kinds of shacks all over the country, courtesy of Mr. Foxworth himself, which would be built whenever his mission dragged long enough to require them. He also stayed at a small apartment close to the edge of the forest, where he would live a quieter life whenever he had the chance, and where he'd sleep and cook and store most of his possessions if he wasn't traveling. It had been months since he'd gotten to Adler, so he had grown increasingly familiar with the small town and its people.

The hunter left for his cabin after the encounter with the wolf, Taylor. His boots and jacket felt extremely heavy, and relieved him of great pain the moment he took them off, but not his gauntlet – never his gauntlet. There was a small table with two chairs, a single bed and a chest, and not anything else; his laptop laid open on the table, all beat up but running nevertheless. There was running water and electricity, all of which was provided by Mr. Foxworth, allowing Elijah to focus solely on his work, and not the paying of bills and taxes.

The hunter sat down at the table and opened his collection of digital books. After scanning through different sections without finding anything, he ended up in the "Camouflage and Disguises" section of *European Demons*.

Elijah started reading. The little hope he had for sleeping more than a couple hours that night was now completely gone.

George, April 3rd, late afternoon

I checked my phone the moment I left school, but saw no message from Andrea. Slightly disappointed, I proceeded to start my walk to Steph's house. Steph lived a lot closer to school than me, so it was just quicker and easier to walk there instead of taking the bus. Must have taken me like six minutes from the school doors to her front lawn, and still no text from Andrea.

Steph's house was one of my favorites in Adler. Nice brown roof and big windows with red frames. Steph's mom's SUV usually stood outside of the red garage door, but she was working by then so it wasn't there.

I knocked on the door and heard Steph's granny walk towards it. It was one of the few times I'd seen her outside of bed, or outside of her room for that matter. "Who is it?" she asked.

"Hi granny, it's George."

"George Burns from church? It's not Sunday yet, is it?" I smiled and prepared to reply, but I heard Charlie's footsteps approaching before I could.

"Granny, what are you doing out of bed?" I heard him ask. I waited as I heard him take her back to her room. Moments later, Steph's kid brother opened the door. "Hi, George."

"Aren't you supposed to ask who it is before you open, mister?"

"Nah, I knew it was you. Granny speaks way too loudly." He let me in and we fist-bumped as I entered. "Steph is in her room," he said. He then retired to the living room, where the TV was on with cartoons and there was an open notebook on the carpet. Charlie sort of reminded me of myself when I was 7 years old, before my dad died.

I walked up the stairs and down the hallway to Steph's room and knocked on the door. "Come in," I heard her say, so I opened the door and entered her dark room, where she was in bed, covered in blankets, watching TV. The lights were off, the curtains were closed, and even her laptop was shut down on the desk.

She looked at me and smiled. "Hey, you."

I smiled back and approached her. She got into a sitting position and I leaned down to kiss her forehead. As I did, I felt the intense heat coming from it. "Damn. I could fry an egg on your forehead right now." She laughed lightly and kicked me.

"Asshole," she said. "How was school today?"

I grabbed the chair from the computer desk and sat down as I took off my backpack. "Well, I got into an interesting argument with Larned about the word "ain't," but I'll tell you about that later. I got some news."

"Huh? What news? About what?"

"You know I've been talking a lot with Andrea, right? And we sat together at lunch again today."

"Yeah."

"Well, I realized something today. Something I thought was stupid and impossible but turned out to be–

"Oh my God, George, just tell me."

I took a deep breath. "I have concluded that I'm into Andrea, and I'd like her to be my girlfriend."

Silence. Steph looked at me with curiosity. Then she coughed a bit, but didn't say anything else.

"That's it. That's the news."

"Wait, really?" she replied. "You just realized this? Today?"

"Uh, yeah."

"I'm certainly glad you're not like the President or something because we would all be completely doomed under your command."

"What is that supposed to mean?"

"Dude, you obviously have a crush on her. Ever since like November or something. Those aren't news."

Now I was confused. "Wait, what? I only realized today. How could you know?"

"Seriously?" She rolled her eyes. "I swear. Men are just so incapable of everything."

"Ok missy thank you. How did you know?"

"How couldn't I? You've been floundering ever since that day at the cafeteria about how she's so pretty and funny and an overall awesome person. I don't understand how it took you so long to realize it. What did you think it was?" She got me, as she always did.

"Well, ok. I'm sorry for being this slow."

"Man, you have no idea."

#

I spent a couple hours with Steph sharing my notes about our classes together that day. Ever since we started together at Jefferson we've made sure we share at least two classes together, and this year we shared three: Algebra, Chemistry, and AP French. It's extremely useful to have somebody who speaks the same foreign language as you, especially for gossip.

I stayed so long at Steph's, her mom came back from work before I left. We were together in the living room when she came through the door. She saw me and smiled widely. "Hey, George!"

I smiled and stood up to give her a hug. "Hi, Evelyn."

She put her bag on the table and approached Steph. "How are you feeling, honey?"

"Better," she replied. "But George won't let me forget about school for just one day."

"That's good. At least you listen to him." Evelyn left for the living to see Charlie, and Steph looked at me.

I smiled and sticked my tongue out. "*Connard,*" she called me.

I chuckled. "Language." I took a look at the window and saw how dark it was outside. "Oh crap. What time is it?"

Steph checked her computer. "Almost eight." I panicked and started putting my stuff away in my bag. "What's up?" she asked, concerned.

"Robert's probably gonna murder me now. You know how he gets." Steph sighed and stood up. Evelyn saw me from the living room.

"You sure you don't wanna stay for dinner, sweetheart?" asked Evelyn.

"I would love to, but you know how Robert gets." Evelyn walked to the door.

"Ugh. I've heard," she said. "Well, whenever you feel like bailing out, you know you're welcome here."

I gave her a sad smile. "Thanks." She then gave me a hug and opened the door for me. I turned to Steph. "See you tomorrow?"

"Probably," she answered. "Love you."

"Love you too," I replied, and left.

Even though I had to run home, I felt like walking as slowly as possible. It's weird sometimes to think that school is my favorite time of the day, simply because it means not being home with Robert. I had to resist the urge of turning back and staying at Steph's for good. Really resist it.

The only good thing to come out of the walk home was the text I got from Andrea. "Hey sorry I didn't text back. Had to run some errands for my mom and got stuck with this stupid algebra homework. Did you start already?" I smiled widely when I saw her name pop up on my screen.

"Hey. No worries. I was at Steph's until now, sharing our notes from class. No, I haven't started. I'll tell you if I need your help."

"Sure. Because my math skills are so superior to yours." I chuckled, but instantly froze when I looked up and saw that I was home.

It was revolting to think of the front lawn of my house, especially because it used to remind me of my mom and her obsession with the color green. Green grass decorated with green garden windmills. A green "Welcome" mat in front of the door. She even got a green abstract painting from an independent art gallery back in Pennsylvania that she brought all the way here, because she loved it so much.

But now, it just reminded me that she was gone. Now when I saw the front of the house I thought of her last days, when she was so skinny she couldn't even raise her arms to pinch my cheeks. I would see the green front lawn and I be reminded of the last time she ever took care of it, the morning of the day she collapsed and I had to call the ambulance. I would see the green painting and think of our life in Penn, before everything got ruined in an instant and our lives changed forever, for the very worst. I would see this house, and I would feel pain.

I walked to the door and inserted the key. I could hear Robert in the living room, watching TV. I took a deep breath, and opened the door. The millisecond I did, Robert started screaming.

I looked down at the dirty green mat. "Welcome."

Chapter 2
Home

Elijah, April 3rd, night

The hunter woke up with a jump, as he wasn't used to sleeping on a chair, much less with his head lying on the table. He'd left his computer open in front of him, and now it had run out of battery. Elijah looked at his watch, marking 8:25PM. He remembered it was the 3rd, which meant that he hadn't gone back to the apartment in two days already. With as much energy as he could muster, Elijah stood up, cracked his back, and gathered his things. He turned off the lights and left the shack, heading towards the town. He had forgotten about how unusually cold it was, even with his heavy jacket on.

Elijah walked with ease, being absolutely sure that nothing was going to happen to him. He'd prefer it if it did, though, so he could get the job done already. Nevertheless, if whatever he was chasing hadn't had appeared in all the months he had stayed in Adler, it would be of terribly bad taste for the things to come out the moment Elijah decided to take a stroll by the woods at night.

He had grown extremely familiar with these woods. The 2 mile walk from his shack to the apartment was always a way for him to relax and think about what had to be done next. On this specific occasion, he used the time and silence to review everything he had gathered on the present case.

According to his studies and observations, whatever he was chasing had been hiding around Adler for at least seven months, but waited until the night of March 22nd to get their first victims, and fallen back dormant ever since. The only way Elijah was sure the creatures were still around was the unusual cold, which was uncharacteristic of the area. He also found it hard to believe that the demons would wait so long, only claim two victims and then disappear. If it wasn't for the wolves assuring him that they'd been chasing them since October, he wouldn't believe they'd been there for so long.

The first victim was a middle-aged woman by the name of Barbara Hawkins. She was assaulted while on the road from work to her apartment, where she lived with two cats. Both of her children were off for college – one in New York and the other in Texas – and she had been divorced for about ten years. Her assault resulted in a reported possible car accident that night, which was reported by several passersby who clarified that no person could be seen near the vehicle, but were too scared to get out and confirm that everything was alright due to the circumstances surrounding the vehicle; middle of the night, lonesome road, poor lighting. Sadly, the situation is what ultimately got the demons their second victim.

Alan Maffei was a 32-year-old Park Ranger who had the misfortune of being on duty that night, and being tasked with investigating the possible accident. Maffei was notified of the situation and drove to the place, but no other thing is known about what happened after that. Maffei was married to a public accountant named Eliza, and they had a baby boy called Thomas.

The police believed it to be the work of several kidnappers that work in the area, but after not receiving any kind of ransom note, they had no clue of what could have happened. Others speculated that it was the work of a serial killer, who made Barbara his first victim and then stumbled upon Maffei when cleaning the scene. No matter what they say, however, Elijah knew that's not what happened.

But, what exactly were they? That's what Elijah had trouble pinpointing at first. After all, most of the things he had fought throughout his career were only the remains of species that were now pretty much extinct. It wasn't until Elijah sat down with the wolves that they unanimously decided what their new threat was.

This was the work of the last group of bloodsucking demons, and their leader, believed to be called John.

George, April 3rd, night

I came in and tried to get to the stairs in one motion, but Robert wouldn't let me. As I closed the front door he stood up from the couch and approached me, screaming all the way.

"Do you know what time it is, boy?" he asked. "Haven't you read the news? What am I gonna do when the police come knocking?"

"I was at Steph's doing homework."

"Did I ask you were you been? I don't care where you've been unless you get here after dark."

"You don't care either way. I don't know what you're talking about."

He slapped me in the mouth. "Don't talk to me like that, boy."

I pushed him away. "Don't talk to me like *that*, asshole."

Robert's face turned red. His short military haircut let me see his scalp, which was almost as red as his face. "You didn't just do that," he said, taking a step towards me.

"I think I did," I replied, getting uncomfortably close to his face. He was only a couple inches taller than me, but probably thought he looked like a wrestler. He was fit and well gained, but he wasn't winning bodybuilding contests any time soon.

Robert pointed his finger at my eye. "Don't ever do that again, and don't get so late home either," he said. I just turned to the stairs. He grabbed my arm to turn me towards him. "Are we clear?" he said.

I gathered all the fluid I could and spit directly into his left eye. He groaned and yelled, which gave me time to run upstairs and into my room. I could hear him chasing me.

"Come back here!"

I just kept going up the stairs, past the bathroom, unlocked the door, and into my room. I relocked half a second before Robert tried to open it. He tried several times until he gave up and punched the wall.

"No dinner for you today," he said.

"I'd rather starve than be anywhere close to you," I yelled back. I wasn't sure if he heard me, but it was irrelevant. I'd gotten back into my room, safe and sound.

I was fortunate enough to live in an old-school house, where the walls were not made of paper and I could isolate myself from any noise Robert would make. It also helped that he wasn't able to break the walls with his fists the few times he tried.

On a scale of 1 to 5, this encounter was maybe a 3 in terms of intensity. We usually never fought this harshly, but when we did it often had consequences. Most of the time they were level 1 or 2 fights, 3 if he wasn't feeling good that day. Today, it was a combination of him not feeling well and me not having it this time. Last time a level 4 fight happened, I didn't leave the upper floor in a day and a half.

The only time a level 5 broke out was after my mom's funeral. Long story short, Robert got a headbutt to the nose and spilled blood all over the floor, and I got a black eye. The circumstances of that fight are very painful to remember, so we'll leave it at that for now. Since then, though, nothing as serious had happened between us. Not yet, at least.

I always locked my door when I got out of my room, no matter what I was doing. If I go to the bathroom, to the kitchen, to school, my door remains locked. My room was the only place where I felt safe inside the house, and there's no way Robert would take that away from me. I didn't care if he wanted to clean, to grab a book, look out the window into the street, he was not getting in my room. For the past two years, I hadn't given him any excuse to want to go in, and that's just the way I liked it.

It's very hard to explain exactly how Robert came into our lives, particularly because I wasn't very bright or attentive when it first happened. I must have been around 11 years old when my mom first brought him to the house. Even then I thought it was a very obvious attempt from my mom to introduce me to a possible new boyfriend, which had been increasingly tedious since her last boyfriend wanted to convert both of us to Mormons. But that guy, Harry, at least seemed like a human being with a heart, unlike Robert; the moment I saw Robert, I knew he was no good.

We'd bought the house a couple years back, with my dad's insurance money. My mom had made sure we moved to a nice neighborhood for her job, and not just another hectic city full of cars and irresponsible drivers. Robert came to our house on a school night, while I was doing homework in the kitchen. He knocked on the door and I stood up to open it, but my mom rushed to it and opened it herself, almost like she didn't want me to see Robert – or him not to see me.

I stood between the kitchen and the front door, wearing my signature blue basketball shorts and a themed T-shirt – knowing myself, it was probably *Star Wars* or video-game related. Robert came through the front door and kissed my mom's cheek. I saw how she reddened instantly, and knew this was probably the guy she'd gone out with the week before, the one that took her to dinner and made her stink of wine when she got home.

Robert came in and saw me, and smiled. My face didn't change at all. I just stood there and looked at him, trying to figure him out.

"George, don't be rude," my mom said. "Introduce yourself."

I stretched out my hand. "George McKnight," I said to Robert, with as much character and conviction as an 11-year-old could muster. He shook my hand.

"Robert Gil. Pleased to meet you," he said. He then proceeded to the living room, and my mom offered him a seat and a drink. I still wasn't convinced.

I remember we had fish for dinner that night, which my mom knew I didn't like very much. She'd been trying to introduce me to some "adult tastes," as she called them, now that I was almost a teenager. She succeeded in many ways, but making me like fish wasn't one of them. Little did she know, that fish dinner would be one of the worst decisions she'd make in her life.

"George, why aren't you eating?" she asked me.

"I don't like fish. You know I don't like fish," I answered. "I don't know why we couldn't have the nice chicken filets that I marinated last night."

"Well, because Robert really likes fish, and I wanted to show him that you're a grown-up who can eat fish, just like us." She knew those comments drove me nuts. If I was a bit older, I probably would've been able to hold my tongue. But I was 11.

"Grown-ups eat avocados and you don't like avocados. Are you not a grown-up either?"

"George," she started. I wish I had turned to see Robert's expression. He was probably thinking of how much he'd educate me once he finished romancing my mom. "Stop showing off in front of Robert." Now *that* really drove me mad. Even after I grew up, it never, ever stopped infuriating me whenever my mom suggested my replies to her stupid mom-comments were me fanning out my feathers.

"Oh my God, mom," I replied. I slammed my cutlery on the table and stood up. As I walked away, Robert grabbed me by the arm.

"Excuse me," he said. "That's no way to talk to a lady, much less if she's your mother." I tried to shake him off but he held on. "Apologize."

"Excuse you," I said. "You're neither my dad nor a teacher." I shook his hand off my arm. "I don't have to answer to you."

I walked to the staircase and went upstairs, but sat at the edge of the last step and listened. I listened to my mom share her frustrations with her new boyfriend, and I listened as he consoled her and gave her hope. I listened how he essentially finished the application to become the new man of the house, and now, in retrospect, I wish I had done something. I wish I had been more open with my mom about how Robert gave me bad vibes, about how he sometimes looked at me with repugnance and seemed to want to send me away.

He stayed in that night. Lucky my mom's bedroom is downstairs.

#

When I say my room was my sanctum, I'm not kidding. There are few places in the world where I felt safe and secured, and one of those was my bedroom. My bedroom is where I could relax and find some zen after school or after being in contact with Robert.

Ever since we moved to the house I decided that my room would be the one upstairs, accepting the fact that I'd have to get out of the room every time I wanted to go to the bathroom. That's a decision I felt thankful for after Robert came into our lives, because being the only person upstairs gave me enough freedom to disconnect from the rest of the world.

Inside my room there's a bed, a night stand, a walk-in closet, and a giant desk where I kept my laptop, my TV, and my console. But my favorite part was the enormous bookshelf that I placed next to the closet, where I was slowly starting to run out of space for the ever-growing book collection that I was amounting.

My love for books started with my mom. She was an avid book lover herself, and used literature to connect with me when my dad died. She would sit by my side and read to me, usually making voices and sound effects as the story demanded.

She read half of the *Harry Potter* series to me by my bedside, but I eventually picked them up myself because I got too engrossed in the story. After that, it was all reading for me and my mom.

She gave me her old copies of the books she read in high school; *Catcher in the Rye*, *The Great Gatsby*, all the American classics. She tried to get me into poetry as well, but that is something she never achieved to do. Just like I could never get her into graphic novels, though I think that was more because of her stubbornness.

A couple months before she died, she started insisting that I read more mature books. I started reading young adult novels when I was about 10, so she thought it was time for me to venture into more adult content. So at 15, she let me read her copy of Stieg Larsson's *The Girl With the Dragon Tattoo*, and that's when I knew I wanted to be a writer.

The way Larsson's words – albeit translated from Swedish – went through the page in such a dominant and factual way made me feel I was reading a newspaper, and gave me a new perspective into what written text could do. My mom never had a chance to read David Lagercrantz's follow-ups to Larsson's novels, but I'm glad, because they don't do justice to either the characters or Larsson's prose.

But my favorite adult writer, hands down, had to be Gillian Flynn. My mom discovered her first novel, *Sharp Objects*, before any of the adaptations of her other books had been released. Since then, she fell in love with her writing, and she transferred that love to me.

I specifically say "adult writer" because JK Rowling held the favorite spot in my heart for years, though I was well versed in the concept of "Death of the Author" by the time my mom was gone, thankfully. Rowling's books were what got me into reading, and opened the way for other authors to catch my love and attention, like Sanderson, King, Atwood and McCarthy.

My mom was the head nurse at the hospital, and she used her down time to read, so she soon developed a fast reading pace. I would sometimes go to the hospital to do homework or something, and soon she and I started sharing books. We used to keep separate bookmarks, so when she was working I'd grab a book from her purse and read it myself. That's why she kept one book in her purse and a different one by her nightstand, in case she felt like reading something inappropriate for my age.

Being at the hospital always made me feel safe, even before Robert came into our lives. Most nurses knew who I was, and so did the janitors and some of the staff. It's a small hospital for a very small town, after all, but it's always nice to feel at home somewhere other than your actual home. Funny enough, most of the time I would've rather been at the hospital than in my house.

After my mom died, Mercedes became the new head nurse. She was always very nice to me and made me feel welcome and safe after my mom left us, but I didn't visit the hospital very often anymore. I would instinctively look for my mom, and I would never find her.

#

I was playing *Overwatch* when I got a text from Steph. "Yo," she said. "Guess what I forgot."

"What?" I eventually replied.

"The Spring Fest is this Friday right after the game." Somehow, I had forgotten too. It was part of Steph's master plan for me to invite Andrea to go to the Spring Festival, and now Steph had realized that it was also occurring after the street football game at school.

"Seems like a golden opportunity, huh?" I said.

"It is. You will take it."

"I don't know about that. Don't you think it's a bit precipitated?"

"Uh, no. It's not like you just met her, dude. Seriously. Grow a pair and invite her to the festival."

"You're so sweet."

"Sweet as a kick in the teeth if you don't act, McKnight. I'm serious."

"Ok, ok. I'll tell her tomorrow after class."

"At lunch."

"You're not coming tomorrow either?"

"I am, but we'll sit with her and any friends from whatever class she's in. And you'll tell her."

"In front of all her friends? That fever really fried your brain, woman."

"You will. You'll see."

And I knew she meant it.

April 4th, noon

Andrea usually sat with her friends from her English class, Stacy and Roger. They were nice, but I'd never really sat and talked to them before.

Right after we got our food, Steph made me go to where Andrea was sitting, and ask if we could sit with them. They all smiled and agreed.

With Steph in front of me, I felt the pressure of her gaze as time went by and I didn't ask Andrea out for the festival on Friday. And then, right before I said it, somebody tapped my shoulder.

"Excuse me," said a male voice. I turned to see a fellow junior. A tall, blonde guy called Antoine.

"Oh, hey," I said. I stood up and shook his hand. "How are you, Antoine?" The rest of the table kept on talking.

"Well, that's kind of what I'm here for. Could I talk to you outside?" I raised my eyebrows and looked at Steph, who wasn't paying attention.

"Uhm, sure," I said. "Steph," I called to her. She turned to see me. "Please take my bag. I'll be outside." She nodded, and I left with Antoine.

We stood right by the cafeteria door.

"What's up?" I said.

"Were you planning on going to the game on Friday, by any chance?" he asked me.

"Well, yeah. I usually go support my year. Why?"

"Jimmy has the flu, and he's positive he won't be able to play with us on Friday."

"Oh no. Are you cancelling the game?" I knew they weren't, and I was sure where this conversation was going. I guess I just didn't want to believe it.

"We're trying not to. That's why I'm here. How tall are you, if you don't mind me asking? About 5'8"?"

"5'9". Why?"

Antoine smiled, which pretty much confirmed my theory. "Awesome. In that case, would you like to be one of our playmakers for Friday's game?"

Elijah, April 4th, afternoon

Elijah had a very friendly and collaborative relationship with the wolves. He'd known about them for years, but only met them when he settled in Adler and coincided with their migration. Whenever they spoke, Elijah had to hold his urges to ask them infinite questions about their kind, their powers, their personal history, and their daily lives. Of the latter, Elijah had had more than a taste, sharing weeks worth of interactions with them during his work in Adler.

Elijah was woken up by a banging on his door. He jumped off the bed, confused and groggy, and put on a robe over his scarred and swollen body. He looked through the peephole, and opened the door.

In front of him was a tall, 40-year-old man with a long, black mane of hair that ran past his shoulders. He was wearing a simple black shirt that really highlighted his musculature. On top of that shirt was a long black trench coat, on his legs were blue jeans, and on his feet were heavy boots. The man had what looked like a plastic bag hanging from the side of his jeans.

"Gray," exclaimed Elijah. "Didn't expect you."

"Taylor told me you may have found a lead," answered Gray, entering the apartment without any explicit invitation. Elijah closed the door behind him.

"That's a bit of a stretch. Yesterday I got an idea about what may be considered something. I wouldn't exactly call it a lead."

"But it's something, isn't it?" Gray sat on the couch in the living room. The small apartment didn't have a lot of space for much, with the kitchen separated from the living room by merely a countertop.

"I guess. Let me show you."

Elijah picked up his computer and sat next to Gray. He opened it, where the digital version of a book was on display on the screen.

"Here," pointed Elijah. "Here's what I think I got." Elijah handed the computer to Gray and went inside his room.

"Taylor mentioned something about hiding their scent," said Gray, doubtful. Not at all hopeful.

"From what I've gathered," said Elijah from his room, "he may not be too wrong with that assumption." The hunter came back to the living room, with a physical book in his hands. A very old book that looked taken directly from a museum. "Check this out."

Gray grabbed the book and read. After a moment, his eyes widened. "Are you sure?"

"No," answered Elijah. "But it's something."

"And when do you think this could happen?"

"If everything my gut tells me is correct, probably this week. On Friday, at the Spring Festival."

Chapter 3
The Game
George, April 7th, afternoon

To summarize what happened on Tuesday after Antoine approached me: I accepted his proposal; I asked Andrea out for the Spring Festival and she said yes; Steph didn't murder me. When Friday afternoon finally came, though, I was about to die from a panic attack.

Me and Steph walked from class to the parking lot. "You need to get your head in the game, dude," said Steph. "Those seniors are going to destroy you if you don't focus."

I hopped and punched the air, unsuccessfully trying to imitate Rocky. "I'm ready for this."

Steph squeezed my cheeks with her right hand and pulled my face to hers – all six inches of difference in our height. "Cut the crap and listen to me."

"Yes, boss," I tried to mutter. She let go of me.

"You need to take advantage of the playground. Antoine is the quarterback and he sort of likes you."

"I laughed at one of his jokes once, and I'm not even sure if I got it right."

"Not relevant. You're taller than most of the other juniors and have the quarterback's trust. That should be enough for you to shine."

"Are you sure this is a good idea? What if I get hurt like a little girl?"

Steph turned red and pulled me down by the ear. "I'm a little girl and I'm hurting you right now." She let go, but didn't give me time to react when she pushed my chest. "Go talk to Antoine and set up a play or something. That could really put you on the spotlight."

I half smiled and ran over to Antoine and the other juniors, who were gathered behind the school building, where the game was to take place. I couldn't believe how cold it was that day – that week. Usually by April it already started to get warmer, but the breeze and cold air were rushing through my nose like it was November all over again. This cold made it more difficult to play football on the street, but I felt safe assuming that it also made me look cooler, somehow.

For years, the students at my school accustomed to organize underground football games that usually took place in the school's parking lot after class. Ever since I got to the school I was always a part of the crowd that went to watch, because it's just too interesting to miss. But I had never been invited to participate nor did I show any interest in doing it.

Teams were usually groups of five men from the same year, who went against other groups of five, sometimes from other years. Twice every month, a secret group of students would gather some money and pay the evening janitor so he would ignore us while we stayed inside school grounds; some speculate that the school board is fully aware of these activities, but choose to ignore them because nobody has gotten hurt. Antoine was the one who started it all, and now it was a privilege to be selected to be in his team. Everyone knew this, so I hoped that Andrea noticed and thought it was totally rad.

"Yo McKnight!" called Antoine as I walked to the group. I smiled and waved. "C'mere, we're discussing some plays."

The guys were in a circle, like we use to see in movies. Backs bent, heads together, arms around each other's shoulders. Antoine opened the circle so I could join him on his left side. Completing the circle from my left were Peter Cready, a total hulk of fat and sweat; Panju Kalil, who had gained a reputation thanks to his speed when running when his mom got pissed; Ed Boon, who I didn't know very well but sat two desks to my right in history class; and Antoine, the most liked guy in the whole year, and the Mayor's grandson, of all people.

"Let me recall your rolls so that George understand our dynamic," started Antoine. "Panju, you're fast as hell, so you're our runner. Be sure to never get caught by anybody because you'll be easily taken down." Panju nodded nervously. "Peter and Ed, you're the defenders." Ed and Peter fist bumped. "Be sure to protect us from Mike and Ryan, especially Panju."

So that meant that I...

"George," continued Antoine, "you and I are the heart of the team." I started sweating, but nodded. "Either of us passes it to Panju so he can run and score for the team." I nodded again, wanting to ask a million questions but staying silent. "How good is your throw?"

I zoned out for a second before responding. "Wha– Uh, pretty good, I guess. I'm more of a kicking guy." I've never kicked a football in my life. I don't know why I said that.

Antoine was a little confused with my statement. "Uh, well, we ain't kicking in this game, so we gotta rely on your throw. Are you right-handed?" I nodded. "Good. I'm left-handed, so I think there could be a strong dynamic between our passes." I nodded again, starting to regret ever saying yes to Antoine's proposal.

Because I've never been a sporty guy, I only understood what was happening during these games because they're extremely simplified. To me, the big guys that stand in the back are called tanks, those who throw the ball around are throwers, and those who run are runners. So much for coming every month to watch.

Antoine put his hand in the middle of the circle, and so did everyone else. My hand was on top of all the others, feeling very uncomfortable.

"Who runs the world?!" yelled Antoine.

"Us!" screamed everyone else but me. I just raised my hand and tried to look tough, probably unsuccessfully.

The members of the circle spread to talk to their friends, as the game wasn't going to start just yet. When I turned to walk to Steph, I saw she was talking to Andrea, and I instantly froze. Andrea was facing the other way, so Steph could see my expression of desperation and panic from where she was standing.

Very subtly, Steph used her eyes to command me to approach them as she nodded to whatever Andrea was telling her. They were both equally short in height, but Steph was slightly skinnier.

"Hey, guys," I said, approaching the pair. Andrea turned and she was already smiling, so she just kept her expression intact.

"Hello Georgie!" she exclaimed. "You look right at home with Antoine's team. I hope you kill it today!"

Say "thanks," you idiot, I told myself, but the words couldn't leave my mouth.

"He will," said Steph. "His passes are masterful. That's why they got him."

Andrea turned to me again. "Are they really?!" I wasn't sure why in the world she was so excited by this.

"My wha- Y-yeah," I stammered. "Pretty nice right curve." That's a baseball term. She didn't notice.

"That's great! I'm so excited."

"You just wait," said Steph. She smiled at me, but her eyes were telling me to really do my best in the field. I didn't know how I would, but I had to try something.

After ten minutes or so, the referee called the teams to the center. Jonathan Walker was a senior, part of the group responsible of creating the tradition of street football. He was one of the few to remain from the veterans, and so he decided to be the referee for what was left of his high school months. The coincidental likeness of his name with the famous whisky brand got him the nickname "Scotch," though he couldn't look further from a scotsman with his dark skin and deep voice.

Juniors and seniors stood in front of Scotch. He was averagely tall, a whistle hanging from a cord around his neck.

"Alright guys," said Scotch. "We have a couple of newcomers, so I want everyone to be at their politest today. I'm talking to you, Fallon," Scotch looked at one of the enemy tanks. "The fact that this is street football doesn't make it less honorable."

The field we were going to play on was right outside of the school building, inside the grounds, next to the woods. About forty feet wide and over two hundred feet long, there was more than enough space for ten teenagers to sweat and punch each other.

"Both touchdown areas have been set," continued Scotch, pointing at the tape lines drawn at each end of the field. "And, as usual, there are no field goals in this game.

You have thirty seconds to assemble, gentlemen." This caught me by surprise.

Antoine patted my shoulder twice and turned with the rest of the team. I followed him, turning to my far right to see Andrea, Steph, and Andrea's friends, Stacy and Roger, sitting together. Andrea waved from afar and smiled, and I waved back. Steph looked at me and signaled me to breathe.

The team stopped halfway between the end and center of the field. The tanks at the end of each side, Antoine and I in the middle, and Panju right in front. In this game, teams don't start at the center, but instead the referee throws the ball in the air and the team has to fight to get it, like in basketball. That first throw is usually when most of the ugly injuries may occur, so I was extremely nervous about even starting the game. Luckily, it was poor Panju who was going to get the most hits, not me.

Apart from having a team of only five people and the exclusion of field goals, there are barely any pauses; if the ball falls to the ground, it's whoever gets it first. After a team scores, the opposite team gets to throw it from the center, and the game restarts. If a player falls to the ground with the ball and an opponent throws himself on him, it must be solely to recover the ball; if the opponent remains on the player without any other purpose, the victim's team restarts the game from that place in the field.

Scotch stood in the center of the field, holding a smaller-than-usual football. I started trembling. "Don't worry," said Antoine. "I'll let you score the first point so you can impress that redhead over there." I tried to answer but just stammered. Antoine smiled and winked. "I've got you."

Scotch lowered the ball and blew his whistle. As the teams accelerated towards the center, Scotch threw the ball in the air and left the field, watching from the side opposite to the spectators.

There were at least fifty people watching the game, from all years. Probably not, but the moment the whistle blew, I felt all hundred eyes were watching my every move. Either way, there was only one pair of eyes I wanted to be watching, and a quick turn to my left assured me that they definitely were.

The ball went into the air and I felt a big rush of wind through my body. Instinctively I ran towards the center along with my team, and I saw the seniors were doing the same. Their formation was different from ours; they didn't appear to have a runner but the two throwers and three tanks instead. One of the senior throwers – Miles, Monica's boyfriend – was very fast, and almost got to the ball before Panju.

In a second, Panju jumped and grabbed the ball, dodging the incoming senior that was surely going to hit him hard in the face. Almost instantly, Panju turned as he fell on the ground, and threw the ball at Antoine, who grabbed it and took a step back.

I never stopped moving towards the center, but slowed down when I saw Panju fall. As Antoine grabbed the ball, he looked at me. "Run!" he yelled, and so I did. I ran towards the other end of the field and dodged one of the tanks, who almost grabbed me by the shirt.

Antoine had thrown the ball towards me. I carefully looked up and forwards at the same time, and, somehow, grabbed the ball. The moment the ball was in my hands, I heard a cheer from afar.

As I ran towards the touchdown area I saw that one of the tanks was running to me from my right side. I accelerated as much as I could but I was getting tired.

Before the tank could tackle me, I saw that Panju was outrunning him and signaling me to throw the ball. Very clumsily I threw the ball from bellow my waist, making it go very high but not too far, and provoking the tank to run away from me and after the ball. Thankfully, I instinctively launched myself to the tank and stopped him from grabbing it.

The ball fell on the ground and bounced once, its distinctive shape making it move closer to Panju's approaching hand. He grabbed it and sprinted the few remaining feet towards the touchdown area. I was too focused on pushing the tank to see what happened, but Scotch's whistle made me stop and look. We scored.

There was a huge cheer from the audience; I turned to look at them applaud. I cleaned the sweat from my forehead and smiled, looking at Steph and Andrea smile back and wave. I made eye contact with Andrea for a few seconds, and saw her mouth, "That was great." I blushed, and moved back into formation.

"Nice pass," said Panju, as I got into position.

"Th-thanks," I answered.

Antoine grabbed me by the shoulder. "Good one, McKnight. Next time I'll make sure *you* score the point." He smiled, and I smiled back.

The enemy team got into formation and Scotch blew his whistle. One of the throwers gave the ball to the fastest tank, and he ran directly towards Panju. Our two tanks clashed with the remaining tanks in the enemy team, so it was up to Antoine and me to do something, so we ran backwards and took a defensive stance.

Panju didn't even think of trying to take the ball away, so he positioned himself behind the enemy team and waited for our throw. The two enemy throwers ran towards our end of the field, as the tank moved slowly but steadily towards us.

"Go back and cover the passer," said Antoine. "I've seen him play; he can't pass to save his life. I'll try to slow him down and signal you to take the ball from him." I nodded and ran to our end of the field, where I saw the enemy throwers preparing.

I got there and didn't say anything. They both looked at me. "Look, Ryan. It's the new face," said Miles.

"I don't know about you, but he seems scared to me," said Ryan. I ignored them and focused on Antoine. I heard the throwers walking towards me, as Antoine clashed with Fallon and was struggling to keep his stance.

"You know, it's funny how this game works," said Miles. "We can assume any role we want. Just like a defender can decide to pass the ball real far," he said, as he grabbed me by both arms and didn't let me move.

Ryan laughed and ran towards Fallon, who was still struggling but clearly winning against Antoine's resistance. Ryan got close enough for Fallon to pass the ball at him, and he ran back to our end of the field. I tried to move but Miles' grip was too strong for me to do anything. Fallon was now holding Antoine, and Panju was too far to catch Ryan, although he tried. A moment later, Ryan scored.

Another big cheer from the public, probably even louder than the last one. I looked at Steph as soon as Miles let me go, and she looked optimistic. She smiled and held two thumbs up. Andrea was saying something to Roger and didn't see me, but she didn't look too happy.

"I have a plan," said Antoine as we moved back into formation. We formed a circle and Antoine laid out his plan. It seemed okay to everybody, but it implied assuming that the enemy team was going to apply the same strategy again, and we couldn't be sure about that. "Trust me," said Antoine. "I know these guys. They really like to stick to their plays."

Scotch blew his whistle twice, indicating that the timeout was over. We got into a different formation, with Antoine in front and Panju right behind him. I stood behind

Panju, and both our tanks – or defenders, I guess – were to my sides. Scotch blew his whistle and Antoine delivered the ball to Panju, who ran for the other end of the field. The four side defenders clashed with each other in what sounded like a duel between bulls and rhinos.

Panju was greeted by Ryan right after we broke formation, but Panju was fast and agile enough to dodge him with ease and run towards the point. Miles was waiting at the end just like a goalkeeper, but I ran towards him without him noticing, and covered his side. Meanwhile, Antoine was holding Fallon, who was being pulled by Ryan.

Panju was about to pass me and get to the point, but Miles broke free of my grip and grabbed Panju by the shirt, pulling him to the ground. Just then, Ryan ran towards us and the forces changed directions, as now Fallon was pushing Antoine away. The ball flew from Panju's hand and bounced three times before Ryan grabbed it and ran towards our end.

Antoine got away from Fallon's grip and tried to block Ryan, throwing himself to the floor and grabbing Ryan's legs. Ryan fell to the floor and the ball bounced away, getting very close to our end. At the last second, Fallon sprinted towards our end and grabbed the ball. Both Panju and I ran for him – without any resistance from Ryan or Miles – but he was already too far and scored easily. Scotch blew his whistle.

I was sweating a lot and covered in dirt, which I hoped made me look cool rather than childish. I turned to see Steph's and Andrea's faces, both looking back at me and smiling. "You got this!" I heard Andrea yelling from her seat. I waved and ran back into formation.

"Again," said Antoine. "Let's wait for them to pull the same move and counter it."

"What if they don't?" I asked.

"They will. Trust me."

We went into the same formation as last turn. Antoine had the ball ready for Panju, waiting for Scotch's whistle. I was sweating profusely, hoping that Antoine's plan had at least some probability of working, and it wasn't just him trying to brag about his advanced quarterbacking skills.

I'd seen Antoine play in this field before, ever since we both entered the school as freshmen. He was practically the founder of our class' team, and because he was always the tallest amongst all, he was always the quarterback. Although he never won against any of the older teams before, everybody gave Antoine props for taking his sophomore team as far as tying and losing at the last second to last year's juniors. For most of the current year, Antoine had been trying to defeat the older students without any success, and this game was his last chance before the school year's end and there not being anyone older than himself to defeat. I guess that's why it was such a big deal for me to be handpicked by him for his team, and part of why I was so nervous.

Like in slow motion, Scotch blew his whistle and Antoine gave Panju the ball. The two pairs of defenders clashed with each other again, and Fallon went straight for Antoine. Just like Antoine told me, I stayed in position and waited to see if Ryan and Miles would try to tackle. When I saw one of the throwers moving towards Panju, I sprinted towards their general direction.

Panju got close to being tackled by Ryan, but dodged him and kept running towards the end; Miles was guarding it, like before. I sprinted as fast as I could and I quickly passed Ryan, who looked confused; before he could start chasing me, Antoine got free of Fallon's grip and tackled Ryan.

I ran steadily towards Panju as he got close to Miles. Miles jogged towards Panju and was agile enough to secure a grip, but right before he grabbed his shirt, Panju passed the ball blindly to his right side, where it bounced once on the floor and finally landed in my hands. I heard a fierce roar from afar, and a confused curse from Miles as he took Panju to the floor. I jogged the remaining feet left, and scored for our team. Scotch blew his whistle.

I walked triumphantly back into position, smiling at the rest of my team. Antoine looked at me and nodded approvingly, and I returned it. I turned to my right to see the crowd, who were still clapping and cheering, to my extreme delight. I saw Steph howling and cheering me on, and Andrea doing a strange dance with her friends, like trying to spell my name or something. I blushed, and tried to hide it by running back into formation as quickly as possible.

Before I went back to Antoine, Ryan walked towards me and stopped me with a hard shoulder push. "Who do you think you are?" he said.

I was distracted by the hit and didn't get everything he said. "Excuse me?" I asked.

"This is our field, our game. I don't know what you think you're doing." I couldn't help but smile.

"I believe what we're doing is playing as a team and climbing over your ego." I wanted to say that and walk away, but Ryan didn't let me. As I gave my first step, Ryan grabbed me by the shoulder and turned me to him.

"I'm gonna–" he growled, but was interrupted by Scotch's whistle. Ryan and I turned to see him.

"Back into formation, players," he said, with no emotion on his face. Ryan scoffed and moved back to his team. I looked at Scotch, waiting to see if he would say anything else. "McKnight, back into formation," he repeated. I nodded and turned back to my team.

I went into the circle my teammates had already formed. "What did that guy want?" asked Peter, one of our defenders.

"Probably nothing," said Antoine before I could speak. "He just needs someone to rub his face with when he's feeling insecure."

"That's exactly right," I said.

"Let's forget about him for now," continued Antoine. "This is the winning point, and they're clearly very angry." He turned to Panju. "How are you doing on energy?"

"Are you kidding?" smiled Panju. "I could run a marathon and come back for dinner later."

"That's good. We're gonna need that energy if we want to get this last point. They're probably thinking of the most unpredictable strategy to bring us down, so we have to do the same."

Antoine then proceeded to lay out his plan, and we all agreed with both its boldness and unpredictability, but also with how improbable it was for it to work. "Trust me on this one," insisted Antoine. I just nodded, sweating from the nerves and the overactivity, but the cold breeze made me feel fresh instead of hot.

Scotch blew his whistle again to indicate that timeout was over. We got into formation, mixing things up a little bit. Antoine and I were in front, with Panju behind us, and both defenders behind him. The seniors kept the same formation as before, looking confident. My hands were trembling as I locked eyes with Ryan; his gaze felt like a gun being pointed directly to my mouth.

The next were the longest 90 seconds of my life.

The whistle blew and the seniors passed the ball. Antoine and I ran for Fallon, who had the ball, while Peter and Ed, our tanks, grabbed Panju and ran behind us. This caught the seniors by surprise, and messed up with their strategy, whatever it was going to be. Ed and Peter dropped Panju and defended from the enemy tanks, and Panju quickly ran towards the end of the field, awaiting a pass. Fallon had no option but to pass it back to Ryan, who ran to one side as Miles ran to the other. Antoine and I split up and went chasing after one each, with Ryan running extra fast when he saw that I was the one chasing him.

Ed freed himself from the senior's grip and grabbed Ryan by the shirt, making him slide and drop the ball. I quickly passed his falling body, grabbed the ball, turned, and sprinted towards Panju. I heard the crowd roar and Steph shouting something like, "Run, you idiot!" Ryan got out of Ed's grip and ran after me, so I accelerated.

I could see Panju waiting for me at the very end, and Miles running back from his position to block him. Panju noticed and got closer to me to make the passing easier, but before I could aim or anything alike, Fallon appeared from out of nowhere and tackled me so hard on my left side, I felt numb for a few seconds. The ball dropped from my hands and bounced to right side, but Ryan couldn't grab it because he tripped with my fallen body before he could stop his sprinting.

I raised my head and saw Panju getting knocked back by Miles, who quickly ran for the ball. I crawled, with my ears beeping, and got to the ball before him. My feet slid on the grass as I tried to start sprinting before I was fully standing up, but I had no time to fix myself with

Miles getting so close to me. I took two steps before I saw Antoine to my left, and passed the ball to him, making Miles change course and instead try to cover him.

Antoine didn't see Miles coming, as he was focused on looking at me when I passed him the ball. When Antoine turned to look straight, he was surprised by Miles tackling him aggressively, and pushing him to the ground. Antoine instinctively threw the ball to his right before he was hit, and it landed in my hands after only two bounces. So I ran.

I sprinted as fast as I could towards the end of the field, where I saw Panju trying to get back up; but as I ran, I felt Miles approaching to my left. Before I could dodge him, his arm grabbed my arm and pulled, but I resisted as much as I could and I didn't fall, miraculously. I pulled so abruptly Miles' hands slipped from my arm and I kept running, catching Fallon's and the audience's attention.

I could hear shouting and gasps from the audience, but I couldn't turn to see if Andrea was among them, because now Ryan had stood up and was also chasing after me. So I ran faster.

Panju got back on his feet and attempted to get closer to me, but Fallon literally picked him up and walked with him past us, to where his defenders were. "You got him, Ryan!" he shouted, as he passed me with Panju. Fallon got to the middle of the field, dropped Panju, and ran back to where I was.

Before Panju could move, he was grabbed by one of the senior defenders, at the same time he struggled with Ed.

Antoine stood up and ran for Fallon, who – according to Antoine's recollection – looked like a mad lion running towards his prey. Antoine got to Fallon and tried to block him, but Fallon just grabbed his whole body and pushed him aside, and kept running towards me.

I was but a few dozen feet from my goal, but I had both throwers pulling me without getting me to stop. "Contention grip," said Ryan, and Miles nodded. Suddenly, Ryan kept pulling me while Miles positioned himself in front of me, and started pushing me instead; now I had two overwhelming forces trying to stop my movement, but somehow, I didn't stop. I just kept going, holding the ball as close to my chest as possible, and using all my strength to just keep going forward. I couldn't focus my hearing enough to get any noise the audience was making, but later Steph told me that she'd never heard such a perfectly synchronized gasp as in that moment.

"There's no way I let you past here!" exclaimed Miles, his face turning red as he kept pushing me. "There's just no way." I couldn't help but smile. With my steady pace I slowly got closer and closer to the finish line, and I could feel Ryan's pull getting weaker and looser as I progressed. "Ryan, step it up!" Miles yelled at him, but Ryan was almost out of breath and couldn't keep going.

From afar, Fallon was quickly approaching me, but I couldn't see him. I just knew he was there the moment he arrived, as he tackled the three of us to the floor. I couldn't hold the ball any longer, and it got out of my hands as soon as I touched the ground. The four of us where laying down, me with my eyes closed, too confused to understand what was happening, and the ball bounced away from us in front of me, in the direction of the touchdown area.

Bounce. Bounce. Bounce. Bounce. Bounce. And then, it was in.

I opened my eyes and looked up to see the ball resting idle inside the touchdown area, and quickly saw Panju picking it up, and stomping the ground. Scotch blew his whistle, followed by a tremendously loud roar.

"George!" he called for me, excited. He did all he could to get Fallon off of me, but Fallon just pushed him and stood up himself.

"You two are useless," he told Ryan and Miles. "Just useless!" I'm not sure if the two throwers where conscious enough to catch whatever Fallon told them.

Panju helped me stand up and clean off the dirt from my shirt. I felt this sharp pain in my right leg, so Panju helped me limp back to where the crowd was seating.

Antoine, Peter and Ed greeted me with smiles and joy, and soon they raised me into the air and sat me on their shoulders. I was still fuzzy from Fallon's tackle, but I remember seeing Andrea and her friends cheering and trying to touch my hands.

The defenders lowered me and I sat next to Steph, still sweating and panting. She hugged me, kissed my cheek and handed me a water bottle. "You stink," she said, as I drank the whole bottle in one gulp. I just smiled.

Andrea approached me, hyperactive and joyful as usual. "Georgie, that was amazing!" she said, looking down at me sitting on the bench. I started to get up but she sat next to me before I did. She hugged me from the side. "You're the real MVP!"

I laughed nervously. "I'm all sweaty. Don't want you to–"

"Don't be silly!" she interrupted. "You deserve hugs from the whole class!" I smiled again, and hugged her back.

As I shook hands with everybody in our class, Miles and Ryan walked towards me and stood in front. I looked at them without any expression, and so did they. Then, Ryan stretched out his hand.

"Good game, McKnight," he said. I looked at his hand, then back at him. I stood up and shook his hand.

"Thank you," I replied.

Miles stretched out his hand too. "Those last few seconds were amazing. I hope you lead your class next year into victory." I shook his hand and smiled.

As soon as they left, I heard someone calling me form afar, interrupting once again my interactions with Andrea. I turned to see who it was and saw Scotch.

"McKnight," he said, overly serious like he always spoke. I stood up once again. "That was one of the most incredible resistances I've ever seen in my years of playing football at this school." I blushed slightly, and the crowd around me cheered. "I want to formally congratulate you and let you know of your amazing feat," he said as he stretched out his hand and I shook it. Sometimes I forget he wants to be a lawyer and that's why he speaks so robotically, or so he says.

That afternoon had one of the most unpredictable endings I could have thought of, with lots of cheers and pats on the back and chants. But the very ending, the icing on the cake, was the last thing Andrea said to me before we all left. "Wanna walk me home?"

Chapter 4
The Annual Adler Spring Festival
George, April 7th, evening

I liked to talk with Andrea because of how well our personalities flow together. Not only is there never a dull moment, but we also really listened to each other and never tried to interrupt or diminish what the other is saying. Like we usually did during lunch, we spent all of our walk talking, mostly about the game. I told her about our strategies and Antoine's leadership skills, and she recalled how everyone around her reacted at specific moments, including the great collective gasp near the end of the game.

It wasn't until we got to Andrea's front door that I dared to remind her, just in case I could sound the least bit over-insistent.

"So, see you in a couple hours?" I asked.

"Yes!" she exclaimed. "I'm *so* excited."

I smiled. "Why? Don't you go every year?"

"Yeah, and I'm this excited every year as well. What about you?"

In my mind, I took a deep breath and grew a metric ton of chest hair instantly. "I'm excited because I'm going with you." Judging by the sudden redness of her face, I concluded I made a good move.

"I'll see you there, then," she said as she opened the door. I smiled and waved as she went in. After the door closed, I exhaled for what felt like minutes, and walked back home with a stupid smile on my face.

The Spring Festival was one of my favorite traditions in Adler. Every year on the first Friday of April, the Mayor's office would close a couple of the largest streets in town and give way to what was essentially a small county fair. There was lots of food, light shows, shoppes, and different sorts of attractions. I used to go with my mom every year, but I hadn't gone back ever since she died. Not even Steph could get me to do it.

But now it was different. Andrea and I were going *together*, as a… couple of friends, I guessed. But it was still exciting and different. And who knew, maybe the night could end as unpredictably as the day did. There were really no words to accurately describe what I was feeling.

"She'll see me there," I texted Steph.

"Awesome. So will I, ditcher," she responded.

"That's not fair. I have never ditched you."

"Not yet, you mean."

I got home to see that Robert wasn't in, which made me immeasurably happy. I went upstairs and took a long, hot shower. I shaved the shadow of a mustache I had achieved to grow, tendered my hair as delicately as possible, and made sure every single inch of my body smelled of greatness.

My mom always insisted on remembering everything that's great about myself so that I don't fall into a hole of negativity. She always reminded me of my deduction skills, my great memory, and ability with words, and that is something I still hold dearly. Something I do not hold dearly is the way my body looks; it's not as bad as I sometimes feel it is, but I could definitely use more exercise in my daily routine. Still, every time I make Andrea laugh sincerely, I forget about how I look, and I know my mom would be very happy about that.

When I got out of the bathroom with my bathrobe on, I saw that my bedroom's door was open. "Shit," I muttered. For the first time in months, I had forgotten to lock the door after leaving. As I entered my room, I saw that Robert was sitting on my computer chair, apparently waiting for me.

"Can I talk to you?" he said.

"When, in the past six years, have you ever been inside this room?" I said.

"Are you going out tonight?"

"And when have you ever been inside this room without being explicitly invited in by me?"

Nobody answered any questions.

"I need you to cancel your plans tonight," he said. "I need your help fixing the garage."

My scoff was unreal. "And I need you to renounce your guardian rights and leave the house to me. Who goes first?"

He stood up. "I'm asking you nicely. The garage door is stuck and I can't park my car inside the house."

"You're not asking me for anything. You're demanding to cancel the first plans I make in weeks for no reason." I walked further into the room and opened the closet door. "You can fix the door yourself. I'm going out."

He approached me. "Well, I'm not letting you."

"What are you gonna do? Tell my mom?" I took out some nice clothes and threw them on my bed.

"I'm serious, George. I need your help fixing our hou–"

"*Our* house?" I raised my voice. "Excuse you, this is my mom's house. You have had no interest in sharing anything with me unless you need my physical help with something." I flaunted my chest unto him and slowly pushed him to the door.

"George–" he started, but I wouldn't let him finish.

"Shut up," I said. "I'm going out tonight, and you're gonna make me late. Get out of my room."

I saw how he clenched his fist.

I raised my voice even higher. "Get out of my room before I let you punch me while I'm in a towel and I call the cops. Then you can tell them all about it. Cool?"

He unclenched his fists and looked at me with rage. "Your mother would be so disappointed."

"Disappointed that I still allow you to exist less than a hundred feet from me. Out."

He turned and left my room, and I slammed the door. I would not let him ruin this for me with this Level 1 encounter.

#

A few days after we arrived in Adler, I decided to establish an average biking time between my house and important places around town, including the very edge of its limits. From my calculations, it took me about 3 full minutes of biking to get to downtown from my house, and about 15 to reach the town limits. So, yeah, Adler is pretty small.

That night, I walked out of my house at 7:28PM and got to the festival by 7:39PM, because I didn't want a particle of sweat to be visible or smellable in my body. It was a bit counter-intuitive to be carrying a sweater, though, but the cold breeze wouldn't let me survive otherwise. So much for "Spring" Festival, huh?

When I got there, I spotted the Kim family walking by the cotton candy stand. Even after all these years, it was weird seeing Steph's dad wear anything other than his white coat.

"George!" exclaimed Charlie from a distance. He came running towards me with a piece of cotton candy that was easily larger than his head. "Look at this thing!"

"Are you sure you can eat that all by yourself?" I asked him.

"I'm not giving you any, if that's what you mean." I laughed and stroke his hair.

The rest of the Kim family approached me. "Good to see you, George," said Steph's dad, stretching his hand to me.

I shook it. "Likewise, Dr. Kim," I said. "Didn't expect to see you here at all."

"I was fortunate enough to get the night off today," he smiled. Before I could answer, Evelyn barged in.

"Hi, Evelyn," I said, muffled by her shoulder crushing my face as she hugged me.

"I'm so glad to see you here," she said. Before I could answer, Steph grabbed my hand and pulled me away.

"We'll be back by midnight," she said. I heard her parents respond something but I couldn't make out what.

"Somebody's in a hurry," I said to her as she dragged me through the crowd.

"It drives me nuts how they treat you like a charity case ever since your mom," she answered. I sort of agreed with her, but it didn't bother me.

"Well, I haven't been here in two years."

"And you'll use your newfound wisdom to complete tonight's task," she said. She pointed towards a small crowd to my left, where I saw Andrea and her friends at a juice stand.

I took a deep breath and looked into Steph's eyes, which always proves to be reassuring and comforting, even with her tough love methods of helping.

"Go," she said. "I'll be right behind you."

I walked towards Andrea. It didn't take her long to notice me, and she walked to hug me when she did. Her friends stayed behind her, almost mirroring Steph.

"I'm so glad to see you here!" she exclaimed. For what I could see and smell, she was drinking fresh apricot juice from the stand.

"Me too," I said. I looked at her friends and waved, and they waved back.

"Hi, Steph," said Andrea to her. Steph smiled and walked towards Roger and Stacy. She turned to me. "Wanna walk around?" she asked. I got stuck for a second, not expecting that proposal at all.

"Go ahead," said Steph. "We'll see you around, right guys?" she asked to Roger and Stacy. They both nodded.

"It's not like we'll get lost or anything," said Roger.

Andrea giggled and waved them goodbye. I looked at Steph with panic as Andrea and I walked away. Steph, Stacy and Roger gave me collective smiles of approval, and so I was dragged away by Andrea.

#

After trying out spicy apples, playing darts, and appreciating the beautiful light decoration around us, we sat at a bench. The firework show would start in a few minutes.

"How are you doing?" I asked her.

"Uhm, I'm good, how are you?" she answered.

I waited a moment. Then said, "Okay, I have two things to say to you. One is a terribly obnoxious, grammar-Nazi correction that will make you hate me." I stopped to let her giggle. "And the other is some real talk. Which one do you want first?"

"Real talk is never priority, really," she laughed.

"Okay. So, "good" as a noun is like the action of doing good things. Like, doctors do good, superheroes do good, cops do good. Likewise, when you say you're good, you're saying that you are well-capable of something. You're good at singing, sports, cooking. If I ask you how you are, and you want to answer positively, a more adequate response is to say that you're "well," not good."

She looked at me for a few seconds without saying anything. "You seriously wasted this past precious minute telling me that?"

"I told you you'd hate me," I said, insecure of what she was actually thinking. She smiled, and I felt my heartbeats reset.

"I'm doing *well*, how are you?" she said.

"I just wanted to tell you that I'm really glad to be here with you," I mustered to say. Her cheeks got slightly red.

"I'm glad to be here with you too," she answered.

Before I could say something else, she slowly grabbed my hand with hers. I swallowed harder than I ever had, and felt my forehead start to sweat. But, right before we could say anything else, something behind me caught her attention.

"Oh, shit," she said, looking past me. I turned to see Monica and Miles holding hands, walking past the stands and outside the festival. They looked to be going towards the forest.

Monica looked reluctant, but Miles was all smiley and touchy. I could feel the doubt on Monica's face from where I was sitting, but in the end, she went with Miles.

"I need to stop her," said Andrea. "She may be Gone-Mon right now but I'll give her time to thank me later." She stood up, and I stood up with her.

"I'll go with you," I said.

"Oh, Georgie, no," she said. "Go back to Steph. You don't have to deal with all this drama."

"I want to help you help your friend," I said. "It's no bother." She suddenly and without hesitation gave me a quick kiss on the cheek, and I almost lost it.

"Thank you," she said. She grabbed my hand and started walking to where we saw Monica. I was still in shock, but followed suit.

I knew we were out of festival grounds when I felt the floor switch from a solid concrete foundation into mushy, humid dirt. The cold had prevented us from going into the forest for months already, but this kind of environment felt very unfamiliar to me. I had been into the forest many times with school, but never at night, and never this cold. As we approached the limits, I felt the breeze rush through my nose, and it actually hurt.

Andrea stopped and looked at me for reassurance. "I'm here with you," I said. She nodded and kept walking, and I followed.

Monica, April 7th, night

Even though they had been together for a couple months, Monica was not at all comfortable with the idea of sneaking into the forest with Miles. Although it was a fairly normal thing for women to be independent of anyone else's desires for them, she still considered it very awkward to take such an important step into adulthood on a cold night outside the forest. Still, she agreed, because there weren't many reasons not to, at least not many that sounded coherent in her mind.

It was cold outside. If there was a phrase she was tired of hearing, thinking and feeling for the past six months is that it was very cold outside. Of all her years living in Adler, she had never felt so disgusted by the Minnesota cold until that evening. Although it was unanimously agreed that 27 degrees Fahrenheit for an April night was quite ferocious.

Her boots felt uncomfortable on the humid ground. She disliked the idea of being pushed against a mushy tree and made to breathe more heavily in the cold air. Add the pitch blackness of the moonless sky, and you got a recipe for disaster where Miles was the final ingredient. And yet, for some reason, Monica agreed.

As they entered the forest, the music and lights from the festival slowly decayed into silence, making her feel slightly more anxious the longer they walked.

"I got a surprise for you," said Miles, and she believed him. She knew this was supposed to be romantic and sweet, and maybe, if the climate was its usual self, it would be.

Unlike what some people had tried to tell her, including Andrea, Miles Goodman was actually a very sweet guy. He was good enough at math to help her with her homework, his parents were attentive and caring, and he had ambitions and desires for his future. He had also never, ever done anything to her without consent, not even taking her hand the first time. His bad boy image confused many, but she knew him for real. Even so, if he was planning what she though he was planning, it was a bit much.

"Are you sure this is the right way?" she asked him, hoping he would realize his honest mistake and walk back.

"Just be patient," he responded, making her sigh. "I promise it'll be worth it."

And so they walked for a few minutes, deep enough into the forest so that the lights from the festival weren't visible at all, and the music and crowd was almost completely drowned out by the sounds of the forest.

Then, Monica jumped with the thunderous sound of an explosion in the sky, which made her trip and fall to the ground. Miles turned to help her, and held her hand.

"We gotta move," he said, dragging her deeper into the forest. "It's already started."

The unbreakable trust Monica had bestowed unto Miles was starting to crumble. She started thinking about all the terrible situations that could follow, including the most outrageous things, like cult sacrifices, kidnappings, and so. It felt irrational to think so, but she could not understand what kind of surprise could be awaiting for her at that moment.

And then she saw it. They got to their destination and Monica gasped. Her pupils dilated and chills went down her spine as she slowly let go of Miles' hand and walked into their destination.

They found themselves in the middle of a clearing, where the forest stopped for a small circular area that allowed them to see the sky and the fireworks. And as soon as she realized that all of her horrible assumptions were completely wrong, Monica bounced back into Miles' arms, more passionately than she had ever done.

"I wanted to watch the whole show with you, here, all by ourselves," he said.

And after they kissed, they turned to the sky to watch the fireworks, completely engrossed in themselves and the lights and the sounds of explosions.

Monica sighed with relief and looked him in the eyes. "Miles Robert Goodman," she said, "I think I love you."

Miles smiled and put a hand on her cheek. "I think I love you too," he answered.

And, as their faces moved towards each others to embrace in a long, tender kiss, they felt a rush of freezing breeze pass through their bodies. A massive force separated him from her, making him fly away to the edge of the clearing.

Monica was out of air. Between the fireworks and the sudden tossing of her boyfriend, she felt awestruck with fear and confusion. With the little air that remained in her lungs, she called out, softly. "Miles?"

But before she took the first step in his direction, she felt a strong, aggressive force grab her by the shoulders. Like if the sharpest knives in the world were suddenly stuck to her back. And then, suddenly, she was flying into the air. So she screamed.

George, April 7th, night

The fireworks started shortly after we entered the forest. I used my phone's flashlight to light up Monica's track, but it was so dark and the floor was so moldable that we weren't even sure if we were on the right path. The explosions in the sky also made it very irritating to try to talk.

If it wasn't for the very specific situation we were in, I would've thought the scene had potential to be romantic. But Andrea was in absolutely no mood for anything other than chasing her friend, and I was committed to helping her.

More and more fireworks were exploding in the sky. I took quick glances above to see the different colors between the branches, but soon enough it was impossible to see anything. The deeper we walked into the forest, the least I could hear any sound from the festival between the explosions, and it made me a bit tense.

But then, finally, we caught a glimpse of where Miles had taken Monica. From a distance we could see what looked like a small circular clearing, and we stopped moving. I looked at Andrea, whose eyes were locked on Monica.

"What do you think?" I asked her.

She took a while to respond. "I think Monica might be in love with this guy," she said. "And that maybe I shouldn't have chased her. I don't even know what I was thinking."

"You were trying to protect your friend from what looked like unideal circumstances," I said. I grabbed her by the shoulders. "You were being a good friend to a pretty bad friend."

She smiled and hugged me, her face buried in my chest. "Thank you so much," I hardly heard her say.

But then we heard it. The screeching sound of a woman's scream, coming from Monica's general direction. It suddenly felt like the temperature had dropped ten degrees in a second, and I was convinced that it would start snowing right away.

We both jumped where we were standing and ran towards the sound. The limited light from the fireworks didn't allow me to fully understand what had just happened. From where I was, it looked like Miles was unconscious, but I couldn't see Monica anywhere.

In the seconds we reacted to the scream and ran towards it, Monica screamed some more. The sound echoed through the forest and into our bodies, but we couldn't see her. It was so dark we could barely figure each other out. But as suddenly as it had started, the screaming was gone.

I ran to check on Miles.

"Mon!" cried Andrea. But we couldn't see her. I could barely hear Andrea's calling over the fireworks.

Miles was completely unconscious, not responding to my shaking or my calls. And before I could lift him up, I felt a sudden, massive force push me on my chest and into the center of the clearing. Andrea turned and ran, but before she could get to me, we heard something come out of the forest in Miles' general direction.

The firework show was now ending, but the moon was slowly creeping from behind the clouds, and more of our surroundings were becoming visible. I could see almost clearly, with my own eyes, how Miles was floating in the air. Then, the final set of fireworks exploded all at the same time, and I saw it.

A shirtless man, with grayish skin that covered all of his naked body, short brown hair and very sharp features, was holding Miles with one of his hands. I thought I was hallucinating, but later I understood that what I thought I was seeing was exactly right: the man had large, boney wings.

We both panicked as the man flapped and flapped his wings, getting more altitude and taking Miles with him. He looked at us and grinned.

"What the hell?" is all Andrea could muster. I didn't say anything. What could I have said? What was I even seeing?

Then, I heard movement coming from all around the clearing, and I turned in every direction, trying to see it coming. But it got Andrea. Whatever was lurking in the shadows got Andrea instead.

I ran to her and jumped in the air and grabbed her hand as she was floating away. She screamed desperately, and I pulled as hard as I could, but it was useless. The soft moonlight allowed me to see what was holding her; it was a woman this time.

A thin, pale woman with bright red hair and the same boney wings was flapping, like making a serious effort to lift Andrea off the floor. Before I could try anything else, I felt something grab my right shoulder.

The sharpest feeling I had ever felt, like four daggers stabbing me in the back and dragging me away from the clearing, away from the light. I tried to fight it, but the force was too strong. The cold air made it feel ten times worse, with my skin getting rigid and my throat burning, gasping for air.

I looked up to see a man, a different man. This one had a blonde ponytail and a short beard, but the same grey skin and wings as the other two... whatever they were. I punched him with my left arm, but it was useless.

He grinned when I looked him in the eyes, but didn't say anything. Instead of flapping his wings, he got close to a tree and used his free arm and his legs to insert his claws into the trunk, and started climbing.

I screamed for help, but the pain from my arm was draining my energy, and my throat got so sore so quickly, it felt as if I had been already screaming for hours. I saw how the floor got farther and farther away as he climbed the tree and dragged me with him. And then, a sharp sound, and I fell into the ground.

Chapter 5
The Night Of

Elijah, April 7th, night

Adler's Annual Spring Festival was in full flood when the hunter left his apartment. He had shared his theory with the wolves, and now they were all alert, walking around the forest, waiting for something. Elijah felt very tempted to go to the festival for recreational purposes, to enjoy himself for once. His will was stronger than that, but he was thinking about it a lot.

His typical mission attire included his blood red trench coat, combat boots, moderately elastic jeans, and comfortable torso wear under his coat. Tonight was no different, but he also went out ready for full combat. A crossbow on his back, arrows on his left hip, a small revolver, bullets on his right hip, a medium platinum sword, bandages, and, most importantly, his gauntlet. And a crucifix hanging from his neck, of course. He knew he probably looked ridiculous to anybody who would see him on the street, but he wasn't on the street and nobody would see him, so he couldn't care less how he looked.

His watch marked almost 10PM when he heard the first scream. He reflexively aimed his crossbow in the general direction of the sound, but quickly realized that it was not within shooting distance, and so he ran. He ran as fast as he could to the source of the noise, taking out a dog whistle from his pocket and blowing it as he went through the forest.

As he got closer to the clearing, he could identify the voices of at least two people. The fireworks were almost completely drowning the sound, but the rush of freezing breeze assured him he was running in the right direction.

And then, after running and running, he saw them. He saw two of the demons, in the flesh, dragging away what looked like teenagers.

Two demons, a male and a female, both with grey ash skin and big, boney wings that made the hunter almost gasp with amazement. He had read endless descriptions and seen interpretations in films and literature, but never like this. Never could he have imagined that his life would allow him to see one of these demons in the flesh, let alone two.

Elijah fired an arrow at the male, but missed by a couple inches. The male noticed, so he flew into the deep forest, and Elijah lost him. When he turned to see the redhead female, she was gone too.

Elijah walked into the clearing to see a third demon, another male with a blonde ponytail, dragging another teenager. For some reason, the demon decided to climb the nearest tree instead of flying away, which gave Elijah enough time to run to the monster, unsheathe his sword, and cut the monster's arm in half.

The sound of the demon's arm separating from its body was something Elijah was quite familiar with. What he wasn't ready for was the minuscule amount of blood that came out of the severed limb. The demon squealed like a pig and released the boy, holding the rest of his body to the tree with his other arm.

The boy fell to the ground, too stunned to do anything but lay there, waiting for everything to be over. The demon used his legs to launch from the tree into Elijah, making him drop his sword.

Elijah rolled on the floor with the demon, avoiding its teeth as effectively as possible. When he got the opportunity, Elijah launched the demon off of him and into the ground, giving him enough time to stand up and run for his sword.

When he turned to face the demon again, he was already in the air, about to bite him. Elijah dodged the demon's bite and used his sword to slice him in half. He could feel how his sword sliced through the skin and bones and organs like nothing, as if they were pieces of old clothes. But, again, only a gush of blood came out of the demon's torso, instead of the gallons anybody could have expected.

The demon fell to the ground, cut in half. His torso moved just as if he was perfectly alive and born without a lower half, which Elijah was not fully ready for. It reminded him of lizards and worms when they lose parts of their bodies, but seeing a human-like thing do ti was on another level of nastiness.

The demon's upper half used its arm to quickly crawl, not to Elijah, but to the boy, who was now leaning against the tree, trying to tend to his bleeding shoulder. Elijah threw his sword to the demon, but he just deflected it with its arm, and kept crawling towards the boy.

The boy quickly realized what was happening, but his panic and pain didn't allow him to do anything but scream in terror. Elijah fired an arrow into the demon's head, but after it came through his skull and got stuck, the demon completely ignored it, crawling to the boy with an arrow through the head. As Elijah ran towards the boy, the demon launched his torso into the kid, with his teeth landing right into the kid's leg.

The boy screamed in panic and tried to shake the demon off, but couldn't achieve anything. Elijah grabbed the demon by the neck and threw him away from the boy. Meanwhile, the boy cried and snotted in pain, attempting to apply pressure to his leg. A significant amount of blood did come out of his wounds.

"I got you kid," said the hunter. "Don't worry. I got you." Elijah grabbed the kid and put him over his shoulder. He turned to see the demon, who positioned his torso right back with his legs, and started fusing them. The arm Elijah had cut remained on the ground, but the demon slowly regenerated another arm, like a worm coming out of the ground and stretching. Soon, the demon was whole again, the arrow stuck in its forehead pushed out by the regenerating skin.

Before Elijah could do anything else, the demon stood up, cracked its neck, and leapt into the air. The hunter saw how the demon flew with ease and liberty, and soon he disappeared into the dark forest.

#

Elijah put the boy down, using the limited moonlight to study his wounds. He unsheathed the blade from his gauntlet and cut off the boy's pant leg, where he could detail the bloody bite marks of the demon. He grabbed the bandages from his coat pocket and rolled them over the wound. The kid groaned in pain, and cried miserably.

Elijah slowly took the boy's jacket off and raised his shirt up to his neck, where he could detail his shoulder wound. It looked like he had been stabbed by Freddy Krueger himself, with four aligned cuts over his shoulder. He switched his priority to that wound instantly.

"Stay with me, kid," he said. "I'll help you if you let me. Okay?" The kid just nodded, his face bloated with tears and snot and fear.

Elijah took the dog whistle and blew it again.

"S-sir," started the boy. "What's happening?"

The hunter wasn't sure what to respond. His answers could go from scientific to worrying to optimistic, so he opted to abstain from answering.

"Sir, please," the boy insisted. "Who are you?"

"My name is Elijah," he answered. "And I promise I'll answer every question you have, but not now. You gotta trust me, okay?" The boy nodded. "What's your name?"

"George," answered the boy. The hunter applied pressure to the wound, making George moan in pain.

There were noises coming from the edge of the clearing. Elijah jumped up and pointed the crossbow at the sound, but stood down as he saw the giant black wolf that came out of the forest.

"Excellent timing," said Elijah.

"Do you know how hard it is to single out that whistle with all those damn fireworks going off?" answered the wolf.

George's eyes widened at the sound of a clear human voice coming out of a wolf. And an incredibly big one at that. "Wha-what the hell?" he managed to say.

From behind them came another sound, and out of the forest an equally big red wolf. "Holy shit is it cold tonight," said the red wolf.

George was about to say something, but he drifted into unconsciousness and fell to the ground. Elijah picked him up.

"He got bit," he said to the black wolf. "Not five minutes ago. In the leg."

"Bit? Are you sure?" asked the black wolf.

"Yes. We need to treat him right now. I need you to take him to the shack before anybody realizes they're missing."

"They?" asked the red wolf. "How many people got kidnapped today?"

"There's no time for this," interrupted the black wolf. He walked to George, each step making his paws transform into hands, his snot into a nose, and his body enlarging into a torso. When he got to George, he looked like a humanoid bear, with hair still covering all of his skin, and his hands rough, with nails like claws.

"His back is hurt, Gray," said Elijah. "Hurry to the shack and start tending him. I'll be there as soon as possible."

Gray took George from Elijah and put him over his shoulder. "Be quick," he said. And just like that, Gray started sprinting southeast, at double the speed of a regular human run.

"Where are the others?" asked Elijah to the red wolf.

"We've been separated all night, patrolling," answer the red wolf. "I wouldn't be surprised if Alex got to the state line."

And right as he said that, a brown wolf came out of the woods and into the clearing. "Not quite," he said. "But almost." The brown wolf looked around the clearing, noticing the blood, the arrow, the severed arm. "What the hell happened here?"

"I'm not sure yet," answered Elijah. "I want to investigate, but the boy got bit and I need to treat him."

"A boy?" asked the brown wolf. "What boy?"

Gray, April 7th, night

It had been years since the wolf had had to partly detransform, and it didn't feel right for him. Usually, if he needed to run, he would just go full dog and sprint, easily and effectively. If he ever needed to carry somebody, it was always easier for the person to ride him like a horse, but this boy was unconscious, bleeding out, and poisoned. There was no horse-riding chance tonight.

Gray ran the half mile from the clearing to Elijah's shack in about six minutes, which angered him. He had run double that distance in half that time, and would be happy to do it right then and there, if it weren't for the boy and his wounds.

The door to the shack was unlocked, so Gray carried George inside and closed the door behind him. He had been in the shack before, and he knew that it was protected against anything that would want to come cause trouble, including the demons they had been preparing to fight.

It was warm inside the shack thanks to a small chimney that Elijah had turned on before leaving for his patrol. On the table was a computer and some books, and hanging by the ceiling was a lightbulb that could be turned on by a switch, right beside the door. The windows were covered by small burgundy curtains, and the wooden walls and floors creaked as the big, heavy wolfman carried George inside and put him on the table.

As Gray walked around the cabin, he detransformed with every step he took, chunks of hair falling off his skin. He grabbed a knife from the kitchen, and bandages and alcohol from the bathroom. When he got back to the boy, he was again a muscular man with a long, black mane of hair. He was also naked.

Gray cut the boy's shirt open and analyzed his shoulder, which was dirty with blood and dirt, with four aligned, deep cuts. George started to wake up when Gray prepared to clean the wound.

"What's happening?" asked the boy.

"Hang on, kid," said Gray. And without any preamble, he poured alcohol directly into the boy's shoulder.

George jumped up and screamed from the searing pain. Gray was strong enough to hold him to the table with one hand, but the boy was giving a good fight. Gray used a tablecloth to clean George's back as he groaned and cried in pain.

"Please, stop," said George. His face was bloated and red, his eyes almost indistinguishable from his cheeks.

"It'll be over soon," answered Gray, coldly and without looking at him.

The wolf took a closer look at the boy's shoulder, noticing how clean the cuts were, with no signs of any foreign objects except for some pieces of cloth. Gray continued cleaning the wound, indifferent to George's moans of pain.

After a couple minutes, Gray used some bandages to cover the shoulder. "I'll be right back," he told the boy, as he left for the kitchen.

Gray took a syringe from inside the refrigerator. It was a small syringe with a medium tube, filled with a yellowish substance that looked semi thick. George flinched at the sight of it.

Gray grabbed George's bitten leg. "What the hell are you doing?" exclaimed George, with the little energy he could muster.

"Saving your life," said Gray. "Stay still."

"Uh-uh. I'm not letting a naked, burly stranger inject me with anything."

Gray looked down at his nakedness. "Would it help if I put on pants?"

"You're still a stranger."

Before Gray could answer, the door opened and Elijah walked in.

"You're awake," said Elijah. "Good." Elijah took a look at Gray's naked body. "Would you mind?"

Gray walked to the door, curving his back with each step and getting more and more hair all over his skin. When he stepped out, he was a wolf again. A giant, black wolf.

"You're welcome," said Gray to the boy. Before the boy answered, Gray pushed the door close with his paw.

#

Outside the shack were Alex and Drake, waiting for him.

"How's the boy?" asked Alex, the brown wolf.

"He'll live," answered Gray. "The poison didn't seem to affect him. He just lost a lot of blood."

"The poison didn't affect him?" asked Drake, the red wolf. "How is that possible?"

"I don't know," said Gray. "Maybe he didn't get poisoned at all, just bitten."

"Do they do that?" asked Drake, confused.

"I have no idea. We can question the boy tomorrow, after he rests."

Elijah, April 7th, night

Gray had treated the boy well enough. A little rough with his shoulder wound, but it was still effective. He noticed the syringe on the table, still full.

"How are you feeling?" said Elijah.

George sat as straight as he could. "Confused," he answered. "Worried." The sharp pain in his back didn't allow him to say much else.

"I understand," said Elijah. "It's a lot to take in at once. But I need you to tell me something." Elijah paused to allow George to focus on his words and his words alone. "Do you have any clue of what your blood type is?"

"O positive," said George without thinking.

"Alright. Give me a second." Elijah turned to the refrigerator and opened it. On the bottom rack were what must have been dozens of blood bags. He grabbed one marked with "O+" and closed the fridge.

Elijah put the bag on the table and took the syringe filled with the thick substance. "I need to inject this in your leg," he said, looking at George. "There is a strong probability that you're poisoned."

George took another look at the syringe and cringed. "Go ahead," he said. "But I won't look."

"You don't have to," answered Elijah. He grabbed George's bitten. George was vocal about his pain, but looked like he was actively trying to be as quiet as possible..

The leg was red and swollen, with two small holes dangerously close to his tendon. It looked like blood had stopped leaking for a while, and there were no signs of any other strange colors that Elijah was expecting, like yellow or grey.

"Take a deep breath," said Elijah.

"I know how to take thick injections," answered George. "Please, just get it over with."

Elijah inserted the needle in the closest vein to the bite, and slowly pressed for the liquid to get inside George's calf. George looked like he was holding a scream as the thick yellowish substance entered his body. After he finished, Elijah took the syringe out and cleaned George's calf as delicately as possible.

"You should lay down and rest," said Elijah.

"I can't," said George, getting off the table. The moment his leg touched the floor, he lost all balance and fell to the floor.

"You won't be able to do anything if you don't rest," said Elijah, as he picked the boy off the floor and walked with him to the bedroom. "You've lost too much blood."

"I need to go back," said George. His voice seemed to be losing potency with every word. "They took Andrea. I need to tell Steph."

Elijah put George on his bed. George was so entranced he didn't even seem to notice he was laying on his back.

"We'll be back tomorrow," said Elijah, rolling George over on his chest. "You need to sleep now." And without anything else to say, George fell into a deep sleep. Elijah set an IV next to George's sleeping body. He hung the blood bag and let it slowly drip into the vein.

#

The hunter and the wolves walked back to the clearing, where the blonde wolf Elijah had seen days before was sniffing around. He turned to see them when they got there.

"Anything?" asked Gray.

"Many things," answered Taylor, the blonde wolf. "Blood, skin, sweat. There were four different people here, if I'm not mistaken."

"Four?" asked Elijah. He turned to see Gray. "George mentioned the name of one girl. Andrea, I think."

"There are two and two, I think," said Taylor. But before they could discuss any further, all wolves turned abruptly to the south. "There's someone coming."

"I think it's the police," said Alex, the brown wolf.

"Oh shit," started Elijah. "They must be looking for the missing kids. I need you guys to clean and take George to the cave." At this, Gray scoffed.

"Excuse you," he said. "We–"

"They're going to see me and search my cabin," interrupted Elijah, urgently.

"I thought you knew the police," said Drake, the red wolf. "I thought you were cleared."

"I am," he answered. "But that doesn't save me from being a potential suspect."

"We shall go back, then," said Taylor. "And take the boy." He looked at Gray for approval, who nodded, with clear annoyance.

Elijah was still wearing his battle attire, which he took off almost entirely and handed to the wolves. The four wolves turned to the east and left. Elijah kept his jacket on, as well as the crossbow and his gauntlet.

Soon after, he could distinguish flashlights coming from the south, and heard several voices. He crouched and pretended to be looking at the crime scene, keeping his hands off the ground.

"Freeze!" he heard somebody say, behind him. Elijah put his hands up and stood up slowly, as if he knew he was going to be told to do so.

"Put that down," he heard another, gruffer voice order. "That's Peter Anderson." Elijah turned slowly to see a familiar face. A buff, middle-aged black man with a well-kept mustache was leading a group of four officers.

"Good evening, Terrence," said Elijah to the leader of the group. "May I lower my hands now?"

"Yes," answered the Sergeant. Elijah lowered his hands and walked to the group. "I thought I'd see you here." The Sergeant stretched his hands so Elijah could shake it.

"Heard a bunch of funny stuff," said Elijah, shaking the Sergeant's hand. "Wanted to take a look. Took you longer than I expected to get here."

"The Festival was a real mess," answered the Sergeant. "Made even messier after people realized four teenagers went missing."

Elijah faked surprise. "Four teenagers? Missing in the woods? Are you sure they're not just hiding?"

"I would like to think so," said the Sergeant. "But it's been over an hour now, and they won't even answer to their friends' calls. So we're assuming they're missing."

Before Elijah could retort, one of the officers called for the Sergeant's attention. "Sir," he started. "I think there's blood here."

The Sergeant walked to were the officer was and pointed his flashlight at the spot. Agreeing that it, indeed, looked like blood, he called on his radio.

Elijah stood there, waiting for the Sergeant to finish his call. He looked around, seeing how the police took all of the evidence he was about to analyze.

"You didn't touch anything, I assume," said the Sergeant."

"No," answered Elijah. "I just got here, not a minute before you did."

"And I take it you didn't see anybody either."

"Not at all. Just the fireworks, really."

The Sergeant took a look at Elijah's crossbow, hanging from his back. "What's that for?" he asked.

"Oh, nothing," answered Elijah, uninterested. "You know. In case a wolf or a bear goes astray. Merely for my own safety." The Sergeant looked doubtful, but Elijah knew he believed him.

"Well, we're closing all of this area," said the Sergeant. "I need you to go back to your apartment tonight, not your cabin. Can you do that?"

Elijah kept his annoyance to himself. "Yes, no problem. I'll go get some important stuff and head to my apartment at once."

"I actually need you to go right now," said the Sergeant. Elijah was not expecting that.

"Can't I go to the cabin to grab a book? I just got to the best part."

"I'm sorry, Peter," said the Sergeant, regrettably. "I'm actually closing a perimeter and your cabin is inside of it. I can't let you tamper with it."

Elijah, thinking that arguing more would make him sound more suspicious, just nodded. "Alright. Whatever makes your job easier."

Elijah started walking south, into the town and to his apartment, when the Sergeant stopped him. "Peter," he called, and Elijah turned. "I trust you. These are orders from higher up."

Elijah gave an honest smile. "I know, Terrence. You do your job. I'll be back in the morning." The Sergeant nodded, and Elijah resumed his walk.

The hunter left for his apartment. He knew the woods like the palm of his hand, so it wasn't very difficult for him to evade the police perimeter and get to town without any interruption. Once there, Elijah noticed that there were people walking around, as if the Festival had only ended minutes before.

He rest assured that his cabin and things were safe with the wolves, and that they had taken George, his things, and the IV to their cave, where he would rest and heal until the morning. He knew the wolves were smart enough to know what things to leave and what things to take so it didn't look too clean and cause suspicion. What he didn't know, and wouldn't know, was who the demons had taken and what exactly had happened. At least until the morning, when the boy woke up.

Chapter 6
Caved In

Monica

Black. That's everything she could see. She didn't know if it was night or day, if she was still in the forest or a hundred miles away. There were few things she was sure of: she was still dressed, all her limbs were still in place, and she could still talk. She knew the latter because the first thing she did when she woke up was scream.

Monica was encapsulated inside a strange material, something that felt like millions of threads of cloth, but stickier. Not as sticky as a spider's web, but it wasn't a regular bedsheet. And as she tried to free herself, her movement helped her notice that she was actually not on the ground, but hanging in the air.

Her screams felt muffled even inside her capsule. Aside from the very low energy that remained within her, she felt a sharp pain on her back. She remembered she had been grabbed by the shoulders a while ago, and figured that she was probably bleeding because of it. What she couldn't figure out was how much time had passed since then.

All of a sudden, she heard voices, so she kept quiet. Three distinct voices were talking right outside Monica's cocoon, two men and a woman. They all sounded rough and tired, but somehow, at the same time, not human at all.

"How could you get a bite and at the same time let him escape?" asked the woman voice.

"I already told you I didn't," answered one of the male voices. "It was the hunter."

"You already had the boy," said the other male voice, a deeper one. "I saw you dragging him inside the forest."

"I couldn't lift him," said the higher male voice.

"You couldn't lift a fucking teenager, Jason?" asked the female voice. "I took care of the two girls and you couldn't handle one boy? You're pathetic."

"Listen, bitch," started Jason. He was abruptly interrupted before he could continue.

"Do not call me that," said the woman voice. Monica could make out some moans of pain coming from Jason.

"Leave him, Arabella," said the deeper voice. "He'll have to deal with our Master now. No need to punish him ourselves."

"There's no need to punish me either way," replied Jason. "I didn't eat the boy, nor did I turn him. I just… needed a little fuel."

"And now you have an escaped witness who is probably with the wolves," answered the deeper voice. He seemed to be a lot calmer compared to the rage Arabella was portraying in her voice. "You may not think our Master will punish you, but I assure you, he will. He doesn't like being disobeyed."

Arabella gave a screeching laugh that gave Monica chills. She felt her skin tighten as she started crying inside her sack.

"Oh," started Arabella. "I think someone has woken up." Monica's eyes burnt with pain as a big cut was made to the walls of her sack, letting in a ray of moonlight that heavily contrasted with the pitch blackness she had gotten used to.

After her eyes adjusted, Monica saw Arabella's face inches from hers. It was the face of a formerly beautiful woman, with a perfect nose and a delicate pair of cheeks that were now grey and dry. Her eyes glowing, her teeth shining.

"Hello, precious."

George, April 8th, early morning

I woke up feeling I'd been having nightmares for 12 hours straight. I was lying on my chest on a thin mattress, covered with three or four blankets and sweating as if I had a horrendous flu. There was a gas lamp illuminating part of the place, which kind of looked like a cave. To the other side was a big fire.

There was an indescribable number of things on my mind. Where was I? Was last night real? Is Andrea okay? I wondered what Steph was doing, what she thought had happened to me. All of Adler must've flipped over its head with the disappearance of four high school students.

Police must be looking for us like crazy, not knowing that they were at the mercy of whatever attacked us the night before. Scotch's dad was probably on the case, and I wondered if Scotch would tell him anything useful. And then my mind jumped to what everyone would say, if people outside my extremely small circle at school knew who I was, if they would even notice I was one of the kids missing.

The moment I tried to turn my body on my back, it felt like somebody stabbed my shoulder with a thin, long nail. In answer to my groans of pain, I heard a voice. "Do you need help standing up?" the voice asked. A male voice.

I was breathing very heavily and couldn't see much. "Where am I?" I asked. I could make out the man in front of the fire, looking towards me.

"We brought you to our cave," answered the man. "You've been sleeping for a while." As I tried to sit up again, I realized there was an IV pumping something into my arm. It looked like blood.

Then, I remembered. I remembered that I was on a table and I had been poisoned. I remembered that, before that, I was being tended by a big man with long hair. And before that, I remembered I was at a clearing, with Andrea looking for Monica and Miles. Something attacked us.

Something took them and bit me. The man with the burgundy jacket saved me.

"Where's Elijah?" I asked, not completely sure if I remembered correctly what his name was.

"He's with my pack," said the man. He was walking closer to me. "I'll take care of you until he gets back."

The light from the lamp let me see his face as he gave me a slight smile. He was a young man, maybe late 30s, street clothes, with long blonde hair, very dark eyes, and an enviable goatee. He looked a lot friendlier than his other wolf friend.

He crouched next to me. "I'm Taylor," he said, stretching his hand to me.

Still on my chest, I stretched my IV'd hand and shook his. "George," I said. "Can you help me sit up?"

Taylor stood up and grabbed me by my armpits. Seemingly without any effort, he lifted me up and sat me on the mattress. It wasn't until this moment that I realized I was shirtless.

"Let me take a look," said Taylor, leaning down to look at my shoulder. He didn't touch it, just handled me a bit so he could get more light on the wound. "Looks like it's healing very well. Maybe a nasty scar, but you'll survive."

At this comment, I remembered everything I wanted to ask. But I still felt groggy, similarly to when I woke up after my wisdom teeth got taken out when I was 14. "I need to go," I said. "I need to find Andrea." Before I tried to stand, Taylor held me down.

"You're not going anywhere until Elijah comes back," he said. He looked me in the eyes and I think he felt my frustration and confusion. "Meanwhile, you need to recover. It was a nasty bite that thing took."

This made me look down at my ankle. Half of my pant leg had been cut out completely, leaving anything below my knee uncovered. There was a strange mark, like two small holes.

Before I could say something or choke up with my frustration, Taylor spoke. "I know how you feel," he said. "If you have any questions, you can ask me." He smiled again, which felt surprisingly comforting at that moment.

But I had to consider many more things before continuing. This was a complete stranger in front of me, and I was about to open my head for him to say whatever he wanted. He could've told me horrible things to confuse me and take me on the incorrect path. But it was a risk I was willing to take, seeing how I had gotten that far and seemed to have been taken care of very well.

"What happened last night?" I asked. Taylor stood up and walked a couple steps away, grabbed a chair, and sat down on it.

He sighed. "You are simply the victim of a combination of bad luck and the corrupted desires of terrible people." He was completely serious, but his voice felt kind and understanding. "Last night, these individuals used the Spring Festival to take advantage of the abundance of people and noise to take your friends, and they would've taken you as well, if Elijah hadn't intervened."

Now I had a hundred more questions, and didn't know which one to ask first. So I opted to stay quiet and let Taylor speak freely.

"Elijah had reason to believe you had been poisoned by the bite you received, so we took you to his headquarters and treated both of your wounds. After these many hours, we don't think you were actually poisoned, but you lost a lot of blood. Hence the IV."

I looked back at the IV. The almost-empty blood bag helped me remember how I had told Elijah what my blood type was. Good thing my mom was a nurse.

"My instinct tells me you have three major questions right now," continued Taylor. "Who we are, who those people are, and what they're doing to your friends." I nodded, surprised at his level of intuition, one I could only hope to get to. "To the third question, which is probably the most urgent for you, I have no clear answer. We're sure they're not dead, and we believe they won't get killed any time soon, because there's no reason why they would kidnap them otherwise."

I gave a sigh of relief. I was, in fact, wondering if Andrea and the others were still alive. Even though I had only words as evidence, it felt good to have an authoritative figure tell me somewhat good news. Andrea was alive.

"I think you have some understanding of what Elijah is," said Taylor, his tone conveying that he was waiting for an answer.

I thought about it, and I realized that I actually did not know what Elijah was. I didn't think he had special powers or anything, but he wasn't just a passerby who happened to have an arm-cutting sword.

I shook my head. "My experience with him has been very limited," I answered. "As far as I know, he's a doctor."

Taylor chuckled. "Elijah is, actually, not a doctor." He waited, possibly for me to guess again, but I didn't speak, so he continued. "Elijah is, for lack of a better term, a hunter, George." He waited again to see if I had any comments or questions, but I didn't. "It's not a real title that he holds. There's not an Order of Hunters that he's part of. Everything is really unofficial, but he's a real professional."

I felt Taylor could read my mind. After this, he gave me a couple seconds to take the information in. Then, he continued.

"Elijah answers to a man who we appreciate very deeply. You could call him Elijah's sponsor, again, for lack of a better word. We call him Mr. Foxworth."

I wasn't very impressed by the revelation that Elijah was some sort of hunter. But I would've never guessed that he answered to a sponsor, though it made sense. I don't imagine you'd make a lot of money by being a clandestine monster hunter.

"Elijah isn't part of our clan," continued Taylor. "We met him some time ago, when he moved up here to hunt down your attackers. It took us months to gather clues, but we hadn't seen them until last night. You probably heard of the disappearance of a Park Ranger a couple weeks ago?"

I nodded. I remembered seeing it in the news and how people in school were jokingly speculating that there was a serial killer in the forest. If only they had known.

"Are you," I started asking, to Taylor's surprise, "what I think you are?" Taylor gave me a slight smile.

"There is a lot of mythology available. Most of it is very incorrect, but it gives you a good sense of what it is we are and do." He waited for me, but I didn't say anything else. "There is a specific question you want to ask me. Go ahead and ask."

I swallowed nervously and looked at Taylor. His eyes looked kind and comprehensive, like a teacher waiting for their pupil to ask the greatest question in the history of the subject.

"Are you guys werewolves?"

"You could say so. Yes."

Elijah, April 8th, early morning

The hunter and the three wolves went back to the cabin. A note stuck to the door, detailing that a search of the premises had occurred, and that Elijah was free to go back in. It didn't seem like much had been done. The wolves had gathered the blood bags, weapons and books the night before and taken them to the apartment, which didn't leave much for the Police to investigate.

Elijah had made sure to get to know Sergeant Walker as soon as he got to town. He knew it was important to have the favor of the authorities, seeing that his mask as a "for-pay fauna researcher" was very strange and sounded as fake as it was. Fortunately, with Mr. Foxworth's financial backing, most fake things could be made to look as legit as any other thing.

The wolves were sitting around. It was only the fourth or fifth time that he saw Drake and Alex detransformed into humans, as they were never the ones to go to town for anything.

Alex had a long mane of brown hair that he kept tied. His dark skin and green eyes contrasted heavily with the rest of his partners, who were all white and somewhat pale. Alex looked more like the lord of a villa.

Drake appeared to be younger than his counterparts. If one spotted him walking by the street, it would be impossible to assume that he was any older than 25. He was also the only one with red hair, and it was relatively short at that too. He was also skinnier, had a lighter tone of voice, and kept mostly quiet.

"How much longer do you think we should wait?" asked Gray.

"I don't think it will be possible to return until much later this coming week," answered Elijah. "They're shutting down the whole area and they won't take very kindly to wild wolves hanging out either."

"What do we do, then?" asked Alex.

"I need to take care of the boy," said Elijah, with much concern. "He must be so confused and angry, and his parents must be going insane looking for him."

"Are we returning him to them?" asked Alex.

"No," said Gray, before Elijah could answer. "He knows too much, has seen too much, and could be in even more danger if we let him go."

"That's nuts," said Drake. "We can't take a kid away from his parents. That's savage." Elijah wasn't sure, but he felt an air of relatability in Drake's tone.

"We have no other choice," said Gray, authoritatively. "Do you really want a scared and ruthless child running around town with all that he's seen?"

"What are we gonna do, then?" interrupted Alex. "Train him?"

A brief silence. The wolves looked at each other and turned to Elijah. "Mr. Foxworth is on his way," said Elijah. "We'll have a solution to this in no time."

"What solution?" asked Alex. "Are you really going to train this boy? He's hurt and scared. He's probably never punched anybody in his life. Do you expect him to fight John at our side?"

"Nobody said anything about him fighting John," said Gray.

"Then what? He's going to be a squire? Or bait? Come on, Michael. Think."

"I already thought about this," said Gray, irritably. "The only thing we can do is hope for the best with this kid. But we cannot let him go."

"This is madness," said Alex. "Elijah, you can't be serious."

The hunter didn't answer. He was listening to the discussion but thinking about Mr. Foxworth's arrival and whatever he would do when George woke up.

"I gave Taylor instructions to answer all of his questions," said Gray. "When we get back, he should be well informed about everything."

Alex scoffed. "I'd love to see his face when he finds out what attacked him last night."

"Speaking of that," interrupted Elijah, "I want to discuss something with you." The wolves looked at him. "Do you know how many of them are? Because I think they're three."

The wolves kept quiet. They looked at each other, waiting for the other to answer. "I think I smelled two," said Drake, unsure. "But don't take my word for it. We didn't have time for anything."

"I think we should focus away from the clearing," said Gray, "and start thinking about our next steps. We need the evidence they took, we need to take care of the kid, and we need to find out how the town is doing."

"That's not too hard, is it?" said Drake. "The town must be ballistic looking for those kids. Elijah would probably be the main suspect if it wasn't for Walker."

"Still," said Elijah. "Gray's right. We should forget about the clearing and start dividing some tasks."

"Shouldn't we discuss this with Taylor, then?" asked Alex.

"Definitely," answered Gray. "Time to head back."

George, April 8th, early morning

Surely the antidote Elijah had given me was holding me back, because I couldn't understand how I wasn't totally freaking out right then and there. Taylor's calming tone and personality also helped a lot.

"I understand you're in shock," said Taylor, "but try to understand. Legends and folklore are usually based in reality. Time usually distorts reality into poetry and literature, and that's how you get to what you know about our kind."

"I understand," I said. "I'm just... I can't believe it. This sounds so made up, and yet, I've seen you do incredible things. I saw and felt incredible things last night. It cannot be made up."

"It is certainly not," said Taylor. "And trust me. I felt the same way as you the first time. You get used to it."

I kept quiet for a moment. The effects of the drugs were wearing off and I started to think a bit more clearly.

"Wait a second," I said. "Does that mean..."

Taylor waited patiently for my question. It looked like he knew exactly what it was.

"Does that mean the things that attacked us last night were... Were... Oh my God, it feels so stupid to say out loud."

Taylor chuckled. "I know. But the sooner you accept it, the easier it will be to start recovering."

I took a deep breath. "It means that what attacked us last night were, for lack of a better word, a real, non-poetic example of what is commonly known as..." Taylor waited for me. I exhaled. "Vampires."

Taylor smiled and nodded softly. I could see the sunlight starting to creep inside the cave, and I heard footsteps from outside. Seeing Taylor's calm reaction to simply turning and walking, I assumed it was Elijah and the other wolves.

Sure enough, I heard them muttering something before the lamp let me see them properly. Elijah walked inside the cave, accompanied by a brown, a black and a red wolf.

"You're awake," said Elijah. "Good. We need to talk about some things."

Elijah kneeled down to look at my shoulder wound and disconnect my IV.

"Taylor just told me everything," I said.

"Trust me," he answered, "he hasn't."

He put away the IV and walked closer to the fire where, as I hadn't noticed, was a chair with my shirt and jacket. He threw them to me.

"Put those on. You must be freezing." I put them on with effort, still feeling pain in my shoulder. At this, Elijah took a pill from his pocket and gave it to me. "Take this. It'll help you."

I looked at the pill and recognized it immediately. It was Vicodin. I took it and swallowed it dry.

"George," called Taylor, and I turned to him. "I'd like to introduce you to my pack." The three wolves were standing next to Taylor, all looking at me. "This is Drake," he said, referring to the red wolf. He vowed to me, and I did the same. "Alex," referring to the brown wolf, who also vowed. "And you've already met Gray," he finished, signaling the black wolf. He vowed as well, but somehow it didn't look or feel as polite as the others.

"I'd also like to you meet somebody, George," said Elijah. "Come take a walk with me."

Chapter 7
Mr. Foxworth
George, April 8th, morning

Elijah brought with him a pair of crutches, which I used to stand up and move out of the cave. I could recognize the early rays of the dawn. For what I could calculate on the spot, it had been around ten hours since Andrea's kidnap.

"How are you feeling?" he asked me.

"In short, I'm alright," I answered. "Thanks for your treatment."

"No problem," he said. "I've been thinking a lot about that, actually." He stopped, so I stopped. "You said Taylor told you things. What, exactly?"

"The basics," I said. I was sure the combination of drugs in my bloodstream was keeping me from fainting in shock. "The wolves, the bats, and you, the hunter. And your sponsor, who I assume is who we're meeting."

Elijah didn't expect this. "You're very clever," he said in astonishment as he resumed the walk. "I was expecting we'd have to walk you through it very slowly."

"I'm not stupid," I said. "Everything you did in order to save me proves to me that you're the real thing."

I had never been to this part of the forest before. It was very cold, as usual, but it looked nicely different. I felt there were less trees, that sunlight could seep through the foliage more easily and into my skin, warming me as I walked. To my right, I could see a long downward slope.

"I've been wondering about that," continued Elijah. "All night I've been thinking how you must feel. What you must be thinking about your friends and your parents. The town is surely in total chaos."

"I don't have any parents," I said, coldly. So coldly, Elijah stopped again and looked at me, as if to see if I was messing with him. "Dad died ten years ago, mom a couple. I live with my stepdad." Elijah stood there, speechless. Knowing his stance and expression all too well, I kept walking.

"I'm sorry to hear that," he said, catching up to me. "Surely, he must be worried sick about you."

"Probably doing everything in his power to clean his name so they don't suspect he did it," I answered. Elijah stopped yet again, stunned.

"I-" started Elijah, truly speechless.

"Don't worry about it," I said, not stopping. "Let's get on with this walk. It's too cold to be standing here."

Elijah resumed his walk. "I thought I'd have to talk you into not going back home."

"Well, you don't have to," I said. "I know I'll never find Andrea alone, so there's no reason for me to escape anywhere."

"How old are you?" he asked.

"Seventeen. How old are *you*?"

"Thirty two. I guess we both look older."

We both walked in silence for a moment. I figured he was figuring out what to say.

"Aren't you scared?" he finally asked me.

"Last night was the scariest experience I've ever felt," I said. "Even scarier than seeing my mother collapse and calling the ambulance. The only person I would like to go back to is my best friend, Stephanie. But I'm not stupid enough to put her and you in danger."

I could see slight twitches on Elijah's face that made it seem like he was smiling. "I underestimated you, then."

He kept walking, and I followed.

#

We walked to the edge of this forest, to a place that was definitely not Adler, and I had never seen before. It looked like the edge of a very small town, where there was a main street and a gas station across it. On our side of the street was a 1-story house that lied alone on the block.

"Where are we?" I asked Elijah.

"Foxworth, Minnesota," he said, without looking at me or stopping.

We went around the house to the front porch, where I could see the town more clearly. In front of the house was what looked like a family diner, and beside it was a small credit union. To the other side was a park, and besides that, I couldn't see clearly. But it did feel very strange to not have anything on this side of the street other than this big house.

The house had no lawn, but no fences either. All the grass connected with the forest like there were part of the same lawn, like the forest was the house's backyard.

Elijah knocked the door with a pattern that I recognized as the first line of the "Happy Birthday" song. Without any verbal response, I heard the door unlock, and Elijah pushed it open.

The inside of the house looked like nothing special to me. The door lead directly into a small living room with a couch and a red velvet armchair. A big rug decorated most of the living room, with the naked floor looking like recently-waxed dark wood. There was a white wooden door to the left that, I assumed, went into the kitchen, leaving the oak door to the right as the bedroom door.

As we entered I could see there was a big painting of a green field to my right, and I stared at it. I think it reminded me of my mom. I would've probably stayed on the painting for longer if Elijah hadn't called my name.

"George," he said. I snapped and turned to him, and I saw another person. A fairly old gentleman of at least 70, holding a cane. He was slender, wearing small, round spectacles. "I'd like you to meet my mentor, Peter Foxworth."

The old man looked friendly and inviting. His face was wrinkled and worn, the few hairs remaining on his head completely white. Green eyes and white teeth, dressed in a business suit without a tie, as if he had just come from a meeting. His cane looked solid and sturdy, made of dark wood. He wasn't very tall, but it looked like he had been before.

"My pleasure, young man," said the old man, stretching his hand. I shook his hand, feeling all of his wrinkles and roughed skin against mine.

"Good morning," I said, quietly.

"Please, sit down," said Mr. Foxworth, his hand inviting us to the big central couch. In front of us was a coffee table with a green bowl, filled with what looked like car keys. Elijah took off his jacket and sat down next to me.

We sat down and I rested my crutches on the arm of the couch, and the old man went straight for the red armchair. He sat down with difficulty, really putting his cane to work.

"Do you name yourself after the town you move to, or was this town named after you?" I asked. Mr. Foxworth chuckled and looked at Elijah, who seemed a lot more concerned about my manners.

"You failed to mention he was this observant," he said to Elijah.

"I only found out this morning," he answered. "Lots of surprises on the walk here."

"I would be grateful," I said, "if you didn't speak about me as if I'm not sitting right here."

For some reason, I thought of Mr. Larned. I imagined what he would think of my approach to this conversation, probably commenting on my abundant *logos* and almost complete lack of *pathos*, which is clearly what Elijah and Mr. Foxworth were expecting to deal with.

Mr. Foxworth chuckled some more. "Oh dear. I guess our job won't be as difficult as we thought, eh?" he said, looking at Elijah.

Elijah nodded. "Taylor already laid the most difficult part for him."

Mr. Foxworth looked at me, with slight surprise. "How is it that you haven't ran away yet, young man?"

"Because I'm half drugged and I'm not stupid," I answered. I looked at Elijah. "Are we gonna go through the same conversation again?"

Elijah shook his head. "No. We're just surprised that we won't need the introduction before we start the real talk."

I turned to Mr. Foxworth to see if he had anything to say. He stayed silent, looking at me with curiosity. "Could you give me the chance to guess?" I asked.

This, again, caught them off-guard. "Guess what, exactly?" asked Elijah.

"What you're going to tell me. What I'm pretty sure we're going to talk here."

Elijah looked at Mr. Foxworth in confusion. Mr. Foxworth shook his head at him. "Oh, the youth," he said. "I forget how they grow up, so differently to how I did or even you, Elijah. Information and communication surrounds them." Elijah sat silent. Mr. Foxworth looked back at me. "Go ahead, George. Guess."

"Well," I started. "My first guess is that you brought me here because you thought you'd have to slowly explain to me the situation and convince me that going back to town would put me, my friends, and you in danger, but we already discussed that." They both nodded. "I also think that you want to actually protect me, not only protect yourselves. And even though some may call me naive, you have gained my trust. At least you have, Elijah." They both smiled. "No offense, Mr. Foxworth."

Mr. Foxworth gave me a hearty laugh. "Oh, none taken at all. I am actually very glad that you have given your trust to Elijah, and the fact that you don't instantly trust me makes you look, to my eyes, very smart. Continue."

"You're obviously a man of wealth," I continued. "If I had to guess, I'd say you founded this small town in the middle of nowhere and that you own every piece of it. Therefore, this town was named after you, and not the other way around."

Mr. Foxworth nodded. "That is, indeed, correct."

"What I fail to conclude is where both of you came from. I've read enough books to guess many different things, but none of them sound grounded in reality."

"I am very impressed by your use of language, George," said Mr. Foxworth. "Your assumptions about our possible origins are mostly correct. I wouldn't say any kind of fantasy novels would do us justice."

"We are not part of a secret society," said Elijah, suddenly. "We have no special powers, we are not chosen ones and neither are you. We're just people who know some things that most people don't."

"It has run in my family for generations," continued Mr. Foxworth. "It has nothing to do with magic or blood. I just happen to be too old to continue doing the work myself, so Elijah does it for me."

"Did your family become rich by hunting monsters?" I asked.

"Oh, no," chuckled Mr. Foxworth. "My family's wealth and side occupations have little relation to one another. I inherited a construction company that has grown larger and larger through generations."

I sat silent for a moment. Mr. Foxworth stared into my eyes, as if looking for my thoughts inside them.

"What exactly did they do to me last night?" I asked. "When vampires bite you, you turn, right?"

"Not necessarily," said Elijah. "For what we've gathered over the years, it acts as a kind of two-way needle. They drink blood just like bats, but they also poison you like snakes. Yesterday, your blood was drank but you were not poisoned."

"Are you sure?" I asked, doubtful.

"After seeing you this morning, yes. One hundred percent sure."

I sat there, thinking. Thinking of Elijah's phrasing, how they had gathered information but didn't sound like they were completely informed of every aspect on the matter. That meant that they weren't exactly experienced with vampires, so he might be wrong. Still, apart from the pain of my wounds, I felt physically fine.

"Why are they here?" I asked.

Another moment of silence. "We don't know," said Elijah. "But we've been chasing them for months."

"Are they the reason for this unusual climate?" I asked. They both nodded. "Why did they take so long to strike?"

"That is a great question," said Mr. Foxworth. "We are not completely sure. We have theories, but just that. Elijah and the wolves have been working very hard, investigating."

"And how did you get in contact with the wolves?"

"Oh, that's a very different story, for another time," said Mr. Foxworth. "All you have to know is that every single one of them is a valuable ally and a trusted friend. I implore you to open up to them as much as you have to Elijah."

Another story, for a different time. That sounded almost too convenient, but I didn't have time to ask them further. I had many more questions to ask them.

"What are they gonna do to my friends?"

Silence. Not good for my stomach, but I kept my breathing steady as they thought of what to say.

"We are not sure of that either," said Elijah. "The few things we know is that they don't just kill people for sport or for food. It's more than that."

"Through our studies we have determined that they probably have some kind of ritual to complete," added Mr. Foxworth. "We're just not sure what that is, yet."

"Wait a second," I said, in disbelief. "You mean, you're not even sure of what you're fighting?" This didn't make much sense, though, since they knew what had happened to me last night.

"Oh, no," said Mr. Foxworth. "We know what we're fighting. We know how to protect ourselves from them, and we have very solid ideas on how to kill them. We just don't know what they want."

"These things aren't exactly common, George," added Elijah, solidifying what I'd thought earlier. "It's certainly my first time having to deal with one of them."

"And mine too," said Mr. Foxworth. "And I have seen a lot of things in my lifetime."

I swallowed hardly. "So, we're protected, you say?"

"Yes, we are," said Elijah. He pulled up his sleeve to reveal a strange tattoo on his shoulder. It looked like a strange combination between the Eye of Horus and the Christian cross. But, at the same time, it wasn't like anything I'd seen before. The black ink looked like it had aged a bit on Elijah's skin.

Mr. Foxworth rolled up his sleeve to show me the same tattoo on his wrist, with a lot more age and slightly altered by the wrinkles on his skin. "Like I said, I've been on this business for a long time."

"What about me?" I asked, half scared, half angered at their failure to give me as much protection as they had.

"Check the back pocket of your pants," said Elijah. I put my hand over it and felt something odd, like a piece of plastic that I hadn't noticed when I sat down. I stood up and took out a small, fine necklace with the same symbol as the tattoo. "I obviously wasn't gonna tattoo you in your sleep."

I looked at the necklace and rubbed my thumb against it. It was solid, but very small. It didn't feel heavy or warm or powerful in any way, just a necklace.

"So, what now?" I asked. "Am I part of your group of hunters or something?"

Elijah was about to answer, but was interrupted by another of Mr. Foxworth's laughs. "Is that what you want, young man?"

This looked to impress Elijah even more than it surprised me. "I do," I said. "I want to rescue my friends." Referring to Monica and Miles as 'friends' felt really weird, but saying that I wanted to rescue my friend and the two other people who I didn't know that much didn't really roll off the tongue.

"We can't let you in combat, George," said Elijah. "You're hurt and inexperienced. Letting you fight alongside us would be even riskier than letting you go back to Adler."

"Then why the hell did you bring me here?" I asked, the disappointment and anger starting to rise up from my stomach.

"We wanted to let you see what everything's about. What's actually going on. I think you deserve that after going through last night."

"This is bullshit," I started. I regretted it immediately, seeing how well Mr. Foxworth was handling the situation. I'm sure having an unknown teenager in your house complaining about his wishes was not something he wanted right then. "Sorry, Mr. Foxworth," I said, looking at him.

Mr. Foxworth smiled at me. "I understand your frustration, George." Me and Elijah waited for him to continue, but he didn't say more.

"Can you at least let me read?" I said to Elijah. "Let me understand what's happening?"

This made Elijah stop to think, and so did I. I wondered exactly what they hoped would happen when they brought me here, probably that I'd be a scared child that they had to force into staying put. But we already went through that, so now what? Did they just want me to sit on my ass and not do anything while they dick around with the vampires? Because I was not okay with that.

"We can," said Mr. Foxworth, finally. "You can read while you recover from your injuries."

Elijah looked at his mentor. I could almost hear Elijah asking him if he was sure about it. But Mr. Foxworth looked very sure of his decision.

I thought of what was at stake. I thought about Andrea and how scared she must have been, if she was even conscious. I thought about Monica and Miles, and how their family and friends must feel like. I thought of Steph and the rest of Adler, and wondered if I was declared missing along with the others, or if it had been Steph who had brought it to the town's attention.

Either way, something had to be done. I needed to know exactly what was going on, and if they would allow me to at least read my way into this world, I was going to do it. I had to do it.

For Andrea, for Steph, and for myself.

Part Two

Never in the history of the world had these many eyes been set on the town of Adler, Minnesota. The very next morning after the disappearance of the four kids, there were headlines all over the state, and by Monday, all of the country had heard of it. From Point Roberts to Key West, the whole country was shaken by what the media had nicknamed "The Missing Four."

The story of The Missing Four was very relevant at the Canadian Border as well, where triple security had been established and transportation in and out of the country was being overseen very carefully. Discussions took place where people would point fingers to any logical culprit, usually ending on blaming the government for poor vigilance of their forests, or the community of Adler for poor vigilance of their young. The latter sat particularly bad with the Mayor of Adler, Elliot Robbins.

Mayor Robbins was reaching the end of his career at this point in time, and had been very publicly criticized for this "slip," as some called it. Mayor Robbins was generally liked across his county, with his plans on renovating the roads and a shift on public spending towards the school system, where his grandkids spent their days. But then, in a span of 12 hours, Mayor Robbins became the target for critics around the state and the country, because he liked to keep the forest open, like it had been since the founding of the town.

Experts from corporate media companies chimed in, some defending the Mayor during this terrible situation, feeling compassion for him and his office as they had to deal with these missing children. One way or another, it had been decided by individuals superior to Mayor Robbins that the Adler Natural Conservation Preserve was completely out of bounds, and a curfew was in place for anybody without adult supervision. This, aside from the increasing government presence around the area, was very worrying for young Stephanie Kim, whose best friend had just disappeared.

During the final hours of the Spring Festival, Stephanie had grown concerned for her friend, George McKnight, whom she had last seen leaving for the festival attractions with another lady, Ms. Andrea Clinton, another victim. After the fireworks ended and the festival was closing, Stephanie tried calling her friend, with no success. After getting back home she tried again, and it still didn't connect. George's phone was off, which she found very strange, as she told the police that night.

The next day, before the news broke around the country, Steph took it upon herself to make sure George was okay. She put on a heavy jacket and walked all the way to George's house, and knocked on the door.

Standing on the green mat, she heard screaming from inside the house, getting closer. "I swear to God, if you just came back from–" screamed Robert Gil, McKnight's stepfather, stopping abruptly at the sight of Steph.

Her eyes filled with tears. "He's not here?"

"No," sighed Robert. "I called the police earlier. There's some other kids missing."

Steph didn't want to hear it. She turned away and ran back home, crying in desperation. She entered her living room and turned on the TV, changed the channel to the local news, and sat on the floor. Hopeless.

Sergeant Terrence Walker lead an investigation the night before, forming a perimeter close to the edge of the forest. No more information was shared by the police, making the town explode in chaos. Soon after the briefing, the news broke to outlets outside of the state, and it was the new national story before lunchtime.

Further investigation would let them arrive at better conclusions, but for now, it was evident that this case was not simply a disappearance. Along with the recent cases of Barbara Hawkins and Officer Alan Maffei, it was more than clear for everybody that these cases must have been connected somehow, because Adler was not the type to have this kind of crimes. The Missing Four – Miles Goodman, Monica Lee, Andrea Clinton, and George McKnight – had been kidnapped.

Chapter 8
The Missing Four

Monica

No identifiable characteristic could tell her if it was day or night. The usual cold of the past months couldn't be felt inside her cocoon, and it was almost as if her own body heat was warming everything up.

She awakened to noise. Then, movement. She felt how something grabbed her cocoon and moved her from where she was hanging. Again, she screamed, but she knew it was useless. It was more about letting out her frustration than anything else.

After feeling movement for a few minutes, she was laid down on the floor, and her cocoon collapsed on her, like the walls of a bag. Now that she wasn't being pulled down by gravity, she realized that her cocoon was much bigger than she thought; she could almost stand up inside it.

Without any warning, a claw ripped the front wall of the cocoon and went down, opening it up to the blinding light of day. Monica felt her eyes burn, so she closed them suddenly. The cold breeze blew through her face, making her nose feel like it was about to explode.

Slowly, she reopened them to see where she was. She was still under the trees of a forest, and could see a lakeshore in the distance. The light that blinded her eyes appeared to had bounced from the lake, because not much sunlight penetrated the foliage.

Monica looked around. She couldn't see anybody but herself, and yet, she felt she was being watched.

"On your knees," she thought she heard a deep, growly voice say. This made her jump in surprise and fear, looking around some more in search for the source of the voice. "On your knees," the voice repeated. She didn't know why or how, but suddenly, she felt compelled to kneel, right then and there.

Monica started weeping. "Please," she said. "Please, don't hurt me."

"Silence," she heard again. She still couldn't tell where the voice was coming from, but she felt it was, somehow, right from under her scalp. And, again, she felt compelled to stop talking.

"My Lord," said Arabella, from somewhere Monica couldn't identify. "You have done it. The ritual has worked." Monica wasn't sure she was hearing right, but Arabella's tone sounded happy. Glad.

"Girl," said the voice, seemingly ignoring Arabella. "What do you see?"

"I see…" started Monica, unwillingly. As if a force beneath her was forcing her to speak. "I see a lake."

All of a sudden, Monica felt Arabella's presence right next to her. She looked to her right, and there she was, for the first time in Monica's eyes, standing. She appeared naked, but not exactly; it looked as if she wore a full-body suit of grey skin, but it looked too real and natural. Her breasts were likewise under this grey armor of sorts, and she didn't have any sign of a navel. Her red hair and eyes were highlighted by the sunlight reflected by the lake. To Monica's eyes, she looked like, once upon a time, she must've been a beautiful woman.

"Yes, my Lord," said Arabella, though Monica didn't hear any questions.

Without warning, Arabella grabbed Monica's wrist and pulled her up. Monica felt compelled to keep quiet, to silently drown in her terror.

Then, it all went black again.

Steph, April 8th, morning

Heartbroken as she felt, Steph didn't want to lay down and do nothing. But what could she do, anyway? It's not like she had any kind of influence around town to get some answers. The closest thing she had to any contact was inside the hospital where her dad worked, but that wasn't gonna help anybody right now. The forest was closed, there was a curfew at night, and she had no idea where to start.

Before she could think of something, she got a text from Roger, Andrea's friend. Not exactly the person she expected to contact her at that moment. "Did you see the news this morning?"

"I'm watching it right now. I can't believe it."

"My brother works in the police department. He says they spent all night looking for clues. They may have a couple of leads."

"What leads?"

"I'm with Stacy right now. Meet us at school asap."

That took a turn that she definitely did not see coming. It's not like she expected to find George hidden behind the school or anything, but going out to meet Roger and Stacy somehow felt like progress. Progress in what? She didn't really know.

But before she could get her head around it, somebody knocked on the door, and Steph somehow knew who it was. Evelyn opened to reveal a couple of police officers, one of them familiar to Steph.

"Good morning, Mrs. Kim," greeted Sergeant Walker.

"Good morning," replied Evelyn. "How can I help you, officer?"

"There's a couple things we would like to consult with your daughter. About George." Steph's eyes widened as her mom turned to see her. "If you're both okay with that, of course. We don't want to pressure you."

Evelyn locked eyes with Steph, seemingly reading her mind. Steph didn't want to keep Roger waiting, but also wanted to know whatever she could get from Walker.

"If she's okay with it, you may come in," said Evelyn.

Steph walked to the door. "Hi," she said, nervous. "We can talk."

Sergeant Walker gave her a big smile. "Thank you. Can we come in?" he said to Steph. She nodded, so he and his partner stepped inside the house. Now that they were up close for the first time, Steph was amazed at how amazingly similar Sergeant Walker was to Scotch.

Evelyn showed them to the living room table and they both sat. She then left to the kitchen and started making coffee.

Steph just sat there, listening carefully.

"As you know, we're conducting the investigation to find your friends," started Walker. Steph nodded. "We were told that you were with George and Andrea last night at the festival. Could you tell us more about that?"

Steph stuttered a bit, then felt silent. She didn't feel the natural trust you'd feel towards a police officer, but she didn't know why. Logically, she had no reason to believe they wouldn't want to help her find George. "There's nothing to say," she finally said. "We were there and then he went away with Andrea. Didn't see him after that."

Walker's partner was taking notes on a notepad, but Walker appeared to ignore him. "Did he tell you about any plans that they had?"

"No," she said, sure of her words. "He just wanted to take the chance to be with her alone. I mean, as a boy who likes a girl, you know?" Her mom came back with two cups of coffee for the officers, and sat down next to her.

"You didn't see George and Andrea walking to the forest before the fireworks started?" She hadn't, and she couldn't think of a reason why he would do that.

"I didn't. I was with Roger and Stacy."

"Yes, Jonathan told me about them. They seem to spend a lot of time with Andrea, don't they?"

"Well, yeah. They're like a trio of friends. Just like I'm always with George too."

"But he left you at the festival," insisted Walker, "and now you were with Roger and Stacy."

"Well, yeah. We planned that he would talk to Andrea about how he felt. Thought it would be romantic under the lights and stuff. You know?"

Walker nodded in approval and sipped on his coffee. "This is truly marvelous, Mrs. Kim." Evelyn smiled and nodded. "Just what we needed after last night. Spent a long time walking around that forest."

"Did you find anything?" asked Steph, almost interrupting. She thought she may be able to get some information before seeing Roger at school. She was wrong.

"Sadly, no," said Walker. "That's why we're here. We needed some information on George, and you seem to know him a bit more than his stepfather."

"A lot more," Steph said, almost with disgust. "He couldn't tell you George's middle name if he tried to."

"Do you know if George had any plans of leaving his home?"

This sounded like the most left-field question that could've been asked. "What? No. George would rather die than lose that house. No way."

Walker sat in silence as his partner finished writing his notes. "So, you're sure that George had no intention of going anywhere after the festival?"

Steph got even more confused. "No. Where could he have gone?"

"I don't know, Ms. Kim. We're just covering all possibilities."

Steph thought hard. She analyzed the questions that had been asked and thought of any ulterior motives they could've had. Why would Sergeant Walker imply that George was planning something?

"If he had the intention of escaping anywhere," continued Walker, "you think he would tell you, right?"

Where they really considering the possibility that George was responsible for the kidnapping? Because that would've been very insulting.

Steph wanted to be more mature in her response, but between the recent events and what was just said, she couldn't help it. "I don't like what you're implying, Walker."

"Ms. Kim," said Walker. His friendly tone slipping away just a bit. "We're just covering all grounds. You have nothing to worry about."

"It sounds to me that you think George had something to do with what happened last night, which is an utter lie."

"Like I said, we–"

"Sergeant," interrupted Evelyn, "I don't like what you're implying either. I can assure you, my daughter is not part of whatever you think happened last night."

"And neither is George!" said Steph, standing up, almost yelling. "George wanted to talk to Andrea alone because he has a crush on her and he sucks at talking to girls. That's all."

Silence except for the note-taking by the younger officer. "We're just trying to cover every possibility," Walker repeated one more time. "That's all."

"Well, cover them well," said Steph, standing up from her chair. "George McKnight is the sweetest person I've ever met, and I assure you he's one of the victims of this horrible case, just like the other three." Before Walker could retort, Steph concluded, "Consultation over," and she walked to the stairs.

#

As soon as she saw the cop car leave the front of her house, Steph went out. The walk to school felt almost nonexistent. Her mind was too preoccupied thinking and evaluating the possibilities and consequences of whatever the cops thought George was involved in.

She got to the school gate and saw Roger and Stacy sitting by the steps. They both waved at her.

"I just spoke to the cops," said Steph, without any preamble. "Whatever you know that I don't, please tell me."

"Sit," said Stacy, one of the first words Steph heard her say. For the longest time, Steph could've sworn she was a mute, but no. She just kept to herself and Roger talked double, just how he liked it.

Steph sat beside them. "My brother was part of the search team last night," said Roger. "He was right next to Terrence Walker during the whole thing."

"I just spoke to him," said Steph. "I'm not very impressed."

"The weirdest thing happened when they were looking around," continued Roger. "Chad says he almost arrested a guy who was walking by the clearing they were investigating. Just strolling by, with a crossbow."

"What the hell?" said Steph. "Are you sure that's what Chad said?"

"Positive. But they didn't arrest him because Walker knew him. They even talked for a moment. Chad said they even looked like friends."

This story didn't make a lot of sense. First of all, walking alone at night by the forest sounds so creepy it has to be on purpose. Second, why wouldn't Walker at least suspect this guy, especially if he's armed with a crossbow?

"His name was Peter something, I don't know," continued Roger. "But anyway, Chad said he was going to a cabin close by, but Walker said that he couldn't, that he had to go back to his apartment. A cabin in the woods, okay?" reiterated Roger in disbelief. "Can you believe this guy?"

"Actually, no," said Steph. "It sounds completely made up."

"I know!" said Roger, "but Chad swears it's not. But that's not the creepiest part." Steph legitimately thought the creepy man in the forest was the only thing Roger had to say. She almost wished it was, so she didn't have to learn anything sketchy about George. "After Peter left, they got a full team to investigate the clearing, and they found lots of things. They found hair, skin, and blood."

Steph's stomach turned. "Blood?" she asked. "Whose blood?"

"They don't know yet. They'll announce the finding on the news later today. For now, they sent it to the lab immediately along with the hair and the skin. But before his shift ended, Chad said he heard something else."

Steph felt she knew what was coming, and wished with all her heart that she was wrong. But she wasn't.

"They also found different strands of hair inside Peter's cabin. They think it matches the ones at the scene."

You wake up in the middle of the night for no apparent reason. Baby isn't crying, wife is sleeping sound, but you feel this urge to get up and start walking. You don't, but you must. You have to go outside. You must abide to the request. No; to the order.

It's a strange feeling, but you overcome it. You fall back asleep, and dream of a lake. The lake shines brightly, it burns your eyes with despair, but you can't close them. You stand there, and you wait, while your eyes disintegrate with the radiant sunlight. You can't wake up; they won't let you. All your attempts are useless. The dream is long and slow. It lasts all night.

You wake up again, and it's not nighttime anymore. Your wife is up, the baby's crying.

Chapter 9

Demons

Gray, April 8th, afternoon

It had been a while since Elijah had left with the boy. The wolves used this time to pack absolutely everything they had in their cave and put it in old suitcases they kept for such occasions. Living in the wild for so long and knowing each other so well, it was like they were an actual wolfpack that migrated with the change of seasons.

Gray took a last look at the cave before leaving it for God knows how long. Not only had they had to deal with the cold and the demons, but know the stupid kid made them leave their home for an undetermined amount of time. In human form and fully clothes, the wolves parted ways with their cave and headed West.

Feeling – and smelling – Gray's mood, Taylor decided to chime in. "It'll be nice to see Mr. Foxworth again. That's a funny old man."

Gray barely turned his head to Taylor. "Sure," he said, and nothing more.

Gray looked to his other side at Alex and Drake, and realized that it was the first time in a long time that they were all in human form and fully clothes, probably the first time since they last migrated. In this form, one could appreciate their differences a lot more, not just the color of their pelts. Alex's hair was dark brown, but so was his skin, and it was more apparent that he was older than any of them.

Drake was the complete opposite. Drake looked at best less than a decade older than George, though he was actually much older. His dark red hair matched his pelt's as well, though he kept it shorter than his fellow pack members, but his fair skin could not be noticed when he transformed. They were both tall and fit, though Drake was considerably slimmer than any of them. Still, none matched Gray's physical presence.

If you saw him at a bar, you would think Gray is the prime example of a guy you don't mess with. With his pale skin and long black mane, he can look almost scary from a distance. And his pack know he is actually a very serious person, but they also know that Gray would never beat up an innocent person just for looking at him funny.

Taylor's long blonde mane usually stood out among them. That, and the fact that he looked light-years more approachable than his contemporary peers. Drake, younger as he was, still kept some positivity in his face. The same couldn't be said about Gray and Alex.

Not long after, they arrived at the edge of Foxworth, Minnesota, where they were received by the backside of Mr. Foxworth's house, like they expected. They approached the front door, and Gray knocked the "Happy Birthday" pattern. Seconds later, the door clicked, and the wolves came inside the house.

The entrance room remained unchanged, to what Gray could recall. The big couch, the red armchair, and the two doors at the end. One of the doors lead to a closet where there were some important buttons and switches that Gray didn't know nor cared what they did, and the other door was followed by stairs that lead to the basement, where the real house was.

The basement was thirty times bigger than the house itself, with a complete kitchen, a big central hall with a huge round table, a small office stacked with books that they called library, and rooms. Ten, maybe fifteen rooms that you could access from the main hall. All equipped with a bed, a bathroom, and a small refrigerator that was always full with water bottles.

The dark hardwood floor covered all of the basement, making it feel like a retirement cabin at a mountain top. The ceiling and walls were tall and white, made with what Gray thought could be marble. And in every room there was at least one piece of art. The artificial light that kept the place visible didn't overwhelm the eyes, but it would've been much better to have an actual window somewhere. Not even the welcoming atmosphere of everything with Foxworth's name was enough to make Gray forget that he was underground.

It was difficult for Gray to admit, however, that there were some things that he longed for that the Foxworth Estate could provide. What he didn't like was having to take suggestions – because they were most definitely not orders – and move out of his established hideout. Mr. Foxworth repeatedly expressed his opinion about how ridiculous he found it that the pack didn't just live there permanently, which only irritated Gray even more.

Not much had changed since the last time they'd been to old Foxworth's. The only noticeable difference was the teenager sitting in the library, with two piles of books laying on the table in front of him.

"Welcome, welcome," said Mr. Foxworth, with his typical friendly voice. "Please, sit down and relax. I'm sure your trip was tiresome."

The wolves laid down their bags and sat around the round table. Moments later, Mr. Foxworth came from the kitchen with four cups of hot tea.

"Where's Elijah?" asked Gray, noticing his smell but not his presence.

"I'm over here," said Elijah from the inside of one fo the rooms. "One second." Moments later, Elijah came out of the room in a bathrobe. His hair wet and untidy, his face refreshed.

"Damn. I'd kill for a hot shower," said Drake.

"Come right ahead!" exclaimed Mr. Foxworth. "There are enough rooms for each of you. Relax, eat something, and you can come back later."

"There's no time for that right now," said Gray. "We have important things to discuss."

"Don't be ridiculous, Michael," said Mr. Foxworth. "You've had a long 24 hours. You deserve some rest."

"Go ahead," insisted Elijah. "We'll talk later."

Gray planned to reply, but Drake was more than lenient towards Foxworth's invitation. In no time he had picked what would be his room and took his things inside.

Elijah went back to his room and back out five minutes later, dressed in more casual garments. He approached the round table, where Gray and Alex were sitting, looking at a map of the forest. They still hadn't chosen a room.

"How were your travels?" asked Elijah.

"Same as usual," answered Alex without looking.

"How's the boy?" asked Gray, looking from his seat to the open library door.

"Fine," said Elijah. "He'll have recovered in no time."

"Would you mind explaining the pile of books he seems ready to read?" asked Gray. Alex raised his head.

"What?" asked Alex. "I didn't notice that."

"We are allowing him to spend his recovery reading. So he can understand what's going on."

Gray and Alex looked at each other. Alex sighed. "This is exactly what I told you this morning, Elijah. You can't train this kid."

"I don't have any plans to train him," said Elijah. "He seemed very willing to become part of the team and I shut him down. I don't want him fighting either, Alex."

"I don't think it could hurt," interrupted Gray, "to let the boy learn. It could at least make him ask less questions."

Alex didn't look convinced. "One thing will lead to the other. I'm sure of it."

"It will be you who trains him, then," said Elijah, clearly done with the conversation. "Because I won't."

Elijah proceeded to retire to his room before Alex could say anything else.

George, April 8th, afternoon

For hours I had been glued to the 2000-page book Mr. Foxworth insisted I read first, titled *European Demons*. He said it would be the best place to start, seeing that it was where most of the information we had on the vampires came from.

These books all shared the same basic characteristics. They were all very old, appeared to have no author, and read like scientific papers, but without the boring details that always seem to be on the way from the point. As I read about things that hunt at night, for example, the book didn't proceed to explain the kinds of proteins that formed the beast's eyeballs and how the chemicals in their brain interpreted the low light environments; it just laid out what it was and compared it to an animal we already know.

That's something that really caught my attention about these books; they didn't feel like fantasy, but an extension of our world. One of the few aspects I always disliked about the *Harry Potter* books was how extensive the magical beast catalogue was, because it's just a free invitation for plot holes. The way complete species of magical creatures exist without the Muggles ever experiencing them is interesting and engrossing, but hardly grounded in reality. These books I was reading were very much grounded in reality.

The first books I read gave me a sense of how small our world really is, and how everything hides in plain sight and seems to come from evolutions of real-life creatures. You know how the human mind is so limited, we always imagine aliens as human-like creatures, instead of something that is really out of this world? These books put whatever magical or supernatural creature they spoke about on that same plain. They are from this same planet, after all.

Halfway through *European Demons* I finally got to the part that I thought I would see, the reason why Mr. Foxworth wanted me to start with this book. I read *Dracula* back in middle school for a Winter Break book report and I really liked it, but that book is a clear romanticization of the vampire myth, and has many things that don't do it justice at all.

In *European Demons*, the author – or authors – starts with detailing what is and what isn't real about vampires. Some of the most popular misconceptions adopted from popular media are that vampires are inherent seducers; it's not wrong that they mesmerize some of their victims, but "seducing them" is heavily romanticized for the sake of literary beauty.

Some very false conceptions about vampires include their lack of reflections in mirrors, their apparent allergy to wooden sticks, and their intolerance to sunlight. "While it is true that these demons prefer to strike at night, it is merely out of convenience. It has nothing to do with them being weak to sunlight." At least they don't sparkle under it, either.

What I found strange is that a lot of what is commonly known of vampires is actually true. They drink blood to survive, they abduct people and keep them, and they have big, boney wings similar to bats'. What I couldn't see anywhere was what Elijah had told me about their teeth acting as two-way needled, but I convinced myself that it must have been written in another, more modern book. Because I trusted Elijah.

Other less-publicized aspect of vampires are true as well. They can control small animals like rats or birds, they have increased strength, and are extremely durable; the book went as far as to compare their limb growth to that of lizards, but much, much faster.

It also went into their appearance quite a bit, but there's where the book started going into speculation rather than observations. According to the author(s), the appearance of the average vampire is how I saw them the night before: grey, rough skin that covers all of their body, seemingly hiding their genitals. But sometimes they could go back to looking like a regular human, though the book didn't know exactly how, which frustrated me. It was evident that it wasn't a voluntary, every-day thing like how the wolves transform and detransform at will, but I didn't get any more than speculation.

It was physically impossible to finish reading this giant book in a single day, let alone a single sitting, but I did my best to get as much as possible before having to go to bed. The lunch sandwich I had was eaten inside the library, and I only got up to the bathroom once. The rest of the reading went smooth until I heard voices coming from the stairs.

#

The wolves' arrival was noisy and distracting, making it very hard to focus on my reading. I heard their voices come in, so I opened the door to see and hear better, but I didn't leave my post. I stayed there, and made sure that they all saw me reading. I wanted them to know that we were playing on the same field.

At first, they didn't pay much attention to me. I recognized Gray, now wearing clothes, and obviously Taylor. What caught my attention was how young Drake looked; he could've passed for my older brother, easily. Alex looked much older that Taylor and Gray, maybe in his late 50s.

I stayed seated through Elijah and Alex discussing my possible future training, wondering if they legitimately thought I was deaf. Soon after, Elijah came to the library.

"How are you doing?" he asked, friendly enough.

"Fast and steady," I answered. "Pretty interesting stuff."

"I would agree."

"So, about what Alex suggested," I started, but Elijah wasn't taking it.

"Quit it," he said, not angry, but determined. "Even if I wanted to, you still need crutches to walk."

"Not for long, though," I said, hoping to at least charm him a bit. It didn't seem to work.

"Keep reading," he said as he left the room.

His exit was followed by Drake coming in, wearing a bathrobe and smelling like a fresh shower. His hair combed back.

"Excuse me," he said, as he passed Elijah and laid on the doorframe. "Can I come in?"

"Sure," I said. "Hi, Drake."

"Hi," he smiled. He grabbed the chair on the other side of the table and sat in front of me. "I just wanted to say hi, because we haven't been properly introduced yet." He stretched his hand and I shook it.

"I saw you at the cave earlier," I said. "You're the red wolf."

"I mean, yeah. But that doesn't count." Drake chuckled a bit. "It's not the same meeting a wolf than meeting a person."

That was true, actually. Our introduction had been very quick and included no exchange of dialogue, it still felt very incomplete. Now that I had Drake right in front of me, I didn't exactly know what to say.

"Well, I'll leave you to your books," he said, relieving me of having to think of something else. "Good luck," he said as he stood up and put the chair back in its place.

"Thanks," I answered as he smiled one last time and left the library. "Leave it open, please," I told him before he closed the door.

I could still see Gray and Alex on the table, looking at a map. I didn't know what they were doing nor could I hear what they were saying, but I was still fascinated by their presence. Thinking that the two people outside the door were two living, breathing werewolves was not an easy thing to digest, especially when I had seen first hand how one of them detransformed from a wolf into a… Something. Something between a dog and a human. Like the classical depictions of werewolves at midnight, almost.

I almost wanted to skip the vampire stuff and get directly to the werewolves, but I contained myself. I needed to know everything I could about our enemy if I wanted to let me fight in the team. And who knows, maybe I could find something they hadn't figured out yet.

Gray, April 8th, evening

Gray finally left his station, picked a room and entered. As expected, it was perfectly clean, with white sheets covering the queen-sized bed. Gray laid down his backpack and took off his shoes. He wasn't used to laying down as a man, and every time he did it, he remembered how much he missed it.

The walk-in closet at the other end of the room was empty, except for a couple of bathrobes and two sets of silk pajamas. Not matter how tired or beat up he was, he couldn't bring himself to the idea of wearing a bathrobe, not even after seeing how comfortable Elijah looked in his earlier that day.

After almost falling asleep on the bed, he stood up and went in the bathroom, which was also spotless. The fully equipped bathroom came with two big white towels and a rug, where Gray dropped his clothes.

Michael Gray opened the hot water and stood under it for minutes, enjoying the sensation and breathing in the steam, clearing his nostrils. All of his body was covered in scars that were usually covered by his fur, and his long black mane almost fought against the water, with Gray having to continuously massage his scalp to let it in.

Gray thought he had finished washing and got out of the shower, but the moment he rubbed the towel against his arm, he noticed its whiteness be replaced by a light grey, telling him that he wasn't quite clean yet. So he went back in, for another half hour.

He looked in the mirror after drying, with particular attention to his eyes. He tied his hair in a ponytail and looked closer into the mirror, noticing scars he was not aware of. His eye pockets looked more pronounced than ever, and it dawned on him that he had not slept at all the night before.

He put on one set of silk pajamas and went out of the room, where he saw the rest of his pack was already sitting at the table, having dinner. The boy and the hunter were also there, a pair of crutches leaning against the wall right next to them.

"Michael!" cheered Foxworth. "Please, sit down. Dinner is served."

Gray approached the table and sat next to Taylor. They were having roasted pork with buttery mashed potatoes, steamed broccoli, and white wine. The incredible smell of the rosemary pork made Gray salivate, but he kept his posture.

He was always fascinated by how Foxworth operated. There were obviously servants around the place, but Gray barely ever saw them. They never seemed to interfere with anything, never interrupted, and were always on time. This occasion would mark one of the very few times Gray saw Foxworth interacting with the help.

A short and skinny black woman came out of the kitchen with an extra bottle of wine, and gave it to Foxworth. "Thanks, Rose, dear," he said to her. She nodded and smiled with contempt.

"Won't you sit with us and eat, Ms. Rose?" asked Alex. She shook her head with shyness.

"I already ate, Mr. Chambers," she answered, with a very thick Southern accent. "Thank you for your kindness." And without another word, she retired back to the kitchen.

"I can see your concern," said Foxworth to Alex. "But you don't have to worry. They are well-paid employees, not slaves."

"I wasn't thinking that, Mr. Foxworth," said Alex, and both Gray and Foxworth knew that it was partly true. But a cynical, paranoid ex-servant would always live inside of Alex, and they all knew it.

Gray ate with delight and care, savoring every bite as if it was the last time he would taste anything. As he did so, he looked at the boy, who had been very quiet all evening. Most of the conversations where between Foxworth and either Taylor or Drake, who were always the most interested in knowing about anything Foxworth would talk about.

"So," started Gray, talking for the first time since he sat down. "What have you been reading, boy?" Everybody stopped to look at George.

George swallowed what he was chewing. "Mostly about the different kinds of things you hunt," he answered. "I've been reading since this morning, almost non-stop."

"I think that's great," said Taylor, almost trying to stop Gray from talking. "It's good that you learn about everything we're doing around here."

Alex scoffed, seemingly unintentionally. He caught the gaze of some, but didn't say anything and continued eating. "I'm George, by the way," said the boy to him. Alex turned to see him.

"I know. We've met," answered the black man.

"Not really, though," replied the boy. "Drake came in earlier and shook my hand. This is the first time I see you guys as humans."

Alex looked at Drake, who ate like nothing was being said around him. Nobody continued the topic, so they were all left with an immensely uncomfortable silence.

"What have you learned so far, George?" asked Foxworth, breaking the silence with a sword.

"I just got to the vampire section," answered the boy. That wasn't a word that Gray used to hear a lot. It was archaic, fantastical, a little silly. "But I haven't finished it yet. It's gonna take a while."

"Take your time," said Taylor. "It only works if you understand everything that you're reading. Some things may be hard to fully comprehend unless you put everything to it."

"I think I got to that earlier. When talking about their appearance, I wasn't sure what they meant."

"We can help you wi–" started Taylor, but was interrupted by Alex.

"Could we stop this nonsense?" he asked, getting angry. "We should stop pretending that this is going anywhere, like this boy is going to learn anything useful."

"Alex–" tried to intervene Taylor, but he couldn't.

"No, Taylor. I don't see the point in all of this. This boy was strained from his place and is here temporarily. Why–"

"George," said the boy, very loudly so he could talk over Alex's deep, commanding voice. "My name is George. I'm not a boy."

"How dare y–" but Alex was now interrupted by Foxworth, who stomped his cane on the floor, making them all jump in caution.

"This discussion is over," said Foxworth in his signature friendly tone. "If somebody wishes to stay for desert, we are having creamed strawberries. If not, you may leave our table in peace."

After a brief silence, Alex stood up and muttered something most couldn't hear, but the wolves identified as "bullshit." Shortly after, Gray stood up too.

"Thank you for this wonderful dinner, Mr. Foxworth," said Gray as he left the table.

This would be the first time in who-knows-how long that Gray would be able to sleep on a bed by himself, without any noise to disrupt him. He took off the silk top of the pajamas and laid down on his bed without covering his body with the bedsheet. He didn't feel the necessity to cover himself from the cold of the outside, and soon, he had fallen asleep.

You wake up again in the middle of the night. You feel a force inside your head pulling you up, wanting to throw you outside. The forest calls you. You want to follow.

You get up and get out. It's so cold outside, and you're almost naked. But it doesn't matter. You must obey the call. The forest is calling you, and you must follow. You don't live close to the forest, but it matters not. You will walk as far as you must to get to the forest. You want to go, and so you shall go. Ignore the breeze, ignore the dark; follow the voice.

You're there. You see the trees, the grass, the dark inside. The force grows stronger, it pulls you harder and harder. You feel compelled, convinced that you must go. You take one step, then another, you walk in.

You wake up again. It's daytime, and your wife is up. The baby's crying.

Chapter 10
Three Days Gone
Steph, April 10th, morning

Unsurprising to anybody, there was an assembly at school that Monday morning, first thing. Steph met with Roger and Stacy at the school entrance before the bell rang, and they walked together to the gym and sat next to each other. Stacy was her usual self, letting Roger do all the talking, and was he talkative that morning. He mentioned how everybody was looking at them, which made Steph feel particularly uncomfortable. She wasn't aware of how legal it was for her face or name to appear in the news, but she was sure that, at least in school, everybody would know that she was George's best friend – only friend, really.

It was strange to walk around school without George. Ever since they had found each other in middle school, they had been just inseparable. Although Steph wasn't exactly a socialite, she handled herself a lot better in crowds than George. And after losing his dad in a car accident and moving from Pennsylvania to Minnesota without knowing anybody, who could blame him?

Steph was George's main support after his mom had died. She skipped class to be with them at the hospital, she helped him get dressed to go to the funeral, she made sure he ate, and even got her parents to allow him to sleep on her bed while she slept on an air mattress, right next to him.

After George came back to school, he was quieter than ever. If it wasn't for Steph and some very comprehensive teachers, like Mr. Larned, George would've probably have to redo all of his freshman year of high school. Steph is George's counselor, personal trainer, lab partner, and best friend. And he is hers.

#

Although Jefferson High School didn't have sports teams – aside from the underground football league – it had a gym with a volleyball court that usually doubled as an auditorium. Here is where the assembly was going to take place, and when Steph got there, it was already full of students.

There was a small podium with a microphone, and a bunch of chairs where the teachers were sitting. Standing in front of the microphone was Principal Rodriguez, who seemed to be waiting for the rest of the students to populate the gym. Steph noticed Mr. Larned sitting at the end of the podium, looking unenthusiastic, like everybody else.

Gisela Rodriguez was said to have one of the easiest jobs in town. Adler's reputation as one of Minnesota's most peaceful towns implied certain expectations from whoever was chosen to lead any of its departments. Still, Ms.

Rodriguez ran the school like a well-oiled machine, with a good grip on every student and any event that occurred in and around her school building. It was wildly speculated that she was well aware about the monthly football games, but she allowed it because she thought it was healthy for the community.

A couple minutes after Steph sat with Roger and Stacy, Rodriguez tapped the microphone and everyone instantly went silent. "Good morning," started the Principal. "As I'm sure you all know, our community has been struck with some terrible news this past weekend."

Steph looked around as Rodriguez described the details of what everybody already knew. She was shocked to notice that Antoine was sitting in the front row, next to his grandfather, the Mayor. How Steph didn't notice when she entered the gym, she wasn't sure. Right next to that pair, though, was an even more surprising sight, with a touch of unpleasantness. She saw Scotch sitting with his dad, Sergeant Walker.

Steph caught up with what Rodriguez was saying. "It goes without saying that any information about any of the victims will be greatly appreciated by the authorities." Rodriguez looked at Walker when she finished, and Steph noticed a slight nod from him. "Mayor Robbins, would you like to add something?"

Mayor Robbins stood up and climbed the podium. He looked a lot like his grandson, with the tall, fit figure and the blonde hair. Mayor Robbins was notoriously polite, and he looked like he wanted no more than to make the students of Jefferson feel safe. "Hello," he started. "I always feel very compelled when I visit my grandchildren's school. I'm always proud of our beautiful town and community."

Steph spaced out as the Mayor kept talking. She looked at Antoine, who didn't look like he was enjoying his grandfather's speech, or whatever he was saying. This wasn't strange to Steph, as she had always seen Antoine as a humble kid who never used his name to get what he wanted, except for the empty parking lot once a month.

She turned to Mr. Larned, not sure why. Probably because he was the closest thing George had to any other connection besides her. She saw he was looking around the crowd, not paying attention to Mayor Robbins either. Steph wondered why, maybe not believing that George had disappeared and was sitting somewhere in the crowd, or maybe because he wanted to know if anybody looked suspicious. Or maybe he just didn't care.

"Sergeant Walker," said Mayor Robbins, waking Steph from her daydream. "Is there anything you'd like to say to these wonderful young adults?"

Unlike Robbins, Walker looked like he didn't want to be there at all. He climbed on the podium and stood behind the mic. "The Adler Police Department is conducting an extensive investigation," he said, without any particular feeling in his voice. "In the name of the Department, we ask for your collaboration with information, if you have any, or by following the new, temporary rules we have established around town. Do not go out at night alone, and whatever you do, please stay away from the forest."

Silence. The crowd was waiting for permission to leave or for Walker to say something, but he seemed to have drawn a blank. Rodriguez intervened before it got worse. "Thank you, Sergeant. And thank you for your attention, students. You may resume your school day."

It felt like every person in the gym stood up at the same time, in one motion. Steph, only half there, jumped at the sudden feeling of movement around her. "Finally," she heard Roger mutter.

As they walked down the stairs from their seats, Steph looked at the objects of her attention for the past half hour. Rodriguez looked diplomatic, sharing some final words with the Mayor before he left. Next to him was Antoine, who clearly wanted to leave for class.

Scotch and his dad were not speaking, but rather just listening to what Rodriguez was saying, both ready to go as well. As one of the last people to leave the gym, Steph could faintly make out what they were talking about; something regarding the news, she thought. Soon enough, Antoine and Scotch incorporated into the crowd, behind Steph.

\#

Steph sat alone in chem lab. She took seat at the very back and spaced out into her utensils. By the end of it, she couldn't even remember what she'd done or what had been said. When the bell sounded, she realized she hadn't done any work and started to freak out, but was interrupted by Ms. Waters, the young black lady Steph liked so much. "Don't worry, Stephanie," she said. "I saw you at the beginning of class. I just didn't want to call attention to you."

Steph didn't know what to say. She really hated when somebody took pity on George, and she didn't want the same thing to be done to her. "I'm sorry, Ms. Waters. I–" but she couldn't finish.

"I would like you to visit the Principal's office," she said, making Steph feel even worse.

"I'm so sorry. Please, it won't happen again."

The moment of crisis didn't let Steph see that Ms. Waters wasn't punishing her. She grabbed Steph by the shoulders. "I'm giving you a free pass to go talk to the Principal" she said, calmly.

Steph cooled down and analyzed the words that were just said. "What? Why?"

"Let's walk together, okay?" said Ms. Waters. Steph didn't reply. She just went ahead, in autopilot.

Rodriguez's office was spotless, as usual. Everything was perfectly organized on her desk, the clock was in sync, the calendar up to date, and her books in alphabetical order. Steph and Ms. Waters entered the office after knocking, and Rodriguez received them with a warm smile.

"You may sit," said Rodriguez. Steph thought she was talking to Ms. Waters, but she stood there, waiting for Steph to take seat in front of her.

Steph reluctantly complied and pulled out the chair opposite the Principal's. She laid down her backpack and sat down, feeling a terrible heaviness on her shoulders.

"Thank you, Cassandra," said Principal Rodriguez.

"My pleasure," answered Ms. Waters, and proceeded to leave the office. Steph turned to see her close the door, and looked back at Principal Rodriguez.

"I didn't mean to space out during lab," started Steph. "I promise it won't ever happen again."

Rodriguez's compassionate face didn't fluctuate a bit. She looked at Steph, waiting for another comment. "This is not about that, Stephanie," she said, after Steph didn't continue. "I want to talk about you."

The recent mini crisis left Steph in a very weird headspace. She couldn't connect one thing with another. "About me? What did I do?"

"You haven't done anything, sweetheart. I want to talk about how you feel." Still confused, Steph opted for silence. "I know it must be very hard to deal with your friend's disappearance. I want to let you know that you have permission to stay home until you feel better."

It was hard for Steph to fully internalize what had been said. A combination of lack of sleep and peace of mind that clouded her very own thoughts. "I don't need anything," she said, not fully understanding why.

"We know you are very close with George and understand that it must be excruciating for you. I want the best for your health, Stephanie." Rodriguez had always given her students a sense of security with her speech, and Steph felt compelled enough to at least let go of some of her more private thoughts.

She sighed. "I just want him to be safe," she said. She gathered all of her strength and managed to hold back the tears she felt coming. "I don't want special treatment. Nothing's happened to me."

Rodriguez couldn't help but smile. "I can't order you to skip school, Stephanie. But now you know that you're allowed to go home for the week if you're not feeling well, ok?"

Feeling the ever sensation of pity, Steph had to ask. "Have Roger and Stacy been given the same treatment?"

Rodriguez couldn't contain an even wider smile. "Yes. I spoke to them before you. You can rest easy."

Knowing that Roger and Stacy had been allowed to skip school too made her reconsider taking the offer. But there was one more thing she needed to do without going home for the day. "Is it okay if I leave during lunch hour?" she asked. "I gotta go to French. Take some notes so George doesn't get too behind."

Unbelievable as it sounded, Steph witnessed how Rodriguez's eyes watered. "You may."

afternoon

Steph laid on her bed, reminiscing of her last moments at the festival, thinking of what could've gone wrong. The last three days had consisted of the same thoughts over and over again, not fully comprehending why George had gone to the woods. Sure, it would be more private for him and Andrea, but that didn't sound like something George would do.

She texted Roger. "Did you leave?"

"Yeah. Me and Stacy went home the moment we were told we could. You?"

"After French. I dunno what to do."

Steph waited for Roger's response, but it didn't come. She figured he may have fallen asleep or something of the like. Then, she realized she didn't even have Stacy's number, so she couldn't text her to see how she was.

It wouldn't have been accurate to say that Steph and the pair had become friends over the weekend, but they had grown to know each other a bit. Steph understood the dynamic between the two, how Stacy's comforting silence acted as a support for Roger's anxiety-driven monologues. Before then, Steph only knew Roger as one of the few openly gay students at Jefferson. Not that it affected his social life in any way. This is Adler.

Stacy, Steph knew, came from a difficult household. Her parents divorced when she was 10 and her life was never the same. She had three older sisters, and spoke to none of them. It was easy to assume that Roger was the psychological replacement for whatever fraternal feeling Stacy lacked as she was growing up.

Hours later, after Steph had forgotten about it, she got her text from Roger. "Holy shit. Turn on the news."

Steph changed what she was watching to the local news channel of the area. The anchors were talking about The Missing Four, and the new hot lead, which completely revolved Steph's stomach.

There was a picture of a man she had never seen, with a nasty scar from one side of his forehead to the other side of his chin. He looked about 35 or so, maybe older. He had a gruff brown beard and long hair, but didn't look menacing, somehow. When she saw the name, that's when it clicked.

"The Police have narrowed the list of potential suspects to this man. He is a freelance botanist that had been working under contract in Adler since last year. After biological evidence was found at his residence, a call has been sent for his arrest. The name registered to his likeness is Peter Anderson."

Monica, night

A violent shake woke Monica from her deep sleep. Before she could understand what was happening, she landed on the floor, still inside her cocoon. Then, a huge rip that revealed her to the world, illuminated only by the moonlight. In front of her were Arabella and the other monster she hadn't met, who she had heard being called Marcus.

Marcus was tall and imposing, more muscular than Arabella. What little humanity was left in his face revealed a history of handsomeness, but that was all gone then. The Marcus that stood in front of Monica was a horrific creature of short brown hair and pale grey skin, equally opaque and unrevealing as Arabella's. But, while Arabella showed some personality in her treatment of the prisoners, Marcus remained composed, stoic.

Arabella grabbed Monica by the arm and lifted her up. "Come on," she said. "We got places to be." This was the first time Monica had been made to walk instead of being taken inside her sack, and she couldn't understand why.

Then, it struck her like a club to the head. As she was dragged by Arabella, she could see Marcus carrying somebody else. A sight she had not seen since the night of, and who she honestly thought was dead. "Andrea," she tried to call to her friend, but her voice proved too weak, and Andrea was unconscious.

Andrea's limp body was being dragged by its arm. Her usually shiny auburn hair was almost black with dirt, her skin bruised and untreated, and her clothes almost ripped apart. Had she been going through the same things as Monica? Because she looked like she'd been there for longer.

They got to the lake that Monica had seen the other day, and were thrown there on the spot. Monica stood up and ran to Andrea's body, spending half of her energy keeping herself from falling due to how weak her legs felt standing. She inspected it to discover she was breathing, but felt very light and skinny.

Before Monica said anything to her unconscious friend, something fell to her other side, making her jump in surprise and horror. The scarred and beat up body of Miles Goodman laid next to her, and looked even worse than Andrea's. Monica quickly inspected him as well, and discovered he, too, was alive.

Confused, Monica dragged Miles to the lake to try and clean him. She touched the ice cold water and washed their faces. As she washed her hands and cheeks, the water in front of her turned darker and darker, revealing how much dirt and blood must have accumulated on her skin.

Monica dragged Andrea as delicately as possible to the lake, and tried to clean her as well. But she was abruptly stopped by Arabella, who grabbed her wrist and raised her in the air. "Bad girl," she said, throwing her away from the lake.

As Monica regained balance, she saw Marcus had arrived with two more bodies. These she did not recognize, but noticed they looked much older than her and her friends. One was even wearing a police uniform. The other looked old enough to be her mom's older sister.

"My Lord," said Marcus, seemingly to nobody. His deep voice resonated inside Monica's chest. "Your tributes await."

A sharp cold breeze cut through Monica's nose. She covered her face, but now every part of her body was trembling. The remaining water on her face felt like it was slowly freezing.

Then, she heard it again. She heard the voice coming from inside her scalp, but this time way louder. "Stand," commanded the voice, and so she did. Without question, without hesitation, Monica stood up on her two feet, like she wasn't hurting or scared for her life.

She turned her head to her friend, who was still unconscious on the floor. To the other side, so was her boyfriend, but not the two strangers. The two strangers stood up, and Monica could've sworn she saw them floating inches from the ground.

A mysterious sound came from the forest, something Monica had never heard in her life. It sounded almost like water running, but not quite. Like millions of gallons of icy water flowing through a grater, almost. The sound became louder and louder until a black cloud came floating out of the trees. A murder of crows, flying from outside the forest and surrounding the group, covering the moonlight and keeping the cold air inside. The way they were flying looked unnatural, unreal, like they were robots and not birds.

Monica felt her temple palpitating, convinced her brain was going to spill out of her ears. Yet she didn't flinch or moan, but stood there, quiet. Tears rolled down her cheeks, but she didn't disobey. She couldn't.

Out of the shadows, she could see a shape. The silhouette of a man came closer from inside the forest, until it shined with the reflected moonlight from the lake. Monica looked him straight in his blue eyes, and thought he was the most unbelievably handsome man she had ever seen in her life. Tall, with short black hair, and the palest of skins. He didn't look like his servants; he looked like a man. His sharp jawline and perfect lips made Monica dream of kissing him, of dying in his strong, muscular arms. She imagined what it would be like to feel his big hands around her neck, her waist.

And when he spoke, Monica felt shivers. "Come here," he said out loud, with a soothing, calm voice that mesmerized her. The voice of a leader, a general, a conqueror. A Master.

She walked to Him and stood still, waiting for instructions from her Master. He did not speak, but instead raised His left hand past Monica's shoulder. She heard the whistle of the wind, and felt how something was flying towards her, a big object that brought with it furious wind. In a moment, her Master's hand was holding the female stranger's neck.

She locked eyes with Him, unable to look away in any form, hypnotized completely by His pair of rounded sapphires. He opened his mouth slightly, revealing two long, sharp fangs. He brought the female stranger closer to his face, and put her neck in front of his mouth, placing His teeth over her scarred skin. In one motion, still staring into Monica's soul, her Master thrusted His jaw to the stranger's neck. A gush of blood flew into the air and landed all over Monica's face.

Her Master drank as Monica looked, helplessly staring at this horrifying act. The stranger didn't even scream, as if she were dead before her neck was violated. But she was alive, made clearly by the thrashing of her limbs that nothing could have controlled. Some of the blood that landed on Monica's forehead went down into her eyes, dripping from her eyebrows to her cheeks, creating a red curtain between her and what she was seeing.

Her Master finished and let the body drop to the floor. Monica mustered enough energy to look at the floor, and behold the body of the stranger. It looked like a plastic skeleton, with her eyes sucked into the skull and her limbs made of skin and bone, with nothing else. She died with her mouth open.

Monica looked at her Master again, who stood still, staring into her eyes. She wanted to scream, to run into the lake and wash the blood off her face. "Sleep," her Master said, and everything went black.

You can't take the nightmares anymore. You'd rather never sleep again than have to endure them. It pains you to close your eyes, to not follow the orders. It gets worse at night. There is only one solution, and you know what it is. Follow your orders. Obey your orders. Hear the call. Listen to your master.

They can't find out. Kill the spare, bring the tribute.

Kill the spare, bring the tribute.

Kill the spare, bring the tribute.

Kill the spare, bring the tribute.

Kill the spare, bring the tribute.

Kill the spare, bring the tribute.

Kill the spare, bring the tribute.

Kill the spare, bring the tribute.

Kill the spare, bring the tribute.

Kill the spare, bring the tribute.

Kill the spare, bring the tribute.

Kill the spare, bring the tribute.

Kill the spare, bring the tribute.

Kill the spare, bring the tribute.

Kill the spare, bring the tribute.

Kill the spare, bring the tribute.

Kill the spare, bring the tribute.

Kill the spare, bring the tribute.

Kill the spare, bring the tribute.

Kill the spare, bring the tribute.

Kill the spare, bring the tribute.

Kill the spare, bring the tribute.

Chapter 11
Wolves

George, April 13th, evening

I couldn't differentiate the past three days if I tried to. They'd all consisted of me waking up and studying, with short interruptions to go to the bathroom or eat, and the occasional checking of my wounds. The room I had chosen was closest to the library, so it didn't take me that long to crutch my way there, thankfully. Still, "monotone" cannot begin to describe how the weekend felt inside the Foxworth safehouse.

And then, the news broke. Later that Monday, after three days gone, the world had a suspect, and he had Elijah's face. We never discussed this, but I was sure that they knew that was going to happen, eventually. I wasn't surprised that they had tracked whatever they found in the clearing back to Elijah's, and after that it must've been easy.

I was reading in the library with the door open when I heard Gray. "Tell Mr. Foxworth that we're leaving. Be back in three days," he told Elijah.

"Are you sure about this?" he asked back, as the rest of the wolves left their bedrooms and gathered by the door.

"We need information, and your face is all over the news now. There's nothing else to do." Elijah nodded and the wolves queued out the door. Only Drake turned to wave goodbye at me.

Elijah sighed and closed the door to the stairs. He saw me looking at the scene, and walked towards me. "What are you reading now?" he asked.

"I finally got to the wolves," I said. I wouldn't say that I was excited, more like morbidly curious to finally understand.

"You've been reading very fast. I believe that's the last chapter."

"Yes." After a moment, I added, "Can you give me a preamble?"

Elijah showed confusion on his face. "Preamble? You want me to introduce you to the book you've been reading for three days?"

"You know what I mean."

Elijah chuckled heartedly. "What do you wanna know? You'll find everything out as you read."

"There isn't enough information on vampires, and I'm sure there won't be enough on them either."

"There will never be enough information about anything in the world, George. Information is infinite."

"But they are different. We live with four of them, one of them pretty old. What better to explain their condition than one of them? But since I'm not sitting with them anytime soon, you can tell me."

Elijah stopped to think about it. "Read first," he concluded. "Any other questions you have, I'll try to answer to the best of my abilities. Sound good?"

"Sure," I said, a bit disappointed.

It had taken me that long to finish reading *European Demons*, and what I had learned was unmeasurable. Highlights include the true science behind exorcisms, the role of the Catholic Church in history across the millennia, and sea monsters. Mother-flipping sea monsters.

The last chapter was on lycanthropes, from the Greek for "wolf-person." The term werewolf comes from old English, and the myth of the wolf man was particularly popular in Medieval Europe. All of this I already knew, but it would be the only true thing that I was sure of before I started reading.

Starting with the curse itself, it can hardly be classified as that. Though, as I had already confirmed through my readings, curses do exist, those are defined by an individual bestowing it upon somebody else through black magic. The "curse of the werewolf" acts more like a virus, being spread from person to person. What is true is that it is spread through biting, but it gets more complicated.

Unlike real-life vampires, werewolf fangs do not act like two-way needles. There is no poison to be injected, sucked out, or cured. If you're bit, you're infected, though it isn't exactly clear how or why; speculation revolves around saliva, bacteria, or actual cursing from the individual, somehow. In popular legend, the curse would manifest in presence of a full moon, where the individual would lose control over his actions and turn into a dog-like beast that ravages for blood. That, like many other things, is extremely poetic and very fictional.

First of all, the moon has nothing to do with anything; that is easily the most romanticized part of the legend. And, as I have already confirmed myself, lycanthropes can transform and detransform at will, in the middle of the day. Noteworthy, also, is that they can transform into full wolves or half-transform into a hybrid between wolf and man, more akin to popular modern legends. The book described the physical process that people go through, explaining that the wolves are so big because the individual's volume doesn't change; they don't lose mass when they transform into wolves, so if you're a 200-pound man, you transform into a 200-pound wolf.

There was a whole section dedicated to the behavior of recently-transformed individuals, and how they can easily lose control over their body for the duration of their transformation. A simple way to put it would be to say that the virus infects you, and your body rejects it, making you curl up in pain, while your brain produces chemicals it's not supposed to, making you hallucinate. This, paired with the intense physical modifications the body goes through, makes the victim go insane. That's why there are so many stories about frantic werewolf attacks.

The infection spreads quickly inside your body, feeling like a flu combined with acute allergies and joint pains. According to the book, most people suffer their first transformation after about a minute of being bit, and they go through the process described above. After regaining some control over themselves, they usually escape, trying to understand what is happening to them and what they'd done.

I don't think it was intentional, but the book really makes you feel sorry for these people. Vampires are painted as demons straight from hell – though no such place actually exists – who become engrossed in their own power and do evil things. Werewolves are victims of terrible circumstances, and many times they do terrible things on accident, and deal with the consequences all their life. The author(s) describe the aging process of lycanthropes as "extremely slow and agonizing," detailing that the lifespan of the individual extends about 40%, bumping up the average lifespan of a werewolf to 110 years.

This last thing got me thinking about the wolves that live among us. Starting with the two extremes, Drake and Alex. If Drake looked roughly 22, he must've been at least 40, right? Or maybe he's like 25 and was bitten not long ago. That's a factor I had to consider, and it messed up all the math I could've possibly gotten right.

Alex was different. Alex was clearly older than his peers, and the way he spoke and behaved signaled that he was from another time. Assuming he was bitten as a young man of, let's say, 18, and that he looks roughly 55, that would make him around 70 years old, at least. My math may have been very wrong, partly because of the faulty data I was working with, but it was still impressive nonetheless. To think Alex may be the same age as Mr. Foxworth, or even older.

The book said that werewolves eventually learn how to control their transformations, allowing them to go into full wolves without the painful and uncomfortable hybrid stage. Nevertheless, they still suffer from considerable pain every time they transform and detransform. Apart from that simple fact, they aren't very different from humans in any other aspects. And they are definitely not allergic to silver.

Their powers were by far the least interesting part of the section. Increased strength and resistance, of course. Better reflexes, speed, and enhanced senses, like dogs who aren't colorblind. Fun fact: they can't control how long their hair grows after they go from wolves to humans, but every time they become wolves, their pelts will instantly grow, and fall off their skin when they go back. That was a very strange thing to read.

They also count with very fast regeneration, though not as fast as the vampires, and not as forgiving. Vampires can regrow complete limbs if they were to feed off somebody, but werewolves wouldn't be able to, under any circumstance. A werewolf's regeneration acts exactly like a human's, but much faster. They also have stronger bones and tougher skin. Some exceptional cases may ensue, but it's impossible to determine what would and wouldn't apply without testing, and that would be some Nazi-level stuff. So, no way to find out, really.

A notable aspect missing from the book was the origins of the virus. There is no documentation regarding how the curse of the werewolf was created, or where. It is believed to have its origins in Europe because of the older folklore, but nothing has ever been confirmed, and probably never will.

But the thing that caught my attention the most was the last thing that the book talked about before ending, which is the state of werewolves in the modern world. This was one of the few times that the book referenced modern times, and it talked about how the curse has almost been completely eradicated from Earth, just like smallpox. With the rise of contemporary societies, fewer and fewer cases where known of and even less where documented, resulting in the fadeaway of the virus.

This got me thinking about Gray's gang again. They were four men, of three different generations, and they all lived together as a pack. How many other werewolves had they met in their lifetime? Could they, possibly, be the last werewolves in the Midwest? In the United States? In the Americas? Or in the World?

Gray, April 13th, evening

The trip to Adler had been long and tolling on the wolves. The close perimeter established by the police made it difficult to move in vehicles, which made the pack drive to the outskirts of town, and then walk the rest of the way in wolf form. They were all grateful for Foxworth's hospitality and his car, of course. But Gray found it increasingly hard to think of anything else that wasn't the Peter Anderson situation and how much that complicated everything even further.

It got dark on their way to the edge of town, where they could faintly hear the sounds of people everywhere, reminiscent to the sounds of big cities. Soon after, they caught sight of the operation, where dozens of people where gathered around the police station in what looked like a protest of some sort.

For what he could gather from signs and people's screams, the town was protesting the police for not suspecting Peter Anderson earlier, calling them incompetent, among other things. Gray had to admit, Anderson would've been his first suspect if he were in Walker's shoes. But the two of them were friends; that was the whole point.

The wolves crawled away from the crowd and deeper into the forest, going around town until they got closer to the clearing, where they started listening to people again. In the short distance they noticed a pair of young medical examiners inside the clearing, locked away only by a very ignorable police line.

In the dark, Gray's black pelt was almost invisible to the unaware human eye, with only his yellow eyes easily giving away his location. He used this to get closer and inspect, confirming that, in fact, there were only two men at the scene.

Gray went back to his pack. "Only two," he whispered. "Drake, scout East to make sure. Alex, stay here. Taylor, with me."

Drake went around the clearing to the other side, his red pelt more noticeable, so he kept to the farther shadows. Alex remained in place, turning West. Gray and Taylor, with each step, detransformed from wolves into hybrids, using the trees as cover.

Smoothly, the hybrids used their claws to grip the trunks and slowly climb the tall trees, under cover of darkness. After a moment, they were on top of the clearing, hiding between the branches. The medical examiners didn't notice; after all, why would they choose to look up at that exact moment?

Gray analyzed the scene, looking for anything that may help them understand the situation. The examiners weren't talking about the job, and didn't seem to be doing anything but waiting. With no evidence, Gray signaled Taylor to get down.

From the top, the hybrids jumped from the branches of one tree to another, further from the lights. Then they descended to the ground, and transformed into wolves again. The pack walked away from the clearing back West, where they had originally come from.

"It still smelled like George," said Taylor. "And like the other kids. We could potentially get to them from there."

"Yes," answered Gray. "But we need to know what their plan is first. Or at least how many they are." After some silent deliberation, Gray concluded his thoughts. "We should go back to Elijah's, to see if we can get anything there."

#

The way to Elijah's cabin felt instantaneous. They stopped a hundred feet away, where they could hear more people around. These were wearing FBI vests.

"If the FBI is here," said Taylor, "that means there must be a national manhunt. Elijah cannot leave the safe-house at any cost."

"You're right," said Gray, almost without paying attention. He was listening in on the agents, but they weren't saying anything interesting or relevant to the case. "The apartment may be a better suit."

"Are you sure?" asked Alex.

"I'd prefer to walk straight into the police station, but we can't do that."

They all started walking South, back to the town limits. Except for Drake. Drake remained standing, thinking. "Can't we?" he asked.

"What?" asked Gray.

"Can't we… break into the Police Department?"

George, April 13th, night

The moment I finished the last page of *European Demons*, I crutched straight to Elijah's room. I knocked on his door and he said to come in, so I did.

He was sitting on his bed, reading what looked like a novel. "Are you done?" he asked me.

"Yes. I still have questions."

"Of course you do," he said, putting away the books. "Asking questions is mostly what you do best."

"Well, I'm sorry," I said, irritated. "There's a lot of things I naturally don't unders–" he raised his hand to interrupt me.

"That was meant as a compliment. You ask very good questions."

Now I felt like a dumbass. "Oh," I said, not knowing what else to retort.

"Let's sit outside."

I crutched my way to the round table and sat on the nearest chair. Elijah sat next to me.

"How's your leg?"

"Better. I think it'll be good to go on Monday."

Elijah looked at me, unbelievingly. "Good to go for what?"

"You know. To walk again."

A moment of silence. Then, "What questions do you have?"

I went through my thoughts to determine which question to ask first. I couldn't decide until I thought of this one. "How old is Alex?"

Elijah looked almost astonished. "Hundreds of years of research are in that book, and that's the first question you come up with?"

"Insatiable curiosity."

Elijah half sighed, half chuckled. "I don't know how old he is. What do you think?"

"My rough estimates put him in his seventies, but I'm probably wrong."

"I think he's a bit older than that. Doesn't look like it, huh?"

"The book mentioned that their existence is painful, that the fact that they age so slowly makes them hate life. Why is that?"

Elijah stopped to think for a second. "Well, I'm no expert, but I would have to guess that most werewolves are born from very unfortunate circumstances. Maybe those circumstances dictate the rest of their lives."

I wasn't exactly sure what he meant. "You mean, whatever they do during their initial hysteria defines the rest of their lives?"

"Think of it this way. You're a young man with a wife and a baby, until one day you go berserk and kill both of them, alerting the whole town not only of your terrible act, but also of the curse that now lays upon you. Don't you think your life is over after that?"

"I could run. The village would never catch up to me."

Elijah looked disappointed in my response. "That's not the point, George. You're seeing it through the eyes of an outsider who has a lot more information than the poor man whose soul has been poisoned forever. They don't know what's happening, or that they can eventually control it. They just see themselves as monsters from one moment to another, and live with the consequences of their actions for the rest of their lives."

Mr. Larned would scold me for my complete lack of *pathos*. I guessed being glued to the book for so long disconnected me from the real world for a second. I don't consider myself to be that insensitive.

"Any other questions?" asked Elijah after he saw me deliberating.

"How do we kill them?"

"The wolves? Like anything else. You just need to try very hard. Silver won't help you."

"No," I said, hastily. "I meant the demons. The vampires. The book didn't mention it."

Elijah looked at me in silence. He did that a lot. "We don't know exactly how," he answered. "But in my experience, if you cut something's head off, it's not growing back."

I smiled slightly. "Guess we'll have to find out."

"We'll see," he said, returning the subtle smile.

Gray, April 13th, night

The walk to the Adler Police Station had to be done as humans, which made the wolves go back to where they had parked the car and take with them four plastic bags. They kept clean clothes on plastic bags for occasions like these. As they got closer to the edge of town, they detransformed into humans and got dressed.

The four-men group walked slowly out of the shadows, but anywhere they looked, the way into town was blocked by the authorities. "Are you ready?" asked Gray. The pack nodded, and so they walked to the edge of town. This would be the fourth or fifth time that Gray had walked inside the town limits.

A pair of armed uniformed men stopped them. One pointed a flashlight directly at their faces, the other, a rifle. "Put your hands where I can see them," signaled the flashlight officer. The pack raised their hands into the air. "Don't you know there is a curfew?" he asked them.

"I'm sorry, officer," started Taylor. "We're just passersby that heard about the kids and wanted to help."

The flashlight officer searched the pack's pockets to find nothing, not even cellphones or wallets.

"You are in direct violation of the curfew established by the Police Department. I'm gonna have to ask you to come with me." The flashlight officer made a call on his radio for a pickup of four suspects. The wolves didn't mutter a single word.

#

The pack was driven in a reinforced truck to the police station, handcuffed. They sat in silence all the way from their arrest to the station, where the doors were open and they were escorted out by two uniformed men, each with a shotgun. As they walked out, Gray could hear the driver speaking on the radio. "Four suspects, shabby looking. They had nothing in them. It's like they wanted to be caught." Gray smiled softly and kept walking with his pack, into the station.

The minuscule station was almost empty, noticeable especially by the impressive amount of echo that every one of their steps made. The walls were clean, but looked old and worn out. The low ceiling lights illuminated the building with a white hue that made it look depressing and lifeless.

After they entered, Gray scanned the area around him, noticing two men behind the registration desk, another one sitting to their right, and another one interviewing a crying woman to the left. Six cameras covering all angles; nothing to do about those.

The escorting guard talked to the man behind the desk to register them into the station. Gray expected the station to be a lot busier, which made the plan a lot easier than expected. Feeling how his pack was ready to strike, Gray snapped his fingers and, instantly, they were all moving.

They had practiced this move a lot over time. It all revolved around where Gray was standing, which at that moment was behind, South point. If Gray was South then Drake was North, Alex was West and Taylor was East.

The millisecond Gray's fingers snapped, the wolves broke their handcuffs and formation. Gray used his elbow to hit the officer behind him, shattering a couple teeth and breaking his nose, with only one hit. Stunned, the man couldn't help but be pulled into Gray's knee, receiving a hit directly into the forehead and falling unconscious.

At the same time, Taylor slid on the floor to where the lone officer was sitting. As the noise alerted him, the officer stood up but his reflexes weren't enough to dodge Taylor's kick to the shins, and he fell. Taylor pulled his head up by the hair. "Sorry," he said, as he punched the man into unconsciousness.

Alex used the registration desk as a point of impulse, jumping on it and impulsing his body towards the interrogating officer, falling on top of him. The woman screamed in panic, but Alex covered her mouth. The officer groaned in pain until Alex kicked him in the head.

Drake's job was easily the hardest. He first had to take the guard in front of them, which he did by kicking the back of his legs and smashing his head on the registration desk. Then, he jumped over the desk and smashed the two men's heads against each other.

After five seconds, there were five people conscious in the room. Gray turned to the screaming woman, who looked like she was about to faint. Alex was still covering her mouth. "We're not going to hurt you," said Gray. The woman sobbed desperately, turning red. "Alex, you stay with her."

Drake went to the door to keep a lookout. Alex stayed seated with the woman, who looked about the age he looked like. "I'm going to release you now," he said. "But don't scream." Alex softly lifted his hand off the woman's face, making her gasp for air. But she didn't scream.

Gray went on the computer on the registry desk, to see if he could find anything. He was not very good with computers, but it shouldn't have been too hard to at least find a file about Elijah or something. But after what felt like an appropriate time trying to navigate, he couldn't figure anything out.

"Let's go," urged Taylor. "We're running out of time."

Before he turned to leave, he noticed the time and date on the computer. It was 8:53pm, April 13th. "It's my father's birthday," said Gray, seemingly to nobody. After a second, he snapped and followed Taylor.

Gray and Taylor went to the back, to the evidence room. Although he suspected that the FBI had taken most of the valuable evidence, he knew there had to be something left at the station.

The room was dark, lit only by a single lightbulb hanging from the ceiling. The shelves were dusty, the floor felt sticky. There wasn't much of anything on the shelves, so a search of the room would be quick and easy. Aside from the obvious drug confiscations, there were a couple of containers that stood out, but not much else.

There was a locked silver suitcase resting in the corner of the room. Gray opened it by force and analyzed its contents. There were small vials that looked empty, but Gray looked closely to find that there were hairs in each of them. There were labels on the suitcases, marking: Goodman, Lee, Clinton, McKnight, Anderson, and seven others with "Unknown." Seven others, which meant they had also found hairs from the pack, but also the demons. This could be huge.

"Michael," called Taylor. He was analyzing a small yellow biohazard container. "Take a look at this." Gray looked over Taylor's shoulder. He was holding a plastic bag with a white… something. He couldn't identify it. It looked like a piece of cloth, but also like an enlarged piece of spider web. "This smells funny," he added.

"Let's go," said Gray. "We'll talk on the way back."

Gray and Taylor reunited with the rest of the pack, who were still in their positions. The woman wasn't calm but she was quiet, looking down at the floor and trembling.

"There's nobody outside," said Drake. "We could walk out."

"Let's do it quick, then," ordered Gray.

Alex stood up from his post and looked down at the woman. "Sorry for the disturbance, ma'am," he said as he walked away. The woman, horrified, broke down into a desperate sob.

#

The pack ran out of the station, the curfew making it easier for them to get to the forest without interruptions. The streets where completely deserted, aside from police patrols driving around, but those were easy to avoid. They would run a stretch, hide behind parked cars or within alleys until the patrols went out of sight, and keep going.

They continued running until they got to the edge of town, where two armed officers where standing, as they would've thought. Quickly and silently, Taylor approached them and knocked them out with a strong punch to each. The pack then sprinted into the forest until they got to the car, where they sat for a moment, without driving off.

"They're bound to start a search soon," said Drake. "When they realize they're not getting a response from home base."

Taylor took out the white thing from the plastic bag. "This smells funny" he repeated. "Like one of the kids."

"What is that?" asked Alex, in complete confusion. "Is that ripped clothes?"

"No," said Gray. "It looks organic."

"Organic? You mean this came from them?" asked Alex. "You mean these are remains or–"

"I don't mean anything. I don't know."

"We should go back," urged Taylor. "We have to show this to the others. Maybe they'll know."

"Yeah. Maybe."

You've done it.

You've obeyed your Master.

But it's not over yet.

You cannot die just yet.

There's still more work to do.

You have to do it.

Serve your Master.

Chapter 12
Out of the Shell

Monica, night

Monica was woken up by the rustling outside her cocoon. Arabella let her out to pee twice a day, and it hadn't been long since the second time, so it must've still be night time, she figured.

Monica heard the rustling stop, and felt how Arabella came down from her nest on top of the tree and onto the ground. "Have you been to Jason?" she asked out loud.

"Yes," answered a voice Monica had never heard in her life. It didn't sound any different to a normal human voice, unlike Arabella's or Marcus' or Jason's, which sounded gruff and damaged.

"Good. How is he doing?"

"He's getting ready," answered the voice. A man's voice, a young adult. 30s, maybe.

"What are your orders now?"

"To bring as many tributes as possible before the ceremony." No emotion, no voice inflections. Like the most human robot in the universe.

"Go ahead," ordered Arabella.

"I must speak to our Master first," retorted the voice.

"You can tell Him whatever you want from wherever you are. You don't need to go to Him."

Silence. The only thing Monica could her was her own breathing and the palpitations of the thin veins in her ears. "Yes, Master," said the strange man after a while.

day

Monica woke up with a bang, her cocoon falling from the tree where it was hanging and opening up to reveal fresh sunlight into Monica's skin. As usual, it hurt her to fully open her eyes after so many hours in complete darkness.

She inspected her body with her hands, rubbing the areas where she felt pain from the fall. At that moment, she touched the side of her ribcage and gasped in horror, realizing how skinny she was. Her clothes where still the same she'd worn when she was captured.

"Move," ordered Arabella. Monica moved behind the trees and did her business, like nothing had happened.

#

The daily routine inside their cocoons was repetitive and frustrating to everybody involved. After the morning stop, Monica would be put asleep by Arabella's mysterious methods, and wake up shortly after, inside a new cocoon. They did this every single day, twice a day. But that day, something changed.

After what felt like six or seven hours, Monica heard the stranger's voice again. "Jason is ready," said the stranger.

"Good. What about you?"

"Still researching. I'll be finished shortly."

"Our Master doesn't like waiting."

"I've already settled it with Him. You don't have to worry about anything I do."

Monica could only think about what they meant by everything they were saying. Who was this person? Was he one of those monsters? He didn't sound like them. Then again, neither did their Master.

"You are very smart," Monica heard from inside her scalp. She jumped in horror – or would've, if she were standing. "All of that thinking that you're doing will prove useful to me, someday."

"What do you want?" she said, out loud. For the first time, she answered to the voice.

"You will know, very soon," answered her Master.

Monica sobbed out of control. She had never gotten used to listening to the voice inside her head, nor did she know how long she would have to stay there, imprisoned. Nor who the stranger was or what was happening. She didn't know anything at all.

George, April 14th, morning

I didn't hear the wolves arrive the night before. I wanted to stay up until the small hours, but the toll of the past week had finally settled in, and I couldn't resist laying in bed after dinner until I fell asleep. I slept for nine hours, maybe, and when I woke up, everybody else was up and about, talking about the night before.

Though I had healed well, my leg was still bothering me. I think the urgency of listening in made me forget that, because I limped my way from bed to the round table. Only Elijah turned to see me come in.

"I agree with you, Michael," said Mr. Foxworth. "This definitely looks organic." He was handling a piece of what looked like white cloth.

"But what do you think it is?" asked Alex. "Have you ever seen something like this?"

Mr. Foxworth didn't answer. I could see he was thinking, but I don't think I'd ever seen him so determined. It was maybe the first time that I saw Mr. Foxworth with an expression that didn't represent some kind of positivity.

"What about you?" said Taylor to Elijah.

Elijah clearly didn't expect to be asked something like that. "No idea," he said, reluctantly. "It kind of reminds me of a butterfly cocoon though."

At this comment, everyone stopped and looked at each other. "Have you ever read about something like that?" asked Taylor.

"Not that I remember," said Elijah.

"I don't think so," I said. Because nobody had seen me come in, they all jumped at the sound of my voice. Except Elijah. "At least not yet."

"Well, we wouldn't expect you to have," said Alex, begrudgingly. "Elijah has s decade of studies more than you, boy."

"Still," interrupted Taylor. "George, you've been reading everything we have on vampires, and still no sign of anything like a cocoon?"

"Can't think of anything like that," I answered. Taylor's calm tone made me feel safe from Alex, though he was still staring at me with resentment.

"Wait a second," said Elijah. "George, do you remember what the books say about how they keep prisoners?"

This sparked an idea in my mind, which I thought was what Elijah was trying to do. Maybe to give me some credit in front of the wolves. "It doesn't really say," I answered. "That is one of the aspects with the least information."

"Exactly," continued Elijah, now to the wolves. "Let's take a wild guess. What if they keep their prisoners in cocoons, like spiders do?"

Silence. I could tell everybody was thinking at double their regular rate. I looked around to see the wolves' faces, but it was Mr. Foxworth's which caught my attention the most. He looked concerned, curious, and a bit confused. I assumed he was trying to remember if he had seen anything like that in his decades of experience, which would surely be very hard to survey.

"It makes sense, though," I said, finally. Everybody turned to look at me, and I got nervous again. I felt specifically uncomfortable by Gray's attention, not sure why. "If they wanted long-term sources of fuel, they wouldn't just suck their victims dry and dump them. They'd need constant refueling all the time."

"So they keep them in cocoons and... what?" asked Alex. "You think they absorb their energy through that?"

"Whatever it is," said Elijah, "I think we're onto something. We should investigate."

"Agreed," said Drake, standing up. "We should trace them and go where they are."

Gray stood up too. "Let's go, then."

Almost reflexively, Elijah turned to his room to get his stuff, but Gray stopped him "What are you doing?" Elijah was about to answer, but he didn't. He had forgotten about it, but he soon realized that there was no secure way for him to accompany them into Adler, especially in broad daylight.

"I'm sorry," said Elijah, putting down his things. "The habit, you know?"

Gray nodded and left for his room, followed by his pack. I looked at Elijah and felt the frustration coming from his eyes. "Hey," I said to him. He turned to me. "You should sit with me today so we can read some more."

And just like that, the wolves were off again.

Steph, April 14th, morning

It was the first time Steph noticed FBI presence around school. She knew they were part of the investigation and that a national manhunt was on the way, but she, not once, felt she was being observed. Until that morning, when she got to school for the first time since Monday and she noticed a black van parked across the street.

Stacy and Roger were walking with her, but they were too distracted to notice. Steph stopped and looked at the van, wondering if it had been there all week, or if it was the first time they came, because they knew she was going back to school. Either way, it felt ominous and unnerving, a feeling she kept with her all morning, even during class. Though she wasn't sure if the atmosphere was really that tense, or if it had been her lack of food and sleep during the past week.

Then, in the middle of class, the news broke out. It spread across everybody's phone before the authorities gave an official statement on the matter, and soon after, the whole school knew about the assault at the police station the night before.

"All of the evidence involving the Anderson case has disappeared," read Roger out loud from his phone. Him, Steph and Stacy were sitting together at lunch. "Though none of the guards were badly hurt, they were all unconscious during the event and for much after. It was Mrs. Carol Sanders who brought attention to the matter, after she'd been kept held inside the station for about fifteen minutes while the assailants ransacked the evidence room."

"That's insane," said Steph. "How could they let something like that happen?"

"Chad says that it's been very difficult for the police with the FBI on their ass. That most of the men are patrolling the streets and surveilling the town limits"

"What is the FBI doing, then?" asked Steph.

"Searching the forest and towns around us, mostly. The security of Adler is none of their concern."

"So why was there evidence at the police station? It makes no sense. They should've taken it with them."

Roger lowered his voice and pushed his head closer to Steph. "That was Walker's insistence. He wanted to keep some evidence for the records. I guess it really backfired on him."

"Poor Scotch," said Stacy, out of nowhere. Steph turned to see her in surprise.

"Yeah," said Steph. "I hope it doesn't come back to them too harshly."

#

There was an emergency assembly at the gym again after lunch hour. Steph, Roger and Stacy walked together and sat in the back, almost exactly where they had sat earlier that week. This time, Principal Rodriguez was accompanied by a man Steph had never seen, but she recognized his jacket as FBI-affiliated.

"Good afternoon," said Rodriguez. "We're very sorry to interrupt your school day again, but we have some news to share with you." Rodriguez signaled to the FBI agent beside her. He was tall, muscular and imposing. "This is detective Roland Michaels from the FBI. Please listen to what he has to say."

Rodriguez stepped back and Michaels stood in front of the microphone. The gym was completely silent as he spoke. "I'm sure you are all aware of the event that occurred last night. It seems the media is having trouble containing themselves at the sight of sensitive information." Steph agreed. Whoever was behind all of this, it seemed that they could easily use the news to know how their own manhunt was going. "Something that you have not been told, however, is that we have another set of disappearances."

Gasps from everybody, including Steph. Rodriguez looked down to the floor, clearly trying not to cry. "What the hell?" muttered Roger.

"Please settle down," ordered Michaels. The gym got progressively quieter, but there was no complete silence anymore. "The FBI and the Adler Police Department are currently investigating the disappearance of Mr. Earnest Erb and his family, who have not been seen since this Tuesday. The only reason the FBI has decided to tell you this personally is because, starting today, the school shall remain under constant surveillance from the Bureau."

More surprised gasps flooded the room. Steph could even make out some people sobbing. She remembered the black van outside school that morning, and it all made sense. Though she wasn't completely convinced that it was just guarding the school entrance.

She searched the back of her head, trying to remember if she knew Earnest Erb, or anybody with that last name. She couldn't think of anybody, and by the looks of them, neither could Roger or Stacy. Nobody around Steph seemed to know who Earnest Erb was.

"No student or staff member is allowed to leave the school on foot. The Mayor's office will provide you with transportation to the bus stations across town, where patrols will be set vigilant." It started to sound wrong, all of a sudden. "In the meantime, be wary of your surroundings and keep your phones charged, in case you have anything to inform. Mr. Erb has a wife and an infant son, possibly with him."

Steph couldn't speak, couldn't think. The assembly finished with some final words from Rodriguez, but she couldn't hear them. She sat on her place, looking to the void, unable to breathe. Then, like a brick wall, she fell to the floor, fainted.

George, April 14th, afternoon

The house felt very quiet without the wolves. Mr. Foxworth's employees had clearly been trained to mind their own business and remain invisible, because I didn't even hear them making lunch and yet there it was. Wild jasmine rice with grilled honey chicken and zucchini purée, all smelling delicious and looking like a picture off a magazine.

The three of us sat down at the round table to eat. Since the wolves had left, Elijah had sat with me at the library to review everything we had on vampires. At this point, I had already read one of the shorter books on the subject, but there was no mention whatsoever about how they keep prisoners. I could only hope that our wild guess was somewhat correct.

"Can I ask you a question?" I said, to the wind. Any of them could answer it.

"Sure," said Mr. Foxworth. "Anything you need."

"Why does Alex hate me so much?" I didn't want to sound or feel victimized. I just needed to know if I was maybe doing something wrong or if there was going to be a problem in the future. I really needed to secure my active place in the team, after all.

"He doesn't," said Elijah. "He's just a grumpy old man."

"You know that's not true," I said. I looked back to Mr. Foxworth. "Do you know why?"

Mr. Foxworth finished chewing and took a sip of water. "I can't tell exactly why he treats you that way," he started, "but I can guess a couple of things."

"Sir," called Elijah, his voice asking for caution.

"I will tell him, Elijah," said Mr. Foxworth. Not angry, but firm. "I think George is mature enough and knows many things that someone his age wouldn't even imagine. I think he deserves it."

Elijah sighed with concern and doubt, but didn't say anything. Mr. Foxworth was my best bet at being accepted by the others, apparently.

I had analyzed this many times over the past week. From my interactions with them, I could easily determine that Taylor and Drake definitely liked me, and Alex and Gray did not. What differentiated Alex from Gray was that Alex saw me as an obstacle, while Gray seemed even open to the idea of training me. Maybe he wouldn't see me as a team member, but at least as an asset.

"Alexander is very old, George," started Mr. Foxworth. "Older than I am, and with much more experience out there. He has seen a lot of things I've merely just read about. And has gone through something we can only imagine." Mr. Foxworth looked at Elijah to see if he had something to add, but he kept quiet. "What do you think he thinks about you?"

I should've expected that. Mr. Foxworth always did everything possible for me to learn, including not giving me the answers to simple questions. He always made me think and rationalize, which is something I felt really helped me, but it wasn't what I wanted to hear right then. "I honestly have no clue. I haven't done anything but read ever since I got here."

Mr. Foxworth looked disappointed, but not at me. More like disappointed at what he was about to tell me. "You're right, George. You are so right, and that is exactly why it saddens me to see him treat you like that." Again, he turned to Elijah, and once more he didn't say anything. "Alexander thinks it illogical to have you informed about what we are doing, because he doesn't think you deserve it."

I knew that already. My frustration didn't let me think of a polite way to say it, so I kept it to myself. But that I already knew. Mr. Foxworth had been impressed with my observation skills since the beginning, so he should've known too.

"He thinks that you don't have enough reason to be involved in all of this," said Mr. Foxworth.

"What?!" I exclaimed, a bit too loudly. "I was fucking bit by a vampire last week. What else does he want?"

"George," said Elijah, firmly and dominantly. He didn't need to say anything else. I recognized my mistake and felt very ashamed about it.

"Sorry, Mr. Foxworth," I said. Mr. Foxworth seemed to have not heard me, though that was impossible. "My anger should be directed at Alex, not you."

"You need to understand something about him, George," continued Mr. Foxworth. "Alexander comes from a place and time where he had to fight a lot for what he deserved, even when it was crystal clear. Even though he is old, he has it engrained in his brain."

"With all due respect," I interrupted, "I don't care about what Alex has or hasn't engrained in his brain."

"But you should, because they are the ones who will help you in the field, not me. If you don't understand how they think, how they would react, you will all fail as a team and crumble."

I was thinking so hard about what to say next that I didn't notice the huge implication in that statement. But Elijah did. "Sir," he said, "are you serious?"

"Absolutely," said Mr. Foxworth, standing up from his chair. "I'm tired of seeing George's potential wasted in countless hours of reading. He needs to be prepared, because bigger things will come unto us very soon."

"Wait, what?" I finally said, after they finished arguing. I stood up from my chair. "Are you allowing me to train, Mr. Foxworth?"

"I am ordering the beginning of your training for today, after you've digested what you just ate," said Mr. Foxworth.

I smiled wildly, and he chuckled. I looked at Elijah, who looked back at me with concern. "How's your leg?" he asked me.

"Perfect," I answered.

Steph, April 14th, afternoon

Steph woke up, slowly and clumsily. The room where she was glowed with white fervor, almost blinding her delicate eyes as she opened them. The sheets she was lying on felt harsh and used. After a moment, she realized she was in a hospital room, wearing a gown.

"Sweetheart," exclaimed Evelyn, who was sitting beside her by the window. Steph hadn't noticed her presence. "I'm so glad you're awake." Evelyn's makeup was ruined by the path of her tears, and her nose looked runny and red. Evelyn stood up from her chair and hugged her daughter.

"What happened?" asked Steph, hugging back.

"You collapsed at the assembly. They brought you here afterwards. Your dad's on top of it."

"Wh-why? What happened to me?" insisted Steph, not understanding the concept of just collapsing.

"We will see after the tests are done," said a voice from the door. Standing under the frame was a middle-aged black woman nurse. Tall, sturdy, and with the sweetest face imaginable.

"Mercedes," called Steph in surprise. Evelyn smiled at her daughter's wholesome expression of joy. "What are you doing here?"

Mercedes entered the room. "When I heard that Stephanie Kim was in, I had to take care myself."

Mercedes wasn't only head nurse at the hospital, but also George's unofficial godmother. Steph was very familiar with her through both her dad and George, but this was the first time she would be under her care.

"Give us until tomorrow and we'll give you your results," said Mercedes. "Meanwhile, your father said that you are to stay here and rest."

Steph still felt lightheaded, but understood enough of what was just said. She nodded with her eyes almost shut, and laid back down into her pillow.

George, April 14th, evening

At the end of the hallway where the doors to the rooms where there was another door that I had never payed attention to. Turns out it was the door to a huge gym area, where there were weights, machines, treadmills, and open areas for combat.

Mr. Foxworth had provided me with a lot of clothes since I got there. For this occasion, he gave me three sets of gyms clothes, with sleeveless shirts, shorts, and running shoes. I was voluminous but never muscular, and the past week I had done nothing but read and sleep, so my arms looked really small inside the shirt. I wanted to change that.

Elijah told me to meet him at the gym at 5pm, and so I did. I opened the door to presence the gym for the second time in my life, first time having been a couple hours prior when Mr. Foxworth authorized my training. On the spot, I thought I would never stopped being mesmerized by the size of it.

Elijah was already in, wearing the least amount of clothes I had ever seen him in. Shorts and sleeveless shirt, just like me, but he could definitively fill them. For the first time, I noticed his scars all over his body. From afar it almost looked like he had a tattoo sleeve, but when you got closer you could clearly see that it was the abstract design of scars made sporadically by a variety of sharp objects.

"Come in," he said when I opened the door. The ceiling was so tall, I thought it was probably the forest floor itself, covered with some cement.

I walked to Elijah, who was standing in the middle of the open combat area, where training mats covered the floor. His hair was held back with a ponytail, and he didn't have any weapons on him. It was weird seeing him like this. He looked almost vulnerable.

"Why didn't you want to train me?" I asked. Elijah sighed with some annoyance.

"Do you ever get tired of asking questions?"

"Do you ever get tired of dodging them?"

Elijah chuckled. "Fight now, talk later. Okay?" I nodded. "The very basic principles of combat consist of using your mind to predict what your opponent will do next and using your body to counter it."

I nodded again and listened carefully. I completely forgot about my leg, which was almost completely healed, but still bothering me a bit. Still, I couldn't waste a second more. And, also, I wanted to learn as much as I could before the wolves got back.

"Have you ever been in a fight?" asked Elijah. From somebody else, that question would've sounded intrusive and skeptical. From him, it sounded curious and friendly.

"Not really," I said. "I played street football last week and killed it, thought." Elijah's face filled with visible confusion.

"Street football?" he asked.

I dismissed it. "The point is, I'm stronger than I appear. I promise. I held my place against two seniors who were trying to overthrow me."

Elijah looked a little impressed. "When faced with life-or-death situations, animals tend to fill with adrenaline and do things they may not be able to do otherwise. That's why you hear of mothers lifting cars to save their babies trapped beneath them."

"Are you implying that I'm not strong enough?" I asked, feeling insulted.

"You need to stop that," said Elijah, now with a clear tone of annoyance. He walked closer to me. "I'm one of your few allies in here. I'm trying to help you, so let me. Your smartassery and stubbornness could get you in trouble out there."

He was right, and I knew it. At that moment, however, I only felt insulted and dishonored. "But what are you saying, then?" I asked, seemingly ignoring his previous comments.

"I'm saying that sometimes we do things that are out of character, and we cannot always trust our instincts.

You cannot depend on the things you've done under pressure right now, because what you will feel won't be pressure, but fear."

He stopped to let me respond, but I didn't. I looked into his eyes, taking in what he just said. Trying to breathe and understand the situation. I just... I wanted to fight. So badly.

"Can you try me?" I asked him.

He nodded and took position. His legs open, one in front and one back, his arms almost perpendicular to them. He looked perfectly in balance. "Push me," he said.

I took a deep breath and prepared myself. I saw him and his perfectly stable body, and suddenly regretted ever implying that I could fight even a bit. I got close to him and held his shoulders, and used my legs and back to push him backwards, but he didn't move. He was a statue.

Without warning, his back leg swiped under my feet, making me fall on my ass. "You were as vulnerable as you could've been," he said, offering me his hand.

"That was so dirty," I said, not taking his hand and standing up by myself. "You told me to push you, so I did."

"Contrary to what movies or sports might teach you, there are no rules in combat, George." He stood in peace, with his hands behind his back. "There is no honor in fighting for your life and doing everything you can to survive. Save that to the samurais and war heroes. If you're getting assaulted and the only way out is to kick the man in the balls, you do it. There is no time for shame."

I wanted to laugh, but I was still working on taking in what he was saying. The idea of fighting without honor sounded wrong and dirty, but I couldn't exactly pinpoint why. I guess storytellers really romanticize combat as well.

"Remember that you need to think what your enemy will do next," continued Elijah after a moment. "Be three or four steps ahead of them."

"Wouldn't they be three or four steps ahead of me as well, if they were competent fighters?" Elijah gave me a slight smile, which relaxed me greatly.

"Finally, a good question. If you're both competent fighters, you'll have to keep each other guessing every time, until one of you slips. If not, you'll never stop."

"Interesting," I said, though I meant to just think it.

5pm was the time I entered the gym, and we didn't leave until Ms. Rose called us for dinner, almost four hours later.

Everything is going well.

You've done well.

Master will be pleased.

And it will all be over soon.

You can be with them again.

Soon.

One more day.

Chapter 13
The Night of April 16th,
Part 1

Gray, April 16th, the small hours

The trip had been four times as long as they had expected. After reaching Adler again, they had to cut corners due to the heavy police presence in town. Gray knew it had to do with their break-in, but he honestly didn't expect as much outrage. He guessed he had underestimated the modern authorities.

After two days of walking around, trying to eavesdrop on conversations, and even considering breaking into the police station again, the wolfpack redirected their efforts towards following the trail left by the demons and their strange organic cloth, which was very faint. After animals and humans and countless tempering, it was hard following such a unique and delicate smell.

By what Gray counted as Sunday, they had explored probably 20 miles in and around Adler, looking for anything of value. It wasn't until that early morning that something appeared, seemingly out of nowhere. Taylor walked by it as he was returning to the pack. Another piece of cloth, that looked about the same but smelt fresher. That would surely give them a better idea of where they had headed, so they made their way into that direction.

George, April 16th, noon

It had been the most intense two days of my life. After dinner the first night, we went back to reading anything we could find to confirm our suspicions about the cocoons. Then, next morning, Elijah woke me up at six to run an hour of treadmill, and then train for another hour. After breakfast, we read for a couple hours and trained again for about three hours. Lunch, read, train, shower, dinner, read, sleep.

That Sunday morning I woke up with everything hurting like crazy, especially my back. Before restarting training after our first reading session, Elijah approached me while I was warming up at the gym. "I want you to try something different today," he said.

"What?" I asked. We'd been doing basic hand-to-hand since the beginning, and I was nowhere near close of dominating it. Not even the most basic things.

"Come with me." Elijah opened the doors and left the gym, and I followed him in confusion. We walked past all the bedrooms and past the main hall, to the other side, where there was another door that I had never opened.

Elijah pushed the door open to reveal what I could only identify as an armory. A small shooting gallery with targets and an incredible variety of guns placed on the wall. "Wow," I let escape me. Elijah chuckled with delight.

We walked in and I stood in front of the gallery, inside one of those cubicles that you get into when you go to a shooting range. I had never held a gun in my life, but I thought I'd seen enough pictures to kinda understand what was happening.

"I want to test your aim," said Elijah. I thought he would say something like that eventually, but I didn't expect it to come so soon after we started training. "Grab the silver handgun." I scanned the wall for it and found it near the bottom, hanging next to some scary-looking rifles. "That is a Kimber 1911. Basic, reliable and easy."

I grabbed the gun. I'd always read that guns were always a lot heavier than what they appeared, but this was an understatement. The gun didn't only feel heavy; it felt massive and powerful.

I knew enough about guns to know that there was a small thing you pushed to take out the cartridge, so I did. Unsurprisingly, it was completely empty. I pulled back the cannon to check if there was a bullet in the chamber, and there wasn't.

"Have you done this before?" asked Elijah, trying to hide his surprise.

"No," I said. "But I watch lots of movies."

Elijah took the gun from me and loaded it. "Extremely careful," he said as he gave it back to me. I grabbed it, feeling how it was heavier than before. I stood in front of the gallery, back straight and arms firm, doing everything I could to hide my trembling.

Elijah pulled static targets first. I'd read and heard countless times to "squeeze not pull" and I tried, but it was a lot harder than it sounded. I shot once, and realized that whenever someone shoots a gun one-handed and lands any shot, it's complete bullshit. The kick was so strong, I thought my shoulder was gonna pop out of place.

In that same steady position I tried a very slow-moving target, some farther targets, and a combination of everything. By the end, in total, I had fired thirty shots, or two clips. The total number of shots that hit a target in any spot: four. Amount of shots that hit a target's head: zero.

"Not bad for a first-timer. Put that back and meet me at the gym," said Elijah, leaving the armory. I felt the impulse to disobey and try out other guns, but I wouldn't dare. It would be dangerous and stupid, and would make Elijah very mad.

The amount of guns hanging on the wall was too impressive. I identified three different rifles, four shotguns, six handguns, two sniper rifles, and even a crossbow. I felt very compelled to touch them, but I couldn't even do that. I just placed the handgun back and left for the gym. "*Another day*," I thought.

#

Training with Elijah was intense, to say the least. It was definitely a lot heavier than however many PE classes I ever had in school. It wasn't only the physical activity of standing and strafing and punching and kicking, but all the mental games he played with me. It was truly exhausting.

"Predict what I'm going to do, and counter it," he said, taking his usual fighting stance. We both knew I wasn't gonna be able to do it, but I tried anyway.

He stood, solemn in his pose, and stroke my left cheek with his right hand, almost like a slap. I saw it coming, but my reflexes weren't nearly good enough to block it in time.

I exclaimed in pain. "Can't we start easy?" I asked.

"This is easy," he answered. I wanted to laugh, but it also made me really nervous for whatever awaited me.

He went back to his stance, and I waited. Right when I thought he wasn't going to move, he made the same move as before, but with his other hand. I almost managed to block it, but his hand overpowered mine and I ended up hitting myself. I also couldn't block the low kick that came afterwards, making me fall on my ass.

"Again," he said, not helping me up.

Steph, April 16th, afternoon

The Adler/Morrow General Hospital was very small, as the area it served was very small too. The four-floor building was notoriously underfunded and understaffed, having to constantly ask for help from the Twin Cities whenever there was any kind of outbreak, and during important holidays where people were likely to cause mayhem, like the 4th of July or Halloween. But, even with all of those issues, nobody could deny that the teams that served at the hospital were professional and efficient.

Dr. Kim had given orders for his daughter to stay in bed until Monday morning. Her test results had come back with shocking connotations, showing dangerously low levels of iron and sugar, and moderate dehydration. After being seen by a resident psychologist and her father several times, she decided that she wouldn't fight it anymore, that she would fulfill her father's wishes and stay one more day at the hospital.

The look and smell of the room was getting to her nerves. She had already memorized the magazine Evelyn bought her a couple days before, and there was nothing interesting on TV aside from more and more news about the Missing Four and now Earnest Erb. She stopped at the local news channel while zapping, being able to see Earnest Erb's face for the first time. He was white, tall, with short blonde hair. His wife was Asian-American, and their little boy looked absolutely adorable in the picture they showed. This made Steph feel weird, so she turned off the TV.

Evelyn had brought Steph's computer the day after she was taken in, but the hospital's internet was so bad, the only thing Steph could do without everything crashing was check her email. Soon, she started doing something she had thought of doing for a while, but never brought herself to it.

She opened a blank document and started typing. "Dear George."

What was she going to say? Could she express how much he missed him and worried for his safety? Or maybe tell him how angry it made her that the police were actually considering him a suspect. Perhaps she could tell him that the whole school is worried about him, that he isn't alone like he probably thinks he is.

But she also wanted to tell him about herself. About how all of her world turned upside down after his disappearance, and she felt without purpose. That so much of her life felt destabilized without him, even walking through school. That, deep inside, she wished he would knock on the door of her hospital room. But that was not possible, and she knew.

She wrote for about an hour. Then, Steph decided her letter was finished.

"Dear George,

I don't really know where to start. I've never been the writing type, that's your thing. But lately I've had to be everything for both of us, because you're not here. It's so strange not having you around, regardless of the circumstances. You know? Not seeing you in French or at lunch, it's just weird.

I don't think it's possible for me to ever get used to not having you by my side. Sure, maybe when we both get married and live in separate countries, you being a famous writer and I... whatever it is I end up being. For now, it has been so hard to walk around without you. To check my phone and know it's simply impossible that I have a text from you, but I wait for it anyway.

You are innocent. I know that. There is no doubt in my mind that you have absolutely nothing to do with this. Walker can suck it because he's wasting everybody's time by going after you when it's that creepy-ass forest dude they should be chasing around. I'm so worried about you, I really hope he isn't doing anything to you. Every time I think about it I squirm, but I just can't do anything. How can I help you? What do I do?

I'm a lame-o who fainted and now I'm at the hospital. I guess I forgot to eat this past week, thinking about you and how to help you. I don't know what to do besides wait for any news, and it breaks my heart every time I get the feeling that I will never, ever see you again.

But that can't be true. You cannot be dead. I need to know if you got to kiss Andrea at the festival. And finish that novel chapter you said were starting soon, remember? I also need somebody outside of class to practice my French so I don't get rusty. You're so much better at it than me; that's why I need you to listen and correct me whenever I make a mistake.

Sometimes I think of you in ways I don't like to. In ways I absolutely abhor (see? I can use fancy words too). I think of you lying cold and grey on the ground, not breathing, your eyes completely white. I think I may have had a nightmare about it or something, because the thoughts are sometimes so overwhelming, my eyes tear up. It has to be some kind of sick moment of imagination, right? I'm not a psychic. Or a psychopath. I guess I'm just too worried about you. I don't think I've ever been so scared for somebody else's life, not even when your mom was here, where I'm sitting right now.

You are my best friend, and I love you so much. Please come back soon.

Love,

Steph."

Monica, twilight

Violent shaking woke Monica from her sleep. She was dreaming of flying away on top of a golden eagle. Instead, she fell to the ground from the bottom of her ripped cocoon, and was raised up by Arabella in typical fashion.

The sky was orange with the last sun rays of the day. Monica couldn't think of the last time she'd seen a sunset, much less one as beautiful as the one she was witnessing right there. "Move," ordered Arabella, pushing her deeper into the woods.

Monica heard rustling in the shadows and jumped at the sound of a body dropping right next to her. Miles Goodman had been pushed to the ground by Marcus. "Miles," whispered Monica, though it was barely audible anyway. It burned to use her vocal cords.

Miles turned his head up to see her, but couldn't speak. She lifted him up and put her on her back, though he was considerably taller than her, and none of them had had any muscle stimulus in more than a week. Needless to say, Monica's efforts to carry Miles were completely nullified by his weight and her weak state.

They both fell back to the ground face first. Monica rolled over on her back and laid down, breathing heavily, her eyes full of tears. She turned to look at Miles, dirty, pale, and skinny, barely breathing.

"Miles," she tried to whisper again, but her voice broke. She felt an unbearable pain on her foot which made her look up to see Arabella stepping on her.

"I told you to move," she said. "You can't make our Master wait for you."

Arabella grabbed both teenagers by their hair and raised them to their feet. Monica screamed with pain, and could barely remain standing. Miles didn't last a second and fell to the floor again. "Miles," tried to call Monica, still unable to get enough air in her lungs.

Then, out of nowhere, Miles opened his eyes and stood up with a jump, like nothing had happened, as if he had been eating, sleeping and breathing normally for the past week. Monica looked at him with horror and confusion, until she heard it. "Move," said the voice in her head, and so she felt instantly compelled to walk. She didn't know where. She just walked.

George, April 16th, night

The shower I took after the last training of the day felt like a blessing from the Gods. My muscles ached and I felt bruises developing all over my legs and hands, due to all the punching and kicking I'd been doing for the past couple days. According to Elijah, there was still a very long way to go. Understandable, seeing that it was only the second day.

In their usual fashion, Mr. Foxworth's employees had dinner ready by the time I got out of the shower. Roast turkey with russet potatoes and a garden salad with walnuts and honey. Stunningly delicious, really.

There was something in my mind that couldn't escape me, though. Even with the training and the great environment that I felt in thanks to the lack of wolves around the place, I still found something kind of uncomfortable, and I couldn't continue without clearing it with Elijah.

After dinner, I brushed my teeth and went back to the library to continue studying for a couple hours. When I entered the room, Elijah was already there, reading. "No time to waste," I said, trying to somehow start casual banter.

"None at all," he said, not taking his eyes off the book. He pointed at a couple books I hadn't read. "You can start off with those and see where you end up."

I sat down in front of him, but didn't start reading. I stared into his eyes, trying to somehow connect with him in a physical way, to literally form a connection between our brains so I could have my answers instead of having to ask him and possibly annoy. Alas, there was no other way.

"Hey," I started, "I wanted to ask you something."

Elijah looked up from the book to me and saw my concerned expression. He put the book down on the table. "What could that be?"

"I want you to be honest with me, okay?" I said.

Elijah sighed. "I'm always honest with you, George. What is it?"

I swallowed hard. I was never someone to fear asking provocative questions, but, for some reason, Elijah was different. It ashamed me to bother him, to feel I wasted his time. "Why... why didn't you want to train me?"

Silence. Silence I felt lasted ages, waiting for Elijah to analyze my question and answer me. He looked me in the eyes with that comprehensive look of his, but he didn't make me feel safe. On the contrary, I felt that he, for some reason, was going to snap.

"Never mind," I said before he answered. "It's nothing. Don't worry about it."

"I don't think you're ready," he said. I had already assumed that was going to be the answer, but ever since they started saying that, I took it as a euphemism for "*You are a bother and a waste of space.*"

"I know, I know," I said, regretting I asked and trying to end the conversation. "Forget about it."

"You are very smart," he continued, as if I didn't say anything else. "I'm sure you would be a great hunter when you reach a certain age, after you've trained and studied a lot more than you have now."

I sighed. "It's okay," I said. "You don't have to cheer me up. Let's just read."

I grabbed the book he'd pointed to before and started reading the first page, but I could still feel his gaze upon me. "You're doing great," he said. "Especially considering the amount of time you've spent here. It's truly marvelous."

I didn't know what to say. I guess I just needed to be sure that they thought I was a bother, so I could stop torturing myself, wondering if they actually thought that way. But he wasn't confirming any of my theories.

"I'm gonna pull a 'George' and try to guess your motives, alright?" he asked, smiling slightly. I wasn't sure what he was talking about, but I nodded. "My guess is that you don't feel like part of this team, and that you have a lot more to give than what you've had the chance for. Is that correct?" I nodded with embarrassment.

"You don't have to keep going," I said, but he ignored me.

"That teenage brain of yours is so complex, so vicious. It makes you think really stupid stuff, and therefore do stupid stuff." He stayed silent for a moment, waiting for me to answer, but I didn't. "I know you want to fight. I know you want to help your friends and save them from these horrible situations. I get it. But you're not ready."

"But what am I supposed to do?" I snapped back, more aggressively than I intended. "I can't just sit here and wait until you solve everything."

"Sometimes there is nothing you can do," he said. He kept a consistent relaxed tone throughout. "We've already started your training, but it takes time. It will be a while until you can help us out in the field. If that time ever comes."

"Why wouldn't it come?" I asked, feeling nervous all of a sudden. I expected to be yelled at.

"Have you thought about what you're going to do after we're done here, George? Have you thought about what will happen after we save your friends?"

"I'll stay here with you," I said, not even thinking about another answer.

Elijah sighed and shook his head. "You're so young. You don't know what you're getting into. Staying here means being in danger every second of your life. Not sleeping or eating for days. Constantly reminding yourself of who you are and that the world is real. I don't want that for you at such a young age."

"What do you think my life is out there?" I snapped again, this time with a lot more strength in my voice. "What do you think I do during a normal day, out in the world? I have no family and one friend. I don't have a future anywhere out there. Or do you think Robert is going to work to pay for my education? Or that I could get enough help to get myself out of this shithole in the middle of nowhere? I am nobody and have nothing, Elijah."

I started crying, even though I did everything to hold it. I couldn't take it anymore. Elijah's silence only made it worse.

I stood up and left for my room. I didn't want anyone to see me like that. All vulnerable and weak, helpless and scared. I couldn't allow it.

I laid face down on my bed with my head against the pillow. I gathered all of my strength and screamed against the soft pillowcase, feeling the inside of my neck tense with all of the rage I had been containing.

There was a knock on my door, but I didn't answer. Another knock, but I ignored it. I heard the door open and felt weight settling in at the end of the bed, next to my feet. "I want to show you something," said Elijah.

I raised my head off the pillow and looked at him, sniffing. My eyes red. "What?" I asked.

"Come with me," he said, standing up and going for the door. I followed him.

Elijah's room looked clean and organized. Of course, I didn't expect it to look like he had been living there for days without getting out, but it was way more presentable than I thought it would be. The bed was made, his weapons were all aligned against the wall, and his red attire was hanging from a perch, along with his hat.

"Sit wherever you like," he said. I grabbed a chair that was by the desk at the end of the wall and sat on it. Elijah went to where his weapons were laying, and grabbed from the floor what looked like a wooden suitcase.

"What's that?" I asked.

"You'll see." He put the suitcase on the bed right next to me and opened it. Inside was something made out of brown leather, with carved diamond shapes. A gauntlet.

"I've seen you wearing that," I remembered out loud. "Ever since I first met you."

"Yes," he said, taking it out of the box. "I never go anywhere without it." He put it on his right hand and it fit perfectly, as if it had been made especially for his hand. The moment he put it on, it's like he was himself one more time, like his physical identity that his casual clothing had concealed was back to him.

He turned it for me to detail, and for the first time I noticed the blade that was attached to the upper wrist. "Oh, it's a weapon," I noted.

"Yes. A concealed weapon." He pushed the blade out of the wrist. It was as bigger than a regular knife, but thin like a glass. "I carry this gauntlet everywhere I go, and I feel incomplete without it. Vulnerable, almost."

"Why?"

"Why do I carry it everywhere or why do I feel incomplete?"

I chuckled. "Both, I guess."

"When you go into this world, this kind of job, you need to find something that keeps you grounded. Something that reminds you that there are things bigger than you in this world, and no matter how many things you kill or how many ancient texts you read, you're only human. This gauntlet is one of the few things I owned before Mr. Foxworth took me in. He recommended I keep it to remind me of who I am."

I didn't understand what he was trying to tell me. I just told him that I wanted to stay here because I didn't have anything outside of it, and he explains that I need something to remind me of that? It felt almost like a sick joke.

"You are too young to renounce to your life," he continued. "I don't want you to make a decision based on raw emotions when you're not thinking clearly. Like I thought you'd do when it all started and I feared you'd want to go back to your family."

"You're telling me that in this world I'm coming into, I will forget about my previous life and need something to go back to it?"

Elijah realized right there that he had made a huge mistake. He sighed heavily. "Yes."

I stood up. "Then I'm definitely staying," I said, and turned to the door.

Elijah, April 16th, night

He knew he screwed up. His attempt at making George appreciate his life had the opposite effect on him, and he felt horrible. He felt he had personally thrown George into this world and that if anything happened to him, it would be his fault. This kid, who just happened to be in the wrong place at the wrong time.

Without putting anything away, Elijah stood up and went for the door to chase George, but he was stopped by the sound of his phone. The phone that never, ever made a sound unless there was an emergency. A real emergency.

Terrified and confused, Elijah turned back and walked to his nightstand, where the phone was glowing and vibrating. It could only be one person calling, and that was exactly who it was.

"Gray," answered Elijah. "What happened?"

"It's me," said Taylor from the other side of the line. "You need to come here right now."

They're here.

It's time.

Chapter 14
The Night of April 16th,
Part 2

Gray, April 16th, night

Following the tracks, the pack got as far as the outskirts of Morrow, the nearest town North of Adler. They had been walking for so long, their paws had started to bleed out of excessive use.

At one point they had to stop and rest, something they didn't use to do at all. "I'm getting too old for this shit," said Alex, laying down on the ground, breathing heavily. The travel had taken a particularly heavy toll on him.

"It'll all be over soon," said Taylor, laying down as well. Gray could hear all of their stomachs roar with hunger.

"Taylor," called Gray. Taylor turned to him. "You got the bag?"

"Yeah," said Taylor.

"I'll go hunt for something. Be right back." Taylor nodded, and so Gray left his group, heading West.

He could hear the distant cars and people of Morrow, and he almost considered approaching town to look for food, but he wouldn't. It would be stupid for a 250-pound black wolf to appear in the middle of the night, especially with all the tension around the area lately.

Gray walked peacefully, for the first time thinking about something other than the case, the travel. He needed to find food for him and his pack, or it would all have been for nothing.

But he couldn't smell anything. Not squirrels or birds or deer, nothing. His pelt protected him from the cold, but he could still feel that it was almost unbearable for that time of year. Nevertheless, that was no reason for animals to be completely absent. They were part of the forest, they were used to it.

In the distance, Gray thought he heard something. He raised his head and listened carefully, noticing every little sound available, until he identified what sounded like small steps, typical of small animals. The black wolf walked slowly, muting his steps as effectively as possible, approaching his probable prey.

Suddenly, the cold got worse. Way worse. His pelt couldn't protect him from such breeze. His snot felt like it was being pierced with a meat hook. Gray started feeling dizzy, but it wasn't the hunger or lack of sleep. And he had to do something before he fell.

The black wolf stopped walking and contained himself from dropping on the ground. With a big breath of freezing air, he looked to the sky and howled. He howled as loudly and clearly as he could. It was his only chance for survival. And he trusted that his pack would do the rest.

Elijah, April 16th, night

"What happened?" asked the hunter on the phone.

"We don't know," answered the blonde wolf from the other side. "We're running there right now. We're just outside of Morrow, half a mile West. Hurry." And he hung up.

Fear and confusion invaded Elijah's thoughts too quickly. He undressed and put on his combat attire in seconds. His vest, belt, jacket, boots, and all of his weapons. He put on his gauntlet last, as he had forgotten he'd taken it out of its case.

Elijah left his room to find George reading in the library with the door open, his eyes still teary. "Where are you going?" asked the boy.

"Something happened," said Elijah, not looking at George. "I'll meet the wolves in Morrow."

"Morrow?" George stood up from the desk and walked to the door that Elijah was opening. "You're not going alone, are you?"

Elijah's instinct told him everything he needed to know right then and there. He turned to George. "Don't even think about coming with me," he said. For the first time, he showed legitimate anger in his voice, though he didn't mean it. The haste of the moment didn't allow him to control his emotions.

"I can't let you go all by yourself," argued George.

"You are staying here safe and sound," said Elijah, authoritatively. "End of story." Before the boy could reply, Elijah opened the door and climbed the stairs out of the basement.

He hadn't been to the ground floor ever since he got there with George the week before. He'd almost forgotten that there was a house façade before you entered the safe house, where he had introduced the boy to his mentor.

There was a bowl on the coffee table in the middle of the living room where Elijah knew were the keys to the vehicles. He grabbed one for a sedan and went out of the house. The Foxworth Estate keeps vehicles parked near the safe houses for emergencies, and this one was parked right outside the diner across the street.

Elijah had forgotten about the incredible cold outside. He almost couldn't believe that it could be that cold in the middle of April, and all of the hate he felt towards the climate came back all at once, frustrating him.

He opened the door to the blue car and got in. He turned on the engine, making it come to life with a potent roar that told him the car hadn't been turned on in a while, probably weeks.

Whatever it was that happened, he had to fix it. No matter what, he needed all of the team to survive the night.

George, April 16th, night

I was shocked by Elijah's tone. I just couldn't believe how angry he looked, how worried. It didn't even cross my mind that he may have received bad news and that's what made him angry. I just instantly thought that it was me, the argument we had right before he left, and my overall uselessness.

"Don't worry," said Mr. Foxworth from behind me. I wondered how much he'd heard, how much he knew. "They're a team of very capable hunters. They'll be fine."

"I need to help them," I insisted.

"You help them by staying here. Letting them know that you're safe." Mr. Foxworth kept calm and friendly, as usual. But it wasn't working. There was nothing that could prevent me from wanting to go. I needed to go.

"They need help," I repeated. "I need to help them."

"George." Mr. Foxworth got closer to me, staring into my eyes, into my soul. "You shall stay here and keep studying."

"I can't," I said. "I need to do something. They may be in danger."

I walked into my room and put on clothes right over my pajamas. A pair of jeans, a shirt, a hoodie, and shoes. Mr. Foxworth walked slowly but surely to my door. "I can't let you go, George," he said, standing by my door.

"With all due respect, Mr. Foxworth," I said, pulling up my sweater's zipper. "There's nothing you can do to stop me."

"There is a lot that I can do," replied Mr. Foxworth. For the first time in my life, I felt a threatening undertone in his voice. "Please. Stand down."

I did my best to ignore him and walk out of my room, but he blocked the way with his cane. His brown hardwood cane that looked like it could break a baseball bat in half. "Let me go, sir," I said.

"You will not go anywhere, young man," said Mr. Foxworth.

I had to think. My room was the first one in the hallway, so from my door I could see the round table and the exit, the kitchen, the armory. What would I do? What could I do? I wasn't going to hurt Mr. Foxworth, nor did I think I could, anyway.

I thought of Mr. Larned again. I remembered one time we were discussing about something I didn't know much about – and I actually can't remember what it was – and how he said that he really admired my ability to improvise. "The way you bullshit your way through an argument is fascinating," he said to me.

So I improvised. I pushed the cane away from my way and ran to the armory door. Mr. Foxworth almost grabbed my arm, but his hand slipped. I opened the armory door and got in, and closed it from the inside.

I looked at the wall full of weapons and felt terrified, but curious. The wall looked almost like a piece of art, with different tones of silver and black shining across a bedazzled canvas.

There was a hard knock on the door that couldn't possibly come from Mr. Foxworth. "Open up, George," he said, still sounding uncharacteristically menacing.

"I'm going to Morrow," I said. "You can't stop me."

"I have a couple people here that think otherwise," he responded, without any doubt in his voice.

I took the deepest breath of my life and grabbed the gun that Elijah had lent me earlier. "Get away from the door," I demanded. I took out as many clips as possible from the cabinet parallel to the wall on the other side. I loaded one and put the others in my pockets.

"Stand down, George," said Mr. Foxworth. "I don't want you to get hurt."

I quickly opened the door and saw two men in suits, each pointing a similar gun at me. Two tall men, fit, looking like stereotypical FBI agents from the movies. But they felt almost robotic, the way they didn't blink for a millisecond, watching me constantly.

My gun, however, was not pointed at them, but at myself. At my own head.

Mr. Foxworth turned whiter than he usually was. "What are you doing?" he asked, terrified. "Stop that right now."

"Let me go," I said, trembling. The weight of the gun was tiring to my already burned out arm, and the clips inside my pockets made me feel unbalanced. All of the exercise of the past two days was taking a toll.

"George, please stop. You don't know what you're doing."

Very slowly, I walked out of the armory, making the men in suits step back, still pointing their guns at me. "Where did they come from?" I asked, legitimately curious.

"You don't think we're here in the middle of nowhere unprotected, do you?" asked Mr. Foxworth. He had a point. I should've seen it coming.

This made me think of Ms. Rose and the other servants. Were they secret agents too? Did they know how to fight, how to shoot? Where did they go after they finished dinner? Where did they live? How did Mr. Foxworth hire them? But there was no time for that.

I continued walking, redirecting my steps towards the exit door, never taking my eyes off of the guards. "You take one more step and I shoot," I said, still trembling. "All of what you're doing will be for nothing because I will be dead."

Mr. Foxworth sighed and looked down. "Please don't do this. I beg you."

I didn't answer. I continued walking backwards towards the door until I felt it against my back. I used my free hand to open it and get on the staircase.

"George," insisted Mr. Foxworth. "You can't go alone. It's dangerous."

"I'm not going alone," I said. "I'm joining the team who's already there."

I climbed up two steps backwards, which made me feel ridiculous and awkward. But Mr. Foxworth's expression of terror never changed. "Please," he begged again.

I wasn't going to stop. I was getting out of the house and helping the wolves. Helping Elijah. I was a worthy part of the team and I would be helpful. I was sick of staying in, studying like a crippled child.

"I'm going to close this door now," I said from two steps up, where I could still reach the door. "If I hear you open it again, I will shoot myself. I swear to God."

Mr. Foxworth looked into my eyes again, trying to reach in. I blocked him. "Please," he begged. I pushed the door closed and ran upstairs.

When I got to the living room upstairs, I grabbed one of the chairs and pushed it to the door, doing everything I could to make it block the way. It was probably not going to be very effective, but it could give me a moment to think.

I remembered they told me that the car keys where on the coffee table at all times, so I walked to it and checked the only thing that was on it. The small green glass bowl had three different sets of keys, and I grabbed them all and put them in my pockets.

I walked out of the house for the first time in almost two weeks. I felt the cold breeze hit my face, hurting my eyes and nostrils. I used the hoodie to cover half of my face as I walked out and figured out which car to take.

I clicked one of the car keys and heard a beep to my right, where I saw a red motorcycle flash its lights. I'd never driven a motorcycle and the cold air would surely burn my face off, so that wasn't an option.

The second key I pressed showed me a white truck parked on the other side of the street, in front of what looked like a bank. I ran towards it and opened it. I'd driven cars before because Steph insisted that I learn, so Evelyn gave me some lessons the year before. I knew the basics, but I wasn't an experimented driver by any means. But I had to go, so I turned on the engine and the truck roared to life. I took the deepest of breaths, and drove off.

Elijah, April 16th, night

The hunter drove fast and recklessly. The way to Morrow was probably 25 minutes away, but he didn't have that kind of time. The wolves didn't have that kind of time. So he drove, and got there in 18 minutes instead.

The outskirts of Morrow were deserted. Understandable, seeing it was late at night and there was barely any light outside. The moment he got close to town, Elijah felt a knot form in his stomach, as if his intestines were being pulled out right through his navel.

He parked and got out the moment he saw the familiar car the wolves had taken days prior. He instantly took out his crossbow, ready to strike, grabbed the dog whistle he kept hanging from his neck and blew it, hoping for the best.

As he walked, he could see the remains of tracks, and he followed, hoping they were from the pack and not some wild animal. But apart from that, the forest looked completely deserted. It didn't appear that any sentient being was around him for miles and miles, which made him very anxious.

He blew on his whistle again, hoping for something. Then, he felt his phone vibrating in his pocket. He hastily took it out and checked it, only to see that it was a message from Mr. Foxworth. "George ran away. He's going to you. He took all keys."

That was probably the last thing Elijah wanted to find out at that moment. Before he could think of an answer to give, he heard something behind him, making him drop the phone and point the crossbow at nothing. He was relieved by a familiar silhouette of blonde pelt.

"Taylor," he sighed, putting down the crossbow and picking up the phone.

"They got Gray," said Taylor, breathless. "We don't know where they're going. Come quick."

Gray, April 16th, night

The black wolf had been half-conscious for the better part of the last hour, barely able to see where he was or in what direction he was moving. Still in wolf form, he was being dragged by a person he didn't recognize. A tall man, early 30s, who wore no expression on his face.

Gray thought it prudent to play dead for the remainder of the trip, and then run or fight whenever they got to where they were going. Still, the most curious aspect about everything was that Gray could smell something. Sure, the ground and the trees and the insects among the leaves, but now he could also get a scent from the demon closest to him. Their scent that had disappeared was back, possibly proving Elijah's theory about their weak state.

The stranger mumbled something that Gray, at first, thought was directed at him. But no. The stranger was just talking to himself. "One more night, then it's over," he repeated, over and over again. His face still expressionless.

They stopped, and the stranger dropped Gray's paws. Still playing dead, he opened his eyes ever so slightly to try to see around him, but he couldn't identify anything particular. It was just more forest.

"Jason," called the stranger. "I got one."

Gray heard something peculiar. He still couldn't smell anything, but he heard rustling in the wind, as if a giant bird had flapped its wings. The cold intensified, and Gray had to hold on to everything he had so he wouldn't shiver.

Even though Gray closed his eyes shut, he could still understand exactly what was happening. The demon had landed right next to him, and was walking around his body. "Where are the others?" said the demon. His voice sounded weak and impatient, not at all what Gray had expected.

"They'll be here soon. We must be patient so everything goes well."

"I've waited long enough," said the demon. "I think this one is mine." Gray felt how the demon got closer. He was probably crouching, almost on top of Gray's black wolf body.

He couldn't hold it any longer. As he felt the demon's respiration on top of his pelt, Gray jumped out of his resting position. He stood five feet away, ready to attack, growling like a wild wolf.

The demon smiled with delight. "Glad you could join us." Gray analyzed the situation. He took a good look at the demon, with long blonde hair and grey skin, smelling of ash and rotten meat. The man beside him looked apathetic, unemotional.

Gray could finally take a good look at the demon and study his external anatomy. He was particularly fascinated by his wings, which were not at all like a bat's or anything he'd seen. They were like two long extremities that came out of his back, with leathery membranes going from the tip of the wing to the lower back, like some kind of organic glider. Most interestingly, at the tip of the wings were what looked like long rhinoceros horns, which Gray assumed served mainly for stabbing or impaling.

Before anything else could happen, Gray looked up to the sky and howled.

Steph, April 16th, night

Steph hadn't been able to sleep all day. Miraculously, the internet improved that afternoon, so she used it to catch up on some homework before going back to school next week. Her mom had spent the day with her, but she was gone by then. She was under the care of her father and Mercedes, which didn't bother her at all.

Mercedes came in to check on her after dinner. "How are you feeling, sweetheart?" she asked.

"Better," answered Steph with a sigh. "I just wanna get out of here. Be in my room."

Mercedes sat at the edge of the hospital bed. "It will all be over soon. Don't you worry."

The Head Nurse stood up and prepared to leave the room. "Wait," said Steph, making Mercedes stop on her tracks. "Can you stay here a bit longer?"

It wasn't normal for Stephanie Kim to feel so vulnerable and alone. She always kept her back straight and priorities in check, but she hadn't been herself for a while now. She felt allowed to feel weak, to ask for comfort.

"Sure thing, baby," answered Mercedes with a warm smile. Mercedes sat on the chair next to Steph. But before any of them could say something, every light in the room flickered. "Strange," pointed out Mercedes.

"You think there's something wrong with the generator?" asked Steph, more worried than she thought was reasonable.

"I don't know," answered Mercedes. "It's probably nothing."

But, again, the lights flickered, this time for longer. Steph looked out to the hallway, where the lights were also failing. Before she could say anything else to her comforting nurse, the lights went off entirely for a couple seconds. They, they restarted, though with a lot less potency.

"The backup generator is on," pointed out Mercedes. "I need to go check with the higher-ups."

"Please don't leave me," asked Stephanie. Her childish request and the tone she made it with threw her off immensely, but she didn't have enough energy to correct herself.

"I'll be right back, okay?" said Mercedes warmly. Steph nodded with doubt, and Mercedes left the room.

Steph looked around her room. Half of the lights were lit by the backup generator, and not to full power either. In another situation, Steph would've thought it had potential to look romantic, with the soft lighting and yellowish hue. But right now, she was just terrified.

She heard crackling to her left, where the window was. She turned to look at it, and she noticed the glass slowly filling with ice crystals. She gasped with horror, but couldn't speak.

Elijah, April 16th, night

As Taylor and Elijah sprinted to where Alex and Drake were last seen, they heard another howl. Elijah's hearing wasn't as acute as Taylor's, so he couldn't identify that it came from Gray. But Taylor was sure, and so they switched directions from Northeast to Southwest, away from town.

Elijah's body was starting to fail him. He was young and in shape, but the cold and heavy clothing he was wearing to fight it didn't make it easy to keep up with a wolf. Still, he ran as fast as he could.

"I can hear the other two," said Taylor, lowering his speed and looking to his right. Moments later, a brown and a red wolf appeared from the dark.

"Did you see anything?" asked Alex.

"No. Nothing at all," answered Elijah.

The group continued their way to where Gray had alerted them, noticing the artificial light bleeding from between the trees. "It's right there," said Drake, with a hint of fear in his voice Elijah had never heard before.

They got closer and closer to the lights until the forest was no more. They were right outside a four-story building with flickering lights. "That's the hospital," said Taylor. "Adler-Morrow General, I think."

"What do you think they're doing here?" asked Elijah. His question was completely ignored, as the three wolves turned abruptly to the left and started running. This made Elijah realize that this was the very first time he and the wolves were chasing something at the same time, and it was exhausting.

The hunter ran behind the wolves and progressively started to hear what they were so shaken up about. He heard rustling and groans and growls, but couldn't see much. Then, he witnessed it. He saw the hybrid body of Michael Gray fighting with the same monster Elijah had encountered at the clearing. The one that bit George. His boney wings opened fully, his grey body opaqued even with the hospital lights shining upon him.

"Gray!" cried Taylor as he ran towards them. With every step, he became more manlike, until he adopted a form similar to Gray's, but with blond hair. A majestic beast that looked almost like a lion.

The demon kicked Gray away and into Taylor's running body, making them hit each other. Alex and Drake jumped in and transformed in midair. Alex's hybrid form look very much like Gray's, save for the lighter pelt color. Drake, on the other hand, look really strange. He wasn't as muscular as his peers, and the color of his pelt reminded Elijah of a fox. Soon enough, Elijah. had four fully-transformed werewolves in front of him, for the very first time.

The demon laughed out loud. "How fortunate," he said. "We will get all of you at once."

Then, a black cloud of a strange material came out of the forest at top speed. Elijah couldn't identify exactly what it was, or if it was even a cloud. Like a black mist made out of giant particles, almost. Or like a swarm of millions of bees flying in sync towards them.

The cloud revolved around the wolves, separating them from Elijah. The hunter took out his sword and swung it around, trying to kill whatever it was that clouded his vision. Not even the hospital lights could help him see, and now whatever the cloud was made of was cutting him rapidly, hitting him with speed and precision, making small incisions in his attire.

As he swung his sword, he felt he hit solid objects. One of those times he turned his head to the floor, and noticed that the cloud was nothing more than a group of hyper-coordinated crows. A magnificent murder of crows that was flying around him and his team, creating confusion. In joined a couple of bats as well, creating a tornado of black sharp particles.

He looked at the dead bird for a moment. There didn't seem to be anything interesting about it. Its black feathers and small beak looked perfectly normal, its tiny eyes without any brightness at all. The hunter almost felt pity, having to kill a wild animal like that who probably did not intend to hurt them, but couldn't help it.

The demon used this moment to jump high into the air, flapping his giant wings, creating hurricane winds that blew Elijah off his feet. "Feast, children!" screamed the demon as he flew away to the hospital building.

Still on the floor, Elijah tried to distinguish what was happening, but he was feeling dizzy. A sensation that reminded him of the first time he smoked a cigarette; how his head felt light and fragile, and his mouth became dry. The crows were not paying much attention to him, but focusing solely on the wolves. From the floor, Elijah could see the small wounds they were giving his friends, surely debilitating them slowly.

"They're going inside the hospital!" yelled Gray to the group as they tried to shake off the birds. "We need to go in!"

George, April 16th, night

I didn't know where I was or where I was going. The decision I had taken 20 minutes before was starting to feel very, very wrong. But there was no going back. I needed to get to Morrow as soon as possible. I just needed something to help me understand where I was.

The driving part of the plan wasn't as bad as it could've been. Good thing the truck wasn't a stick because my escape would've been cut short before it even started. I just kept to my lane at a decent speed and hoped for the best. Luckily, the recent events made people scared of going out at night – or at least that's what I thought – so there were barely any other cars on my way.

After what felt like an eternity driving aimlessly, I finally found a sign that said that I was approaching Adler-Morrow General, which was a good point of reference I could start from. But it wasn't necessary. The moment I saw the hospital, I knew. I knew they were there.

As I drove closer I noticed the poor lighting coming from inside, which was not normal at all. But what really gave it away was the giant thing flying in the air close to the windows of the fourth floor. That really let me know that I was at the right place.

Gray, April 16th, night

There was no time to lose. The moment the demon called for his army of… whatever those things were, Gray felt the presence of dozens of creatures, all going into the hospital. His eyes allowed him to see the vampire flying into the building, breaking a window in the process. Seconds later, the screaming of the people inside was unbearable to the wolves' ears.

"Let's go!" screamed Gray. In a single movement, he spun around, lashing at the creatures. It gave his team enough space to jump out of the cloud.

"I'll secure the entrance!" Elijah yelled back. Of course, he was unable to follow the pack inside the hospital the way they were planning to go inside, so it was reasonable for him to use the front door.

Each wolf jumped as high as they could. Drake achieved to break into the second floor on his first try, which saved time. Alex couldn't jump very high, so he used all of his claws to quickly climb the cement wall and go into the first floor, where a window was already broken.

Gray and Taylor took the fourth and third floor, respectively. Gray jumped high enough to almost get to the second floor window, and he climbed the rest of the way. He felt the hundreds of flying things hit him in the back of the head as he climbed to the fourth floor, and it wasn't until he released one of his hands to cover himself that he could grab one of the flying things and notice they were birds. Crows, acting as bullets.

Gray gave one last jump to get to the fourth floor windows, where he heard intense screaming from the people inside and the chaos the crows were causing. Gray could hear glass shattering, bottles dropping, people running. He wondered what would happen when they saw a giant wolf man as well.

Gray climbed through the window into a vacant hospital room, where there were no signs that a person had been staying there before the invasion. He opted to stay in hybrid form, and so he walked out of the room in this way, feeling uncomfortable and unnatural.

Elijah, April 16th, night

The thing that would've made Elijah the happiest in that moment was a flamethrower. He needed something to get rid of the crows faster than the swing of his sword, but there was nothing on him that could've helped him. He gathered his strength and ran to the front of the hospital, where he saw something that truly confused him.

"Hey!" yelled Elijah to the people outside the hospital doors. Five people, three men and two women of different colors and ages, blocking the glass hospital doors for the people who were trying to open it from the inside. Elijah's call for attention was useless.

The hunter ran to the group of people and tried to push them, but they were static in their positions. They didn't even seem to notice him, as if he was a ghost or an insect.

"What are you doing?" asked Elijah to the first person blocking the door. A tall, black woman of about forty. She, too, ignored his words.

Elijah's head was starting to play games on him. As he touched the group of people, trying to push them out of the way, he felt dizzy, drugged.

"Come on!" he yelled in desperation. The crows flew around him, not enough to block his way but enough to disrupt him from thinking straight. He took out the handgun he kept on his belt and fired one shot into the air. The echo of the shot almost drowned by the rest of the noise surrounding him. But the group of people didn't leave their positions.

Elijah then opted to shoot the lower part of the hospital door, hoping it would shatter and let everybody out. It didn't work, but it did get the people's attention. The two men in the back turned to Elijah and stared, not quite into his eyes, but beyond them. As if they were looking at something behind Elijah, and his body was invisible.

Without any warning, the two men, both tall and white, sprinted towards Elijah. Elijah's first instinct was to point his gun at them, but they didn't react in the least, which told him it was useless. He was already suspecting it, but this further confirmed that these people were being controlled, in some kind of a trance.

Elijah quickly put away his gun and took out his gauntlet blade, but the two men didn't have any weapons. They were just going to attack him with their bare hands, and Elijah did not want to hurt them at all. The two men jumped on him at the same time, but Elijah was fast and strong enough to use their momentum to his advantage, making them fall to the floor as he dodged their tackles.

The two Entranced men stood up and kept going for him as if nothing had happened. They didn't seem to feel any pain or to be thinking of strategies to actually catch Elijah. As if they were just chasing him instinctively, without thinking of how or why.

Before Elijah could think of something else to do, there was a thundering sound, probably the loudest he had ever heard. The two Entranced men both aimed to punch him at the same time, to which Elijah, half stunned, responded by blocking their punches and swinging their arms in the air, making them fall hard on the floor.

Elijah used these spare seconds to turn to the glass doors and see that they were no more, replaced by a white truck that smashed through them. Then, the truck's door opened, and George McKnight came out of the driver's seat, visibly confused and disoriented.

Catch the wolves.

And it'll all be over.

Chapter 15
The Night of April 16th,
Part 3

Gray, April 16th, night

The soft lights flickered. The hospital hallways felt mostly empty, probably because whoever remained in the building was hiding behind closed doors or ran down the stairs. But Gray knew the demon was in there. He'd seen him enter through the same window he did. And he could smell him, finally.

It was a smell even more repulsive than the demons themselves. It wasn't only of rotten meat, but of meat that had rotten under a very damp and dark sewer, absorbing whatever other wastes flew down the drain and creating its own kind of bacteria within its ligaments. Then, it was as if that meat was burned at extremely high temperatures and left to decompose.

The relative silence was counterintuitive to what Gray thought should be happening at the moment, especially because of all the screaming he'd heard moments before. He could barely hear the water running through the pipes, or the lightbulbs buzzing. What he could hear with clarity, though, was somebody's breathing. As he walked through the deserted hallway he sensed the presence of a person, a smaller person, in the room right next to him.

With his huge hybrid hands he grabbed the doorknob and opened the door to his left, slowly, preventing it from creaking. He heard a muffled gasp from behind the hospital bed, and how the person's breathing got heavier and heavier by the second. He noticed a laptop on the bed and a backpack on a chair by the other side of the room.

"I'm not going to hurt you," said Gray with his deep, commanding voice. He could hear how the person muffled another gasp, and was probably holding back weeps. "There is something out here that does," continued Gray. "I need you to stay here and don't go out, no matter what. Okay?"

Gray heard how the person remained still, doing everything in their power to not hyperventilate. He didn't expect them to answer, but he had faith that his warning had been enough. He turned back to the hallway and closed the door behind him.

Gray opted, for the first time in his life, to walk on four feet as a hybrid. He felt that it gave him more control over the sounds he produced, and would let him jump unto the demon if he happened to appear out of nowhere. But the hallway was still empty. And then, what seemed like an explosion on the ground floor.

Elijah, April 16th, night

The glass doors were completely destroyed. About a dozen nurses and people in gowns came out of the building, running and screaming in all directions. Some were stepping on the glass completely barefoot, but that didn't stop them.

As George got out of the car, Elijah had to run to him and cover him from the remaining three Entranced people who were pushing the door. George's stunt had allowed everyone at the entrance to run free, but that meant that the five Entranced humans were now unto them, and George had only a day and a half of training.

But even if he had had two weeks or a year, George didn't look good. Elijah didn't know if it was the car crash or something else, but George's head kept drifting, like he was seasick. "Wake up, buddy," alerted Elijah. "You're here now. Time to get to work."

They were slowly getting surrounded by the five Entranced men and women. Elijah analyzed their faces one by one, and none of them seem to be focusing on anything in particular. They were all looking beyond Elijah. Then, all at once, they ran towards them.

"George!" screamed Elijah, as the boy seemed to still be disoriented. In one motion, Elijah dropped George to the floor and launched himself into the small black woman, the only one he thought he could lift.

Using his momentum, he grabbed the small black woman and launched her into her partners, smashing them all like bowling pins. Elijah grabbed the dog whistle around his neck and blew it, hoping for the best.

"I need you to wake up," he told George. He crouched unto him, trying to feel his forehead for fever or palpitations.

"Elijah," called George, but he couldn't say more. He was too weak. He was drifting away.

"What can it be? What did yo—" but then he got it. He reached into his pocket and took out a small golden necklace, the same one he had put inside George's pants the week before. "Take this," he said, giving the necklace to George and wrapping his fists over his.

Elijah squeezed George's hands into the necklace. "*In nomine Patris, et Filii, et Spiritus Sancti,*" started Elijah, in perfect Latin pronunciation. There was a prayer he had learned a long time ago, during his early studies. He knew it by heart, even though this would be the first time he would use it. It translates to: *In your trust I leave these hands for you to sanctify. In your heart I leave this soul for you to purify. In your eyes I leave this body for you to clean. In your power I believe, please believe in mine.*

George's hands started burning. Elijah held them tight and close, looking over the boy's shoulder, seeing how the Entranced were getting back up. Elijah squeezed George's hands until the burning feeling started to hurt him as well, and then George screamed. He looked up into the sky and screamed his lungs out, maybe in pain, maybe in frustration, or maybe literally letting out whatever was inside him that intoxicated his system. One way or another, after screaming, he fell to the floor.

Out of the building came a figure, a fast, relentless figure that jumped between the Entranced and Elijah. The brown wolf growled at the possessed individuals, who seemed to not even notice he was between them and their objective. "What is he doing here?" asked Alex.

"He escaped," said Elijah, picking George up. "I need to get him to safety."

"We need to secure the building," replied Alex. Anger in his voice like Elijah had never heard before.

Before Elijah could reply, Alex jumped in the air, stretching his body into hybrid form, and landing on top of the slow-walking Entranced. In one swift movement, Alex knocked all of them out with a hit to the head.

"Leave the boy and help us, Elijah," demanded Alex. "There are dozens of people inside who did not choose to be here."

Elijah wanted to reply, because he was sick of Alex's attitude towards George. It infuriated him that Alex implied that George was in it because he chose to, that he asked to be bit and for his friends to be taken away. But there was no time to argue. Fortunately, George was waking up.

Gray, April 16th, night

The thundering sound from downstairs distracted Gray long enough for the demon to lunge at him from out of the shadows. The soft backup lights malfunctioned as the two monsters rolled on the floor of the hallway, trying to bite each other's throats off. Moments later, the lights went off, the hallway illuminated only by the reflecting moonlight coming from outside.

The demon pushed Gray away with his long legs. Gray's body flew away to the other end of the hallway, next to the room he had come in from. Before Gray could stand back up, the demon lunged himself on him again, wrapping his wings around his body like a bullet, flying too fast for the black hybrid to react. The demon flew headfirst into Gray's chest, leaving him out of air.

The demon used the tip of one of his wings to stab Gray's stomach, making him roar in pain. The demon opened his mouth, showing his terrifying white fangs ready to strike at Gray's neck. The demon flinched, but Gray grabbed the demon's throat and held him away. Gray squeezed as hard as he could, trying to break the demon's jaw. Before he could achieve it, the demon stabbed Gray with his other wing and lifted him off the floor, throwing him inside the room right next to them.

George, April 16th, night

Surreal doesn't quite describe how it felt when I crashed the truck into the hospital doors. It wasn't the crash that made me feel dizzy, though. It's as if the air was toxic, like I was drugged with every whiff of oxygen I took in, and it got worse after I got out of the truck.

My hands were steaming hot, red with inflammation. My left hand even had a cut in the form of the necklace Elijah pushed into my skin, and it stung really badly. Disoriented and confused, I heard Elijah arguing with Alex as I opened my eyes.

"There is no time for this, Elijah," yelled Alex. As my eyes opened, I identified Alex's werewolf form in the flesh, and if I had been more conscious, I would've probably jumped in terror at first. It was a truly magnificent sight; looked a lot like what I remembered from Gray's, but with a lighter pelt. I don't know if I would've recognized him as Alex if I didn't know it was him beforehand.

"Elijah," I called, with all the energy I could muster. He was holding me in his arms, but he put me down when he heard me speak.

"Can you walk?" he asked me. Concerned, not angry. Not at all angry at my presence.

"I think so," I said, slowly regaining balance as I stood up. As I tried to stretch and recover control over my body, I felt the gun in my pants and the cartridges in my sweater. I took it out and showed it to him. "I got this."

Elijah sighed. "Keep it. You'll need it."

"You're awake," said Alex from behind me. "Do something. Go make sure everybody escapes. There should be a lot more people running out of the building."

Without waiting for any of us to answer, Alex turned and left for the side of the building. As I looked at him go, I noticed a huge black cloud moving around the building. "What the hell is that?" I asked Elijah.

"Crows," he said. "Now we know *that* specific power is real."

Gray, April 16th, night

The black wolf felt he had broken something. His powers allowed him to heal quickly and not feel as much pain, but it was still a very hard hit, and he had certainly lost the habit of fighting. His stomach wound bled profusely as he applied pressure with his hands.

"I was ordered to not kill you," said the demon, walking towards Gray. "Doesn't mean I cannot turn you." He showed his fangs again, white and sharp, ready to strike.

Gray crawled back against the wall, stretching his arm to the side, looking for something to throw. The chair and hospital bed were too far away for Gray to reach, and when he tried to stand up, his back cracked and he moaned in pain.

The demon got closer. Gray's wound was hurting him, preventing him from moving. He wasn't ready for this fight, he was too out of practice. He hadn't slept or eaten, and it was taking a toll on him. For a moment, he felt as old as he actually was, and thought about what could've been different. He remembered New Hampshire, and the shoes, and his father. Alice. The river.

Out of the shadows jumped another figure. A hybrid, just like Gray, but with blonde hair. Taylor tackled the demon into the floor and punched him repeatedly. Every punch sounded like a cannonball, like Taylor wanted to mash the demon's face to a pulp, but he wasn't doing much apart from disorienting him.

The demon rolled on the floor and kicked Taylor off of him, but he landed right on his feet. The blonde wolf launched himself unto the demon again, with such force, they both flew through the air, and out the window.

For the third time that night, Gray gathered his forces. He had two enormous stab wounds on his stomach but he couldn't think about that. He had to save Taylor, kill the demon, and look for the people he could not hear or feel. With a breath of air that felt like his last, he howled again.

Steph, April 16th, night

The horror Stephanie had felt when she heard that door opening was unlike anything she'd ever felt in her life. Whatever it was that was outside her room looked like nothing from this world, and she even wondered if she may be hallucinating. But no. The thing was real, and it was inside her room. And it spoke. It told her to be quiet, to be safe. That he would protect her.

What did it even mean, he would protect her? As far as she was concerned, whatever entered through the window at the end of the hall was that thing. The black thing that looked like a bear, with a long snout and hair all over its body. But his voice was that of a human man, and it didn't sound menacing at all. It sounded sincere and concerned for her safety.

Steph stood up from behind the hospital bed, but everything went dark at that instant, with the sound of an explosion making her fall on her back all of a sudden. Terror went through her veins, making her tremble, her teeth chatter as if the room's temperature had dropped 20 degrees in an instant.

Still on the floor, she heard a crash right outside her door, and she understood, somehow, that the black bear was being hurt by something else. She could see shadows in the low light of the hallway, but she couldn't distinguish what was happening. Then, the shadows moved to the end of the hallway, and she stood up to try and see.

Stephanie felt dizzy. At first she'd thought it was her condition or the medication, but she had started to suspect that it may be something else, though she couldn't know why. Dismissing her dizziness, she walked to the door, slowly, not knowing what to expect. But before she got there, there was a rush of wind that shook the windows, and another big shadow went running through the hallway. Steph felt like she was going to pass out on the spot, but she composed herself before that happened. She took a deep breath and put her hand on the doorknob, turning it at a steady pace, taking in the low creaking like it was a nail scratching a blackboard.

But she couldn't finish the action. She froze where she was, trying to tell her hand to finish turning the knob so she could go out, but she couldn't. She suddenly didn't feel like opening the door, like all of her will had been taken out at once and she didn't want nothing except to stand there in silence.

Elijah, April 16th, night

George was not completely recovered yet. It was Elijah's first exorcism, after all, so he didn't really know how long it took victims to recover, even if they had only been possessed for less than a minute. "We have to go in," said the hunter to the boy. "I don't know why the people aren't coming out. We need to help them."

George nodded, but didn't answer verbally. His hand was cut and blood was coming out of it, but it didn't seem to annoy him as much as Elijah would've thought. Though Elijah could barely feel his own hands in the outside cold.

"Come on," insisted Elijah, trying to guide George inside the building. The boy walked alongside his mentor, slowly and steady. Elijah had almost forgotten that he was not feeling well either, and after he saw George was fine, everything came back to him all at once. But he couldn't pay attention to it; he had to find the nurses.

The ground floor of the hospital was completely dark and silent. There didn't seem to be anybody else inside, but Elijah took George in anyway, walking down the dark hallway. He took out a flashlight from his pocket and aimed it at their path, lighting up the very normal hospital floor.

They looked inside the rooms as they walked by, but couldn't see anybody inside any of them. "This hospital isn't usually very full," said George, faintly. "We should check the nurse room at the end of the hallway."

"*Good idea*," thought Elijah, but he didn't say anything. His mind was flying, trying to see fifteen steps ahead. He had to protect George from harm and save whoever may have been trapped inside the building. Good manners where not his priority at the moment.

At the end of the hall were double doors with a sign that read "Nurse Room." Elijah handed the flashlight to George. "Light my way," he said, as he pushed the doors open and grabbed the crossbow hanging from his back. He aimed his weapon at the darkness, barely illuminated by the flashlight. There didn't seem to be anyone in.

"Where's Mercedes?" asked George. Elijah didn't know who Mercedes was, so he opted for ignoring the question. They moved in, looking around for any signs of life, but there were none. Tables and chairs, spilled coffee everywhere, a TV that was probably on before the lights went out. But no people. Had Elijah seen them run outside earlier, when George destroyed the doors? He saw a couple of nurses, but there was no way those were all the nurses in the hospital.

Then, George jumped in terror, making Elijah turned abruptly and point his crossbow in the direction of whatever George had seen. With the faint light from the flashlight, Elijah could see the body of a person, standing straight. It wasn't hanging from a rope or levitating, just standing, breathing very softly, not saying anything. It didn't even seem to be aware of their presence.

George got closer to the body, inspecting it with the flashlight. "It's a nurse," he observed. "I don't know this one."

"Why would you know her?" asked the hunter. Flooded with confusion about what was in front of them and George's background with the hospital.

"My mom used to work here. I know a lot of people," said the boy, nonchalantly.

Elijah leaned forwards to the person standing in front of them. She was looking down, and breathing ever so slightly, almost unnoticeable. "Ma'am?" asked Elijah, but, as expected, the woman did not answer. She didn't even seem to know she existed. "Ma'am?" insisted Elijah, waving his hand in front of the nurse's face. No response.

"Is she alive?" asked George with as much concern as he could muster in his weak voice.

"She's breathing," answered Elijah. "I don't–" but before Elijah could answer, he heard a sound he wished he hadn't heard. He identified it immediately as a howl of pain, coming from somewhere outside the hospital.

"What's that?" asked George. He had probably never thought of the wolves still howling to call for help, much less after he'd met them as humans too.

"We need to go," said Elijah, turning rapidly to the door. "I'm not sure where that's coming from."

"What do you mean?" said George, following Elijah as quickly as his body allowed him. "Are we just leaving that nurse there?"

"Whatever did that to her is probably around here," thought Elijah, but, again, did not say out loud. His thoughts were racing, wondering who it was that howled so loudly. Wishing it was only a cry for help and not a last breath.

The boy and the hunter ran outside the hospital. The five Entranced lied unconscious on the floor, and there were strange sounds coming from around the corner. Elijah dragged George to the source of the sound to see the full hybrid form of Taylor getting his ass kicked by the demon.

The same demon Elijah had dismembered a couple weeks ago. Under the moonlight and in the flesh, he could detail him a lot better. Now that it wasn't the first time he saw him, he could really pay attention to his features, and just one second was enough to completely fascinate him. The demon's skin looked coarse, like sandpaper. His legs and arms were boney, and his wings did resemble that of a bat, kind of. The sharp horns that came out of their ends really differentiated them from any other kind of wings he had ever seen.

Taylor crashed against the wall. Elijah ran towards him, but Taylor signaled him to stop. "Gray is hurt," he said. "Fourth floor. Quickly." Then, without any more, he pushed himself off the wall and to the demon again. The hybrid and the vampire exchanged punches, kicks and slashes, but Taylor seemed to be taking a lot more damage than the demon.

"He needs our help," said George, moving his hand towards his sweater to take out the gun.

"Gray needs our help," said Elijah. "We have to go." But before he could drag him again, George sprinted towards the fight. "George!" yelled Elijah, running after him. He was still feeling nauseous and uneasy, but George's sudden flight made him forget about everything.

Taylor got a good punch to the demon's jaw, giving him an open to stick his claws into his stomach and try to rip him in half. The demon, for the first time, showed signals of pain, but was quickly relieved by a strong headbutt to Taylor's nose, breaking it and making him bleed profusely.

Right as the demon kicked Taylor back again, George got closer to him and aimed his gun. The demon took a second to recognize him, and then laughed. "Is that Georgie who I'm seeing?" he said, mockingly. "How adorable."

"Fuck you," said George, pulling the trigger once. The bullet flew by the demon's face, grazing his neck slightly. Elijah was now standing about 10 feet away from

George, and he could see how the demon's neck wound slowly closed by itself.

"That was not very nice," said the demon.

Steph, April 16th, night

All of a sudden, Steph felt she had control over her body again. It had been more than a moment, maybe like fifteen minutes. She didn't know what it was or what had happened, but the feeling was now replaced by terrible nausea that made her want to stay put before her head exploded. But she knew she had to go out, because she heard a strong howl in the wind and knew that the black bear was hurt.

She finished opening the door and went out into the hallway. The ceiling and walls were very damaged, with holes and stains all over. A dripping pipe hanging from the ceiling, and no lights whatsoever. Steph could barely see anything, with only the reflecting moonlight lighting her way to the end of the hallway.

The wall to the end was almost completely destroyed, with two huge holes and blood everywhere. The window next to it was also destroyed, letting in a rush of freezing wind that made Steph shiver. But between her shivers and the wind, she could hear breathing. Heavy breathing that made her stop in horror for a second. *"It's the black bear. You have to help him,"* she thought, and so she sighed and moved into the room at the end.

In there was a very big man of about forty, maybe. Long black hair, white skin with a lot of scars, and blood everywhere. Blood all over his body, a puddle of blood on the floor, and stained all over the walls. He breathed heavily, laying down on his chest, almost trying to crawl. He was also naked.

"Hey," said Steph, not knowing how else to break the silence. The man jumped in surprise, clearly moving muscles he didn't mean to, making him growl in pain. "I'm sorry," cried Steph, walking slowly towards him. "Where are you hurt, mister?"

The man looked at her with uncertainty. He stretched his hand towards the hospital bed next to him and pulled off the covers. He covered the lower part of his body and sat up against the wall. Steph could see two huge wounds on his stomach that almost made her faint in shock. She had experience looking at nasty wounds thanks to her dad, but never had she seen them so close before.

"I'm going to get something from the box, okay?" she said to the man. He nodded, and so walked to her right, where there was an emergency box that was, fortunately, almost intact. She opened it and took out everything there was: rubbing alcohol, cotton balls, bandages, a packed needle, a bottle of penicillin, and some tape. "I'll do my best," she reiterated, walking closer to him, making the contents of the box rattle as she trembled.

His breathing had not steadied at all, making her nervous. "Breathe," said the man, maybe to himself as much as her, making Steph almost drop everything she was holding. His voice was deep and soothing, exactly like the black bear's.

Steph slowly crouched in front of the man, taking a closer look at the wound. Two holes the size of baseballs, covered in red and still bleeding a bit. "I'm going to clean you a bit, okay?" she said.

"Let's do it together," answered the man. "Faster."

Steph felt muted. She didn't feel able to do anything but nod.

Elijah, April 16th, night

The demon stretched his wings wide open, the sharp points shining bright with the light of the moon. George's trembling hand shot two more shots, one missing entirely, the other hitting the demon's chest. He looked down to his newly-perforated chest plate. "You truly are special, boy."

Elijah saw how one of the demon's wings was about to stab George, so he ran to him. In one motion, Elijah unsheathed his sword and blocked the horn from perforating George's side, making the demon stumbled slightly. With his sword raised in the air, Elijah hammered it down, aiming at the demon's head.

The demon used both of his horns to block it, holding it up as Elijah pushed with both of his hands, applying as much force as he could. "They didn't give me any instructions about you," said the demon. He crossed his horns around Elijah's sword and snapped, breaking the sword in half and making Elijah lose balance for a second. In shock, Elijah couldn't react quick enough to the demon's kick that would send him flying back what felt like a dozen yards.

These should be enough for them.

You counted sixteen. More than enough.

But now he's calling you.

He isn't satisfied. He expects more.

So you must do more.

The hunter.

Chapter 16
The Night of April 16th,
Part 4

Steph, April 16th, night

Everything in between the first and last application of alcohol to the man's wound was blurry. She just knew she grabbed the needle and the bottle of penicillin and was ready to inject him when she was interrupted. The man grabbed her hand. "Wait," he said.

Before she could ask why, she heard steps from behind her. She thought everything was lost, right then and there. The monster that attacked the black bear was now going to kill her, and finish him off. But what she saw wasn't a strange figure at all, except for its size. The biggest wolf she had ever seen, with beautiful red pelt.

"Drake," called the man. "Where's everybody?"

"Alex is trying to secure as much people as possible, but they're not making it easy." Stephanie heard the voice coming from the wolf, and saw his mouth open and close in sync with the words being spoken, but she was convinced she was hallucinating. She couldn't have just witness a wild wolf speaking.

"Give him the needle," said the man to Steph. She snapped back from her thoughts and turned to him. "The needle. He'll use it."

Steph turned back to look at the wolf, who wasn't a wolf anymore, but a grown man that looked 30 at the latest, but probably younger. Jovial face, red neck-length hair, not not handsome. He was also naked, but he covered himself with a loose bedsheet that she wasn't sure where he got.

The redheaded man stretched his hand to Steph, delicately, as if she was a little girl. Though that is exactly how she felt. "Here you go, sir," is the only thing she was able to say.

"Thank you," answered the redheaded man, Drake. He smiled, wordlessly assuring her that nothing wrong was going to happen while they were close to her.

Elijah, April 16th, night

It was merely a brief moment of disorientation, but it was enough to throw the hunter completely off his game. As he flew through the air and hit the ground, he saw the blonde figure of Taylor's hybrid form flying in the opposite direction, going back to the demon.

George ran back to his mentor to help him up. His eyes were teary, maybe because he was nearly stabbed to death, or maybe because he feared for his mentor's life. "Are you okay? I'm so sorry. I just-" he started, lending his hand so Elijah could get up. But this time, Elijah was actually angry.

He grabbed the boy by the shoulders. "Don't you ever pull that shit on me again. Got it?" he screamed into the boy's face. "We're trying to protect you, and it's like you want to get in–"

But before he could finish, George pulled him out of the way, making both of them fall to the ground. Elijah turned on his back to see a man with a hammer standing beside them. A man he thought he may had seen before, but wasn't sure.

The man was young, about Elijah's age. Fair skin and hair, moderately tall, but he was clearly under the trance. He didn't seem physically able to take his eyes off of Elijah, and he swung his hammer mindlessly at him. George crawled back far enough to stand up and point his gun at the man. "Stop!" he screamed.

Elijah crawled back and stood up as well, grabbing the gun, still in George's hands. "No," he said. "He's not himself. He's innocent."

The strange man continued his walk to Elijah, clenching the hammer like his life depended on it. With a huge swing and without hesitation, the man almost hit Elijah's face, but he was able to dodge it and tackle him to the ground. Elijah smashed the man's hand to the ground until he released the hammer, and reached into his jacket pocket.

George, April 16th, night

Everything was happening so fast, I just didn't know what to do. I was still thinking about the howling we'd heard before we saw Taylor fighting the vampire, and now there was this man fighting Elijah, and no sign of the other wolves. I couldn't shoot the man, and my aim wasn't nearly close to alright to help Taylor, so I was useless. I just stood there, watching both fights, unable to do anything.

Taylor and the vampire seemed to be evenly matched most of the time, though the vampire took the lead once or twice while I looked. Taylor dodged his wing spikes with finesse, but he was starting to get tired, unlike the vampire. Taylor would punch him in the face with what felt like all the strength in his body, but the vampire wouldn't even flinch.

The advantage of having Taylor fight the vampire was that he seemingly forgot about us. He was solely focused on getting to Taylor, which allowed me to have my nervous breakdown and for Elijah to hold down the stranger.

Elijah reached into his jacket pocket, but couldn't find anything. I was still planted on my feet, immobilized by everything that was happening. I slowly heard Elijah calling my name. "George!" I heard one time, loud enough to snap me out of my daydream. "I need your necklace," he said, as he saw I was paying attention.

I instinctively put my hand on my chest and felt the necklace, the same necklace Elijah had used earlier to… burn my hands and make me hurt a lot. I don't know.

"George," called Elijah again, holding down the man, who was really struggling to get out of his grip. "I need your necklace. Quick."

Without asking any of the questions I had, I took off the necklace and tossed it to him. Elijah placed it on the man's forehead, pushing it in like he was trying to plant it inside his brain. I heard him saying the familiar Trinity prayer in Latin, but everything else he said afterwards was completely foreign to me. My knowledge of Latin went as far as whatever sounded kinda like French.

I could see how Elijah's hands started glowing as he said whatever he was saying. At the same time, however, I started feeling dizzy, like I did when I drove into the hospital. As if whatever had got me then was getting me again, but faster.

My face suddenly felt cold and my hands started to get numb. Seconds later, I was imagining the most horrible things, out of the blue. I saw Elijah being burned to a crisp, the wolves being decapitated one by one by an unknown figure in the shadows, and I was standing there, staring. I couldn't control these thoughts, they just invaded my mind like a virus.

I could only stand still until Elijah finished his prayer. Then, I dropped to my knees, gasping for air as I heard the strange man scream in pain, just like I had. As

Elijah held him, he turned to see me choking. "Five seconds, George," he said, holding the man as he shook violently. A thin line of blood dripped down his forehead, though I wasn't sure if it was his or Elijah's.

Then, there was a flash of light that made me cover my eyes. It was as if whatever was inside of me was instantly punched out in a second. After his hands stopped glowing, Elijah tossed me the necklace and I held it to my chest, feeling relief almost immediately. I laid on my back and breathed heavily, holding the necklace as if it was the very last bottle of water in the desert. My face slowly heated up again to a regular temperature, and my mind was clear of almost everything I had thought. Somehow, I knew right there that there were many other, more horrible things that had crossed my mind, but the necklace made me forget them.

Steph, April 16th, night

Drake treated the man's wound with care and precision, clearly having done it many times before. Steph sat against the wall, just thinking about the last hour and all that had happened. She also wondered where all the people were, because, surely, there should be chaos outside, but she couldn't hear anything.

"Where's Elijah?" asked the black-haired man as he groaned in pain from his double stab wound.

"Haven't seen him in a while," answered Drake. "But Alex mentioned that he and George were clearing the ground floor."

"George?" asked the black-haired man, and almost so did Steph. But she couldn't find the breath to say it out loud.

"Yeah. I don't know how, but he's here."

"Fucking kid," said the man with great annoyance. "He's gonna get us all killed soon enough."

"Excuse me," is all that Steph could muster. They both turned to see her, almost as if they had forgotten that she had been there the whole time.

"Yes?" asked Drake, still with a very approachable tone. But Steph fell mute. She just couldn't bring herself to say any more. "Now that I think about it, we don't know your name," continued Drake, stretching his hand. "I'm Drake. And this is Michael."

Steph's trembling hand moved closer to Drake's and shook it slightly. She felt his rough skin, immediately sensing the wear and tear of the man's whole body, and only able to imagine what else had happened to these two strangers she had encountered.

"What's your name, girl?" asked the black-haired man, Michael.

"S-s–" started Steph, really doing her best to get it out of her. "Stephie," she muttered, still trembling.

"Stephanie?" asked Drake. Steph nodded. "My pleasure, Stephanie."

"Wh-who–" she started asking again, but was interrupted by a thundering scream of pain that also alerted the two men.

Michael flinched, making the preliminary movements to stand up, but the pain did not let him. Drake did stand up, holding the sheets on his hips and tying a knot around it. Steph stood up as well, sticking to Drake's side like he was an open furnace and she was caught in the middle of a blizzard.

Drake looked out the window with curiosity, pointing his face down at the ground, where the sound had most likely come from. Steph couldn't bring herself to look, so she stayed behind Drake, waiting to hear what had happened instead.

"Elijah just exorcized a man," said Drake. "And George seems to be having a tough time handling the curse."

"Where's Taylor?" asked Michael, still on the floor.

"He and Elijah are fighting the other guy."

Steph slowly walked to the window. This was the first time she had heard of an actual exorcism in a completely serious context, so she didn't know what to expect. But what she actually saw was nothing she could have ever imagined.

In the distance she could make out a man in mostly red attire. This man was on top of blonde man, holding him down as he screamed his lungs out. She had seen that face so many times, she recognized him without much effort.

Though the red-dressed man's face was not visible, Steph identified the screaming face of Earnest Erb.

About ten feet away from the two, she saw someone she could not believe was there. She had imagined, fantasized about him just reappearing out of nowhere, but she knew deep in her heart that it would be impossible. Yet, there he was, laid on the floor, seemingly in pain, clutching something to his chest.

"Georgie," Steph gasped.

George, April 16th, night

I struggled to stand up after catching my breath. Elijah was completely unaware of my discomfort, instead focusing on reviving the man he had apparently just exorcised to death. But, in the middle of CPR, a yellowish blur interrupted Elijah's concentration, making him tilt his head up to see Taylor flying through the air, covered in cuts. As I looked around, I noticed the cloud of crows had dissipated.

Elijah stood up and turned to me. "Take care of this," he told me, pointing at the man.

"Wh- What?" I said, confused.

Elijah took out his gauntlet blade and a gun with his other hand, and started walking towards the vampire, who was standing in the distance, possibly recovering from throwing Taylor so far. "30 pushes, then breathe in. Blow delicately."

Without letting me ask anything else, Elijah sprinted to the vampire. Before the demon had a chance to do anything, Elijah fired at him God knows how many shots, pushing him back with each bullet landing on the demon's chest.

I turned back my attention to the man on the floor, who didn't seem to be alive at all. I remembered what Elijah said to me moments earlier, and started doing CPR for the first time in my life. Or I was about to and couldn't, because the man woke up all of a sudden, startling me like nothing had ever done.

I couldn't tell how it happened, but after I composed myself, I saw I had blood over my face. Judging by the man's expression, he had probably coughed it on me. "They're all here," said the man, still coughing between words. "The four of them. They want you."

"What do you mean?" I asked him, forgetting about the blood on my face.

"They're getting people. Food. Army." I felt the man was going to puke his lungs out. He tried to reach for me, so I leaned down. The man held my shirt tightly, and I felt his grip get weaker and weaker with every word he said. "Earnest Erb," said the man to me. "Don't let me go back."

Before I could think of a reply, his hand let go of my shirt and fell on his chest. I was frozen, not able to understand exactly what he had said or what had just happened. And it just occurred to me that, right there, was the first time I saw someone die with my own eyes.

But I didn't have time to think about that, because there were other very pressing matters happening a hundred feet from me. Not only were Elijah and now Taylor fighting the vampire to my left, but to my right I heard a sound that, come to think about it, I should've wondered about a while before. Police sirens.

Elijah, April 16th, night

It had been enough. Characterized by his seemingly infinite patience, Elijah felt, at that moment, that he had lost his mind. Seeing Taylor flying away again, now covered in his own blood, was the last drop. He couldn't take care of the poor possessed man, George, and Taylor at the same time. And it would all come to an end if the demon was slain, so that's what he wanted to do.

He sprinted to the demon with his gauntlet blade out and a gun in his other hand, ready to do whatever it took to destroy this thing that had caused them so many problems. That bit George. That terrorized and possibly killed or captured the people at the hospital. That shredded his dear friend to unconsciousness. It all had to end, right then and there, for his mind's sake.

The demon took the four shots like bee stings, then proceeded to open up his wings and welcome Elijah's physical efforts. "Are you sad about your sword?" taunted the demon.

But Elijah knew better. He knew it was suicide to just charge at the vampire out in the open, so he waited for the vampire to motion his body to stab him, and Elijah dropped to the floor. In the momentum he gained by his drop, the demon's horn passed by above his head, giving him the opportunity to use his gauntlet blade to slash at the horn, creating a gash and spraying blood everywhere.

The demon fell to the floor, for the first time screaming in pain. "What the fuck did you just do?" he asked Elijah. His voice was nothing but pure fury, startling even the hunter, who was used to that kind of disturbing noises.

Elijah raised his right forearm, showing the blood-soaked blade in all its glory. "This one you can't break," he stated.

The demon roared in anger. The horn at the end of his wing bled profusely, creating a puddle of blood where he was standing. "I'm done playing games with you," roared the demon. But right before he launched back at Elijah, his arm was held and pulled back with great force by Taylor, who proceeded to spin him and slam him to the floor with incredible force, making the ground shake.

The demon laid face down on the ground, with Taylor kneeling on top of him and holding his face up. "I'm done playing games with you, too," growled Taylor, with hate in his voice Elijah wouldn't have thought he'd ever hear from him.

Taylor sunk his claws in the demon's neck, slowly but surely, holding him tight. The demon screamed and shook, but he couldn't get the hybrid off of him. His wings were trapped under Taylor's knees.

Elijah walked to the two, his blade still out, dripping thick, red blood. He crouched down when he got to the demon, seeing him in all his weakness and helplessness. Elijah wasn't one to feel satisfaction in foreign pain, but this was a very notable exception. He saw the demon's neck being slowly ripped off his torso, and he prepared to finish the job with his blade, cutting off the demon's head.

But, alas, he was interrupted by a sound he had not thought about, and was ultimately embarrassed by it. Embarrassed by having overseen such an obvious thing to plan for. It ruined everything, in an instant, including the advantage they had on the demon.

As police sirens blasted in the distance, Taylor got distracted and lost his grip on the demon, allowing him to jump up from the floor, making Elijah fall on his back and Taylor to lose balance. Instead of attacking, the demon jumped high in the air and, in one motion, flew into the forest.

The hunter, still on the floor, felt disoriented for a second as he saw the pale figure flying away. He stood up and looked to the hospital building, where, in the distance, he could see police lights illuminating the dark road.

"Taylor!" called Elijah to the blonde hybrid, who was standing up as well.

Taylor turned to see the lights. "Let's go," he said, sprinting towards the forest. He jumped in the air and transformed into a wolf, and kept running, this time faster.

Elijah felt almost mesmerized by the sight of the police cars. It took him a second to turn to see George, whose face was splattered with blood. The man he had cleansed earlier appeared to be dead.

At the sound of the sirens getting closer, George looked back to Elijah. His breathing had stabilized, but his eyes wore an expression of fear he had not seen in a while. "What do we do now?" asked George. But Elijah didn't know. He was as stunned as the boy he was supposed to guide and protect.

It wasn't until the first car stopped in front of them that they both snapped. The hunter couldn't tell if they were just exhausted, or if the curse in the air had messed with their senses, but now that they regained full consciousness, he couldn't understand why in the world they stood there instead of running into the woods. "We have to go," said Elijah, walking to George and grabbing him by the shoulder. "Quick."

George didn't reply, didn't fight, he just agreed and followed. Once he had George's attention, he started sprinting, and the boy followed his lead. In the distance, they could hear not only the sirens, but the distorted voice of a megaphone. "Freeze! Both of you!" Elijah did not recognize the voice, but he was absolutely sure that Terrence Walker was among the officers present in the squad.

What did startle the two was the sound they heard later, as they were entering the forest. Not from the forest itself, but from the hospital, from the inside. As they got covered by the shadows of the trees, far in the distance and seemingly from high up, they both heard a cry. A soft female voice that cried the boy's name. And, judging by George's face, he heard the exact same thing as Elijah. But they couldn't stop. They needed to run from the police and chase the vampire before it was too late. The answer to who had called George's name would remain in Elijah's mind for the rest of his life.

Steph, April 16th, night

She tried again and again to call for his friend, but she couldn't find the strength, the air. She completely ignored the red-dressed man, who was now far enough to be out of her vision. She was fixated on George, trying to call his name, to understand how he was there and why he had left. Why he was hurting, and why he was with all these people.

George seemed to be trying to help Earnest, but Steph knew it was too late. He looked lifeless even from a distance, and George looked confused and horrified. He jumped at the sound of police sirens in the distance, and from the window, Steph saw how whatever was haunting the hospital flew away into the forest, and how a yellowish bear just like Michael and Drake ran after it, transforming into a wolf in midair.

"We have to go," said Drake, turning to Michael. "They ran into the forest. The police are here."

"Alex will probably hear them in time," said Michael, making an effort to stand up, not caring about the sheet covering his genitals. Steph turned back to the window, where she saw George and the red-dressed man running into the forest as well.

She couldn't take losing George again. Now that she knew he was alive, she had to see him. She had to talk to him and know he was okay, that he wasn't being tortured or held captive. But she couldn't jump from the window and land gracefully on the ground.

"George," she tried calling again, but her throat closed on her. A combination of fear and held-back weeps made it impossible for her to project her voice. "George," she tried again, only a little louder.

"Let's go," said Michael, now transformed into a full black wolf, but considerably bigger than any Steph had ever seen.

"It'll be safer for you to stay here," said Drake to Steph, though she was still not fully aware of what was happening. She didn't notice Drake going back into wolf form either, and felt panic flooding her bloodstream as she saw George's figure disappear in the shadows of the trees.

"George!" she managed to shout, even louder than she had imagined. As if the flooded gates of her throat had been opened at once and let everything out. A scream so loud, it made George stop and turn.

But the red-dressed man did not allow him to be still any longer. He dragged him by the arm, not letting him take a good look at her. She couldn't muster the energy to call for him again, and so she sat down against the wall, not caring about the broken glass all over the floor, and cried. She cried all of what she hadn't cried in almost two weeks since her best friend's disappearance. Tears and snot making her face look swollen.

"Stephanie," said Drake. "George is safe with us." She didn't expect to hear that, and by the sort of expression she could make out in Michael's wolven face, neither did he. "He eats great food and sleeps in a warm bed. He reads a lot, and usually keeps to himself. That sounds like him, right?"

Stephanie was not sure of what to say. That did sound like the George she knew, but she wasn't sure what to respond. What to say to the talking red wolf that just informed her that her best friend was safe, even though she had just seen him run from the scene and into the black forest, after a monster.

"The police will find you and make sure you're safe," continued Drake. "Let them know if you're hurt, but don't tell them about us. Alright?"

Drake's voice was not very deep, unlike Michael's, but it felt soothing and relaxing in the situation. His tone was endearing and caring, and felt almost like a hug to Stephanie's trembling body. The cold breeze coming from the window made it hard for her not to shake, but she nodded however she could.

"Please," she managed to say, right before they left. "Tell him to come to me. We need to talk." Michael did not seem even aware of what she had said, but Drake nodded slightly. "Keep him safe."

"We will," said Drake. "Promise."

George, April 16th, night

It all happened so fast, I wasn't even sure if it was actually true. But it had to be, because Elijah heard it as well. He turned to look for whoever screamed my name, but he knew better than I did, and so he didn't let us get to a full stop. I didn't even have enough energy to retort, I just followed him into the forest.

As we ran into the forest, all the cold I had forgotten about came back to me all at once, making me shake. The breeze got inside my nose, feeling like two butcher hooks pulling up my nostrils. But we had to keep going, because Taylor was in danger.

Elijah took the dog whistle he kept around his neck and blew it as we ran, making a sound I could not hear at all. "Come on, Taylor," said Elijah to himself . "Where the hell are you."

We ran until we got to a clearing, where we stopped. Elijah looked up to the stars and blew his whistle again. Then he looked down to the floor, probably looking for any kind of trace, but neither of us could see anything. All of a sudden, I felt a familiar sensation coming from behind me, and before I could react, I felt four sharp knives stabbing me in the shoulder and dragging me forwards.

The vampire flew up about twenty feet, holding me from my shoulder blade, making me feel ten times more pain he had the last time. In the heat of the moment, I could finally take a closer look at him, even though I was agonizing. I instantly understood why the folklore tales associated vampires with bats, particularly because of the way their wings are shaped and structured. They also have fangs they use to suck blood, but also inject venom like snakes. Apart from that, there is nothing bat-like that relates to them. Their face, as far as I could tell in that moment, looks just like a human's after a lot of bad stuff has happened to them.

Before the vampire could drop me or take me away or bite me or whatever he was planning, I heard a roar coming from behind us, as Taylor jumped from a tree to the demon. He grabbed him by the wings and hung on them, making the vampire descend to the ground and scream in pain. As we descended, he retracted his claws and let me go, making me fall about five feet.

I laid face down on the ground as I felt Elijah dragging me away from the center of the clearing, listening to Taylor and the vampire punching each other nonstop. Elijah used his blade to cut my shirt and sweater open to look at my wound. "This is worse than the previous one," he said. "He did this to hurt you, not to take you away."

I couldn't control my breathing. Sometimes I felt I was going to drown in air, and other times it was like there was not enough oxygen on the planet. My shoulder stung so bad, my head felt like it was going to explode, and I was so tired. I wanted to fall asleep and wake up in a week, when everything would be over and the pain would seize.

A thunderous cry of pain came from the vampire as Taylor covered his neck with his wolven jaw, blood gushing everywhere, covering Taylor and the ground, and the vampire. He used his left arm to punch Taylor's face until he let go, but that same second, Elijah charged at the vampire and stabbed him in the eye with his blade.

The vampire screeched and punched Elijah away, not able to do anything else, completely disoriented. He shook his wings around, trying to find something to stab, his hands covering his bloody face. "Arabella!" he called to the air. "Marcus!" Where these the names of his partners? We were, of course, unsure, but the way he called their names for help was chilling. To think a demon as menacing and horrifying was crying for help just made me reconsider everything I knew.

As the vampire shook his wings around, Taylor grabbed the one Elijah had cut earlier, the gash still bleeding. Taylor held the horn with one hand and the rest of the wing with the other, and snapped the horn out, making the vampire cry in pain and anger. Knowing where Taylor was, he turned his body to him and tried to stab him with the other horn, but Taylor dodged it swiftly and used the opening to stab the vampire's chest with his own horn, creating a huge wound in his sternum.

I was still laying face down on the ground, holding my neck up to see what was happening. I saw the demon fall to his knees, looking absolutely defeated. His grey skin was red, almost every particle soaked in blood, both his and Taylor's, and probably mine, too. Elijah walked back to me now that the fighting was done. "You'll be fine," he said. "It's over now."

I was fixated on the vampire, still on his knees. I stared into his remaining eye, trying to understand him, like I was going to connect with him, somehow. My dizziness wasn't letting me think straight, clearly.

But he turned his head and saw me. As Taylor prepared to interrogate him, the vampire looked into my eyes as I did his, and I could physically feel his anger. It was like a soft burning feeling all over my body, making my shoulder sting even more than it already was. I could even hear his voice inside my head, somehow, and I even knew his name all of a sudden.

"Jason," I whispered, low enough so that nobody could hear me. But Jason did. He heard me calling him, and his rage grew even bigger. His expression changed from neutral to absolutely furious, and I instantly felt his intentions boiling inside him.

In one quick motion, Jason launched himself to his left, in my direction. Too fast for Taylor to catch, Jason used his long legs to push himself into us. But he didn't go for me. He went for Elijah.

Elijah, who was standing next to me, checking my shoulder wound, was violently tackled by Jason against a tree. Before he could use his blade or Taylor could pull Jason away, the vampire sunk his sharp fangs on Elijah's neck, making him scream in horror, his arms shaking uncontrollably.

Only about a second passed, but it felt like an eternity. Taylor pulled Jason off of Elijah's neck, literally disconnecting the fangs from the vein. Elijah fell to the floor and applied pressure to his neck with his hands, as Jason was slammed to the ground face down, just like I was. Taylor put a foot in the space between Jason's wings and pulled both of them, tearing them off the vampire's back.

"It's over," said Jason, laughing. Laughing as he saw his wings dropped on the floor, completely separated from his body. Laughing as there was no more grey in his body, replaced by red. Laughing as he knew – and therefore, I knew – that he was about to die. He looked at me. "I hope it hurts you half as much as it'll hurt him."

At the sound of these words, Taylor looked back at Elijah, who was still speechless, leaning against the tree, trying to contain the blood dripping from his neck. Taylor's breathing sounded like that of a bull at the sight of red as he stomped on Jason's lower jaw, chattering it completely. Using his foot to hold it to the ground, Taylor grabbed Jason's upper jaw from inside his mouth, and pulled it back, tearing it off the neck.

Taylor dropped the upper half of Jason's head and ran back to Elijah. "We're going back to the house," said Taylor. "You'll be fine."

Elijah was still struggling to speak. I could barely hear what he said. "We both know that's not gonna happen."

Still on the floor, I looked at Jason's head. It felt surreal, like a movie prop and not a real head. The pale skin and the ridiculous amount of blood just made it look fake, but I knew it wasn't. I knew it wasn't fake because I stopped feeling his mind as soon as Taylor ripped his head off.

Chapter 17
The Small Hours of April 17th
Monica, night

There had been no other time when Monica felt
Arabella even half as anxious as at that moment. What
started as a short mobilization ended up being a three hour
walk to seemingly nowhere. It was also the first time since
their capture that Monica was kept out of her cocoon,
though she still had no freedom to do anything but wait.
She also wasn't stupid enough to try to run – not that she
would've gotten anywhere in the state that she was.

After hours sitting against a tree, waiting for
instructions, Arabella came out of the shadows. "We're
moving," she said. "Move." Monica could notice how
nervous Arabella was, and she knew it had something to do
with the blonde man and whatever he was doing with
Jason. But there was no way to tell, and she wasn't gonna
ask.

Monica was pushed by Arabella as she walked,
holding Miles up as much as she could. The imposing,
muscular figure he used to carry had been replaced by a

skinny and shabby boy that seemed taken straight out of the streets of Aleppo.

On the other hand was Andrea, who Monica had still not seen awake ever since their capture. She was always being carried on Marcus' shoulder, along with the older man who looked like a cop. Marcus did not seem to be concerned about anything at all, which brought her even more curiosity to Arabella's behavior.

They stopped walking, eventually, and she laid down against a tree, putting Miles right next to her as he fell asleep almost instantly. Monica had no idea where they were, not even in what direction they had been walking. For all she knew, they could already be in Canada. What she did identify was the sound of footsteps at a distance, all coming from one side of the forest.

Soon enough, Monica saw a group of people, maybe a dozen, walking to the sort of camp they had established. People she did not know, of all ages, sizes, genders. People in hospital gowns, some that looked like nurses, others just wearing regular clothes.

After scanning the group, she could only recognize one person; Steph's dad, Dr. Kim. At the sight of him, Monica gasped, calling for Arabella's attention.

"Know any of them?" asked Arabella. Not menacingly, not tauntingly. She actually sounded curious.

Monica wasn't even sure if she and Arabella had ever exchanged dialogue before. It was so surreal, having her talk in such a neutral tone. "A couple," answered Monica, almost to just herself.

"Our Lord will be very happy when he sees them," replied Arabella. Her red hair blew with the light breeze, reminding Monica of how beautiful she must have been before she was turned into a monster.

"I am, indeed," said a voice from out of nowhere. Monica jumped in her place, startled by the sudden sound of the familiar voice. Miles remained immobile, unaware of whatever was happening around him.

Arabella kneeled on one knee at the sound of the voice, and she pulled Monica out of her resting position so she could kneel as well. Monica's skin and bones were so brittle, she felt kneeling on one knee was going to tear her leg muscles apart. But she did it, and looked down to the ground, not wanting to see her Master's face. She felt how the people who had just arrived had formed a circle around them, and knelt on one knee as well. The only individuals not doing it were unconscious.

She heard how a presence materialized in front of her, her face still down. "Look at me, Monica," said the voice, and so she looked up, unable to resist the urge to do so. She looked at her Master, just like she saw Him last time. Perfect eyes, clean skin, soothing voice, shining hair. He was wearing a full suit, and looked as handsome as any human man could wish to look. Absolutely irresistible in His impressive height and fit physique, calm demeanor and imposing presence.

"Master," called Arabella, almost thirsty for His attention. "Look at what we've collected." It gave Monica the impression of a little girl trying to show a handsome teacher a drawing she made. That's the exact thought Monica had.

"I agree," said their Master, looking at Monica. Neither her nor Arabella understood exactly what He meant. "You're trying so hard, Arabella," he continued. Arabella's eyes glowed with regret and fear.

"Master, forgive me," she said, face to the ground, begging. "I don't mean to disturb you."

"Then don't," He said, coldly, sharply. If words could hurt, that would've been a swift cut to the jugular.

Their Master walked past them, to the group. Arabella raised her head to look at Him go, suddenly looking heartbroken, to Monica's confusion. Arabella looked at her eyes. "What did you say to Him?" she asked, at the edge of either breaking down into tears or stabbing Monica dead.

"I didn't say anything," cried Monica.

Their Master looked at each person kneeling. Turning and walking slowly by them, stopping on only a couple. "Marcus," called the Master.

"Sir," answered Marcus, still knelt where he was, about five places away from Arabella.

"Escort these lovely people out of here, to the cave." The Master's tone was not demanding at the slightest, although one could almost feel how He expected His word to be followed to perfection.

"Yes, my Lord," answered Marcus. He always looked unworried about everything, and that did not change with his Master's request. Unlike Arabella, Marcus seemed to not need to impress Him.

Monica had turned her head back to the ground, holding in the tears as she heard the exchange between the two male creatures. She heard how every person stood up at once and started walking, reminding her of the military marches she'd seen online, where thousands of North Korean soldiers march at a rhythm without missing a single beat.

But, as the people left, there was a series of sounds coming from the trees ahead that she could not identify. It sounded like something coming to them at a very high speed, which got Arabella's curiosity, making her stand up and turn. Monica turned as well, but remained on the floor.

Soon enough, the speeding, bleeding body of Jason flew high into a tree, then falling down to the ground. He was covered in blood, breathless, and scared. He actually looked scared for his life.

"Master," called Jason. His Master had stopped moving when he arrived, but did not even flinch at the sight of his critical condition. Jason composed himself and knelt on one knee like everybody else had, even though he was clearly in a lot of pain. "Master, please help me."

His Master looked at him with pity and shame. No words were necessary to understand that He had no intention of doing anything for Jason, not even take him back into the group. But He spoke anyway. "You have allowed the wolves to interfere with our plan," started their Master, bringing every single individual around him to their knees. "You have compromised the secrecy and efficiency of this clan twice already. You lost your grip on a defenseless teenage boy."

"The hunter attacked me!" replied Jason, still on one knee, but without any care in his tone. His Master raised one of his hands to neck length, demanding silence. Jason stopped speaking as if a switch had been turned off.

"Marcus, continue your procession," said their Master, still looking at Jason. Without any words, the newly-captured people stood up at the same time and resumed their walk, with Marcus in front.

Monica wanted to burst into tears, but she couldn't. She was paralyzed by fear and despair, looking at the innocent people as they were taken who-knows-where. She feared for her own life as well, and her friends'. She looked on as Marcus left with the group of people, Arabella still kneeling and not doing anything else.

"You have disobeyed simple instructions since the beginning," continued their Master, now to Jason. "After being given a second chance, you fucked it up yet again. I have to admit you impress me, Jason."

Jason's face looked like it was going to explode. His veins were highlighted in purple on his grey skin, and his eyes looked desperate. "Master, please," begged Jason.

"Now, you couldn't even finish what you started. You let Earnest die, and couldn't even get the boy back." Monica wanted to turn and ask them if they were talking about George, which she was almost certain they were. That meant he was alive, but also that he was probably not back in Adler.

"I'll kill all of them!" cried Jason, dragging his knees on the floor and resting his head on his Master's feet. "Please, forgive me."

"You also brought one with you," said the Master. At this, both Arabella and Jason turned their heads to Him. Monica found this very odd, and she didn't understand what He was talking about.

"What do you mean?" asked Jason. His desperate tone now complimented by one of confusion and uncertainty.

"Arabella," called their Master.

Arabella turned her head back to the ground. "Yes, Master?"

"Take the children. A wolf is on his way."

At the sound of these words, Arabella stood up and pulled Monica up, like if suddenly there was an alarm alerting of an upcoming tsunami.

Almost on cue, more sounds of fast movement came from where Jason had first arrived. Jason and

Arabella turned in the direction of the sound, and started panicking. Arabella grabbed Miles and put him on her shoulder. "Move," she demanded to Monica.

Out of the shadows came a figure that Monica didn't quite understand at first. It looked like a very big blonde wolf on first sight, but soon it changed shape into something completely foreign to Monica. She didn't get a good look at it before Arabella grabbed her arm and flew away.

The last thing Monica could see was their Master disappearing into thin air as the new monster attacked Jason. But the last thing Monica thought as she was taken away was that there were no hands to take neither the cop, nor Andrea.

George, April 17th, the small hours

Taylor turned his head quickly as he heard something in the distance. I managed to sit up, still feeling immense pain in my shoulder. Soon enough, I saw the remaining part of the wolfpack arriving, and even in the dark and from a distance I could see that Gray was hurt. Drake had what looked like several bedsheets around his torso.

"What happened?" asked Alex.

"He's bit," said Taylor, with embarrassment and regret in his tone. "Demon's dead."

The wolves looked at the center of the clearing, where Jason's body was splattered on the floor, wingless, headless and lifeless. "Are you sure, Elijah?" asked Gray, his tone assuring me that he was in a lot of pain.

Elijah nodded slightly, still holding his hands against his neck. "We can treat him," I said. The way the wolves turned violently towards me demonstrated none of them had even noticed I was there. "He has potions back in Foxworth. We can save him."

Taylor sighed and walked to me. He put his hand on my good shoulder and took a look at the other one. "That won't be enough, George."

"What do you mean?" I asked. Between the anguish of the bite and the pain in my shoulder, I was starting to lose consciousness. I felt my head drifting away, but I did everything I could to focus. "You guys can run to the car and get him."

"The roads are blocked and Foxworth is too far away," said Alex. Tactless, as always. "There's nothing we can do about this now."

"Wouldn't he happen to have an antidote in the car, though?" asked Taylor. I wasn't sure if he was saying it to give me hope, or if he actually thought we had a chance.

"It needs to be stored in freezing temperature," continued Alex. "You know this, Taylor. Don't pamper the kid."

"Fucking do something!" I snapped, furious at their indifference. "You're just gonna stand there and let him die? Or turn? Are you even concerned for his safety? Or sad because you're going to lose a friend?"

"This is part of the job, boy," said Gray. "The sooner you understand that, the better it will be for you."

"So he's dead, then," I said, standing up with the most effort I'd ever put into it. My shoulder stung like I was being burned with melting metal, but I didn't care. "You're just declaring him dead right now, as he's looking at me speak."

Alex was about to retort, but was stopped by Elijah's groan. It looked like he was trying to say something. "You do it, Gray," he said. All of them seemed to understand what he was talking about, except me.

The three wolves stood on two legs and slowly proceeded to transform into humans. This was my first time looking at them do it from such a short distance. It looked very bizarre, like a butterfly coming out of a cocoon, but backwards. Their hair fell off instantly and their snots sank into their faces. It looked kinda painful, actually.

Gray was the one who suffered the most. It was evident that it pained him to stand up in two feet and stretch his back into that of a human. When all of his hair fell off, I flinched at the sight of two huge, disgusting scars in his stomach. They looked just like the wound Jason received to the chest with his own horn.

Drake gave each of the wolves a bedsheet so they could cover themselves. Then, he walked to me and covered me as well. "These are clean except for some hair," he said. "I promise."

Elijah looked at me and smiled. "What is Gray gonna do?" I asked him. He didn't seem to have the energy to respond. Taylor, still next to me, just put his hand on my shoulder. He had detransformed as well.

"Can you give us a couple minutes?" Elijah asked to the wolves. They all looked at me with eyes of pity, which I did not appreciate at all.

"I'll take you to where they were," said Taylor. "You have to see something." The wolves all continued their way on foot, as humans, in the direction from which Jason had previously flown in.

"I understand it now," said Elijah to me. I was focused on the wolves leaving and jumped at the sudden sound of his voice. I turned my head to him. "The feeling of fangs tearing through your skin is very unpleasant."

"Yes," I responded. "I don't know about you, but I could feel how he literally sucked the blood out of my ankle and drank it.

"I did not," said Elijah, "because I don't think he drank any of my blood. He knew he was dead. There was no reason to heal."

"Heal? What do you mean?"

"I finally understood what he did to you, George. I put it together, though it took me a lot longer than I would've liked."

I remained silent, waiting for his explanation. He probably wanted me to try to guess or something, like I usually did. But I did not have energy for that. I was in a lot of pain, physical and mental.

"Sucking blood out of living beings is what they do to restore their bodies," continued Elijah. "You probably don't remember, but, after he bit your ankle, the arm I had cut off regenerated out of the blue. It just grew back."

I did not remember that. I guess I was too busy crying for my life and tending to my stabbed shoulder to have noticed. As I was, sitting with a blanket over my naked back as my shoulder burned in the cold air, I almost wished I was back at that clearing.

"Anyway, he did not drink any of my blood. That was not his intention. He said he wanted me, and you, to suffer."

"What did he mean by that?" I asked, though I already knew the answer. And Elijah knew I knew.

"George," replied Elijah, like skipping through the conversation portion he already knew the script for. "The situation has changed too much in the last couple days." He took a moment to sigh, then continued. "I think it best for you to continue your training after I'm gone."

"I don't understand why you have to go," I said. My eyes started tearing up, which I didn't want to happen. "We don't know if he just tried to kill you with that bite. Or how long it'll take you to turn. We can give you medicine."

Elijah shook his head. "The way the roads are, you may have to spend the night around here before you go back to Foxworth. We cannot take that risk."

"But we're not!" I replied. Snot making it harder for me to breathe. "You don't know if he wanted to hurt you real bad and that's why you're bleeding so much."

"He could've stab me, choke me, rip my eyes out. Many faster ways to do it. He didn't want to kill me, George. You know that."

"No!" I demanded. I even stood up, though the pain in my shoulder almost made me pass out. But I kept my balance. "We are not letting you die because of this stubbornness! We can't."

Elijah never lost his calm, educational tone. "What if I told you," he continued, "that I don't want to be buried with a single trace of vampire in my appearance?"

I was gonna say something, but I didn't. I didn't know what to answer to that. I hadn't even thought of the image of Elijah turned into a vampire. What would happen if we let him? Would he become evil all of a sudden? That sounds ridiculous. But I couldn't know, and neither could any of them.

"If you respect me, you will respect my wishes of dying as a man, and not a monster." He looked up at me as I walked to him, really slowly. The cold was getting on my nerves, and the blanket wasn't doing much.

I sat next to Elijah, to the other side of the bite. "I'm scared," I said, instantly regretting it. How could I be so selfish? How could I be thinking about my own problems when Elijah was about to sacrifice himself in the name of his humanity and our safety? I felt so stupid.

"Me too," he said. "But I want you to continue just like you were doing with me. I'm sure Taylor will teach you well." I was gonna reply, but he didn't let me. "You are very smart, George. But you're a lousy shot," he chuckled a bit, though it was very evident that it hurt him a lot. "You have to use your head a lot more than your heart sometimes, like when I told you to stay and you didn't."

"I'm so sorry," I started, my eyes still glossy.

"It doesn't matter that you're sorry," he interrupted. "What matters is that you recognize your mistake and learn from it. If you can't undo whatever it is you did, then being sorry is completely pointless. You have to learn. Be rational. *Listen to others*."

He smiled as he stressed those last words, but I couldn't. I was trapped in my feelings and in the images that I knew were about to come. I couldn't think of anything else but what awaited me in the near and far future. And I felt so, so guilty.

"Promise me you will learn," he said.

I looked at him in the eyes, into his soul like I usually tried to do. I felt the warmth of his kindness and reassurance, and it gave me enough confidence to answer. "I promise."

Gray, April 17th, the small hours

What Taylor had to show his pack was not a small thing at all. It was probably one of the biggest clues of the

320

entire expedition, and it had to happen the very last night. Of course.

As the pack walked as humans, covering themselves only with the bedsheets from the cold breeze of the forest, Gray wondered what could be so incredibly important. But every thought he had did not hold up to what they actually found at the abandoned campsite.

Two bodies laid down against a different tree each, both covered in the white organic material they had found at the clearing and around the forest. They were well covered, but completely static. It wasn't until the wolves got closer that they could actually confirm that they were alive.

"I saw them when I chased the demon," said Taylor. "I saw the others, too. They were on the run."

"Did you see John?" asked Gray.

"I think I did. Though I'm not sure."

Drake had already walked to the farthest body, also the smaller one. A girl, obviously one of George's friends. "Guys," called Drake. "She's alive too."

"What are we going to do?" asked Alex.

The pack looked at their leader for answers, but Gray didn't know what they should do. He was far more hurt than his teammates, and he just wanted to rest. Obviously, the right answer was to take the two people back to Foxworth and nurse them back to health. But, at that moment, Gray just wished he could teleport.

Elijah, April 17th, the small hours

The hunter hid his incredible pain as much as he could, still applying pressure to his neck wound. He wanted the last image George had of him to be positive, to give him hope for a better future. In the last moments of his life, he felt he succeeded at that.

The wolves walked back carrying what looked like two bodies, which really confused the boy and the hunter. "Who are those?" asked Elijah. "Are they alive?"

"Yes," answered Taylor. "One of them is the missing Park Ranger." Elijah remembered the case that started it all. Alan Maffei was his name. "The other one, we hope you can tell us," he said to George.

George's eyes widened immensely. "Is it one of my friends?" he asked, partly excited, partly worried.

"Yes," answered Drake, who was carrying that body. "A girl."

At the sound of these words, George seemingly forgot about his terrible injury that had the bedsheets soaked in red. He jumped up and went to Drake, where he checked on the body wrapped in the cocoon material they had previously seen.

George's eyes enlightened with joy. "Andrea," he whispered, out of breath not because of the pain or the shock, but the happiness of seeing this girl, still alive.

From the very few conversations he had had with the boy, the hunter remembered the name 'Andrea.' George was walking alone with her when everything went down. It made him happy to know that, just maybe, they could resume that walk some time in the near future.

#

After much talking about the bodies and their next actions, they were all ready. Except, clearly, for George. The ecstasy of seeing that Andrea was alive soon wore off as he remembered that his mentor was about to leave them forever.

They all gathered round him, as he hadn't moved from the tree he was resting against. They formed a circle with him as the parting spot, Drake by one side and Gray by the other.

"It has been an incomparable honor working with you," said Alex. Elijah raised his right forearm, and Drake proceeded to take the gauntlet off him.

"We will never forget how great of an ally you've been to us and to this cause," said Drake, handing the gauntlet to Gray. His eyes got very glossy, but he held back.

"You have been a great companion, and incredible friend," said Taylor. "The things we have lived and learned beside you will remain with us forever. Wherever you go after this, I want you to remember that." Taylor's eyes did let escape tears, though he never lost his posture.

"Thank you for everything that you've done for us and this investigation," said Gray. It wasn't clear if it was his evident lack of energy or the mood of the scene, but he sounded the softest and kindest any of the people around him had ever heard him.

Elijah looked at George, who was right in front of him in the circle. The boy looked to the floor, with shame and sadness flooding his eyes with tears. "You have been the greatest teacher I've ever had," said the boy. "Is 'Elijah' your real name?"

The wolves looked a bit taken aback by such a question at a moment like that, but Elijah didn't seem to mind. In fact, he smiled. "It is," he answered.

"Then I promise you that I'll name my first kid after you," said George. Elijah could not resist anymore, and let his finals tears fall off his eyes and roll down his cheeks.

"Finish training him," he said to the pack. "Remember to care, not just for each other, but for yourselves." He looked at each one of them separately, and stopped momentarily at Gray. "The lives we live are hard enough for you to punish yourselves too. Keep that in mind as you move on."

Elijah let go of his neck wound, but not much blood came out of it. He took one last breath and closed his eyes. He was ready. He had accepted it. He was going to die on that day, as a man.

He knew he had done good in the world. He had saved lives, he had taught others his ways and been taught others' ways. He knew he was going to be remembered fondly, and that his impact on the world would be felt long after he was gone, which gave him peace.

And in peace he would rest, forever.

Part Three

Every day for the past month, Terrence Walker had woken up asking the Universe what he had done to deserve such punishment. Had he been a bloodthirsty dictator who enslaved and killed his people? Had he stolen millions of dollars from people in need for his own gain? Because it certainly felt that way, especially that night.

The night of April 16th was the most horrifying night Terrence Walker had ever lived. Not only had he gone to bed extremely early because of the exhaustion caused by the case, but he also didn't have dinner nor did he take any time to unwind after he got back home. He just arrived, laid down, and fell into a deep sleep, at times wishing he was actually dead, so that everything would be over.

But it wasn't over. In fact, that same night, it got unpredictably worse, if that was even possible. A quarter before midnight, Sergeant Walker was awakened by the phone ringing. He and Mrs. Walker knew perfectly well that a phone ring at that hour meant the most terrible news, but even they weren't expecting such a thing.

Not five minutes later, Sergeant Walker was uniformed and driving to the station to get reinforcements and supplies. Apparently, some kind of terrorist attack was occurring right at that moment at Adler-Morrow General Hospital. A terrorist attack, in a 4-story hospital in the remote woods of Minnesota. If he tried to, he couldn't have come up with something that sounded faker.

A convoy of six cars left the Adler Police Department, packed with weapons and expecting a helicopter to arrive soon. They had also informed the FBI, who were setting a perimeter around the area. Sergeant Walker thought that maybe, just maybe, it could all be over that night. Assuming the unexplainable terrorist attack was somehow connected to the Anderson case, of course.

Peter Anderson. That was a twist Walker did not expect, and one which, deep inside, hurt him. He had formed a strange bond with Mr. Anderson, to the point where he could almost consider him a friend and not just an acquaintance. They had met when Anderson came to Adler for his research, so that the Police force where informed that there would be a strange man walking around the woods. Little did they know, he was a lot stranger than anybody could've thought.

Why would a child kidnapper attack a hospital like that? And how? It sounded so ridiculous, to think that a kidnapper would also be a terrorist and count with an army and weaponry strong enough to assault a whole building. Absolutely none of it made any sense, and Walker's terrible sleeping schedule didn't help make it clearer.

The road to Adler-Morrow General was completely deserted and almost completely dark, which was not common nor safe. The police had almost no information regarding the status of the hospital, except for the 911 report that came in from a supposed escaped hostage. According to her, the lights had gone out, several explosions had occurred, and men accompanied by wild animals stormed inside the building. One of them even crashed a truck into the front door. What kind of wild animals? Were they really wild? Were the men armed? What was their objective? Nothing made a bit of sense.

The convoy of six cars split up when they got to the hospital. One of them stayed back, guarding the entrance to the small parking lot. Two others secured the entrance, where they saw people walking out, some terrified, some clearly disoriented. Another one took around the right corner to secure the area. The final two, where Walker was, approached the left side of the building, where there was audible conflict and maybe, Walker thought, people at a distance.

It was almost like a garden, that side of the hospital. There was nothing but grass, giving the building a little space before the woods started. There was a short walkway for people to take walks once in a while, but it was really just an open space that separated the building from the forest. This side is where everything seemed to be happening.

Once the cars got closer, Walker could distinguish the figures of two people. One of them taller than the other, wearing red. The shorter one wearing grey or dusty blue. Not able to know exactly who they were, he grabbed the car's megaphone and spoke, "Freeze!" he demanded. "Both of you!"

At the sound of his words, the taller one grabbed the arm of the bedazzled shorter one and dragged him away. Walker's driver almost caught up with them, but the small space and unstable terrain didn't allow much maneuverability. Soon enough, both people had disappeared in the dark of the forest.

As he inspected the ground around him, he saw big puddles of blood everywhere, and something that he had not noticed from the car. Slowly, he walked to what looked like a body, quickly identifying it as the corpse of Earnest Erb.

"Redford," called Walker on his radio. "Send as many as you can. This is bigger than we thought." He turned back to the cars, where, in the background, he could see ambulances and firefighters arriving to the front, along with people getting out of the hospital, some wearing gowns.

Right before he spoke again, he heard something very strange. A scream. A name being screamed, from inside the hospital. Walker looked up to see the completely destroyed windows of the fourth floor, where there was another figure. His sight was not good enough to identify who it was, but he was sure of what he had heard. The voice had called for "George," and after turning back to the forest to see the escaping kidnappers for a split second more, he put everything together.

Chapter 18
Michael & Alexander
Rochester, New Hampshire – March, 1938

The Miller-Gray Shoe Company was one of the few remaining family businesses left in town after the Great Depression, which led to most business owners to either move down South or go broke. Miller-Gray, however, had been struck with some of the luckiest turn of events anybody had ever witnessed. After competition disappeared from the area and Miller-Gray were left almost on their own, they went all-in. Working day and night, hiring for what some called "Southern rates," they managed to survive the recession until finally, by the end of '37, things started looking good again, for the state, the town, and Miller-Gray.

Most of this success was attributed to the visionary head of operations at Miller-Gray, the eponymous Anthony Gray, who allegedly gave a speech so compelling, so incredibly inspiring, it took Jacob Miller out of his impending alcoholism. Folks around town said that they heard this conversation take place sometime around

Christmas of 1934, and that, since then, Rochester was never the same ever again.

Come four short years later, and the Miller-Gray Shoe Company was so thriving, there were folks from the big cities coming to buy shoes. Rich folks from New York, Boston and Pennsylvania were all coming to Rochester, New Hampshire to try out them Miller-Gray shoes.

As the business grew, slowly but steady, Anthony Gray's life started getting better, which some would say helped him cope with the apocalyptic amount of work that he had put on himself and his partner. Anthony's wife, Clarissa, gave birth to a baby girl called Alice a few months after that life-changing Christmas speech, and Anthony could not be happier that his 6-year-old boy Michael finally had a little sibling to love and play with. Clarissa was also a terrific mother, wife, and friend, making sure that Anthony always ate and slept at least half of the recommended amount, as well as taking the best care of the children, and being a great conversation partner.

After Alice's birth, however, it did become tougher for Clarissa to keep the household standing on her own. The Gray Family had garnered a reputation for being extremely progressive, especially for their time, but what they decided to do with their household would go down through generations as the most groundbreaking action for racial equality in all of New England.

In the earliest days of the company's rise, with all of those "Southern rates" that allowed in so many workers, there was one beautiful soul that Anthony Gray really wanted to hire, but had no use for. A young, charismatic black man called Alexander Chambers. The day the two met, they instantly liked each other, like an explosion of chemistry had occurred between them.

Alexander was bright, almost literally. He irradiated a sort of positive energy that was unexplainable for Anthony and the rest of the workers. Every room he walked into, he changed everybody's mood for the better. At just shy of 19 years of age, Alexander Chambers could have probably won the seat of Mayor, if the times had been different. The only problem was that he was not bright in the other sense, the sense that Anthony needed in one of his workers. Alexander did not count with some of the most basic education, which was common for the time, but he also didn't show a lot of aptitude for the work the factory demanded. They ended their first meeting promising to talk in the near future.

Now that Clarissa was at home with two children to take care of, and most of the help had gone back South, Anthony saw a golden opportunity to both help his wife keep the household afloat, and give this remarkable young man a well-paid job that included food and a roof. It was, truly, exceptionally convenient, and seen as very charitable by most of the community.

To say that it was uncommon for a black *man* to work as help in a white household is an understatement. It was unheard of, revolutionary, blasphemous for some. But

Anthony Gray never did things based on what some people would think of him, but rather, based on what he believed was the best for everybody involved. It is highly debated if this kind of attitude was developed before he took his company to huge success, or because of it.

Alexander would wake up every morning and start breakfast for himself and the four members of the Gray Family, though, depending on the season, Anthony would sometimes not even show up the night before, opting to sleep – or, probably, continue working – at the factory. Alexander was given the liberty to make whatever he saw fit for each day, and would sit and eat with the Grays for every meal. He would play in the garden with little Michael, who grew to adore him in no time. Sometimes he would take care of baby Alice if Clarissa needed to rest.

As Alice grew older, Alexander started putting both children to sleep, sometimes telling them stories of his family down South, some based on reality, some made up. But either way, Alexander made sure that the children's imaginations were always blooming, which is what he felt his grandmother did for him when he was a child. Alice and Michael grew up seeing Alexander as, essentially, their second father. Some think they almost loved him as one, too.

One night, shortly after Alice turned 4, Alexander was helping her tie up her hair before going to school. Little Alice had always been incredibly intelligent for her age, and it never stopped impressing Alexander. "Alex," said Alice as she looked at herself in the mirror, Alexander behind her. She looked just like her mother, with light brown hair and her exact same pair of eyes.

"Yes, dear?" asked Alex. Even after half a decade in New England, traces of his deep bayou accent could still be traced when he spoke.

"What is that word that the man said to you the other day?" Alexander knew exactly what she was talking about, but he wasn't sure if to change the subject or actually answer. It was a very hard question to answer, especially to a toddler.

"What word?" he opted to ask instead of responding.

"Mommy said I could never, ever say it," said Alice. Alexander couldn't help but smile.

"Your mommy's right about that," he said. But he knew Alice wasn't stupid.

"But what does it mean?" cried Alice. "Mommy was very angry when she heard it."

Alexander finished fixing the toddler's hair and turned her to him. "It's a very bad word that bad people use to make me feel bad," he said, looking into Alice's beautiful blue yes.

"Don't feel bad," said Alice, hugging Alexander around his neck. He smiled widely and returned the hug.

"Don't worry. As long as you're here, I will never feel bad. I promise."

#

Anthony had gone back home very late at night, and had but a cup of coffee for breakfast before he left for the factory. Alexander and the rest of the family had breakfast as usual; fried eggs, juicy bacon strips, orange juice, and Alexander's biscuits that the kids loved so much. It was a Saturday.

"Alex," started Clarissa. The young man looked up to her as he ate. "Could you take Michael out for a walk?" 10-year-old Michael was sitting right next to Alexander, but it was as if he wasn't in the room. He seemed to be distracted looking at his own hands. "I feel he spends way too much time in the house."

"Sure thing, Mrs. Gray," answered Alexander. He looked at Michael as he finished eating, noticing a strange lack of focus in his eyes.

After cleaning the dishes, Alexander looked at the clock. It was almost 10 in the morning, which meant that, if he wanted to have lunch ready in time, he had to take young Michael as soon as possible.

Alexander knocked on Michael's open door, just to call for the young boy's attention. He looked a lot like his father, especially in his shiny black hair that made his fair face features pop, though he did not inherit his mother's eyes. He was sitting on his bed, reading. "What is that?" asked Alexander, walking in.

Michael showed Alexander the thin book with a beautiful purple cover and big eyes floating in the sky. Alexander could read and write perfectly well, but he didn't do it very often. Likewise, he did not know what that book was about, but the title sounded kind of familiar.

"*The Great Gatsby*," said Alexander with curiosity. He sat beside Michael on his bed. "Is it for school?"

"No," said Michael. He didn't sound irritated or annoyed, but his face said otherwise. "I found it in dad's library and felt like giving it a try. It's very famous."

"I knew I'd heard that name somewhere," said Alexander, exaggerating his mannerisms, trying to get a smile out of Michael. It didn't work. "How you like it so far?"

"It's good," said Michael, looking down at the book. "But I just started. I'm not sure where anything's going yet."

"You'll have to let me know when you finish it, so I can read it too." Alexander smiled at Michael, who sort of tried to return the smile at him. "Wanna go out for a walk with me? I feel like taking in some sun."

"I heard my mom asking you to take me," said Michael, with some disappointment in his voice. "You don't have to lie."

"I ain't lying," said Alexander. "I like having some sun on my face once in a while, and I wanna walk before having to come back in to make lunch. I'm simply asking if you'd like to come with me, so that I can also please your mom by taking you out of the house."

Michael stopped to think, still looking down at the book. "Why does she want that?"

"I don't know. Maybe because you read too much."
Alexander poked Michael's tummy, making him jump in reflex, but also smile. "What do you say?"

"Okay," said Michael.

#

It was a fresh March morning, that day. The sun was up and radiant, but not hot. The air felt light and welcoming, birds were chirping for the beginning of Spring. Michael and Alexander left the Gray house and walked down the sidewalk to Bosworth Park, just a couple blocks away from the house. Alexander used to take Michael there all the time when he was younger, when he was happy and full of energy. But they stopped going after some doubtful stares caught Alexander's eyes.

It was as if Michael had forgotten about the existence of the park, even though he walked by it to go to school every day. When he stared at the familiar arch at the entrance, his eyes filled with delight and nostalgia. "We're *here*," he said, emphasizing the last word.

"Yes we are," said Alexander, smiling down at the boy. He proceeded to run inside the park and around the trees close by to the right.

Alexander was delighted to see Michael run with such joy, especially after feeling his bad mood just minutes ago in his room. For a second, he reminded Alexander of the little boy he had helped to raise, and who he loved like a combination of a little brother and his own son.

Alexander sat on the closest bench, watching Michael chasing squirrels around. They would always be fast enough to go up the trees before he even got close to them, but he still tried to catch them, and one could see in his eyes that he truly believed he was going to be able to.

The sun in Alexander's face was suddenly blocked by a shadow. He turned to see three white, brown-haired men, tall and imposing, not much older than him. They looked shabby, like they hadn't showered in a couple days after hiking for long hours. Their nails were pretty long, their hair unkempt. The one in the front spoke first. "Does anything around here say this is a Nigger Park, nigger?"

Alexander Chambers was very used to being called that and treated like a lesser part of society, but it was very, very rare for him to encounter people like that up North. "He asked you a question, nigger," said the one to Alexander's right. "Or do you not speak American?"

He was wiser than to answer to any of the taunts. He was mature enough to understand that he was outnumbered, and nothing was worth getting beat in the street for no reason. So, Alexander stood up, finally revealing how tall he was, though still not as tall as his assailants. "Michael," he called to the boy. "We're leaving."

Michael turned to see his dear friend and the three strangers. They gave him a terrible vibe, like they were planning to do something to Alexander. But he couldn't possibly understand what, or why.

"Wait a second," said the one to Alexander's left. "You're not going now, are you?"

"You go the moment somebody calls you out on your bullshit, huh?" said the one in the center. "That's not how things work around here."

"You three shut up," said Michael, approaching the scene. Alexander was still quiet, opting to leave as soon as possible. "You don't know how things work around here because you're not from here."

The three strangers couldn't hide the surprise from their faces. "You got balls, kid," said the one in the center, the apparent leader. "What's your name?"

"Michael Gray," said the boy. "Son of Anthony Gray, the most important person in this town. And if I ever see you bothering my friend again, I'll make sure it's the last thing you do around here."

The three strangers laughed out loud, though Alexander could see that it was mostly fake. They weren't afraid of Michael's threat, but they still wanted to make him feel terrible, to crush him down.

"Let's go," said Alexander, not looking at the strangers. He grabbed Michael by the shoulder and walked away.

"We'll see you again, Michael," said the leader of the trio. Michael turned to see him, but Alexander insisted in going forward until they couldn't see them anymore.

#

The boy and his friend continued walking past the house to the riverside, where they finally slowed their pace. "What happened?" asked Michael.

"Nothing," said Alexander, catching his breath, even though they hadn't been running. He had just walked all of that distance with barely any air in his lungs. "Just some kids looking for trouble."

"I'm not stupid, Alex," said Michael. "I heard them call you that word. The one mom made a big fuss about."

"Three bored, uninspired kids looking to annoy the easiest prey. There's nothing to worry about. I promise you." But Michael wasn't buying it. Even though he didn't say anything else, he looked at his friend with distrust and insecurity, knowing there was more to it.

#

Dinner that night was interrupted by an unexpected phone call. It was the first time in weeks that Anthony Gray had enough free time to enjoy a peaceful meal at his house, but it was cut short by a panicking Jacob Miller, who called Anthony back to the factory immediately.

"Can't you tell him that you're enjoying some family time for once?" asked a frustrated Clarissa Gray.

"Sorry, honey," answered Anthony, as he put on his coat. "If what Jacob says is true, then I have to go."

"It is so clear that he has no family to take care of," cried Clarissa. Anthony leaned closer to his wife and gave her a kiss.

"I'll be back for breakfast. I promise."

Anthony walked to little Alice and kissed her forehead. "Bye daddy," she said, almost spilling her bean puree over her dress.

"Good night, sweetheart," he answered, as he went by Michael and brushed his hair. "Take care of them, okay?" Michael nodded. Anthony smiled and walked to the door. He turned one last time to look at Alexander, who was cleaning the dishes. "Good night, Alex," he said.

"Good night, Mr. Gray," answered Alex from the kitchen.

"Alex," called Clarissa while massaging her temples. "Can you please get Alice to bed when you finish? I think I need to lay down."

"I got it, Mrs. Gray," called Alex, finishing the last pot of the night. The frequency with which Mrs. Gray was having these terrible headaches was starting to concern Alexander, and Michael had noticed too.

"You okay, mom?" asked Michael.

"Yes. I just need to lay down."

Clarissa kissed both of her children and retired to her room, leaving the young black man to clean up the dining table and put the kids to bed.

"Let's go," said Alexander, raising Alice from her chair. "I'll tell you some more about my Uncle Po."

Michael watched as Alexander took his sister away to her room, and sat still for a moment. Thinking, harder than any 10-year-old boy should have to think. Wondering what was really happening at his father's factory, what was wrong with his mom, what was Alexander hiding from him. But he would never know.

#

Later that night, after only snores and cricket sounds remained around the house, Alexander was left all to himself with a clean dining room and nothing to do but sleep. The only room on the ground floor was his, and so it sometimes felt like he had a whole house for himself, which was not far from a lifelong dream he'd had since his bayou days, when he shared a room with his brother and a cousin.

Not quite ready to sleep yet, Alexander walked around the kitchen, making sure that everything was in order for breakfast the next morning. He liked to know what he was going to do if he could, unless little Alice woke up with a crazy request that would tarnish his plans, but he would make it anyway with the widest smile.

As he checked the refrigerator and counted the fruit in the baskets, he heard a noise coming from outside. From the backyard, closer to the riverside, there was a thump, as if something had fallen down. He looked out the window to see nothing but the yard lit by the light coming from inside the house.

Another thump, then another, then silence. There was no pattern, but also no explanation for what could be out there. Some sort of animal, maybe, and so Alexander grabbed one of the dining chairs and used it to reach to the very top of the cabinet, where there was an old Remington shotgun that he believed had belonged to Michael's grandfather, Mr. Gray's father.

Alexander grabbed the shotgun and only two shells, and loaded it up how he had learned to do when he was hired half a decade before. He opened the door to the backyard and stepped out of the house. "Hello?" he said to the wind, but it didn't answer.

Another step, and now he was completely outside of the house, almost in absolute darkness. Alexander turned left, where the closest fence was. With the limited visibility, he couldn't make up anything specific, but there didn't seem to be anything wrong with the fence or the neighbors.

He looked down at the floor, looking for traces or animals. Maybe they were just raccoons looking for food, or a cat chasing rats. Something that didn't require the use of a shotgun at all. Something, not someone.

But as he turned right to the other side of the yard, he received the strongest punch to the face he could remember at the moment. The shotgun flew out of his hands and he fell to the floor, smashing the back of his head against the ground.

The world spun as Alexander tried to focus his gaze on something, but there was only the darkness of the night. He couldn't even notice the twinkling stars in the sky as everything revolved into a porridge of confusion.

"Got a little lightheaded, nigger?" said the one to his right. He felt his arm being raised violently into the air as he was made to stand up in front of the three white men.

"I hope I didn't hit you too hard," said the one in the center. "You're supposed to be fully conscious for this."

"Wha-" tried Alexander, but the one in the middle hit him in the stomach with something stiff and hard. The shotgun.

"Shut your ass up," said the one to his left.

Unrelated to the confusion of the moment, Alexander couldn't even remember how any of them really looked like. To him, they could've been triplets. Their faces merged with each other in ways he couldn't think of how to describe.

"I just wanted to let you know that you were not welcome here," said the middle one. "But then your little faggot boy had to talk back. And, well, I don't much like being talked back to."

The one to his left put on what looked and smelled like a dirty sock inside Alex's mouth. "You shut up now," he said as he pushed the piece of cloth into the black man's larynx.

Alexander thought the hit to the face had severely affected him, because he could swear that the face of the middle man was changing. His nose turned bigger, light brown hair grew out his pores. His teeth where suddenly sticking out of his lips and shined bright in the moonlight. His eyes looked completely black, directly into Alexander's.

The formless, terrifying thing that stood in front of him leaned forward, making Alexander tremble. Any effort he made was outmatched by the strength of the two other men holding him in place as their leader came closer and closer.

With his transformed mouth, Alexander heard the man's slow breathing into his right ear, and without warning, a pain like no other. The feeling of two sharp swords stabbing his neck, going through his skin and bones and muscles like they were paper, holding in place inside the upper part of his thorax. Alexander screamed and cried, but almost no sounds came out of his moth, even though, on the inside, there was a storm of noise. Of noise he was making and that was being made inside of him.

After what felt like hours, the teeth slid out the way they came, letting out a gush of blood that sprayed all over the man in the middle, still looking like a monster from Alexander's darkest and most repressed nightmares. The black man was let go, falling back to the ground, using his hands to try to stop the bleeding, completely forgetting about the gag in his mouth.

"This is our town now," said the one in the middle, though Alexander couldn't see him; his eyes were closed against the ground. "No niggers allowed."

That was the last thing Alexander heard before immediately falling ill. He took the gag out and vomited all over himself. He tried to look around, but there was nobody, only him. He tried to crawl into the house, but the pain in his neck didn't allow him to even move his right arm.

He didn't have time to keep trying before he started shaking uncontrollably. Like a seizure, but not quite. He was completely conscious and actively trying to stop moving his arms, but he couldn't. The constant thrusting made him feel like the gash on his neck was going to open up and let his guts out. His fists started knocking on the wood of the house, so he used every bit of control he could muster over his body to push himself out of range and back into the ground.

It was too late. As he stopped shaking he noticed a ray of light reflecting on the yard and he looked up to see Michael's bedroom window lit from the inside.

But there was nothing he could do, because his body wasn't finished. Suddenly, his hands felt irritated, his fingertips started to burn. His jaw started moving in a way he had never felt before, as if it had been completely dislocated and now it was floating around inside his skin. His arms and legs itched, reminding him of the time he almost died of smallpox as a boy.

He tried to speak, but couldn't. He started shaking again, more violently this time. He felt how his fingertips opened up, like fruit being peeled, to let out what looked like sharp, shiny claws. His wide nose grew thinner, but also sharper, and out, like someone had hooked it and was trying to pull it out of him. His teeth grew so fast they perforated his lower lip, letting out two fangs.

He could feel hair growing on every inch of skin he had. Dark brown hair, like the one around his head.

Growing from his cheeks, his arms, his feet, his hands, his hips, his neck, he ripped his shirt apart trying to make the itch go. His whole face felt like it was being pulled out of his skull as a snout formed from his bone. He rolled on the ground and unto his knees, where he tried to contain his panicked self into a knelt fetal position. His back cracked with the feeling of an expanding skeleton, and so he ripped his shirt apart with his fangs and straightened his back, letting out a thunderous, pain-filled roar.

"Alex?" called Michael from inside the house. The black-haired boy walked slowly into view, illuminated by the light from inside the house.

Alexander couldn't recognize him. His body itched with the feeling of hair and burned skin all over it, and in the moment, little Michael just looked like the biggest hindrance in his existence. Like an obstacle that needed to be eliminated in order for the world to recover its balance. He couldn't think, he couldn't speak.

"Alex?" called Michael once more. The light from inside the house was not bright enough to illuminate the yard, so he couldn't see what his friend was going through. He didn't understand why he had heard him crying earlier. "Were you bit by a snake?" cried Michael, afraid for his friend's wellbeing. "Should I wake up my mom?"

The thought of Mrs. Gray's presence enraged Alexander like nothing else could at that moment. Controlling himself was hard enough, but having to deal with a grown adult woman was not going to help at all.

Yet, there was another part of him that struggled. A part of him, deep inside, that knew who the boy was and wanted to protect him. Protect him, and the woman, and the girl. Alice. Clarissa. Michael.

The brown wolf looked as the boy walked closer. "Are you okay?" he asked him, but the wolf didn't answer. He couldn't answer. What he wanted most was to talk, to tell Michael to stay away, but he couldn't get the words out of his mouth. He couldn't get his vocal cords to vibrate at a frequency that didn't result in grunts.

Go away, boy. Just leave. Let him drown in the agony he was going through. Let him fight it alone. But the boy wouldn't go. His heart was too pure.

And so, after one step too many, Michael could finally understand what was in front of him. He saw the skin full of hair, the snout, the eyes, claws, fangs, and dark, lifeless eyes, and couldn't help but scream and run away. A scream that lasted a fraction of what it would've if it wasn't for the brown wolf, who launched himself unto the running kid and almost bit off his leg clean.

A maul that lasted but a couple seconds, until the man inside the wolf retook control of the body. He instantly let go of the boy's leg, spraying blood all over his face and on the steps to the house. The brown wolf shook his head and covered his eyes, trying to understand what he had just done and what had happened to him, how to reverse everything, why he hadn't stopped just five seconds earlier.

Alexander picked up the boy, begging every force in the Universe to let him live and take him instead. A moment of silence that allowed him to feel how his whole body hurt, and how he himself was also bleeding. His own face felt unfamiliar, and so did his arms as he held little Michael in them.

Two pools of blood combined into a red puddle. With the boy in his arms, the brown wolf detransformed with every breath he took back into the dark-skinned man he knew himself to be. His shirt was gone, all of his skin was bruised and burned. A whole new animal could be crafted with all the hair that suddenly lied dead on the floor by his knees as he held the child, his eyes full of tears, wishing to wake up every second.

"Michael," wheezed Alexander, barely able to vocalize his words. "Michael," he called again. He scanned the child's leg, practically now half a leg as the calf was almost completely nonexistent.

The black man could not feel the boy's breathing. He forgot about what had just happened to his body, about the assault he suffered right in that yard just minutes before. All he needed was for little Michael to take a breath and assure him whatever had happened wasn't permanent.

The boy snapped awake out of the blue, making Alexander jump in horror. Immediately, the boy started shaking, just like Alexander had done moments ago. The black man held the black-haired boy as sternly as he could, but not even that was enough to contain the shaking. Soon enough there was vomit all over him and the boy himself as he shook more violently, thrusting his limbs around the air, sometimes hitting Alexander's face.

In the chaos of the moment, Alexander hadn't noticed the additional noise coming from inside the house. Right before Michael regained partial consciousness, Clarissa Gray stepped into the yard, barely illuminated by the light from the living room.

"Alex?" called Mrs. Gray, sleepy and confused. "What's wrong? I heard thumping."

"Mrs. Gray," wheezed Alexander. "Mrs. Gray, stay back. Please." The tears in his eyes and irritation all over his face didn't allow him to sound well enough for Mrs. Gray to understand him.

"What's wrong with Michael?" she cried, dashing to her son's dead-like, bloody body.

"Stay back!" called Alexander.

Before the woman could lay a finger on her son, the boy started shaking again, falling off of his friend's arms. He rolled on the ground, this time grunting and crying in pain, not paying any attention to his bit-off calf.

"Michael!" cried his mother.

Little Michael Gray could not stop shaking as the same things that happened to Alex happened to him. Only Alex had been able to contain himself in position after a moment. Michael was not stopping.

His fingertips peeled off. His teeth grew out of proportion. His skull expanded outwards as a snout grew out of his face and ripped the skin off his cheeks. Long, thick, black hair covered every inch of his skin as his mother tried to hold him in place. "Michael!" she cried once more.

The boy kept shaking violently until he wasn't a boy anymore, but a smaller version of whatever Alexander had turned into just moments before. Only Michael had never regained an ounce of control, and was greeted by his mother's desperate screams as soon as he opened his darkened eyes.

The small black wolf didn't stop shaking as his transformation ended. Alexander tried to separate him from his mother before he recovered consciousness. "Mrs. Gray, get away from him," said Alexander, breathing the heaviest air he'd ever felt running through his lungs.

"What did you do to him?!" cried Mrs. Gray, still holding her boy.

"Mrs. Gray. I need to take him away for a moment. Please. Let me have him."

Clarissa hugged her son even harder, looking at Alexander with terror and confusion. "What happened to him? What happened to you?"

"Mrs. Gray," called Alexander one last time. Just as his words dissolved in the air, the woman's cries were silenced by a violent punch to the throat.

Clarissa let go of her son as she tried to breathe through her caved-in throat. She looked at the awakened black wolf, who had nothing but absolute hate in his eyes for his own mother. "Baby," she tried to say. The black wolf slashed his mother's face with his claws, tearing one of her eyes open and deforming her nose.

"Michael," called Alexander, still unable to move or speak loud enough.

The body of Clarissa Gray fell to the ground as a terrifying scream called for all their attention. Alice Gray stood inside the house, letting enough light out to see what had just happened.

The black wolf launched himself to the little girl as Alexander tried to reach for him. "Michael, no," he said, with a lot more potency intended.

The black man couldn't hear anything else as the wolf disappeared with the child, for he passed out on the ground. And he laid there, unconscious for about an hour.

#

Alexander's eyes opened up slowly as he regained control over his body. His skin didn't feel as irritated anymore, and his fingers and mouth had seemingly healed scarless by themselves. But he wasn't thinking about that one bit.

He composed himself and stood up however he could, and limped inside the house, where he fell on the floor again. His legs did not feel strong enough to carry all of his weight, so he opted to lean on every piece of furniture in the house until he walked to wherever the boy had taken his sister. He only had to follow the red path of blood that had been left on the wooden floor.

Alexander got to the staircase, where the red path continued up. He used his arms to push himself up the stairs, but gave up halfway through and started crawling, careful not to touch Alice's blood.

The path lead him to the boy's room, where he could make up muffled cries. Alexander stood up using the staircase handle and walked to the doorframe, where he could see the detransformed Michael Gray hugging his sister's body, crying over her red-stained nightgown.

"Michael," called Alexander, now with enough volume to hear himself.

Michael looked up to his friend. His eyes were red and puffy, full of tears. The area around his mouth and nose was scarred, and there were what looked like pounds of black hair all around him. "What did I do?" asked the boy to his caretaker.

"We have to go," said Alexander, hearing traces of strength in his voice for the first time in hours. "We can't be seen here."

"Why did I do this to her?" asked Michael again, snot coming out of his nose. "What happened to me?"

Alexander walked into the room and kneeled next to the boy. "I don't know what happened to us," he said. He took a quick glance at the girl, but felt too distraught to actually see what happened to her. What he knew for sure was that she was not bitten.

"Alice," called Michael to his sister's corpse. "Alice, please. I'm sorry."

"Michael," said Alexander, putting his hand on Michael's shoulder.

"I can't leave her," he cried. Alexander couldn't resist letting tears out as well, but did everything he could to keep his posture.

"Come with me," he said. "We have to go."

#

Reports say that when the paramedics found Anthony Gray in his house, he was completely covered in his daughter's blood. The investigation on him didn't last very long, because there were more than enough witnesses that assured the police that Mr. Gray had spent all night at the factory, handling a severe case of vandalism and sabotage.

It was unclear exactly what had happened to the Gray women, but police were quick to blame the black man who acted as caretaker for the family. He was wanted for double murder and child kidnapping, as there was no sign of Michael Gray in the house or near the vicinities. The scene of the crime consisted of most of the entire house, with the descriptions of the actions left mostly omitted in light of their gruesomeness.

Until the end of his days, Anthony Gray defended Alexander Chambers, assuring everybody that he was part of the family, that he would never do such a thing. That he loved Alice almost as his own daughter. But, after the comprehensible breakdown he had after seeing his family torn apart, there was little believability in his statements.

Mr. Gray didn't last a month more. At around midnight on April 13th, the day he turned 38, Anthony Gray shot himself with an old Remington shotgun he kept in the house. With his death came the downfall of the Miller-Gray Shoe Company, as there were none left around town that wanted to work for what some called a "cursed factory," even if nothing had ever happened inside or around the factory itself. As the workers left and the clients stopped, not much time passed for the factory to shut its doors forever, and for Jacob Miller to resume his way to alcoholism that had stopped thanks to his partner and friend, who had now left them forever.

Chapter 19
Awakening

Andrea, day?

The softness of the sheets was almost nullified by the pain in every single inch of skin Andrea wore over her muscles. She opened her eyes very slowly, feeling truly awake for the first time in what felt like decades of groggy confusion and exhaustion. The first thing she saw was the white ceiling, which featured a lamp in the middle. There were no windows, but somehow, the room wasn't entirely dark, even though no lights seemed to be on.

Andrea tried to sit up, but was betrayed by her triceps as they burned in soreness the moment she tried to apply any kind of pressure to them. She fell back on the bed, feeling bruises and cuts all over her back and neck. She analyzed her hands, also cut, her fingers looking like stringy worms after all the weight she'd lost.

There was also an IV stuck to her left hand, which didn't alarm her as much as it probably should have. The transparent liquid that slowly dripped into her bloodstream didn't seem to have any conscious effects on her, and somehow she just knew it was nothing to worry about. The needle was set expertly in her hand, and she did not feel any pain or discomfort from it.

But she also noticed something very peculiar, which could imply horrible things. She was wearing clean, comfortable night clothes which she didn't recognize. She touched her auburn hair and felt it soft and puffy, unlike the muddy, awful mess she had grown used to. Her hands weren't covered in dirt, nor did she feel dirty or sweaty. Her nostrils were clear, and she was hungry.

With great effort, she pushed the sheets away from her body and managed to sit up against the mahogany bedframe. Her bed was huge, leaving almost two whole feet of space between her and the edges in every direction. There was a door to her left, and a door right in front of her, both closed. To her right, at arms length, was a small wooden nightstand, where there was a piece of white paper.

Andrea grabbed the paper sheet and analyzed it. Her eyes hurt looking at it, like she had to refocus a camera lens. She also didn't understand how it was possible for her to be reading so clearly without any windows open, but she would worry about that later. Right then, she was thinking about the piece of paper she was holding, which looked like a note.

She wasn't sure if she wanted to read it. She was still convinced that everything was a dream and she would soon wake up inside the cocoon again. But after much deliberation, she started reading the hand-written note. She thought she recognized the handwriting, but wasn't sure, and didn't want to get her hopes up.

Andrea,

I hope you've slept well. As of the writing of this note, you've been in bed for about 15 hours. They told me you were very bruised and about to shut down due to starvation, so they injected you with some vitamins and let you sleep as much as your body required.

Before anything else, I think it's important to let you know that you were taken care of by a team of female nurses who bathed you and put on the pajamas you're now wearing, so don't worry about that part. You were barely conscious during your bath, but they said it's very unlikely that you'll remember anything. Still, they said that you looked a lot better once you were clean, and that your health will recover at a much faster pace now.

Now that I've got that out of the way, I'm gonna try to answer what I would think are your most urgent questions.

1) Where are you?

You are at a safe house in the town of Foxworth, Minnesota, not too far from Adler. I've been staying here since we were attacked, and have been treated as well as I could ask. You are in the safest place you could be right now, and whenever you're ready, you'll eat some of the best food imaginable.

2) What happened to you?

You were captured by someone who you would not believe exists unless I tell you in person. It feels kinda stupid to even write all of this, but you deserve an explanation, even if it's a ridiculous one (though completely true). You and the others were captured by what are, essentially, real-life versions of what we grew up knowing as "vampires." I know. So stupid. I promise it'll all make sense once I see you and explain.

3) What's gonna happen now?

I'm not entirely sure. There are many things to sort out right now, but our priority is for you to fully recover. You were in very bad health when we found you, so it's important that you take care of yourself first. Whenever you're ready, you can come to me and I'll tell you everything that's happened since you were captured. I promise.

4) What about the others?

I honestly don't know. My friends said that they saw the vampires – again, sorry – flying away holding something, and they believe those were our friends. Our best guess is that they are still alive, and they will be for a while. I'm afraid I can't tell you anything else.

I'm sure you have many more questions that need answering. Feel free to head out whenever you feel comfortable and we'll make sure that you get better as quickly as humanly possible. The door in front of you is the bathroom, where you have everything you'll need if you want to bathe or shower. In the nightstand cabinet are a couple of light snacks in case you get hungry, though they said you shouldn't eat too much yet, as your stomach needs to readjust to eating regularly.

My room is three doors to the right from yours, so don't worry about having to walk up to strangers to ask for directions. Whatever *time it is you wake up, feel free to knock on my door and ask whatever you want.*

I'm really happy that we found you. Can't wait to see you healthy again.

− *George*

Steph, April 17th, afternoon

Stephanie woke up in a hospital room – one that wasn't completely destroyed, with no signs of the chaos she had seen the night before. White and clean, but nothing special to it, really. She felt relatively well, apart from groggy due to poor sleeping. Evelyn was sitting right next to her, and hugged her tightly when she gave signs of wakefulness.

"Oh my God," said Evelyn through her tears. "I'm so happy that you're here."

Steph hugged her mother back. "What do you mean? Where are we?"

Before Evelyn could answer, somebody entered the room. It was a young nurse that Steph did not recognize. She used this moment to look out the door, where she noticed there were uniformed men blocking the way. "Mrs. Kim," said the nurse to Evelyn, "they need to talk to her."

"She just woke up!" cried Evelyn in frustration. "Can't you just give her a moment to recover her breath?"

"Where am I?" asked Steph.

"We're in Mother's Mercy in Mankato," answered Evelyn. "Do you remember what happened last night, sweetheart?" asked Evelyn to her daughter.

Steph did remember. She remembered everything, including seeing George. The only thing she couldn't recall was how she got out of Adler-Morrow General, nor how she got to that new hospital where she was now. She guessed she had to find out those details in order to understand what was going to happen next.

She opted not to answer her mother the moment she saw who walked through the door. It was one of the last people she expected to see, and could not think of any logical explanation for his presence. "Antoine?" she exclaimed as the tall Senior entered her hospital room. "What are you doing here?"

"Hey," he said shyly. He was dressed rather formally, ready for a day party at somebody's garden. "How are you feeling?"

Though Antoine was very handsome, Steph had never fallen for his charms. She always saw him as the likable dumb-dumb who every girl wanted to go to prom with. "Confused," she said. "What are you doing here?"

Admittedly, this was a side of Antoine that Steph had never seen. The confidence and air of camaraderie that he used to exhaust naturally were nowhere to be seen, replaced instead by intense doubt on his face. "They told me you were sick so I came to see how you were."

Steph looked back to her mother, who surely didn't even know who Antoine was apart from being the mayor's grandson. Her mother shrugged. "They told me a couple friends were here to see you."

"A couple?" asked Stephanie, even more confused. "Who else is here?" she asked Antoine.

"Scotch," answered the blonde Senior. "And the two weird ones that hung out with you all last week."

Roger and Stacy were there, believably because they were concerned for Steph's sake, especially after hearing what happened at the hospital the night before, and because they were together when she collapsed. But Scotch? That made no sense.

"But why are you here?" insisted Steph. "If Jefferson wasn't such a small school, I'd be surprised that you know my name."

It was evident that Antoine wasn't used to not knowing what to answer. He mumbled something Steph didn't quite catch before he was interrupted by a very familiar voice.

"That's okay, son," barged in Terrence Walker. "She's not feeling well right now."

He had clearly caught Antoine by surprise as much as it had Steph, as the blonde Senior jumped at the sound of his voice and then nodded nervously as he was signaled to leave the room. Antoine left without looking back at Steph.

"Boys can sometimes be so dumb, can't they?" added Walker as the door closed behind him.

Steph stared into his face, changing her expression to one of complete neutrality. "So can men," she answered.

"Officer," started Evelyn. "We have so much to discuss. Can you please give us a moment?"

"I cannot, Mrs. Kim. I'm sorry." Walker grabbed a chair from the other side of the room and sat in front of Steph. "I'm afraid we're going to have to deal with this directly and without much preparation."

Evelyn started to cry, almost uncontrollably. "Mom," called Steph from her bed, trying to reach out to her. "What's wrong?"

"I'm sorry for keeping you waiting for so long," continued Walker as Evelyn cried. "I couldn't think of anything else to soften the blow of the news we need to share with you."

Steph was growing desperate now. "What is it?" she asked, holding her composure as hard as she could.

Walker sighed. "I'm sorry to inform you that your father is part of a group of people that went missing last night at Adler-Morrow General."

It was like being shot with the thinnest and sharpest arrow, clean through the heart. "What?" she mustered to ask. "What group? What do you mean 'missing'?"

"There was a situation last night at Adler-Morrow where you ended up unconscious on the floor, surrounded by broken glass." Walker gave himself a moment, then continued. "Dr. Kim was one of the doctors on duty during the… situation. And he's currently unaccounted for, along with fifteen other people. They have disappeared."

As these last words left Walker's mouth, Evelyn broke into a very loud and heartbreaking sob. Stephanie's eyes filled with tears, but she did not break. "What happened last night?"

Walker sighed again. "We were hoping you could tell us, Ms. Kim," he said. "We don't have a lot of clear information aside from some very specific details. What we do believe is that your father is merely missing, along with the others."

All of the thoughts and ideas she had been trying to juggle had to stop at once. George and the wolves and the screaming and Earnest Erb had to be put on hold. "What do you want me to do?"

"I convinced the FBI to lay off of you for now," said Walker. "I told them it'd be easier for you to talk to a friend, or me, if that failed."

Steph couldn't help but scoff. "Antoine is nowhere close to being my friend. And neither is your son." This seemed to make Walker slightly uncomfortable, though she wasn't entirely sure why.

"Anyway," continued Walker. "I'm here, in front of your mother, asking you to tell me everything you can remember from last night."

The juggling had to start again, this time with the thought of her dad being added into the mix. Yet, somehow, it felt like it had grown exponentially difficult, between her mother's crying and the Sergeant's pressure for answers. She had to help if it meant finding her dad, but she couldn't possibly give away anything about the wolves. Mainly because that involved George as well.

There was that strange moment before she saw the grumpy wolf, Michael. A brief moment where she lost control of her body and couldn't move a muscle. But, apart from that, she couldn't see how any of the other things she saw could help her dad. "I don't remember much," she opted to say. "I was in my room and then I got scared because the lights went out and there was a big bang. I'm not sure about much else."

Walker had started writing stuff down on a notepad. "Did you see anybody after the lights went out?"

"No," she answered, too quickly, she thought. She gave herself a moment. "No, I don't think so. I remember I was looking for Mercedes but I couldn't hear or see her anywhere."

Walker turned his head up. "Mercedes? Mercedes Jackson?"

Another heavy, uncomfortable thought came through Steph's head as she nodded her head. That maybe something had happened to Mercedes. Maybe she was right next to whatever exploded downstairs. Or maybe she had been attacked by one of the horrible things that almost killed Michael. "Is she okay?"

Walker sighed again, putting down the notepad. "I'm afraid she's one of the people unaccounted for since last night. I'm sorry."

Reflexively, Steph gasped and covered her mouth, this time letting go of a couple tears before she recovered her posture. "Are you sure?" she asked. Walker nodded.

From a certain angle, it felt almost unfair for Steph to be pressured into giving all of these important answers to questions she wasn't even sure she understood. How the safety of her father, her nurse, and whoever else was missing was now her responsibility. How she had to lie to protect her friend and her saviors, and still, even if she told Walker everything, it wouldn't make a difference.

"I'm sorry," said Steph. "There's nothing else I can tell you."

"Stephanie," started Walker. "The FBI are going to come on you if I leave here without any information. They'll push you away from your underage shield and treat you much worse than I ever could. Please, be honest with me."

"I am!" she said, a bit louder than she intended to. "If only to help my dad I would give you every answer you want. But I can't. I'm sorry."

Walker looked down at his notepad and then back up to Steph. "What about George?"

What about George, indeed. What did it mean for her to see him with the red-dressed man – who was probably that creepy hobo, Peter Anderson. Why was

George on top of Earnest Erb as he took his last breath? And why were the wolves protecting him, too?

"What's with him? Did you find something about him?" Even though she had had an update on his status, she would have very much liked to know if they knew something more as well.

"You tell me," he said. The familiar friendliness in his voice started to slip away, as she had heard it happen several times now.

Even Evelyn stopped crying for a second to look at Walker. "Excuse me?" she muttered, though he didn't seem to hear her.

"I don't understand your question," said Steph. Which was, in part, the truth.

"Ms. Kim, do you have any reason to believe that George McKnight was present during yesterday's situation at Adler-Morrow General?"

Steph put on her best expression of baffling confusion. "I just told you I'm not even sure what happened after like five minutes. Why do you keep pushing this criminalizing agenda on–"

"I heard you calling his name," Walker interrupted.

And now Steph was, truly, terrified to speak.

"Wasn't it you who called out his name at the end of the attack, as he ran away from the scene, leaving the dead body of Earnest Erb lying on the ground behind the hospital?"

Evelyn gasped between her sobs. Steph remained silent, still trying to keep a neutral expression on her face. Though she couldn't see, she was sure she wasn't succeeding. "I don't know what you're talking about," she finally said.

"We have already talked to Mr. Gil one more time, and he assure's us with strong affirmation that he has no idea about anything related to George." It would be difficult to imagine Robert having any kind of knowledge about George's life even before he disappeared. "Yet he seems to appear everywhere something occurs regarding Peter Anderson and the disappearance of the residents of Adler, and now Morrow."

Walker gave Steph a moment to reply, but she didn't. Evelyn looked like she was trying to say something to her daughter, but couldn't find enough air to make up words.

Sergeant Walker sighed one last time and stood up from the chair. "I believe I can lay the feds off of you for a couple days before it gets serious," he said. He walked to the door and looked back at Steph. "I suggest you revise your statement with me before we get to that point."

Walker opened the door and got out of the room without closing it. From her bed she could see the hallway he was walking to, where his son was waiting for him. Scotch looked into the room and locked eyes with Steph for a second. In his expression she could see worry, but mostly doubt and skepticism. He used their brief moment of connection to mouth two words that Steph wasn't entirely sure if she got right.

Before she had time to think of it, her thoughts were interrupted by Roger and Stacy barging inside the room. Though she was happy to see them, her expression did not change, even as they both came closer to her to hug her. She could barely take her eyes off the spot where she saw Scotch. And inside her head she just kept replaying how she saw his mouth move, and rethinking the meaning of his wording.

"Text me."

Andrea, night?

Now she *had* to get up and out. She had, in fact, recognized the handwriting, and now she needed to know everything. She needed to get out of the room and find George. She looked down at the IV to see that it was installed in a movable pole, so she didn't have to remove the needle from her hand in order to walk out. Thank God for that.

With huge effort, she moved her legs to the edge of the mattress, using all of the strength in her body to do so. Her knees felt atrophied, nonexistent. She could feel the bruises below her pajama pants, burning with every inch she moved on the soft sheets. She managed to put her feet on the floor, and flinched violently, causing all of her lower half to hurt.

The floor felt so cold to the touch, and the soles of her feet – which she hadn't thought about until now – felt like they had been cut with sandpaper. Slowly, she put her right foot on the floor, letting the cold neutralize the burning feeling in her skin. She repeated it with her left foot, and then she had to stand up. She could only imagine how hard it was going to be to walk in her condition; just thinking about how her knees were going to creak made her cringe.

She held on to the IV pole and pulled herself up, but instantly let go and fell on her back on the bed. The effort she had made to lift her body put her back and shoulders to a lot of work, and now she felt she was paralyzed. Like the muscles in her back had all towered over each other and were pushing her spine against her organs.

She had to do what she didn't want to do. Thinking of ways of calling for help, she realized she hadn't spoken out loud yet, so she didn't know how her throat was going to feel. She guessed it would hurt, just like every other thing she had tried since she woke up. Pretty much anything she did hurt her, except for breathing. And blinking.

As quietly as possible, she tried to make sounds with her mouth. "Hello?" she said, almost inaudible to even herself. Still, the vibrations inside her throat felt like lashes against her larynx, so she needed to do something else. She looked around the dark room for something, and ended up holding her pole again. She looked up and down, and grabbed it with both hands.

Without much effort, she pushed it against the wall, making a sound audible enough for the whole room to vibrate. She was sure that this would be enough to call the attention of whoever was outside, and rightly so, seconds later there was a knock on the door. "Miss?" called a young woman's voice. "Miss, are you okay?"

Andrea didn't know how to respond. She could push the pole against the wall again, but that might alarm whoever was caring for her, and she didn't want that. She just wanted enough attention to get some answers. So, she opted to stay quiet.

"I'm going to come in, okay?" said the delicate female voice. The door opened slowly, letting a blinding light through. "Close your eyes, please," said the voice, and so Andrea did. Even with here eyes closed, she could see a burning red coming through her eyelids. She felt a presence standing right in front of her. "I'm going to put on sunglasses on you," said the voice, now much clearer. Andrea could identify a Southern accent.

Andrea nodded, and so she felt the skinny, cold fingers of the young woman touch her face as she put on the sunglasses. As Andrea stopped seeing the red in her eyelids, she opened her eyes to see a skinny black woman, not much older than her.

"Your eyes are very fragile right now," said the woman. "You need protection from the light until you get used to it. Do you need to get up?" Andrea was still thinking about what had just been said. How long had she been captive in the dark that she developed night vision? "Miss?" insisted the woman. Andrea snapped out of her thoughts and nodded.

The woman grabbed Andrea below her shoulders and raised her up as she grabbed the IV pole, making her back crack and shoulders to tense up. The woman, for her size, was extraordinarily strong, being able to carry Andrea all the way to the door, where there was a wheelchair she had not seen earlier. She sat on the wheelchair and cringed in pain.

"I'm sorry, miss," said the woman. "It's going to be hard for about a couple days or so. But you'll get through it."

Andrea's thoughts were racing. She was awake and now had a mode of transportation. She had to decide what to do next, who to see. She looked at the woman and tapped her own wrist, sure that it would be understood that she was asking for the time.

"It's past 10pm, miss," said the woman. "You've been sleeping for a very long time."

Late at night, so George was probably asleep by then. What could she do about that? She didn't want to disturb anyone, but she was so confused. For all she knew, she could be inside a secret government base and George's letter was forged by an expert.

"Would you like me to get you some pen and paper?" asked the woman. Andrea nodded too harshly for her condition, and felt her neck tense up again. "Stay here. I'll be right back."

The nurse left Andrea sitting there, waiting. She put her hands on the wheels and attempted to push the chair forwards, but her arms weren't strong enough for even that. So she just sat there and waited, until she heard a door opening very softly.

"Ms. Rose?" called out a male voice. An adult male voice Andrea was unfamiliar with. She clenched her fists to the chair and flipped the light switch, making the room go dark again, though the lights from the hallway were still on and would still hurt her eyes very much.

Soft steps approached from the right end of the hallway, making Andrea panic on the inside. She couldn't – and wouldn't – scream, but she was also trying to convince herself that there was nothing to fear. She had just read from George and the nurse seemed friendly enough. Then again… government agency.

"Is that you, Andrea?" asked the stranger's voice. Andrea couldn't help but gasp, making her throat burn with the cold air she breathed in. The steps got closer until she saw, through the sunglasses, the man who had that voice. A tall man in his late 30s, maybe, with long blonde hair in a ponytail, wearing a tank top and what looked like gym pants. His body was bruised and filled with cuts all over. He looked at her and smiled. "Hi. I'm Taylor."

Chapter 20
His Third Funeral

George, April 17th, evening

I could barely remember anything from the day before. After Elijah was gone, I fell asleep against a tree and knew nothing more of the wolves or Jason or anything. When we arrived back at Foxworth, it felt like everybody just collapsed. There was no exchange of words between anybody, just a group of tired men arriving at a safe house and each going into their room. Mr. Foxworth had arranged for a mortuary vehicle to take Elijah with us, and he would remain safe until whenever we were prepared for a proper burial.

Apart from my shoulder almost killing me, I just felt extremely embarrassed. I couldn't see Mr. Foxworth in the eye, nor could I even scan the faces of our protectors, even though I didn't even remember how the two suited men looked the night before. It was the heaviest of weights, pulling me down from my neck into the ground. The wolves were hurt, Elijah was dead, and I felt completely useless.

The only thing that kept me from wanting to escape was the fact that we had finally found Andrea. Every time I remembered she was there with us, I forgot about everything else, at least for a moment. She looked so broken, bruised all over, and very skinny. When the nurses – which I still don't know where they came from or where they were staying – took her, I felt they were going to pop her arms out of her joints.

The other person they found was in much more critical condition. The officer that disappeared like a week before we did, that all town had heard about. Alan Maffei. He was in such a bad state, he didn't even seem to be breathing most of the time, nor did he have the brief moments of consciousness that Andrea went through once in a while. He was just there, in a coma.

Even through the incredible pain in my shoulder, I managed to dodge Mr. Foxworth all the way to my room, where I laid down face down on my bed and did nothing for an hour. I just stared at the wall, thinking of everything that had happened. Of what Adler must have been going through then.

Before I fell asleep, however, there was a knock on my door. "Mr. McKnight?" called Ms. Rose. "They told me you were hurt. I need to treat you."

#

I woke up not knowing what day or time it was. The pain on my bandaged shoulder was killing me, and it took everything I had to get out of bed. I looked at the clock to see it was almost 10pm, meaning I had slept for about three hours.

I got out of my room to see the well-lit hallway completely empty. I turned to the main hall to find a silhouette sitting at the round table, seemingly reading. I approached the silhouette.

"Aren't you tired?" I asked, innocently enough. I knew I was.

"Not enough to not pay attention to this," said Taylor. Judging by his looks, it was evident that he had at least showered before sitting to read. He was reading one of the books I rushed through with Elijah, called *Nosferatu Eterna*. I didn't find it to be super useful next to *European Demons*.

"Studying without proper rest is like not studying at all," I said, not sure why. The atmosphere called for me to be many things, but sassy wasn't one of them. I guessed I just needed to fill the silence with something in order to not think about how I got Elijah killed.

"Go to bed, then," answered Taylor, not taking his eyes off the book. "You'll need to be rested so you can continue your own studies. And your shoulder has to heal quickly, too."

I hadn't even thought of that. Elijah and Andrea had been the only things in my mind, really. Never mind studying, much less training or healing. "I don't think I'll be able to sleep right now," I said, looking for some of Taylor's attention.

He wasn't exactly cold – leave that to Gray any day – but the usually optimistic and comprehensive blonde man I'd gotten used to didn't seem to be present either. "Why is that?" he said, still reading.

"I can't stop thinking about Andrea," I said, almost instantly. I didn't even think about my answer.

Taylor looked up at me this time. "She's in excellent care," he said. "They bathed her and dressed her in comfortable clothes and gave her some vitamins. She'll be fine."

"I know. It's not that. It's… you know. All of the crazy shit that's happened lately."

Taylor looked off of me for a second. "I'm sure she has a lot of things figured out already. Don't you think? After all, she was captured by the demons herself."

"I mean…" but he was right. She could probably tell us a lot more about everything that's been happening. How they operate, what they do with the hostages. Clarify our doubts and theories. "What do I do, then? I can't wake her up."

"I don't understand your urge, George," said Taylor.

"I– I don't know. I think I just want to talk to her right now. Not wait until she wakes up. I have so much to say."

"Why don't you write her a letter?" suggested Taylor. Sounded like a stupid idea to me.

"A letter? Telling her what? That I miss her and wish she were awake?"

Taylor put the book down and straightened his back on his chair. "George," he started, "I know you're smarter than this. Don't start blocking your feelings and thoughts just to be quick in your responses."

That was some Confucius-level stuff. But he was right. Totally right. "What should I tell her, then?"

#

I went to Andrea's room with the letter in hand, but Ms. Rose was standing by her door, keeping guard. "I just need to put this on her nightstand."

"I'm sorry, Mr. McKnight," said Ms. Rose, who now doubled as a nurse and a cook. These people never stopped surprising me. "She cannot be disturbed under any circumstances. And you need to wear your bandages or your arm will never stop hurting you." It was as if she was reading my mind, though it was probably just my facial expressions.

"It's just a letter I'm leaving beside her," I cried. "Please?"

Ms. Rose looked at the letter, then back at me. "You can give it to me and I can do it. But I can't let you in."

"Good enough," I said, partially satisfied. "No matter when, let me know when she wakes up, please."

Ms. Rose opened the door very slowly and entered the room in complete silence; it wouldn't have surprised me to find out she was also a trained assassin who could read code and speak Chinese. With the little light that shined inside her room, I could see part of Andrea's face.

She looked much healthier, though still very skinny. I wanted to hug her, tell her she was safe, but I couldn't. Not then, at least.

morning

The following day was a day of getting things done. I woke up obsessed with the idea of getting the symbol tattooed on me, even though the back of my right shoulder was very much in constant pain and would probably end up with a very nasty scar. Still, I was insistent in my request and Taylor got Mr. Foxworth's people to resolve.

It was still very strange how the house was run so smoothly by these mysterious people. With everything that had been happening I hadn't had time to think about it, but it was very bizarre. Cooks and cleaners that came and went without me even noticing, and some of them acted as nurses too, like Ms. Rose. The night I escaped I was almost stopped by two bodyguards who looked like members of the Secret Service, and I had not seen them again since I came back to Foxworth. If only I could see Mr. Foxworth in the eye and ask him, but I couldn't.

Taylor got one of the members of the help to mark me with what looked like a perfectly professional tattoo needle. I don't know where they got it, nor who this person was, but I had seen him walking around once or twice. "Mr. Pearson will do it for you," said Taylor as I walked into the kitchen, where there was a chair waiting for me to sit. This Mr. Pearson was an extremely muscular man of about 50, with tattoos all over his arms that were easily visible thanks to his tank top, including the same one he was going to draw on my shoulder. I wondered what a man with these characteristics was doing as part of the team who ran this house, but I didn't care enough to ask.

Taylor slowly removed the bandages that were covering the back of my right shoulder. I couldn't see, but I knew that my wound was not healing properly – partly because it had only been 2 days, and partly because I hadn't cared for it – and as the last layer of bandages were removed from my skin, I could feel the cold air of the room sliding through the gash. It did not feel well at all.

"Are you sure you want it on there?" asked Taylor. "I'm sure the other arm would work perfectly fine."

"Don't you all have it on your right shoulder?" I asked him.

"Yes."

"Then that's where I'm going to have it too."

Taylor didn't say anything else. I knew he wanted to argue about the permanence of my tattoo, about the pain I was going through to keep with a tradition that I may not end up being part of. But I didn't want to think about that. I wanted to do things right, whether they liked it or not.

"Go ahead, Mr. Pearson," said Taylor. I felt Pearson's giant hand grab my arm and clean my shoulder, not being particularly delicate about it. Something told me he wasn't exactly part of the nursing team.

Gray, April 18th, afternoon

The black wolf had not left his room ever since they got back, and it was driving him insane. He was grateful for the talented and efficient team of medics who tended to him, and he was sure that in a couple of days, everything would be back to normal. But he could not take another day of being a useless, worthless piece of meat, bedridden from his wounds from two nights before, unable to help his team with anything. The pain of his stab wounds wouldn't even allow him to read properly, as just raising his arms to hold the book to his face was very uncomfortable at best.

That afternoon, however, he had to stand up and see it for himself. With a makeshift cane he was given by the help, he left his room at a very slow pace and in terrible pain, walking towards the kitchen to witness the scene at hand. To see how Foxworth's Head of Security, Mr. Pearson, perforated the boy's skin with ink. The same shoulder where he had been ruptured twice now. The black wolf knew, for sure, that the boy was not aware of the next step after getting the physical mark.

After Pearson finished torturing the boy, Taylor proceeded to cover George's back wound with bandages, as the boy's breathing stabilized after minutes of grunting and cringing and a couple of cries. "Who's doing the marking?" asked Gray, knowing full well that Taylor would have wanted to.

"Makes sense it would be me," answered the blonde wolf. Almost without any sound, the couple people who were accompanying Pearson disappeared from sight, leaving only the wolves and the boy to talk.

"What are you talking about?" asked George. He seemed to be a bit confounded from the pain.

"You really thought a simple mark on your skin would be enough to protect you from black conjures? I was starting to think you were smarter than that."

George was clearly not in the mood to take Gray's words without reply, but he seemed physically unable to. "Michael," started Taylor.

"Go ahead then," added Alex as he walked in the kitchen. He had been walking around town, getting some air and keeping watch. Walking as a human, with layers of clothes and winter boots. "Mark the boy so that, when he decides to escape again, at least he can keep his posture."

That was enough to make George stand up from the chair and ignore his pain. Gray saw the boy's shirtless body as he stood up and noticed how much he had changed since the first time he had been attacked. Not only his attitude, but he had also gained a significant amount of musculature, even though he had been training for very little time. His new eating habits and lack of leisure time were probably to blame.

"Calm down," said Taylor, pushing George down by his left shoulder. "If you don't rest, you'll never feel well enough to continue fighting."

"Continue fighting?" asked Alex, not mockingly but almost insulted. "I don't understand what nonsense you're talking about. You were there the last time he was included."

"That's why we're going to mark him," answered Taylor, still calm. "Now that won't happen again."

"I just heard you guys talking," said Alex. "He wasn't even aware that a spell had to be applied on him. This is ridiculous."

"I haven't had time to read," said George, at a very low volume. Though it was clearly because of lack of energy and not intentions of not being heard, all of the wolves heard him clearly anyway.

"Of course you haven't," continued Alex. "You would've had two whole days of studying and *training* if it wasn't for your arrogant sense of self-importance."

Even though Gray had not been very fond of the boy's recent actions, it was never his intention to scold him to the point of making him feel miserable. In his eyes, he wanted to guide him into a better path by pointing out the flaws in his logic and preparation, something he thought Taylor and Elijah did not do enough.

"Alex," started Gray. The boy was still standing and now getting closer to the brown wolf. His face looked red and puffy.

"No, Michael," said Alex, turning to Gray. "I'm tired of all of you trying to protect this kid as if he is some kind of secret weapon that we have to nurture." Alex turned back to George, who was now at spitting distance of him.

Though the boy wasn't short in stature, he paled in comparison to Alex's 6'2"

Without any warning, George gathered impulse with his torso and smashed his head against Alex's chest, taking him by surprise and making him recoil. None of the wolves expected this reaction nor did they know what to do. Almost instinctively, Alex launched himself towards the boy and slammed him against the kitchen wall.

With his right hand, the brown wolf grabbed the boy's throat and lifted him against the wall. Blood from his open back wound now sprayed all over. "How dare you?" asked Alex. Astonished. Insulted.

Taylor tried to push Alex away from the boy but it was of no use. "Stop it!" yelled Taylor. "You'll kill him!"

"He's better off dead than being such a waste of resources," said Alex, with a rage in his voice that only Gray had seen before, in very different circumstances. His eyes were red and his mouth was salivating with anger.

Somehow, in whatever much pain George was in at the moment and with his throat being pushed in, he managed to spit on Alex's face. "Fuck you," he muttered.

The wolves wouldn't find out whatever Alex was planning on responding, because everything came to a halt with a single, potent, imposing scream from the kitchen door. "Enough," resounded all over the house, vibrating on everyone's chests. Mr. Foxworth was standing there, right next to Drake, holding his cane in front of him, back straight and unchallengeable.

Alex let go of George's neck the moment he turned to see Mr. Foxworth. George fell on the floor and Taylor tended to him, particularly his back. Gray looked as Alex composed himself into a normal human being, but didn't say anything himself. He looked at Drake, but was clearly in shock.

"Embarrassing," added Foxworth. "Taylor, please help George back to his room so he can be tended properly." Taylor put George over his shoulders and carried him out of the kitchen, blood dripping from his back. The boy seemed to be almost unconscious. "Drake," continued Foxworth, just turning his head a bit to his right where the red wolf was standing, "tell Father Hanover that they'll need to wait a bit longer for us. That we're sorry to keep them for so long."

"Will do," said Drake. And so he left.

Foxworth looked at the elder wolves. "Michael," he said, after a brief silence. "You should not be out of bed."

"I needed to see if everything was going well with George's marking," answered the black wolf. "Besides, we have a funeral to go to."

"Go get dressed, then," replied the old man, almost tired of even having to reply to any answer he was given. It felt very strange for Gray to take orders or follow directions from someone who was, technically, younger than him and with no relevant strength that he didn't posses – other than money, that is.

Without saying anything out loud, Gray grabbed his own cane and walked back to his room, feeling every single step in his abdomen. This pain he had forgotten about for the duration of the kitchen confrontation, which made him think that maybe, in times of crisis, he would be able to give it his all without worrying about his physical state.

Though he did go into his room and started to change his clothes – as quickly as his abdominal discomfort would allow him – he could still hear whatever was being said in the kitchen. And judging by what Foxworth was saying, he knew that perfectly well.

"I am not here to ask you for an explanation," started Foxworth.

"Good. Because I do not owe you one," answered Alex. He was usually one to keep a very polite tone, and Gray had never heard him speak like that to Mr. Foxworth before. But even in the air, Gray could smell how angry Alex was.

"What you owe me is a minimal amount of respect, seeing that you are in my house. Wearing my clothes. Eating my food and sleeping on my bed. All free of charge, I might add."

"I'll leave if you want, Mr. Foxworth. Just say the word."

"I swear to God, Alexander. Sometimes I can't fathom the fact that you're actually older than me."

Silence.

"What do you get from assaulting the boy? You could at least answer that."

"It was a fit of rage, Mr. Foxworth. I won't happen again."

"That is not enough, Alexander. Ever since he got here you have belittled and scolded this boy to the ground. A breakable promise won't be enough for him or for me."

"I don't understand any of you. Why do you care so much? What has that boy done for us that makes him so important? Is there something I haven't been told?"

"There is nothing particularly special about George McKnight. You know that."

"Then why do you treat him like he's so God damn important?"

"Because, when he grows up to be a responsible, hard-working man, I don't want him to be bitter and angry at the world, like you are."

Gray had to stop dressing to take in what he had just heard. Alex was probably just as shocked as him.

"Have you ever stopped to think about how similar the two of you are? And him and Michael, even more."

At the sound of his name, Gray snapped out of his shock and finish dressing. He was only missing his shoes and his belt.

"I've told all of you since the beginning that this is not George's fault. Taylor and I agree that he was actually behaved extremely well, considering the circumstances.

The difference between him and Michael is that Michael at least had you suffering by his side."

The rage came back to Alex's voice. "You cannot possibly compare what Michael and I have been through with the two inconvenient weeks that boy has had."

"Why not? What qualifies you to be the almighty sayer of what real suffering is?"

"I find that question very insulting, Mr. Foxworth."

"That boy has gone through so much, you can't even imagine. He lost his father when he was seven, his mother at sixteen, almost starved himself to death afterwards, and now he feels solely responsible for the death of his mentor. He doesn't have a real home to go back to, nor an adult he can really rely on for emotional support. He worries that he's not doing enough to save his friends, and I'm sure he feels guilty about having escaped John's grasp when they didn't. Or is that not enough suffering for you?"

Both Alex and Gray had stopped breathing for a moment. Neither of them knew about George's parents, though something told Gray that Elijah did. He could only imagine how Foxworth had found out.

The old man continued. "Ever since he got back, that smart, sweet boy has been absolutely ashamed of looking me in the eye. And now he is to dress up and go outside for his third funeral in ten years. That is not a common number for children in this day and age, mind you. And it's usually for people closer to my age."

Gray finished dressing and walked back to the kitchen. Foxworth didn't seem to care for his presence, for he probably knew that Gray had been listening to everything.

"Both of you have been so hard on him," said Foxworth. "You treat him like a dog," he said, pointing at Gray. "And you," now he pointed at Alex, "treat him like the biggest hindrance. I am ashamed of both of you."

And with nothing more to say, Mr. Foxworth walked away from the kitchen.

George, April 18th, afternoon

Taylor sat me on my bed and helped me put on the dress shirt Mr. Foxworth had gotten for me. We could both see how it was stained with blood and black ink from my shoulder, but both decided to ignore it.

"Would you like to talk about–" started Taylor.

"No," I said. I truly did not, and he complied to my wishes without any reply.

Taylor helped me finish dressing up with a black suit and tie, black dress socks and black shoes, all looking brand new. The only thing that could've been improved was my face; my tired, bruised, tortured face. But that was not gonna change any time soon, so there was no point in trying.

"Marking can be quite painful, so I think it best to wait for the morning so you can rest and the tattoo can set."

I didn't say anything. It sounded good enough for me, and I did not feel in the position to discuss anything about the subject.

"Ready?" he asked me.

"As much as I could be," I answered, truly meaning every word.

#

Taylor helped me walk out of the room, through the hallway, and up the stairs until we went outside. I was still not used to seeing the outside of that house, and in the soft light of dusk, it looked almost unrecognizable from the shack I'd ran away from just a couple days prior.

We turned around the corner of the house to the backyard, just a couple dozen feet from the forest. There I saw everybody whom I knew lived in the house, plus a couple more people. Ms. Rose, Mr. Pearson, a couple other employees I didn't know, and a priest. An actual priest wearing robes and awaiting for Taylor and me.

In front of the priest was a deep rectangular hole, and beside it was a reddish mahogany casket. Around the people were lit torches that gave the blueish atmosphere a bit of yellow around the edges, though the sun had not set just yet.

Taylor walked me towards the middle of the group, where the other wolves were. I stood in front of Taylor, eclipsed by his great height.

"We are gathered here today in remembrance of our lost brother, Elijah Carmellius Pickford," started the priest.

I couldn't concentrate after I heard Elijah's full name out loud.

I noticed I had never asked him about his middle name or even his last name. Elijah Pickford sounded alright, I guess. But "Carmellius" had to be made up, either by himself as an adult or... I don't know. Maybe his parents liked the way it sounded? Or maybe he gave it to himself as a way of hiding his identity? I couldn't even think of Elijah having parents. Or a life before The Hunt. How inconsiderate of me to have never asked or even wondered.

I snapped back into reality as the four wolves moved out of their places. I stopped myself from asking Taylor where he was going, but Mr. Foxworth grabbed me by my good shoulder and pulled me slightly to him. I turned to see his face as he held me in place to give space for the wolves to move, and he looked back. His eyes were glossy with tears and his face showed nothing but pain. I can't even imagine how he must've felt on the inside.

I stood next to Mr. Foxworth as the four wolves grabbed what looked like ribbons from under the casket, each by a corner of the rectangle. In a single motion, they raised the casket up and put it over the hole, and slowly lowered it into the ground.

Taylor and Gray looked very sad, evidently hurting at the loss of their friend. Drake, on the other hand, looked sad in a different way, almost like tired or disappointed. Alex kept a mostly neutral expression, though it was evident that it was not pleasant for him to be lowering Elijah's casket into the ground. And, soon enough, there was nothing left to be lowered, so Mr. Pearson approached the wolves and started shoving dirt into the hole with a shovel. I hadn't even noticed he was holding a shovel when we walked into the backyard.

The wolves went back to their places as we all waited for Mr. Pearson to finish the burial and for the priest to stop whatever he was saying. I wasn't listening. I was stuck on the tombstone that lied against the back wall of the house, ready to be set by the grave after we were all gone. From where I was standing I could read what was carved into it:

Elijah Carmellius Pickford

October 13th 1986 - April 17th 2019

Beloved son, brother,

and mentor

He was a Libra. Just like me.

#

I specifically asked Taylor to leave me alone after we got back inside the house. I told him I could take care of myself for the night and that he should go rest. Because, honestly, I really thought he should have. I always felt he was closest to Elijah, and he was also the only one of the wolves who saw him get bit. Maybe he even blamed himself for keeping Jason alive ten seconds too long.

Anyway, I asked him to leave me be and so I was alone when I heard a knock on my door.

I was trying to put on my night shirt, but my shoulder was giving me a very hard time. "Yes?" I called to the door.

"It's me," said Drake. "Can I come in?"

"One second," I answered. With my dress pants still on, I opted to just finish putting on my night shirt and open the door. So I did.

"I need to talk to you," said Drake, coming in before I told him he could.

"Alright," I said, closing the door.

Drake looked, dare I say, nervous, which made me feel a bit uneasy. He was supposed to be the chill guy of the group. "I haven't talked to him about this, but I'm sure Gray would not want me to tell you. But I think it would be very cruel and unfair not to."

"Tell me what?"

Drake took a deep breath. "We stayed with your friend Stephanie back at the hospital for a while."

And then I just felt as stupid as I ever had. Everything happening with Elijah and Andrea and now Alex made me completely forget about Steph at the hospital. How she recognized me and called me from the top floor. How she probably saw me on top of that dying man. God, did I feel stupid.

As I analyzed what he had just said, my mood went from baffled to confused. "You were with her? How? Why?"

"I'll save the details for later," he said. He looked like he was in a hurry to leave. "She asked me to tell you that you guys need to talk."

I stayed in silence for a moment, thinking about what he just said. Honestly, thinking about everything he was saying. Imagining Steph and Drake interacting in real life just felt and sounded surreal. "Talk about what?" I finally asked.

"She wouldn't say. She asked me to take you to her." This hit me like a shotgun blast to the chest.

In my revolted head, the first thing that felt natural was to complain, for some reason. "And you waited all this time to tell me?" I asked, moderately angry, not thinking very well. "How is she? Why was she at the hospital? Did she see anything? Where is she now?"

"Calm down, man," the said, grabbing me by the shoulders, making me cry in pain at the touch of his fingers on my open wound. "Shit. Sorry," he said, but moved on quickly. "She wanted me to take you to her so you guys can talk. She didn't say what about, but she trusted me."

"Are you sure it was her?" is the second thing that occurred to me to ask. Stupid asshole.

"Asian girl called Stephanie, about your age. Knows your name and recognized you from afar. Pretty sure it's her, right?"

That was her alright.

"Let's go," Drake added to my silence.

"Now?"

"Why not? You can ride on top of me and we'll be there in no time. We'll be back before morning."

I don't know why this sounded like the worst idea in the Universe to me. It would be risky with the authorities looking for me, but that wasn't even it. I think, deep inside, I just thought it wasn't true that she had said that.

"What if we're caught?" I added. "By the Police or the FBI. Or maybe one of *them*."

"Here," he said, reaching for his pocket and tossing the necklace with the strange symbol at me. "You're not marked yet, but that'll me enough for now."

I took a look at the necklace and analyzed the situation. Going out at night again, without Elijah and most of the wolves. "Did you tell anybody about this?"

"Mr. Foxworth and I talked about it before the burial," said Drake. "He approves."

"Really?" I was legitimately surprised.

"We are wasting time," insisted Drake. "I would go myself and ask her what she wants to say to you but I don't know her address. And I'm not sure if she'd talk to me about all that."

I looked down at the necklace again. I imagined Steph at the hospital, alone and scared, wondering what the hell was happening with the crows and the noise and the lights. Wondering what went through her head the moment she saw me and decided to call my name. Did she feel betrayed or relieved? Did she think I did something to that man? Or that I was part of this whole thing from the beginning? This was my chance to find out.

"Let's go."

Chapter 21
Reunion
George, April 18th, night

Riding a giant wolf is weird. Like, really weird. It's not like riding a horse, which is considerably larger than a regular human and feels like a well-oiled machine even with all of your weight on it. Riding a giant wolf feels holding onto a giant teddy bear attached to a wakeboard at max speed. If that even makes sense.

Drake didn't seem to mind my weight at all, nor the weight of everything I had on me: a heavy jacket, a sheathed sword, a pouch with a handgun and bullets, aside from the small bag he asked me to hold for him. I found it very impressive how he was able to run with me on top of him and talk at the same time, almost as if he had two mouths.

He told me everything he'd seen at the hospital. From the hypnotized people to the clouds of crows rounding everybody up. How he found Gray and Steph hiding in the top floor, Gray bleeding to death from a double stab.

As we got closer to the edge of town, more and more activity was audible. Considering it was past curfew, that was very strange to me. And Adler was never exactly a night town either. Besides, that freaking cold that cut through my nostrils with every step Drake took, even though I'd put on full-on Elijah-style clothing, but black instead of red.

"I'm not from around here," said Drake, "but isn't it weird that there are so many people out at this time?"

"Yes," I answered. "What are you hearing?"

Drake stopped for a second and focused on the ambient. "Lots of patrols. On foot around the forest. A couple of cars riding around nearby."

"Nothing not to be expected, I guess," I added, trying to actively cut the tension off my chest. It didn't work a bit.

I got off Drake's back and we walked about a quarter mile together, him still in wolf form. He had not bothered bringing any kind of clothes to change, so I didn't assume he planned on destransforming. After a bit more walking, it started to get difficult to determine where the noises where coming from. "I have an idea," started Drake. "But you're not gonna like it."

After half a minute of convincing, Drake turned into a hybrid and grabbed me whole. He proceeded to climb up a tree and jump around on the high trunks, giving us more vision and keeping us off reach from the authorities. I can't say it felt very good on my shoulder, but I was honestly sick of complaining about it.

Every jump Drake made from tree to tree felt like being thrusted by a bull. I had to focus on my thoughts in order not to break into a cry of pain. "*Andrea is safe. Steph is near. You'll be okay*," I kept repeating to myself.

We got to the edge of town and saw a huge police van driving by, very slowly. Judging by what I recognized from the streets, I figured we were about five or six blocks from Steph's place, but it wasn't easy to identify with certainty.

Adler's streets had changed. What used to be a small and boring Midwestern town was a couple tire fires away from looking like a scene off a bad zombie movie. The streets were completely deserted except for a mix of cops and FBI agents, some walking around, some guarding entrances to the town from the forest. But what really bothered me were the couple of dogs that I saw hanging out with one group of agents at a barricade near where we were.

"Shit," I muttered.

"What?" asked Drake.

"The dog."

Drake looked on nonchalantly, noticing the German Shepard not fifty feet from us. "Have you ever seen a fox take on a bear?" he asked me, almost chuckling.

Drake got down from the tree and left me on the ground, signaling me to stay. He proceeded to walk on four feet, still as a hybrid, approaching the general area where the dog would be able to see him. It was very dark outside, so it was hardly a worry that the guards would notice him at a glance.

Drake started growling like I'd never heard him before. It was the kind of growl that wild animals use to threaten trespassers and such, not something a wolf man would do naturally. From my spot I could see how he had called the dog's attention, and I thought I could distinguish how scared it had gotten, even alarming the guards beside it.

The guards talked among themselves a bit and one of them took the dog away as it trembled and tried to clench to its master's leg. From afar, Drake signaled me to approach him and so I did, with traces of a smile on my face. "Had to show her what a real dog sounds like," said Drake.

With the dog out of the way, I felt comfortable enough with Drake jumping from a tree onto the backyard of a nearby house, for which he waited for another police van to pass so it would cover the thump of our weights falling from so high up. After that was over, it was just a matter of guiding him through the streets of Adler until we reached Steph's house.

After five blocks of turning and backtracking through other houses, I finally saw the outside of Steph's house. The house that had given me asylum so many times before, with its clean brown roof and the red-framed windows that I had climbed in and out of so many times when I ran away from Robert.

Now it was there in front of me, but it felt like a completely different house. Like a house I wasn't welcome in, filled with people that I didn't know. I don't know why, because nothing had happened between me and Steph to justify that way of thinking. I guess it was the anxiety of seeing her after so much had changed. Maybe they would be the ones who didn't know me.

All the lights were off except for Steph's. From the backyard I could see her room lit up and her walking around, which seemed strange to me. Steph usually paces around like that when she's talking about something important or difficult to comprehend.

"What now?" asked Drake. I was thinking the same thing. Climbing and knocking on the window would probably cause her a heart attack, or make her scream so loudly she would wake up half the block and we would have to run away.

So I leaned down and grabbed a rock from the yard we were standing on, and threw it to her window. I saw her silhouette stop moving.

Steph, April 18th, night

After being discharged and going back home, Stephanie did not leave her room for hours. She locked her door and laid on her bed, and cried every tear she had held since she was told about her father's disappearance. She

400

felt sorry for her mom, having to deal with the same thing plus taking care of Charlie and grandma, but Steph needed a break. She couldn't be strong enough for four people at that moment. She needed a rest, and so she fell asleep as she cried against her pillow.

She woke up with the lights on after an undetermined amount of time. She turned to see she had a text from a couple hours ago, from an unknown number. "It's Scotch. We need to talk."

So she had actually understood the mouthed words at the hospital. "Selfie holding up four fingers," she texted back, not taking any chances. She had actually thought of that back at the hospital, before she lost control of her emotions.

Not a minute passed when she received another text from the number. It was a self-taken picture of Scotch, holding up all fingers but his thumb in his right hand. He later sent, "It's important."

Steph took a moment to think. But there was not much more time than that. "Ok," she sent.

She barely had time to wash her face and make her bed when she heard her phone buzzing on top of her nightstand. "Here," sent Scotch.

"Backyard. First room to the right."

There was a very large tree in the backyard of the Kim residence. Through the years it had been used by Stephanie and her friends to climb up and down her bedroom window without her parents noticing. After the children grew up enough to not be silent anymore, they naturally stopped using this method for entering in and out of the house, partially because there was really no need.

Steph opened her window and saw Scotch wearing a black hoodie and blue jeans. His dark skin combined with his clothing and the dead of night made look almost like a ghost that was climbing up the tree to her window. As she saw him struggle to climb, it was clear why he volunteered to referee instead of playing.

Scotch got to the branch closest to Steph's window and she took a step back to allow him to hop in. She ended up having to pull him in by the arm so that he didn't fall off the edge.

The tall black teen shook some leaves off his hoodie as Stephanie closed the window behind him. "People are sleeping," she whispered.

"I'm aware," he said. "I apologize for the disturbance."

Though they weren't exactly friends, Steph had always liked Scotch, from a distance. He was one of the nicest from his class, never seemed to get in trouble. And that extra-formal way of speaking he had was always mildly interesting to hear, especially with his deep, soothing voice.

"Stephanie, I have so many questions to ask you," he started.

Steph held up her right index. "Take off the hoodie," she said.

Scotch flinched. "Excuse me?"

"Take off your hoodie and empty all of your pockets," said Steph continued. "I need to know why you're here."

"I'm here because I want to help you," said Scotch, trying not to sound offended.

"And I won't let you help me if I don't trust you. The quicker you comply, the easier it'll be for me."

Scotch looked at Stephanie's eyes, and she did not budge. She had cried all that she had to cry earlier, and she was ready to be productive again. And the first thing she was doing is stop taking chances with anybody.

Scotch unzipped his hoodie and let it fall to the floor. "Better?" he said, showing his open hands.

Steph grabbed the hoodie and inspected it for any objects attached to it or inside its pockets, but there weren't any. She patted, without permission, Scotch's arms, chest and pants, making him feel visibly uncomfortable, but collaborative nonetheless.

"Phone," demanded Steph, though she didn't wait for Scotch to reach for it in his pocket. She just took it out and turned it off.

"Stephanie, there's not much time," insisted Scotch.

"Okay, dammit," she spat out. "Why are you here?"

"I need to ask you some questions."

Steph felt taken aback by how uncannily he resembled his father at that moment. "Your dad already asked me a lot of questions, and I told him everything I could."

"I don't think he asked the right kind of questions," he answered, keeping his polite tone intact. "Like, how are you feeling?"

Coming from literally anybody else, that would've sounded like either the lamest attempt at charming her or a low-key mock of her situation. But coming from Scotch, somehow, it felt genuine. "Been better," she said. "But that's not important right now."

"It is. Basic psychology dictates that the mental state of the person in question will undoubtedly affect the way they respond to different kinds of stress."

"And your point is?"

"My point is that my father has been pressured by the FBI into insanity, and I don't think he could ever get anything from you until he rests. So I decided to try for myself."

Steph couldn't help but scoff. "Bullshit," she said. "You wouldn't come all the way here just to repeat the same questions your dad already asked me." Steph turned back to the window and opened it. "You have thirty seconds or I'll scream," she said.

Scotch sighed. "Okay, I'm sorry."

"Twenty five," she replied.

"Okay okay." Scotch took a deep breath. "My father didn't have time to piece together the series of events that lead to what he ultimately saw and heard at the end of the assault at Adler-Morrow."

"Assault?" asked Steph, though Scotch ignored her.

"But I did some digging through his notes and found out that you were outside your room, surrounded by shattered glass, with foreign blood all over the walls. First I wanted to warn you that they're ready to come tomorrow and bombard you with questions."

"Thanks, I guess," she said, closing the window.

"Second, I need to ask you how you got to that spot in the hallway. That's one of the things they're going to ask tomorrow."

"How do you know all this?"

"Your answers are way more relevant." Scotch made it impossible to forget that he was aiming for Harvard Law, and had been since he was a child.

"Why does it matter how I got there?"

"Because it can help my father understand your roll in all of this. Clear your name of suspicion."

"Suspicion? Of what?"

"Stephanie," Scotch started, getting closer to her. "I know you know they're trying to prove George has something to do with all of this."

"Which he *doesn't*," she emphasized.

"And I believe you, but they don't. And your insistence is making them think that you may have a part in it as well. Somehow."

"That's ridiculous!" she exclaimed, way louder than it was appropriate at the moment.

"Yet, you have no answers," said Scotch, still keeping his cool. "I'm trying to help you so you don't go down."

"But you're willing to let George go down?" Her eyes started to gloss.

"I didn't say that," said Scotch, almost inaudible under Steph's words.

"It's a misunderstanding and I–" but she stopped on her tracks as she spoke, because there was a sound behind her. A little thump on her window that told her everything that was about to happen. She was that familiar with that method of communication.

George, April 18th, night

It felt like slow-mo how she stopped, turned, and opened the window. I was so nervous for her to see me, I was trembling. In the outside cold I started to sweat and my throat slowly closed as I gasped for air, worse than any time I tried to talk to Andrea or ask something of my mom. This could all end in ways I maybe had not thought about, and it was eating me on the inside.

She opened the window but the light from her room didn't let me see her face as she looked at me, just a black silhouette against the backlight. Yet, somehow, I felt that she gasped, though I didn't hear anything.

Drake stood next to me, still in wolf form, waiting for something to happen. After what felt like a season but was probably about fifteen seconds, she spoke. "Come up the tree," she said. Knowing she could actually see me, I nodded, handed Drake everything but my clothes, and proceeded to go up the familiar tree I had climbed so many times before.

As I moved up the tree, I recalled the past times I'd done it. I remembered the time Robert and I had the level 5 fight, when I actually came to sleep over at Steph's without Evelyn noticing. Or the time a couple days after my mom's hospitalization, when I could not bare to be anywhere near my house. Or any time I felt sad and Steph offered me sanctuary. One way or another, climbing the tree felt like the preliminary phase of being received into her arms. To feeling safe, at least for a moment.

It was harder to climb the tree this time. Not only was my shoulder still stinging and probably bleeding again, but I also felt a huge weight in my chest. Of everything we had to talk, that I had to tell her. Everything I'd been wondering she wanted to tell me.

I got to the branch closest to her window and I could finally distinguish her face. It was evident she had been crying, but not for a bit. And right at that moment, she just looked absolutely joyful. I barely had time to step inside her room when she pulled me in and hugged me with a force she'd never hugged me before, not even after my mom died. She held me tightly and rested her face on my chest, and started to cry. I closed my eyes and took her in, letting her cry on, just feeling the brief moment of pure emotion before the storm.

When I opened my eyes, however, is when I felt the most confused. I almost jumped in surprise. "Scotch?" I asked out loud. He was sitting on her bed, smiling at us.

"Hi," he said, awkwardly.

Steph let go of me and turned to see him. "He's here to help," she said, though I wasn't sure to whom.

Scotch stood up from the bed and extended his arm to me. "It's good to see you're okay, George." I reluctantly shook his hand.

"Is that Drake?" asked Steph, looking out the window and down into the yard.

"Yes. He brought me here."

Scotch walked to the window and looked out. "That is a very big wolf," he pointed out, probably just for himself.

"It's dangerous for both of us for me to be here," I told her. "Drake said you needed to talk to me."

Steph started crying again and hugged me once more. "I'm so happy you're okay," she sniffed.

"I am," I said, giving her head a quick kiss. "But we need to hurry. We need to go back as soon as possible."

"Okay, okay. I'm sorry," she hasted. "So much has happened since yesterday, I just needed to ask about yourself."

"What do you mean?" I asked. Seeing Scotch had really thrown me off, and now my expectations were being defiled with Steph's reaction.

"The Police are rounding up on you as an important accomplice in the kidnapping," Scotch barged in.

"What!?" I exclaimed. Steph signaled me to keep my voice down. "That's ridiculous," I added, at a lower volume.

"I agree," said Scotch. "But they have a lot of evidence that points to you."

"Whatever it is, it's bullshit," I continued. "They have no idea about anything that's happening."

"Then explain it to me," said Scotch. "Explain to me how is it that you had nothing to do with Earnest Erb's death."

"So you don't believe me?" I asked, getting hot in the face.

"George," said Steph, calming me down. "We both believe you. But we have questions. We don't know what's been happening with you, where you've been. I trust you with whatever it is you have to say, but please, tell me."

I looked into Steph's eyes, feeling her confusion and desperation. I could only imagine what it must've been like to be at that hospital without knowing who all those strange people were. If it had been her who was kidnapped and I had had to live my life without knowing if she was okay, I would've lost my mind.

"Okay," I started. "Hear me out."

Andrea, April 18th, night

The conversation – or lecture, as she could not speak – that was had between Taylor and Andrea was fairly similar to the one he'd had with George at the beginning of everything. Or so he said. She had given him permission to enter her room and sit on the desk chair while she went back to bed, already exhausted from the little she'd done since waking up.

"I'm sure you have countless other questions," said Taylor. "When you are able to speak, I promise to answer them all to the best of my abilities. Sound good?"

Andrea nodded. Optimistic, but careful. She still wasn't 100% convinced that all of this wasn't a trick. She had to see George first, then she would believe it. But it added up, it made sense. And it was far easier for her to digest it after the terrible weeks she had been through up until then.

She wanted to tell them so much, about everything. About being shut in, half-conscious in a cocoon for hours on end, without any light coming in. How it felt to be sucked out of life every minute of her existence without even knowing why or by whom. Feeling that there was somebody inside your head at all times, not only knowing what you thought but partially influencing it as well. Planting ideas in your head, making you think they were your own. Making you want to do things out of the blue.

Ms. Rose knocked on the closed door. Though they were inside her bedroom, Andrea had decided to keep the lights on for Taylor's sake, so she remained with her sunglasses on, no matter how stupid it made her feel. "Mr. Kaminsky," called Ms. Rose. "I'm coming in."

Ms. Rose slowly opened the door, looking in Andrea's general direction, probably checking to see if she was wearing her sunglasses. "What time is it, Ms. Rose?" asked Taylor.

"That's why I'm here," she answered. "It's been over an hour now. Ms. Andrea needs to rest."

Taylor looked back at Andrea, who didn't know what to do. It's not like she wanted him to leave, but she was, in fact, exhausted. But she was safe now, and they could resume their conversation in the morning. Maybe, even, including George into the mix.

"I'm sorry to have kept you awake," smiled Taylor at Andrea as he stood up from the chair. "Go back to sleep and I'll see you tomorrow. Okay?" Andrea nodded, with as much excitement as her body allowed her.

Taylor walked out of the room. "I'm turning the lights off now, miss," said Ms. Rose. Andrea nodded again, and so the lights went out and the door was closed.

Without her even noticing, she took off her sunglasses and laid down on her amazingly comfortable, soft, cold pillow, and fell asleep instantly.

George, April 18th, night

I told them as much as I could without getting into much detail, mainly skipping the supernatural aspects of it, giving it more of a "secret society" feel to it. I looked mostly to Steph, who had already experienced what it was to see and hear talking wolves, and surely notice their absence in my story. I wasn't at all sure if anything was making sense to Scotch, who was there mainly because of good faith and nothing else, but he didn't seem to be taking my word any less seriously than before I mixed in talking wolves into the conversation. I almost teared up when bringing up Elijah, but I kept my tone until the end, which brought me where I was at that moment.

"Everything they have on you makes a lot more sense now," said Scotch. "Which is why I came here to see Stephanie. I needed some holes filled in, and now you've done it."

"What is it that they think of me, exactly?" I asked, really afraid of the answer. And it was way more than I expected.

He proceeded to lay down everything the cops had to accuse me of being an accomplice, finishing at the night at the hospital where Steph called out my name and Walker recognized me from afar. Being marked as a suspect was something I had not considered, nor how Elijah's death would change things, if it even would.

"I wanted you to know all this," said Steph after being silent for most of Scotch's tale, "because I know you're innocent, and there has to be something we can do to prove that."

"I don't know if there's anything that could be done right now," I said, very disappointed.

I looked down for a second, taking in everything that had been said. I sat on Steph's bed and took a deep breath. I was ready to say something, but then she hugged me. She held me tight, making my shoulder sting horribly.

"You've been through so much," she cried as she heard my grunt and untightened her hug.

Scotch fell on his back and almost cried in panic all of a sudden. His eyes were wide open, looking at something behind us. I turned to see a hybrid Drake climbing up the last branch before the window. "George," he said. "We have to go."

I think the most surprising part about all of this was Steph's reaction. Of course she would've known who Drake was and how hybrids looked, but I didn't see that happening, so it didn't feel right to see her react so calmly. "Hi, Drake," she said, almost puffily.

"There's no more time to talk," he said to me, ignoring Steph. "We have to go right now." He extended his hand to show me Elijah's phone. The phone that wasn't supposed to ring unless the sky was falling. "Foxworth is under attack."

Andrea, April 18th, night

Andrea, quite literally, jumped out of bed in horror. It felt like a dozen sirens, all ringing in her head at once all of a sudden. Her atrophied muscles didn't stop her from shaking and trying to cover her ears to make the noise stop. Fruitless and painful, but she couldn't think of anything else to do. She tried to scream as loud as possible, but her throat closed on her, like the most violent allergic reaction.

A most familiar feeling invaded her body. It felt like a million spiders crawling up her legs and unto her chest, her neck, her face. She felt compelled to stay put, to not move a muscle. Not because of the pain, but because He asked her to. And she obeyed.

Chapter 22
Tickings

Monica, night

December 21st is supposed to be the shortest day of the year, but for her it was that day, whichever it was. The day after they left Andrea at the forest came and went in what felt like mere minutes. Monica was put to sleep in a new cocoon at dawn, and almost instantly woke up at nighttime again, with new orders, and in a new location.

"Move," roared Arabella, pushing her to walk right after opening her silky casket. But the push was not necessary at all, because Monica was already moving, because she yearned to. She was excited to walk wherever she was ordered to and serve her Master's will.

She soon reunited with the limping, battered up body of Miles Goodman, who clearly could only walk because of their Master's power to will them into do it. Nobody with a full-functioning mind would be able to move much in Miles' condition, even if they really wanted to.

But Miles wasn't the only one around her now. She was ahead of a big group of people she did not recognize, who were clearly under her Master's will as well. People of all colors, ages and sizes, marching almost in-sync as the moonlight shined through the tree branches and the cold breeze ruptured their eyes and lips.

It wasn't long until Monica could identify something other than trees and bleeding moonlight. At a short distance was a cabin, barely illuminated by streetlights and the pale silver moon. The moment she saw it, she knew it was her target. She needed to go inside the cabin, no matter how, and get everybody in there.

No. Not get.

Kill.

Gray, April 18th, night

The three wolves woke up at the same time. The built-up noise coming from outside was too much for their ears to ignore, and they could soon feel the vibrations through the ground into the bunker. Small, very quiet vibrations that only they would be able to identify. But they were there, and getting close.

Shirtless as he was, Gray left his room and got out to the main hall. The bandages covering his abdomen were about to fall off, but he didn't seem to notice. His pack followed shortly after.

"Wake them all up," said the black wolf to the brown one. "Tell them to get ready." Alex nodded and ran to the kitchen, where the entrance to the security room was.

"I'm going to get Andrea," said Taylor.

"What?" asked Gray.

"She can barely walk. I'll get her safe and be back." Taylor left the main hall before Gray could reply, which was probably the smartest thing to do.

Alex came out of the kitchen. "They got Mr. Foxworth to the safe room," he said. "They said not to worry about him at all."

Gray nodded in approval, still standing in the middle of the hall, just listening. Through the ground he heard how the front door was kicked down, and the cabin was being inspected by several people. Impossible to know how many.

"Ms. Rose has her," said Taylor as he came back into the hall. "Along with Officer Maffei." Gray had pretty much forgotten about the existence of the comatose police officer being treated just a few doors down his. "Now what?"

"Now we wait," said Gray, looking at the door. The door that would soon be discovered by the intruders, and in no time would start being forced open.

George, April 18th, night

"What do you mean 'attack'?" I asked Drake.

"They're there," he hastily said. "We're leaving *now*." I had never heard as much seriousness in his voice before. I could see in his face that he was also scared.

I turned to see Scotch and Steph for a second, both confused and terrified; Scotch had not yet recovered from the shock of seeing Drake in full hybrid. I gave myself five seconds to think of what else to do before leaving, because we had to leave, but this couldn't have been all in vain. I had to get something out of the trouble of getting there.

Four seconds left. I thought about staying there and letting Drake go on without me. He could get there quicker and I would not be a nuisance. I wouldn't be present to make more mistakes and compromise the whole situation and the lives of the rest of the team. But I was also an extra soldier that they were probably going to need, and I couldn't leave Drake alone as he went back into the forest.

Three seconds. The police and the FBI were already on our case. I had Scotch right here, who believed me, and I trusted that his dad was just trying to do the best job possible. What if I did something with that? No time to go talk with Walker, and he would surely not listen to me for the first few hours.

Two. Maybe that was it. He would not believe me for a second, but he would trust his own eyes. If I showed him what was happening, if I took them to Foxworth and showed them everything, maybe it would work out. Or maybe it was sealing my fate and all of theirs. Maybe it was nothing. But I had to try.

Yes. I needed to get help, so we didn't have to hide anymore. So we could be more. That was it.

"Scotch," I called him. He snapped out of his shock and turned his eyes from Drake to me. "I need you to tell your dad everything I told you."

"Excuse me?" said Drake, in a tone that reminded me a lot of Elijah.

"Wha-what?" asked Scotch in confusion.

"Tell him everything and make the connections for him. Appeal to his logic and trust in you."

Scotch couldn't find any words for a moment. Then he mumbled, "I'll try."

I nodded and turned to the window, ready to leave. "Wait!" called out Steph. She hugged me again, so hard she pulled the skin below my wound and made it sting. "Please be safe."

"I promise," I said, almost pushing her back as I got out the window. "Scotch, I'm counting on you." Scotch nodded rapidly as I got on Drake's back. He barely gave me time to look at Steph one more time before jumping off.

There were no restrictions in Drake's movement after jumping off. He didn't even transform into a wolf, he just ran as fast as he could from Steph's backyard into the forest, jumping between the shadows with little care. It was very late at night, so it was dark and lonely, but I was sure at least a couple of cops noticed a blur jumping into the forest. But Drake didn't care.

Talkative, kind-hearted Drake was nowhere to be seen. I was being held by a man desperate to be somewhere else, afraid for the well-being of his peers. Not that I thought he wasn't an excellent person and a great partner to work with, but he had his reservations. And right then, he forgot about them.

He ran and ran into the dark forest, through the cold breeze, not paying attention to any patrols that might be close by. Not bothering to jump on top of the trees and be silent in his movement. Thumps with every step he took, never letting go of me as if I and everything I was holding weighed no more than a feather.

Monica, night

Monica was surrounded by the strangers from the forest. They were inside the house all at once, pushing each other as they all tried to reach for the doors. They all seemingly ignored the presence of the furniture, just kicking everything out of the way as they walked by, like it didn't exist.

The door to the right was the one that opened to a staircase. They all clumsily walked past the doorframe and fell down the staircase into a wall. Monica kept to the back of the group as they formed inside the house, somewhat capable of at least doing that for herself. She knew instantly how her objective was now to go down the stairs and open the door. She didn't even know what door, but there was a door that needed to be pushed.

There was a crashing sound above her as she moved into the hallway. At first it sounded like the wind, but it grew way stronger for that to be it, unless it was a tornado. Suddenly, Arabella's fists punched through the wooden roof of the cabin and started pulling. Monica could hear how she flapped her wings, creating gusts that shook the whole structure until a whole burst open.

"Keep moving!" screamed Arabella, and so Monica couldn't help but push on, past the doorframe. She could see Miles just a few feet ahead of her, about to completely collapse.

Just as she passed the doorframe, she heard how the rest of the roof was destroyed, letting the strongest winds possible inside. Turns out it wasn't just winds, but animals. Flocks of hundreds of birds and bats and insects entering the cabin and destroying everything, even pushing the horde of people into the door.

Past the doorframe was a concrete tunnel illuminated by two hanging lightbulbs, that went down about fifteen steps, and then turned the other way and went down for maybe ten more.

At the end of the second set of stairs was a metallic door with no handle. From where she was, Monica could see a keypad to the side of the door and nothing else. She watched as Miles slammed his body against the metallic door, probably his only way of trying to do something about opening it.

Monica felt how the air got short and the tunnel got hotter and hotter with all the people inside. The sheer amount of people inside the tunnel made it feel like the walls were closing in, and Monica, as tired as she was, felt close to collapsing herself just as she saw Miles fall unconscious on the floor.

Monica's teary eyes looked upward to see the terrifying sight of Marcus climbing down the ceiling like a spider. His closed wings in that position with the poor lighting made him look like a cockroach, sneaking through the dark sewers.

From where she stood, Monica saw how Marcus got down from the ceiling and almost stepped on Miles' face. He opened his wings as much as he could, got into position, and kicked the door with resounding force. The whole tunnel vibrated, the walls shook and dust puffed from the ceiling as the kick echoed away. Marcus charged another kick and hit the door, this time making a dent on the door. He kicked it again, and this time Monica heard how the metal had bent. Marcus kicked one more time, and the top half of the door bent inwards, letting her see how a big, hairy arm grabbed Marcus by the throat and pulled him in.

Gray, April 18th, late night

They were not taking any kind of chances, not after what happened to Elijah. The moment they heard the first kick, they knew they had to act quick. The following kicks came in like a ticking clock, and Gray prepared himself to act as quickly as possible.

The three wolves transformed into hybrids, tearing their nightclothes in the process. Gray positioned himself right next to the door, waiting for whatever was going to happen to it after enough kicks. And as soon as he saw the door bend, Gray threw his arm in and grabbed the demon by his neck, pulled him in, and slammed him into the floor, holding him by the neck and kneeling into his chest.

The monster roared as Taylor stuck his claws into his neck and started pulling. The demon shook violently, using his wings to lift off the floor and headbutt Taylor out of his way up, still held by Gray. He jumped into the air, trying to kick Gray off of him with incredible force.

On the ground, Alex was trying to contain the horde of people pushing in, while what looked like hundreds of flying animals entered the room and revolted around them, just like at the hospital. Alex held the horde even through the constant cuts and peaks the animals were giving him, but as he saw Gray being lifted up into the air, he jumped and grabbed the monster's leg, pulling him down. With the same momentum of his initial jump, the demon managed to stab Gray's already open wound, forcing him to let go and fall to the ground. With one solid kick, the demon got rid of Alex as well.

The demon flapped his wings once, covering enough distance to get to the huge candelabra that hung above the roundtable. He looked on as the horde of people pushed each other past the bent door, not caring if they hurt each other or themselves.

Still on the ground and bleeding, Gray turned his head to the other side to see Foxworth's team coming in battle armor. Six or seven soldiers, all dressed up with SWAT-type suits and riot shields.

Taylor launched himself to the demon as Foxworth's team marched in. The horde of people getting close to Gray's hurt self as Alex tried to contain them, with the birds flying around and destroying the tapestry. "Get up, Michael," he growled as he held six people at once, three in each arm. Alex slammed all of them on the floor, incapacitating them for a few moments.

Gray started rising as the candelabra collapsed on the roundtable and Taylor flew off against the wall. At the sight of this, Gray composed himself and stood up as the demon recovered from the smash. He stood up as well, extending his wings and taking out large pieces of glass from around his body.

The demon looked at the three wolves. "Where's the red one?" he asked out loud. His voice was unlike the other demon's, Jason. This one's voice was deep and solemn, and he seemed to keep his cool while being outnumbered. He didn't even seem annoyed by all the cuts he had just gotten.

As he stood there, two of Foxworth's men turned to him and tried to contain him. "No!" called Gray, uselessly reaching for them as the demon used each of his lances to stab a soldier through the abdomen.

The demon raised the two soldiers up and analyzed them. "You," he said to one of the soldiers, throwing the other one into the horde. He grabbed the selected soldier and took off his helmet, revealing a young man that Gray had seen a couple times around the house; white, fit, not older than 25. As the soldier floated in the air, held by the lance in his abdomen, the demon bit into his neck.

After no more than two seconds, he threw the body away. It was physically visible how the demon's cuts were healing at an extremely fast rate, closing without even leaving scars.

The demon extended his wings again, showing off his shining lances and the impeccable state of his body. "Arabella," he said, to nobody in particular. "There's a fourth one coming. Be wary."

Monica, night

Thanks to her positioning inside the crowd, Monica wasn't one of the ones affected by the soldiers that came out of nowhere with riot shields and electric batons. And even though they were doing everything to control the crowd, they would all just stand up again and continue pushing forward.

What would've really messed up with her head if she had control over it was the sight of the hairy monsters that were fighting Marcus. She figured that's what her

Master meant when He talked about "the wolves," but damn. Those things looked arguably scarier than Jason and Arabella. With their huge teeth and sharp claws and everything, they were more like the stuff of nightmares than Marcus was.

As she pushed on, she received an order from her Master. She had to turn back and get the fourth wolf that was coming in. So she and two other people turned back and went up the stairs. As she climbed through the bent door, she saw Miles' unconscious body lying against the wall. His face was stained with fresh blood and he didn't seem to be moving at all, but she couldn't find space in her brain to worry. She had to go up the stairs and find the fourth wolf, and nothing else.

The cabin that used to be upstairs was completely gone, with only the floor and part of the furniture remaining. The walls and windows and the ceiling were all gone, scattered around the surroundings. Car alarms were blasting and a couple people were even running away, but there didn't seem to be lots of people in the town anyway.

Monica turned to her right, where the back of the house used to be. She knew that's where they would be coming from, but she wasn't sure how. Nor did she know what she meant by "they," because her orders were to get a single wolf that was coming back.

George, April 19th, the small hours

It was easy to know the exact moment when we got close to Foxworth, because I started feeling sick. The same sensation that I had felt at the hospital, but less severe, surely because of the necklace in my pocket. Still, it was as if I was hit in the face with a hammer.

"Hold on," pleaded Drake. "We're almost there. You'll be fine." And I was holding on pretty well. But that wasn't what ruined everything.

I kind of recognized the wooded area right before getting to the cabin, but way before we did I'd already started hearing unusual noises, and, logically, Drake had heard them from way farther back. "Do you think they're okay?" I asked him, but he didn't answer. Not because he didn't want to, but because he was hit in the face by a fast-moving flying object that knocked him down and made him drop me at high speed, so I flew about ten feet and crashed into a tree.

Gray, April 19th, the small hours

The chaos caused by the crows alone was enough to drive Michael insane. Between them and the horde of people still pushing against Foxworth's remaining soldiers, Gray was wondering exactly how they were going to fight this new demon, who looked way smarter and stronger than the last one.

He didn't have a lot of time to think about it, though, as the demon, rather than fighting them, instead turned to the hallways where all the rooms were, and launched himself with his wings, flying at top speed down the corridor. This prompted the wolves to frantically run towards them, going around the humans fighting in the middle of the main hall.

Taylor got ahead of the other two, but he wasn't even close to getting to the flying demon, who had gotten to the end of the hallway, were the training hall was. The training hall was considerably taller than the rest of the base, so the demon had enough space to fly around, though Gray couldn't understand why he would take such a tour of the place.

Only a few crows had gotten to the gym when the wolves reunited with the flying demon. He was perched on top of a climbing wall, feeling the ceiling. "I thought it was here, but I was wrong," he said, to nobody in particular. "Past the kitchen? Alright, then."

Taylor had started to run towards the demon and jumped halfway up the wall when he leaped off it and flew out of the training hall. "The kitchen," called out Michael, figuring he was looking for the safe room. But he could not possibly understand how the demon had known about that.

The wolves chased the demon down the corridor as he turned to the right to get inside the kitchen. The speed he flew at was all too fast for any of them to catch him, and so the back door at the end of the kitchen was already destroyed when they got there, and crows were already filling the space in their dark clouds.

"I'll help them," called Alex as he marched on to the horde and Foxworth's soldiers.

Taylor and Gray proceeded past the door and into the dark hallway they were not very familiar with. It wasn't common for anybody outside of Security to be anywhere past that door.

Andrea

The rush of adrenaline between the pounding of the doors and running into safety was enough to make Andrea feel dizzy. As she sat on her wheelchair surrounded by strangers with guns and vests, she struggled to understand anything of what had happened the past 20 minutes, even where she had been taken or how far she was from the room she had awakened in. She even considered she might have fainted for a few minutes.

The room they were all in was cramped and hot, clearly not made for such a number of people. As she woke up she could detail the low ceiling with hanging lightbulbs and big, probably thick metal door at the other end of the room. She could see a makeshift bed made with tables by the wall to her right, where there was a man laying down. A familiar face, which she had seen unconscious many times, but never awake.

The only other person sitting besides her was a very old man with a cane, who sat on a metal chair and looked onward to the door. He turned to see her awake, and smiled warmly. "Don't worry," said the old man. "Everything will be alright."

After a few minutes, she felt an all too familiar feeling all over her body. A specific, punctual sensation that she had grown accustomed to over the past weeks. She could almost see how her thoughts were pulled out of her head. But the worst part was what came next, what she didn't merely see but also took part in and physically hurt her.

Andrea abruptly stood up from her chair, a sharp pain in her joints making her mouth whine reflexively. In front of her was Ms. Rose, looking onwards at the door, who turned as Andrea bumped into her backside as she stood up. "Miss!" cried Ms. Rose. "You can't walk. You'll hurt yourself."

Andrea paid no attention to her words. She stood where she was, waiting for the moment she knew she had to wait for. Not a lot of noise could come from outside of the room, so she just had to wait for the exact moment for her to run. Simply standing was already painful enough on her knees and back, but she didn't want to sit back down, for the sake of her.

"Miss," called Ms. Rose again, but was interrupted by the strongest noise that could've possibly been heard from inside the safe room. A thunderous bang on the metal door that told Andrea to be ready.

She dreaded the thought of having to run in her condition, but there was nothing she wanted more than to escape the room and run outside, where the boy and the red wolf were. Each hit against the door felt more and more flustering inside of Andrea's head as she saw the people in front of her getting ready to fire.

The pacing of each hit increased as Andrea's mind filled with anxiety, as if she was the one who had to break the door down as quickly as possible, because she was being chased. And then, a dent on the lower right side of the door. And the dent got bigger, and bigger, until it became a hole. A hole from where dozens of flying animals started flooding the already crowded room.

The people in front of Andrea started shooting at the ceiling as more and more birds and bats and insects got inside the room, blocking the light from reaching them and eventually destroying the lightbulbs, leaving the room in complete darkness. Andrea used this opportunity to sneak past Ms. Rose and get lost in between the crowd of people and birds, feeling an intense pain in her back as she crouched and moved around in a lower profile.

Gray, April 19th, the small hours

The two wolves found the demon trying to kick the heavy metal door in. Together they both launched themselves unto the demon, crashing with him against the door just as he gave one last kick to dent a hole. As Gray crushed the demon's head against the door, he felt how hundreds of animals filled the tunnel and entered the room.

Taylor pulled one of the demon's wings up and started biting on his lance as gushes of blood sprayed all over him and Gray. With his other wing, the demon pushed himself off the door and kicked Gray away from him. Then, he used his free lance to try and stab Taylor's back, but he blocked it and used his claws to rip a hole in the demon's wing; the wings that looked so much like that of a bat, creating confusing amongst the common folk for centuries.

The demon screamed in pain as Gray recovered himself and ran towards him again, launching one more time at the demon's torso – now turned to the door – aiming his fangs at the back of the neck. The demon used his momentum to turn one more time, giving his free, non-cut wing enough space to hit Gray's body into Taylor's.

On the floor, Gray was almost stabbed in the back by both of the demon's lances, saved only by Taylor's quick reflexes. Taylor gave a quick kick to the sides of the lances, making them pierce the wooden floor instead. Gray used this chance to kick the demon's shins, making him fall to the ground.

Almost perfectly synchronized, Taylor kneeled on top of the demon's back and pressed hard against the floor. Gray sunk his claws into his neck again and started pulling. The demon screeched as the wolves contained him, but managed to reach Taylor's face with one of his arms and slashed. Taylor did everything in his power not to flinch, but after the second slash, it was impossible to keep holding him.

As Taylor reached for his bloody face, the demon opened his wings and pushed him up, slamming him against the ceiling. As Taylor flew up and fell down, the demon grabbed Gray's hands and pushed himself towards him, aiming his teeth at the wolf's neck. Gray managed to hold him in place just inches away from being bit, until the demon was grabbed by his foot, pulled away from the black wolf, and thrown to the other side of the hallway by Alex.

Alex crouched down to see Taylor's slashed face. "I think he got his eye," said the brown wolf.

"And I'll get your throat next," screamed the demon as he flew down the corridor towards the wolves. His neck bled profusely, one of his wings was almost torn in two, and he looked as furious as one could get.

As the demon flew like a bullet, the three wolves braced themselves for him, but Gray was distracted. In position to receive the demon and slam him on the floor, he felt a pair of tiny arms hugging him from behind. He turned his head to see the limp, almost lifeless body of Andrea, holding him like a girl with a teddy bear. Before Gray turned back to the fight, the demon had already grabbed the two other wolves, and smashed them against the metal door at high speed.

George, April 19th, the small hours

The way my skull didn't cave in as I hit the tree should be categorized as a miracle. Not only did I rip several chunks of skin from my shoulder wound, but I also felt, in slow motion, how my elbow snapped in two. Fortunately, it wasn't bad enough to perforate my skin, but my right arm was left completely useless, and I in deep, terrible pain.

I crashed into the tree and fell face first into the ground. After a few moments, I managed to use my left hand to push myself up a bit and lay on my left arm. "George?" I heard Drake calling from a distance. I was still dizzy from the fall and I couldn't find the energy to call him back.

It was very dark and cold outside, so I couldn't see much. I definitely couldn't see Drake, but I could kinda hear that he was to my front-right side. I looked on in the general direction and saw nothing but blurry trees and what kinda looked like a downward slope, which let me know that we were right outside of Foxworth. It was the place where I first spoke with Elijah after waking up that first day. That day, two weeks before, but that felt like a lifetime prior.

I heard an echo of Drake's voice calling my name, but I couldn't tell if it was him or my mind replaying his calling from moments before. I breathed heavily, the cold air coming in and out of my mouth, burning my throat. I was so exhausted, so done with my shoulder and my constant disability to fight or do something. I tried to stand up but the pain on my right side was so bad I didn't even want to move.

I felt movement close to me, like somebody walking behind the trees, hunting for me. I turned my head in every direction, trying to catch a glance of whoever was there, but I couldn't see. It was too dark and my mobility was too limited to see anything.

But then I heard something that chilled down my spine way harder than the cold could've. A voice that I had not heard in years and that made me instantly want to cry. I turned my head so violently to my left I fell back on my chest, and I still couldn't see anything clearly. But the voice was hers, without a doubt. And as it started getting closer, my efforts to stand up grew larger and larger, but I couldn't get myself up.

She got close enough for me not only to see her, but to detail her. She had not gotten a day older. Her hair, her hands, her eyes all looked the same. It was as if nothing had ever happened to her, like the last 2 years of my life were gone and she was just there, with me, no sign of Robert or any cancer. I gathered all of the energy I could muster as she crouched in front of me and smiled. "Mom."

Chapter 23
The Sum of Every Fear

George

At the moment, it felt like the most normal and natural thing in the world. I was lying on the floor, bleeding and in immense pain, but it wasn't relevant in the slightest, like being bit by a mosquito. Nothing had ever happened to us, we were never separated nor did something ever happen to her. There was nothing to think about except that my mother was in front of me, and I was lying down.

Growing up, I was always repeatedly told that I looked exactly like my dad in every single aspect. I never found this particularly amusing, because I never really knew my dad, aside from the 3-4 years of blurred memories I held of him before he died. But I always felt that I was a lot like my mom personality-wise, always thinking ahead and concerned for a million things around her. Physically, though, I can agree; my mom's delicate skin and soft amber eyes are perfectly complimented by a beautiful, joyful smile that I know for a fact I did not inherit. She always liked keeping her hair long, and right then she had it in a bun, like she was coming home from work.

"What are you doing on the floor?" she asked me, half laughing, half concerned. Like what I was doing was just so silly yet a little charming.

"I hit the tree at high speed," I answered. "I think I broke my elbow."

Nurse McKnight took over from Mom McKnight for a moment. She asked to take a look and I raised my arm, almost ignoring the millions of nerve endings being crushed between my bones and my skin as I did so. "You look fine," she said. "Nothing that won't heal with just a little bit of rest." She smiled at me, and made me feel that every word she was saying was true.

"I miss you," I said, though not sure why. She had never gone anywhere.

"I'm right here, sweetie," she answered. "You know I'll never leave you. You know that, right?"

"Of course I know that. You never have. Not once."

She stretched her hand and caressed my cheek, but my face was so numb from the crash that I barely even felt it. It was more like a soft wind.

"Why did you do it, honey?" she asked me.

"Do what?"

"You know," she said, going from jovial and sweet to disappointed, in a quarter of a second.

"Why did I crash against the tree? It wasn't my fault."

"No, not that." She looked like it would hurt her to continue asking. Not even embarrass her but actually physically hurt her to finish her question. "You know."

"I don't, mom. What do you mean?"

She took a deep breath. "Why did you let me marry him?"

I felt like I froze in the cold air. She looked so hurt, like she had been holding tears for years and years. "I-I didn't. I never wanted you to."

"But why didn't you stop me? Why did you keep quiet as he hit you behind my back?"

"Because you looked happy. I wanted you to be happy, mom. I always have, no matter what."

"I would never put my happiness over you, George. Never ever. You should know that."

I started crying. Tears of emotion, this time. I was all out of tears of physical pain by that point. "I know that now," I could barely answer. "I'm so sorry."

"You should've stopped him," she said, crying harder and louder. "You took too long, and now I'm dead. Because you didn't do anything."

"I know," I answered. My voice breaking, barely making any sense. "Every day I wish I could change it. I wish we could trade places."

"But then I would be terribly unhappy," she answered, adding a bit of anger to her voice. "Me, living without my only son? Would you do that to me?"

"No! Absolutely not." I felt like, whatever I said, there was not a right answer. I couldn't win. "I just miss you so much. I'd sacrifice anything."

My mom shook her head. "You still haven't learned anything," she said, going back to disappointment. "Not even after Elijah did you learn to think about others. You only think about yourself. About how you feel, how you look in other people's eyes."

"I'm really trying. I am."

She shook her head more violently. "No you haven't. You were so worried about being seen like a burden that you let that terrible man into our lives and never said anything about it."

"Because I wanted *you* to be happy!"

"You keep making up excuses so you don't have to see how selfish you are. How you only think about yourself. How you wanted to be perceived as strong so you'd rather fight to the death with your mom's boyfriend than tell her he's a bad person."

"That's not true," I said, barely audible.

"You'd rather prove that you're capable of escaping a place where you were safe and put yourself in danger. Show those wolves that you're not a boy anymore, right? Never mind that you've been inside their world for less than two weeks. You have to show them."

"I wanted to help."

"And because of that, now Elijah's dead. And you feel guilty as if you had done it yourself."

I eyes started balling as I spoke. "I did."

"Why do you feel like such a failure, my love?"

"Because I am."

"Why did you and Robert almost choke each other to death the day of my funeral?"

I sniffed as hard as I could, but the cold air made it really difficult. I could barely get any air in my lungs to continue speaking. "Because he said it was my fault that you had died. That I didn't react fast enough."

"And why did you hit him in the back with a chair?"

"Because I agreed with him."

"And you still do."

"Yes."

"And you still think that Elijah died solely because of you."

"He did."

"And now you're worried because Steph was at the hospital, because of how your disappearance affected her."

"Yes."

"When you saw Andrea sleeping, you wanted to apologize for not being able to save her. Or to go back in time and trade places with her, so that you can suffer instead of her."

"She didn't deserve any of that. She's innocent."

"But you're not."

"No."

"Now Drake is trying to defend you, and is probably going to die too."

This made me snap out of my crying for a second. I tried to wipe my tears off and look on in the distance. About twenty feet away was Drake, fighting the female vampire, who I somehow knew was called Arabella. I could barely see anything in the dark and with my puffy eyes, just her bright red hair and his opaque red pelt jumping around.

"You should just stay here, and wait for her to kill him," said my mom. "It'd be easier. Just stop moving, stop intervening. It'll be best for everyone."

And I truly believed her. So I didn't move.

Monica, night

Monica was sure she was going to freeze to death. Between the unusual cold she had not gotten used to since her kidnapping and the violent winds caused by the birds, she almost wanted to just stop and turn completely to ice. Not that she would've been able to.

She was followed by two other people that she hadn't paid attention to before. Turned out one of them was the only person she had recognized amongst the kidnapped people at the hospital. Dr. Kim was still wearing his hospital gown, now almost completely gray and brown, and looked like he hadn't slept in a week while trapped in the middle of a war zone. The other person was an older, black nurse from the hospital that Monica did not know.

The three possessed walked out of the shambles of the house up a small hill that almost terminated the two older individuals, though it was clear that none of them wanted to disobey their orders. Monica saw them struggling to go up the hill, and wondered if she had ever been as blind to orders, if they too could think as much as she could aside from her undisobeyable orders.

They made it past the hill and walked for a couple minutes until Monica could hear something odd. A combination of grunts and thumps and growls, coming from in front of them in the dark. They all knew that's where they needed to go, and so they continued on towards the sounds, hoping to find the red wolf and his companion, whatever that meant.

George, April 19th, the small hours

Though I was not going to move, I could finally focus on Drake for a change, who was having a terrible time fighting Arabella. She was doing everything in her power to get to me, and Drake's sole purpose was to keep her away, not sure for how long. There was no chance that I would be able to call on any of the other wolves to help, nor was there the slightest possibility that I could get up and help him.

For a second, Arabella threw him to the tree to my right, where he took a brief look at me. Without saying anything, he grabbed the sheathed sword I completely forgot was right by my side. "Be right back," he said, as he ran back at Arabella with the sword in hand. Such a big and hairy figure holding a sword looked very unmatched, out of place.

I used this small window to look around me again, noticing everything I had dropped when I crashed into the tree. The pouch with a small handgun and two extra cartridges. Drake's small bag which contained the phone we were called in on – which was of no use at the moment, seeing the house was most likely completely invaded.

In my dizziness I thought to check my neck for the necklace. I felt the cord around my neck but the symbol wasn't on my chest, so I turned it slowly, to get the symbol in front of me, and I realized that it had shattered. Probably when I hit the tree, it shattered into pieces, which helped me understand why I was feeling worse than usual.

I watched as Drake managed to impale Arabella through the abdomen with the sword and charged towards a tree, even letting out a scream of frustration as he pushed the sword against the trunk, letting Arabella stuck between it and the handle. The vampiress roared with pain and anger as she swung her lances, trying to get Drake but missing every time, each time receiving a punch or a slash to the face.

Arabella raised her legs and kicked Drake out of the way, giving her time to use her lances to cut the sword in half, just like Jason had done to Elijah two nights before. It was truly a testament to how hard those lances were, being able to cut a sword that could slice into a tree trunk like that, especially because Arabella was looking more and more tired as the fight continued. The sword handle fell from her abdomen, attached to a blade of about seven inches laying on the ground.

But I couldn't keep watching after I heard steps coming from the direction of the house, followed by the faint, blurry images of three people. Three people I could not believe were together in the same place, all coming towards me. Mercedes was still wearing her nurse gown, and would've probably gotten a heart attack if she'd seen how dirty it was. Same thing with Dr. Kim, who not only looked dirty and beat up but dead tired, almost literally. And Monica in front of them, leading them on, her posture that of a soldier but her face that of a terrified young woman who had lost all control over herself.

"Monica," I called as Drake and Arabella kept fighting. "Snap out of it." I wasn't even sure if my voice was loud enough for her to hear me under the noises of the fight and the wind. But they kept walking either way, and I was running out of ideas.

I could almost physically feel how my will to do something dripped out of my open shoulder wound. I watched as Monica walked towards me and my mom's voice kept bouncing inside my skull. "Let her have you. So you can rest." I stretched my unbroken arm to try to reach for the pouch with the gun in it, but it was too far away and I really, really couldn't move the rest of my body.

Drake took a quick glance at the people coming for me before he had to dodge Arabella's lances one more time. She was beat up, only winning thanks to her biological advantage of regeneration over Drake, but taking a lot more damage than him from his punches and slashes. From where I lay I could see that one of her wings was broken, probably making it harder for her to attack with it and almost impossibly painful to fly.

Drake probably noticed her wing too, as he used the short window after one of his dodges to punch through the debilitated membrane and slash up, tearing the wing like a piece of cloth. In her agonizing pain, Arabella was unable to react to Drake's full-body tackle against a tree, after which he proceeded to sink his claws into her abdomen and slowly go up to her chest, opening her up. Even in the dark, Arabella's eyes shined with horror as Drake grabbed her sternum and pulled it out, making her collapse.

Monica was two feet away from me when Drake managed to get to me and stop her. "Don't hurt them," I implored to him, as if he would ever do so. Monica's instinct was to try to maneuver around Drake to get to me, but he was obviously much quicker and bigger, so he just pushed her aside. It took the other two this long to catch up, and were likewise as clunky in their attempt as Monica, maybe even worse. It was clear that their bodies had taken a lot of damage, and were only standing due to the uncontrollable curse that ran through their system.

"What should we do with them?" asked Drake as he easily held them off of me.

I couldn't respond. I felt so sad, so useless and heavy and just bad. I almost wanted Drake to let them get to me so I could get away from whatever was happening. The cold was sickening, my shoulder was infuriating, and the whole situation was just so much, I couldn't even think.

Drake turned to see me. "George?" he called as I looked at the floor, still lying on my left arm. "Do you have your necklace?" I still didn't answer.

He lifted the three Entranced and took them past Arabella's body, about fifty feet away. The whole thing was kinda ridiculous, and in another context it probably would've been really funny how he had to take them away only for them to stubbornly continue their way to me. But I wasn't able to laugh, even if I wanted to.

Drake came back running on four feet. "That should keep them away for a while. Let me take a look at you." He crouched and looked at the shattered symbol. "I need to mark you," he said, his face full of fear and caution, though I only saw pity. "Let me check your other arm."

"Just leave me," I muttered. "Go."

"Don't be ridiculous," he answered. "The quicker I do this the faster we can go back and help them. Come on." Without waiting for my answer, Drake lifted my whole body and straightened me on my feet, dusting off some dirt with his hairy hands.

Drake cut off the sleeves from the jacket and the shirt under it with one quick slash, revealing my new tattoo, the skin under it still red. "Can I sit down?" I asked. It felt wrong being as tired as I was, seeing how people like Monica or Dr. Kim had probably been through so much more and were still standing. It made me feel really pathetic.

Drake slowly helped me down and I sat cross-legged, close but not against the tree, seeing that my shoulder was probably at amputation point. "This is going to hurt," he said.

"Wouldn't expect any less," I answered, feeling overly dramatic and stupid. I closed my eyes, waiting for the sting, and the words just came out of my mouth. "I'm sorry," I said.

"For what?" he asked me.

I managed to hold in the tears that I felt were coming, though it made it even harder to speak. "Everything."

"Don't be stupid," he answered, dusting off my tattoo with the back of his hairy hand. "None of this is your fault."

A strange feeling went through my body that told me to look past Drake to see Monica and the others walking towards us. Monica, as usual, in front of the other two, though still walking very slowly. It felt like I was tied with a rope and Monica was trying to pull me closer to her, though I couldn't be sure if she wanted me closer to kill me faster or closer so I could help her escape.

For a second, though I would never be completely sure, I thought I heard her voice inside my head. But it didn't feel like my mom's voice from a moment before, but more like a transmission coming from radio inside my skull. I thought I heard her call my name.

Monica, night

The red wolf they had been told to kill was no match for them, not even if they had been twenty and he had been alone. Monica couldn't comprehend why on earth would they be tasked to hold off this individual, especially if Arabella was already up to the task. Then, after seeing George, she understood that He really wanted them to take him instead, and the red wolf would be too distracted to protect the boy. Why He sent her along with Dr. Kim is probably just a matter of sadism.

Monica almost felt her in her own stomach when Arabella was impaled by the red wolf, just as much as she felt her own insides spilling out when she was opened and left collapsed on the floor by the tree. What alarmed Monica the most was that, after being pushed aside by the wolf so he had time to purify the boy, she was still feeling the same uncomfortable sensation of being open.

They walked back to their target, as tiring and painful and agonizing as it felt to take each of their steps on their way. As she heard how the nurse fell on her knees and stood up again to keep walking, she remembered Miles, passed out against the door. Though "passing out" wasn't something very common amongst them, and so her mind flooded with thoughts she'd rather not have; thoughts of death, suffering, complete and utter inability to ever move again. And again she wondered how she could find space inside her mind to think about all of this.

She forgot about everything once they passed Arabella's opened body, which heightened the feeling she already had about her own abdomen. Just past her, though, was the handle of the sword she had been impaled with, which still had a decently sized blade that Monica saw as an opportunity to save time while killing her target, by stabbing him instead of choking or whatever else her nature dictated she do. So she grabbed it, and kept walking.

She walked towards her target, George McKnight. The boy she'd known for years by then, and who she always liked from a distance. The boy who had sparked a new romantic interest in her best friend, Andrea, and so she started paying more attention to him, even though Andrea was never aware. Monica saw him go against two Seniors and win whilst seeming more afraid than determined, and so she knew that he was strong. She knew that, after everything he had been through with his mom, he had to be really something. If one of them had to escape Arabella and Marcus and Jason and become part of the wolves, it had to be him.

So it felt natural for her when, as she walked, she felt their minds linking, just like every other mind under His control was linked somehow. And she tried to talk to him, though he wasn't responding and she wasn't saying what she wanted to say. She did everything within her power to warn him they were coming back, and that there were so many more things coming their way.

The red wolf was doing something with George's arm. She could faintly see that there was some sort of black mark in his shoulder, and her mind instantly jumped to a state of alert, though she didn't know why. She started walking faster and until her foot got stuck in a root and she fell face first on the ground, still holding the sword handle. She stood up again, feeling how her ankle was probably twisted and wanting to cry with every step she took, but she kept going.

She hadn't heard of the other too for a few moments, but she didn't care. She had to stop the red wolf from doing whatever he was doing with George's shoulder. In her hysteria she did not notice that the strange feeling in her stomach had stopped, but her connection with George had not, and she continued sending him signals.

George's shoulder started glowing as the red wolf muttered some things Monica did not understand. George started panting, expressing his pain louder and louder as she approached, limping and twisting her ankle more and more into an unnatural position, raising her right hand where she held the sword handle.

Less than ten feet to go and she would be within reach. But she limped too slowly forward, and there was no way she could make it. Still she moved, almost crawled to her target until the red wolf finished what he was saying, and George's shoulder lit up like a blinding headlight, making him scream deafeningly and Monica feel as though she was drowning. George's high-volume howl matched the way she felt as though smoke left her lungs through her mouth.

She fell down on her back and started shaking violently, appearing to be having a seizure to the common eye. And she shook for the duration of George's scream and then some more, until she stopped suddenly and felt completely powerless. She couldn't stand up, her almost flipped foot hurt like nothing had in weeks. She could barely find the strength to lift her arms, let alone speak. She breathed in and out, consciously for the first time in what felt like ages of darkness and misery.

The red wolf turned quickly to see her on the floor, and then went back to George. Her head was empty. She felt her mind wandering about, thinking about the cold, the dark, her body, the stench in the air, how her eyes were still recovering from the light that came out of George's mark. But she couldn't feel a lot of the things she had grown used to; she couldn't feel the link with George she had formed just moments ago, nor the presence of her two companions whom she had lost in the dark before any of her recent wounds had occurred.

The red wolf was guiding George through some breathing exercises as Monica tried to sit up. Her elbows felt like they were at the brink of exploding when she leaned them on the ground, so she remained on her back until she heard a strange sound. It reminded her of galloping, but it wasn't exactly that. Like an aggressive crawling through the dirt and dead leaves that came from behind her, and so she turned and saw the dirty, bloody, miserable body of Arabella.

Using her wings and her arms, Arabella crawled like an insect towards the red wolf, her red eyes full of hatred and anger, ready to kill. Monica couldn't feel through her anymore, so she wasn't sure how she was able to move so efficiently after the horrible thing the wolf had done to her. But she was moving, and fast.

Arabella looked completely unaware of Monica's presence. She crawled at arms distance of her and looked ready to jump unto the wolf, fangs out. The wolf turned just as Arabella prepared her attack, and Monica used all the momentum she could gather to swing her arm at her and sink the sword handle wherever she could reach, landing on Arabella's lower nape.

The blade made an awful sound as it went in, making Monica cringe in place as she let go of the handle. Arabella stopped on her tracks and screamed like a banshee, forcing Monica to cover her ears. "Master," cried Arabella, but there was no response that Monica could hear. The red wolf turned completely and grabbed the handle, giving it one last push down before he used his other hand to take Arabella's head and pull it clean off.

The banshee was instantly silenced.

Chapter 24
Their Master's Will
Gray, April 19th, the small hours

The auburn-haired girl held onto Michael's fur even after he launched himself to the vampire, who had the other two wolves choked against the metal door, and was about to stab each one of them with a lance. Gray was in midair when the girl on his back yelled, "Marcus, behind you!" Her voice was raspy and weak, and it probably did a lot of damage to her throat having talked as loudly as she had. But not more damage than the kick to the face Gray received from the demon, Marcus, right before they collapsed.

Gray flew back and fell face first unto the floor. Andrea had let go of him somewhere between the kick and his fall, but she was up again and running towards him in no time. Taylor – his face bloody and his left eye closed for good – and Alex had held off Marcus long enough for them to twist his wings and collectively slam him on the floor, retrying their strategy for decapitation. Gray's attempt to join in was interrupted by Andrea getting in his way, making him grab her and toss her to the other end of the tunnel.

Marcus, being pushed against the floor by Alex, was giving a tougher fight than before. "You are old," he said to Alex as he was joined by Gray in pushing the vampire down. As it had been done before by him and Jason, Marcus used his wings to push the wolves up and off of him, but only Alex let go as he was the most tired and beat up of the two.

The loss in weight allowed Marcus to flap his freed wing, turning his body and crushing Gray, whilst Taylor's claws were still sunk into the demon's neck. Marcus grabbed Taylor's arms and pulled him up and slammed him against the floor in front of him like a trash bag. Gray, still under him, pressed his claws into the demon's ribs, but he simply hit the black wolf hard on the face with his elbow and seemingly levitated back to a standing position.

Alex jumped on Marcus again but he grabbed him in the air and slammed him against the tunnel wall, making him fall on top of Gray. The demon prepared both of his lances to pierce the two wolves on the floor, stopped only by Alex's grip of each lance with a hand. His arms shook with effort as the demon pushed down. "You are the weak link of your team," he said with his deep, solemn voice. Alex kept holding the lances, giving away fractions of inches every second. Marcus could've kicked him or pushed harder, but he purposely just let Alex keep holding on to save his and Gray's life. "If you fail, your son dies."

At least one of Taylor's ribs was broken. He stood up with difficulty only to be held by Andrea just like she had done with Gray, pushing in the broken rib(s) and making him growl. He locked his functioning eye with hers and saw nothing; not fear, not anger or happiness, just a blank stare. It would've been difficult to know if she was even aware of what her body was doing, as if her mind was actually asleep.

With Andrea holding on to him, Taylor still ran towards Marcus, only for her to scream his name again as Taylor jumped. Still pushing his lances into Alex, Marcus simply stretched his arm to catch Taylor's throat in the air, stopping his momentum with enough force to break Andrea's grip.

As crows came out of the hole in the metal door, Marcus sank his claws into Taylor's neck and pushed harder on his lances, piercing Alex's chest. At the sound of his teammate's suffering, Gray gathered as much strength as he could and, still under Alex, grabbed the ends of both lances and slashed them, making Marcus recoil.

Still pressed against the wall, Gray used his body to push Alex up, and Alex used his hind legs to push himself from the wall into Marcus, biting most of his neck with his wide open mouth, making him release Taylor. The brown wolf sprayed blood all over himself and the floor as Andrea's skinny arms approached him, but he kicked her away with unrestrained force, making her fly into the air to the other side of the tunnel along with the crows.

Gray jumped up and pressed his hand against his abdomen in discomfort as his stabbing wound bled profusely. He hurried to help Alex as he chewed on Marcus' throat and grabbed his wings with both hands, disabling them for attack and ignoring the countless slashes he was receiving in the back, apart from the hole in his chest. As Alex pushed Marcus against the wall on the other side, Gray grabbed his right wing and slashed through the thick membrane that allowed for flight, then bit the joint that fused the wing with the back of the demon, and ripped it out of place.

Taylor laid on the floor, half blind and barely able to breathe as his throat flooded with his own blood. In his attempt to stand up he saw Andrea walking back into the fight, much slower than she had before. She had a cut somewhere below her hair that let a small stream of blood fall down her forehead, and one of her arms appeared to be broken by the limp look of it. Still, she approached them holding something in her other hand that wasn't recognizable from that distance. A black object that extended past her arm that soon enough was identifiable as a gun. Helplessly miserable, Taylor called on his teammates to take cover, but his throat couldn't properly project his voice, and so gunshots echoed in the narrow tunnel.

George, April 19th, the small hours

I didn't exactly pass out, but it felt like I had just woken up from a very deep sleep. Unconsciously I followed Drake's breathing exercises as I slowly came back into reality, not even remembering how or when the vampiress had been decapitated, nor how Monica was awake. Like, fully awake.

"Are you alright, girl?" asked Drake. I could hear him faintly due to some ringing in my ears of unknown origin to me at the moment.

Monica didn't answer. It didn't look like she could, with the intense panting and sweating she was going through. Drake stood up and walked to her, checking her out as she trembled with panic. "Don't worry," I told her. "He won't hurt you."

Monica and I locked eyes for what felt like the first time since school. Even though she'd seen me moments before, it didn't feel like it was her, but this was. In her glossy and dirty skin, shaggy clothes and still beautiful olive eyes. "George," she managed to say, probably unsure of what to follow it up with.

"Try to relax," I said. "You've been cursed for too long. It may take you a while." It almost felt like I was talking to myself, but there was no way I could compare my two brief experiences with possession to what her and the others had gone through. Unthinkable, really. And as I thought of the others, I remembered. "Where are Mercedes and Dr. Kim?" I asked her.

Her eyes widened. Clearly she had forgotten about them too, and so she turned violently in the direction where Arabella's body had collapsed before she rose again. Drake turned his head too, and quickly leaped off of Monica and approached the bloodstained tree. "They're both here," he said.

From where I sat I could see Drake analyzing the ankles of both adults. "Are they breathing?" I asked.

Drake lowered his head closer to them. "Yes, but barely."

I turned to see Monica, who looked about to start screaming in panic. "I think Arabella used them to regenerate herself. That's how she came crawling towards us." It was so strange saying this to Monica, with whom I had barely spoken in school and by then I hadn't seen since before everything went down. And yet, she not only understood what I said, but probably much better than me.

"I have to go," said Drake. "They need me down there." Monica, still on the floor, tried to sit up but it looked like her back wasn't letting her. "George," called Drake to me as he brought both unconscious bodies to where I was sitting. "There should be enough bandages in the bag for you to seal these wounds."

"Their blood was sucked out, Drake," I tried to explain to him. I had lost track of how much the others understood about the subject, aside from Elijah.

"I know," he replied, with immense sadness and disappointment on his face. "But we can't do much else right now. I'll run to the cabin and help the others, and I'll be back. Maybe we can save them."

Monica couldn't take any more and started balling on the spot. "I'm so sorry," she started.

"I know," said Drake hastily. "We'll talk later. Be safe." And so the red wolf parted ways with us in the direction of the cabin.

In front of me I had a panicked classmate who couldn't stand up, two grown adults in need of blood transfusions, a small bag with bandages, a handgun and bullets to spare, a cellphone I could not use, and the corpse of a vampiress. The back of my right shoulder was ripped and probably infected, and my head was still recovering from the fog.

But then I went through everything again, and I thought of something. Why couldn't I use the phone? It was useless trying to call the team for help but it was still a cellphone. Maybe it could work for a regular call.

So I grabbed it and looked at it for a moment. It was an old cellphone, one of those that was made fifteen years before but still worked almost perfectly with barely any scratches on the screen and incomparable battery life.

Monica desperately reached for the bag with the bandages and opened it up. Mercedes' legs were close enough for her to grab the bit one and roll some bandages around it. "George," she called. "Help me."

I didn't move. I pressed the button to light up the screen and saw that the phone still had 79% battery, and it was 3:27am. Maybe I could call 911 and tell them where we were so that they could come get the two adults, but that could possibly risk them getting into the fight or worse. Or I could call Steph and tell her to call somebody else to come and help. But I didn't want to get anybody else involved, much less Steph, who had already suffered so much because of me. I didn't want to include her or Scotch or any innocent first responder on this; I wanted to solve this by myself, like Drake had asked me to.

Except he hadn't. He never asked me to do it alone, nor did anybody ever since I got to Foxworth the first time. Elijah wanted to protect me and train me right so that I could be independent, and that meant leaving me out of some stuff at first, and I wasn't able to see that. I only saw the shame in being left behind, tagging myself as useless and unwanted when nobody else had ever done so.

I could almost hear Steph inside my head, telling me that she was there because she wanted to, because she cared. Not because she thought I wasn't capable. I remembered how I saw my mom just a few moments before, and how she made me feel so terrible, which helped me internalize that was not my mom, but something the fog had made me imagine, because my mom would rather die than make me feel worthless or unwanted. My real mom would have said everything I was thinking right at that moment.

"George!" called Monica, louder this time. Still on the floor, she was trying to apply pressure to Mercedes' bleeding ankle.

By heart I marked Steph's number on the phone and hit the call button, and it ringed. So I put the phone next to my ear and waited. It ringed six more times, and then I heard Steph's voice. "Hello?"

Gray, April 19th, the small hours

As gunshots suddenly started echoing inside the tunnel, Gray felt the familiar pain of foreign objects piercing his skin at high velocity as he did his best to completely tear off Marcus' right wing. Alex wasn't so lucky as he received most of the shots that would've landed on Gray, making him release Marcus' neck and fall to the ground.

Andrea shot eleven bullets before the cartridge was empty. Two of them landed on Gray, six of them on Alex, and the others missed. As Alex fell to the floor, Marcus used the last of his strength to punch Gray in the face so he would release him. Taylor, still down, started crawling towards his teammates, not sure exactly of what he would or could do.

The girl's attempt to collect another weapon from the main hall was interrupted by Drake, who entered the tunnel just in time to stop her in her tracks. The red wolf grabbed her whole face with one hand as she punched and kicked him to no effect. In this position, Drake started a familiar prayer to all of the people present, but was stopped by the faint cries of Taylor. "You'll kill her," he said, audible enough for Drake to understand and stop. And so he gave her one solid, clean punch to the face, and Andrea fell unconscious on the floor.

Drake ran to his friends, all laying down in one unified puddle of blood coming from four different sources. Every one of his steps sounded like he was walking through a swamp, and Alex's human body seemed minutes away from looking like a floating log.

The demon had slid down against the wall, leaving a trail of blood that went down, forming the shape of a waterfall. His throat was almost completely chewed out, one of his wings was about to fall off, and the rest of his face and body was slashed and bruised like something that should not still be alive, but he was. And he called, lowly and faintly, "Master."

Drake went straight to Gray, who laid face up, in human form, digging into his ribcage for one of the bullets that got him. "Alex," groaned Gray to Drake. "Get to him."

But as Drake turned to the brown wolf instead, the other end of the tunnel went completely dark, blocking half of the light that illuminated the wolves' path. A combination of crows and other flying animals focused on the entrance to the tunnel, creating a small whirlwind as the animals flew in circles over and over again. The wolves could barely see how a shape materialized from inside the whirlwind until the animals slowly flew away, revealing a man.

George, April 19th, the small hours

Listening to her voice was almost deafening, even though I had seen her just an hour before. "Steph," I sighed. I heard how the voices around her faded once I spoke.

"Oh my God," she said. "Are you alright?"

"I'm fine. I need to talk to Scotch. Are you with him?"

Silence. Monica laid next to me, listening to every word I said and unable to move. She had stopped trying to tend to Mercedes' wound.

"We went to Scotch's dad," she said to me, probably expecting me to react negatively, but I kept quiet. "He didn't believe us."

"But he will when you put him on the phone," I replied. From where I was sitting I could just feel how taken aback Steph was at my forward attitude.

"I'm at their house right now. They–"

"Put me on speaker, please," I interrupted. I couldn't tell Steph that her dad was passed out in front of me, probably inches from death, but I really wanted to, if only to accelerate the process.

Steph stayed silent for a moment. "You're on speaker now," she said.

"Mr. Walker, can you hear me?"

Another moment of silence. Then, "Yes," said the voice of an adult man. I wasn't very familiar with Scotch's dad, but I trusted Steph if she told me this was him.

"This is George McKnight," I said, giving him a moment to say something, but he didn't. "I have a lot of explaining to do."

"Young man, it is very late at night and I am busier than ever," he snapped, with an authority in his voice that easily rivaled Gray's. "I gave Ms. Kim the benefit of the doubt but this is too much for me to give right now."

I had to think fast. I remembered Mr. Larned again, and the greek words he always repeated. Use *logos* to appeal to logic, but first comes *pathos* to stir up emotion.

"I understand your point of view, sir," I said, keeping calm. "But I need you to listen to me for a second. There are many lives at risk and I want to save as much as possible, so please listen."

"Ms. Kim, I'm sorry." I could hear his voice changing course as he no longer spoke to the phone. "I'm gonna have to ask you to hang up."

"Peter Anderson is innocent," I babbled, shooting blindly. "So is Earnest Erb. And so am I." The call was still on but Walker didn't say anything else, so I reverted the decision I took seconds before. "Among the people you lost at the hospital are Dr. Kim and a nurse called Mercedes Jackson. They're here in front of me, and they're hurt."

"What?!" exclaimed Steph. "You're with my dad?"

"Is that a threat, mister?" asked Walker.

"No!" I started getting frustrated. "They've been attacked and I'm trying to save them. I need you to come here and take them and all the other people out before it's too late."

I could hear Steph's cries very faintly. "If you are responsible for the kidnapping of any of those innocent people–"

"I'm not," I said. "Here. Listen."

I handed the phone to Monica, who looked at it almost as if she didn't know what a phone was. She took it with upmost care and put it in her ear. "Hello?" she said. She heard whatever they said to her and she replied, "This is Monica Lee."

Monica started weeping and tossed the phone back to me, covering her eyes. "It's me again," I said into the confusing cacophony of voices from the other side.

"I need to ask you to take a picture of yourself and Ms. Lee, please," said Walker, losing a lot of cool in his voice."

"Sir, this model of phone was probably discontinued fifteen years ago. There's no camera."

The silence that usually followed my comments had now changed to endless muttering that I couldn't identify. I heard Walker, Scotch, Steph, and who knows who else.

"Scotch," I called.

After a moment, he replied. "George."

"You're Jonathan Walker. We call you Scotch because of the whisky brand. You want to be a lawyer when you grow up. You're tall and dark skinned, and look just like your dad. You also talk funny."

"Stop it," cautioned Walker. "Do not bring my son into this."

"If it'll make you come help, I'll do whatever is necessary. I really don't want these people to die."

"The Adler Police will not yield to your threats and intimidation, young man," rebuked Walker.

I needed to think of how to convince him. I he hadn't bailed by then it had to be doubt deep inside that kept him in the conversation. Something that would make him believe me other than a picture or my own voice. *Logos.*

"Mr. Walker," I started. "The hair you found at the crime scene. Some of it didn't match at all, right?" Silence. He was listening. "You must've found samples from me, Andrea, Monica and Miles, along with seven others that matched nothing in your records. I bet those didn't even match human DNA, am I right?"

"Young man–"

"Look, I don't know what else you want me to say. I'm giving you everything I've got for you to come and solve the case all by yourself *and* save dozens of lives in the process. Your son told me the FBI was stepping on you, and I'm giving you the chance to prove your worth to them. Leave it, and at least the lives of the two health professionals in front of me will be in your hands."

Silence. Faint sobs from a distance. Paper rustling.

"I'm in the woods North of Foxworth," I sighed. "I'm hurt but I'll be fine. Monica needs water and a blanket. Mercedes and Dr. Kim need blood transfusions at least. Come quick or let us die."

And I hung up.

Gray, April 19th, the small hours

The man was tall with short black hair. He wore a suit that shined in cleanliness and style as He breathed in and out with elegance in an open collar with no tie. His blue eyes were magnetic, not letting any of the wolves take their own eyes off of His, no matter how hard they tried. And His voice resounded in the tunnel and inside the wolves' chests, with a timbre that made Alex recover the rhythm of his breathes.

"This has been an interesting experiment," He said as he walked down the tunnel. Right before He stepped on the puddle of blood that streamed down to the entrance, the mere presence of His foot made the blood flow away, creating holes in the swamp that allowed Him to go without damaging His shoes. "Great things require sacrifices, and this is no exception. A great sacrifice of time, energy, and resources."

Gray leaned against the wall to climb up and stand. His bullet wound in the upper ribcage was bleeding much more than the one right below his elbow, but none more than the stab wound on his abdomen. "John, I assume," he dared to say out loud.

"That is the name I was assigned at birth," He replied, "and one I have chosen for the superior of the lesser to call me by."

"So that the lesser of the lesser can call you Master," said Gray, slowly getting closer to John. The Demon Master had stopped walking after a few steps, standing inside a circle of clean floor about five feet away from Taylor, who was still holding his own neck, trying not to choke on his own blood.

"I'm not naive enough to assume that you would call me your Master under any consensual circumstance," He said, looking around to see the sources of the blood. Drake was still crouched by Alex's side, unable to tend to him, mesmerized by John's voice. "Especially not after everything my minions have cost you."

"You're damn right," said Gray. "Nor will it matter what we call you after you're—" but Gray could not finish his sentence, for he was pushed back and slammed against the metal door with only a flick of His wrist.

"Michael, please," He said. "Don't make me waste the little energy I have left on demanding respect from you." Gray sat back against the metal door, holding his abdomen in excruciating pain. He turned to Drake. "You can't help your eldest anymore. He'll be dead before today's end, no matter how much you treat him. You can only buy him more hours of physical and psychological suffering, letting him know that, if it wasn't for him, you could've been an A-grade team."

"How dare you say that," said Drake, standing up. "After everything this man has gone through, you have no right to call him anything but an inspiration for whatever it is you want to do. Using other people to fuel your body and fulfill your desires. Pathetic."

"I agree with you, Drake," He replied, to Drake's surprise. "Indeed, this was a pathetic attempt at trying to create an army. Humans are so weak, so fragile. Sacks of thin bones and bland meats. Worthless and pathetic, like you said. But, alas, I will learn from my mistakes and be better the next time around. Be more involved in the process in order to assure the quality of my army."

"More involved?" said Gray from his sitting place. "Meaning you will actually do something instead of getting blondie and reddy to do it for you?"

"I do realize my mistake, Michael. Trust me when I tell you it will not happen again."

"Then why are you standing there, talking like a little bitch?" mocked Gray. "Come here and kill me with your own hands."

"Michael," called Taylor from the floor, but he couldn't find space in his vocal cords to say anything else.

"Because I'm not stupid, Michael Gray," He said, not sounding quite insulted but probably starting to lose his seemingly unbreakable cool. "I don't have enough energy left to take on whatever you and Drake can give me and still be able to maintain everything that's giving me control. My servants are dead, my minions are all out. And your dear boy George recently called for reinforcements that will arrive here very soon, and I am not planning on being here when they do." At the mention of George, all the wolves looked at each other in alarm. "I will not destroy my perfect body fighting you, nor will I waste any more energy on this lost battle. I know when to admit defeat, as that is the feat of great leaders."

John fell silent, letting all of their breathing echo through the tunnel walls, especially Marcus', who was still alive, somehow. "Master," called the demon again, though it was barely intelligible with most of his throat gone.

"You have failed me, Marcus," He said to His servant. "You, and Arabella, and Jason failed me. You missed the opportunity of killing your targets due to your unrestrained desire for sadism. You do not even deserve these words I'm speaking." And then the wolves saw something they thought was impossible: Marcus was crying.

"You disgust me," said Gray from his sitting spot.

"In order for my future plans to run as smoothly as possible, I have taken the liberty of handling my minions' memories for you," said the Demon Master. "I can't do anything about Andrea or Monica," He continued, looking back at Andrea's unconscious body, "but everyone else should be right for telling whatever it is you decide. That is your reward for having won."

Gray's breathing stabilized as he heard those words. He had not even thought about the aftermath of the battle until that moment, and couldn't help but wonder why He would do something like that. Maybe He was being honest, after all.

Flying animals started flowing from the tunnel exit and around John. A combination of crows, smaller birds, bats, and insects. "The last words you have spoken were that I disgust you," John said to Gray, looking into his eyes. "I will hold you to those words, Michael Gray," He said as He disintegrated inside the whirlwind.

#

Gray stood up again and walked to Taylor, who gasped for air as he held his own throat. "Alex," Taylor managed to mutter when Gray approached him.

Drake was still trying to tend to Alex's wounds, applying pressure to one of the bullet wounds on his shoulder. Alex's abdomen was almost spilling all over the floor, and a bullet had gone clean through his neck, millimeters away from his aorta. Not that he hadn't already lost an immeasurable amount of blood.

Alex coughed as Gray approached him. His shirtless, hairless dark skin was painted with shades of purple, green and red, slashed all the way from his neck to his hip. His hair, soaked in blood, fell over his eyes and forehead. "I'm right here," said Gray, holding his mentor's hand.

The brown wolf looked into his son's teary eyes. He hadn't spoken in a while, but Gray knew everything he wanted to say just by looking at him. That he was proud of him. That he looked just like his father. That he would go on to do amazing things. That his job as his caretaker had been done well.

Gray failed to notice when Drake stood up to pick up Taylor and bring him into their last meeting, all as humans. Drake held Taylor over his shoulders and descended slowly, getting at eye level with Alex. "We're all here with you," said Drake.

Alex nodded delicately, looking at every one of his teammates for one last time. He stopped at Gray again, still holding his hand. "Thank you," he muttered, too low for any normal person to hear. And slowly, Gray felt how the pressure in his hand got weaker and weaker, until the black man's hand fell limp, and he had closed his eyes.

Gray breathed in and out, trying to keep his posture. Drake put a hand over his shoulder and started to cry, but Gray could not. He was focused on trying not to hyperventilate as he saw his mentor's dead body in front of him. But what finally got him over the edge was the sound of Marcus' breathing just a few feet from them.

Gray stood up and walked ten steps to Marcus. The vampire looked up into Michael's death-ridden eyes as he grabbed his chewed off wing and tear it off completely, making Marcus make the most unnatural sound they had ever heard. "Everything we've studied about you tells me that you'll stay alive as long as your head is still attached to your body." Gray grabbed the detached wing by the lance, and slowly sank it into Marcus' chest, where the heart is supposed to be. "Let's try this out, to know if it's true."

Marcus' body spasmed lightly as the lance went through him and Gray kept pushing, until the tip of the lance touched the wall the demon was sitting against. The puddle of blood turned into a pond as Marcus' eyes locked with Gray's human ones, and he held his position until the demon's breathes stopped completely, who knows after how long.

Chapter 25
Wounds
George, April 19th, the small hours

It was surprisingly quiet after I hung up. Monica sobbed next to me at a very low volume, but I couldn't hear much else around me. The cold had softened, the wind had settled, and whatever animals had been lurking around seemed to have disappeared. It was just me and the eternal pain in my shoulder.

"How are you feeling?" I asked Monica, feeling really stupid as soon as the words left my mouth.

She sniffed and looked at me. Her face was in a very rough state, enhanced by the constant crying she had had going on. "I'm so worried for Miles," she said. "Last time I saw him he didn't look alive." She started sobbing again after that last word.

I had almost completely forgotten about Miles Goodman. Obviously Andrea was on top of my mind most of the time, and I guess Monica was second because she was her best friend and kind of the reason why we both got caught into all of this. But Miles felt so irrelevant to my timeline, and I felt really bad thinking that. It's not like I didn't care for his safety or anything. I just didn't give him much of a thought. Though I'd obviously remembered if we had rescued Andrea and Monica but not Miles. I'm not that big of a dick.

"Did they ever hurt you?" I asked. Stupid question too, seeing how Monica had lost a significant amount of weight. Also, just remembering how Andrea looked when we first got her had to be enough of a clue.

"They mostly kept us in these… bags," she answered, scratching her eyes. "I'd spend whole days just sitting there without doing anything else. No labor, no favors, nothing."

I wanted to ask so many more things. But aside from not being able to sort out my thoughts between my shoulder, the call, and the million other things in my head, something started happening around us. Something I had not seen or even thought about in weeks, and that caught us both completely off guard.

It started to drizzle.

Andrea

It should have been impossible to be in such pain as she was when she woke up. Andrea's whole body ached and burned even worse than when she had woken up hours before, unable to even move her fingers or her neck. She woke up on a stretcher indoors, moving at high speed through a hallway or a tunnel, but there was no way for her to know anything. Her throat stung from the inside, like a cat had scratched her larynx with its paws. The only thing she could feel in her legs was the sensation that they were about to shatter into a million pieces. Then, as she was moved on the stretcher through this corridor, she realized she was wearing sunglasses again, and that's why the lights on the ceiling were not burning away her retinas, which would not stop watering.

The only voice she recognized in the crowd was that of the gentle black lady who had taken care of her before, Ms. Rose. She was saying something about transferring somebody somewhere else, but Andrea didn't catch it. Before anybody noticed that she was awake, she passed out again.

#

Andrea woke up again, this time on a bed. If she had had the energy, she would've jumped out of her sleep, but she still wasn't able to move much more than before. She laid on a bed very similar to the one she'd been in before, including the IV on her left arm, only this time she was accompanied by a shadowy figure sitting to the other side of the room, lit only by a candle. Ms. Rose appeared to be sleeping on a chair, loosely holding a book in one of her hands.

The auburn-haired girl tapped her bed with her right hand, which was as much as her body would allow her to do before making her cry in discomfort, but the sheets were too soft to make any sound loud enough to get Ms. Rose's attention. Before she tried again or thought of anything else, she heard noises in the hallway that did the job. Ms. Rose stood up quickly and opened the door to query about the commotion. Trying to hear what was being said made Andrea realize that her ears were ringing, and as soon as she noticed, it got worse.

Ms. Rose turned to see her patient and rushed to her when she realized she was awake. She took Andrea's vitals while softly speaking about something Andrea could not focus on and so was lost in the ringing as she drifted in and out of consciousness. The only thing Andrea caught was, "This is going to help you sleep," before the nurse injected her with something she didn't see the color of. And so she went back to sleep, only this time she wouldn't wake up for a while.

Monica, April 19th, the small hours

The drizzle that quickly turned into a light rain felt soothing to their ears and skin as George and Monica caught up. They talked for what felt like hours, but was probably 45 minutes or so. She told him everything she could remember about the vampires and the cocoons, and how Earnest Erb simply appeared one day, covered in blood and holding a baby. Fortunately for both of them, she didn't see what happened to that baby, so she couldn't tell him.

About half an hour into their talk, Monica could feel the strength in her body coming back bit by bit. She checked on the two passed-out adults that laid next to them. She had successfully stopped the bleedings from their ankles, but they were still in need of medical attention and the two teenagers were starting to grow impatient.

Monica looked up into the rain and embraced it with her arms open, cleaning herself up off all the dirt and blood and sweat accumulated over the last weeks. She closed her eyes and let the rain fall on her face, feeling every drop of water cleansing her of all the horrible things she had experienced, and, somehow, giving her hope for the near future.

"Something's been on my mind for a while now," said George. "How did you find this place?"

"How did we find you here?"

"I mean, Foxworth. The house and the bunker. How did you follow us here?"

Monica had to stop and think. It wasn't something she had really considered before, just an order she obeyed. She searched deep within her mind, trying to remember, but the only thing that came to her was the image of her best friend. "I think," started Monica, unsure of where she was going, "that it was Andrea."

"Andrea? She told you?"

"Not exactly." Monica couldn't find a cohesive way of expressing what she was thinking, like a toddler without much vocabulary. "I think she was something like a beacon, you know?"

"A beacon?" said George, fascinated. "That's…
Kinda brilliant, actually. So they left her there on purpose."

"I guess," said Monica, full of doubts about her
whole experience now that she was thinking deeply. "I
couldn't tell you if it was part of a plan or not. Lots of
things felt like they were throwing shit at the wall,
honestly."

"Wait," added George, clearly into deep thought, in
the middle of a realization. "Did you not eat during your
capture? At all?"

Monica wasn't sure of how she knew the answer to
that. It was something innate inside of her, like knowing
her own name. "Kind of," she answered. "It's like we were
all nourished through our cocoons. Like we absorbed the
the sap from the trees and they fed through us. Arabella
gave me the occasional piece of bread every couple days,
but I don't know for the others. It's weird."

"Real weird," said George.

She started telling him about her experience at the
lake when they both heard a lot of noises coming from the
North, to George's left. Monica, sitting with a twisted
ankle, leaned over in that direction until two headlights
blinded her. "Freeze!" said a voice through a megaphone.
"Put your hands up!"

Monica froze in place. She put her hands up and
squinted her eyes as the silhouette of a police officer
approached her very slowly. "Identify yourself," demanded
the officer in a deep, authoritative tone.

"M-M-Monica Lee," she stuttered.

The officer, a black man in his 50s, approached her enough to cover the headlights, letting her see his face more clearly. Judging by his extreme resemblance to her acquaintance, Monica deduced this was Sergeant Terrence Walker, Scotch's dad. The man George had called an hour before.

Walker looked up and down at Monica, noticing the two adult bodies laying on the floor next to her. "Kill that," ordered Walker to his men. Not understanding for a brief moment, Monica panicked for a second until the lights were killed and two more officers approached her, now illuminated by the moonlight. "You're alright, sweetheart," said Walker, in a completely different tone. A soothing, friendly tone that made her believe everything she was hoping for just minutes before.

"Glad you came," said George, still sitting against the tree. One of the officers was checking on him when Walker made a hand gesture. She watched as Walker and George talked, almost not noticing how an officer had wrapped her in a blanket, picked her up and taken her to an ambulance that was parked just a dozen yards away.

She stood next to the ambulance as a paramedic checked her vitals. As Walker and George kept talking, two other paramedics took Ms. Mercedes and Dr. Kim away, carrying them inside the ambulance. Monica spaced out completely, faintly hearing the paramedic asking her questions but not answering to even her name. She was focused on the forest that acted as background for George and Walker's conversation.

Monica was exhausted, thirsty and sore all over, but she couldn't take her eyes away from the woods in the distance. It was as if a voice was calling to her, and she didn't know if she should answer or simply go to it. The voice that came from the woods afar, but also from inside her head, was a familiar one that she recognized but couldn't pinpoint from where. As the paramedic snapped his fingers in front of Monica's eyes to call for her attention, she stared in the distance. Until she thought she saw something.

A pair of blue eyes that shined bright in the moonlight were calling to her, pulling her mind away from her body. But she resisted. She stood where she was and kept looking onwards until the voice faded away into a whisper. Before snapping out of her trance, she saw, one last time, the pair of blue eyes in the distance, and the face to whom they belonged to. And she would live the rest of her life remembering those blue eyes and pale skin and perfect dark hair, even though she would never see Him ever again.

Gray, April 19th, the small hours

At some point after Marcus' eyes stopped shining, Gray had fallen to his knees and tightly held his mentor's body in silence. The metal door at the end of the tunnel opened up to let out dozens of people with cuts and bruises who were not prepared to see the carnage right outside the room. The pool of blood extended all the way from the door to the entrance, the walls were almost completely covered in brown and red spots, and the ceiling had the remains of a strong kick the blond wolf had received earlier. The stench of iron made a couple of the hostages cringe in nausea.

Nobody touched or talked to Gray as the scene was cleaned. Drake helped carry Taylor outside the tunnel to get his eye and neck tended, and Ms. Rose placed Andrea on a stretcher and took her away. Mr. Foxworth walked out with his cane and gave orders around to the crew and people moved in and out of the tunnel past Gray, but nobody dared say anything to him. After they organized, the Foxworth crew eventually started cleaning the floor and walls around Michael and Alexander, but they would have to wait until the morning before they could clean every spot. At one point, the demon's dead body had disintegrated into a huge pile of thick, black ash, which was appropriately removed from the scene.

Gray carried his protector's body to the room that used to be his, and placed him on the bed. His eyes were closed and his face looked at peace, not showing the unmeasurable pain he was surely going through at the moment of his death. Alex's body had stopped leaking blood a while back, so Gray arranged him on the bed to look like he could be sleeping, with both hands resting over his abdomen. As Michael left Alex's room and closed the door, he collapsed on the floor.

George, April 19th, the small hours

As the paramedics checked on Monica, I told Walker pretty much everything I could in my state of being. Even as I was tended properly for the first time in what felt like ages, I still couldn't feel entirely safe until Walker explicitly said that I wasn't a suspect anymore. I told caught him up on everything regarding what had happened since I left Steph's house, recalled most of the story I told Scotch, and answered a couple of short questions he had for me. In the end, seeing my state of being convinced him that I was probably not lying.

Shortly after Walker arrived with the ambulance and two patrols, a proper crime scene was established with some other vehicles that got there later. I watched as the forensics team analyzed Arabella's remains, which had quickly decayed into a thick, dark ash. It made it way more difficult for my case, but that was far down the list of my priorities at that moment.

"So the cabin is that way?" asked Walker, pointing south. I nodded. "How come there haven't been any emergency calls from the town, then? I'm sure there was a big enough commotion."

"That town doesn't really exist," I explained. "It's more of a façade for Mr. Foxworth's employees to be on stand-by. I'm sure they were all present in the fight. You'll see them." I was sure Walker was having a very hard time believing everything I was saying, but he was likely doing his best to assimilate it all.

The first ambulance had already taken the two adults away, and the second one was about to leave with Monica, and the paramedic insisted that I go with her. I obviously refused, and Walker gave them the green light to keep going. The two new ambulances that arrived were setting up a sort of medical tent, right next to the forensics's perimeter.

Monica stepped inside the ambulance and looked on to me with worried eyes. I did my best to give her a warm and reassuring smile, knowing full well she was thinking about Miles and all the other people she'd seen since the hospital. From that distance I could barely make up her lips as she mouthed "Thank you" and went inside the ambulance. A few moments later, they left.

As my elbow was bandaged and my arm put on a sling over my jacket, I heard Walker ordering for the reinforcement of the site and for the team of policemen to get ready. This was the moment when I wondered about a very curious detail. "Sir," I called to Sgt. Walker. He turned his head to me. "Why isn't the FBI here?"

To my surprise, Walker smiled. "I wasn't going to risk telling them about your ludicrous tale," he said.

"What if you needed help?" I asked. He didn't say anything. He just called attention to the dozens of people who were arriving at the scene, all part of the Minnesota

State First Responders. A very Mid-Western scene to behold, indeed. "Glad to see you inspire loyalty," I added.

"Comes with the job if you do it well for long enough," he responded.

There was a gasp not far from where I was that made us both turn. One of the forensic investigators had fallen on her back at the sight of a giant red wolf that had suddenly appeared in front of their eyes. The wolf looked around, ignoring the attention he had called on himself and how a couple of officers were ready to pull their weapons on him. When he saw me, he walked to me, as casually as ever.

"Glad to see you're okay," I told Drake. He didn't answer vocally, but with his eyes, sort of telling me that I had to go with him. Though we had never talked about any of this, I assumed they had established a sort of protocol when dealing with people outside of the team. My guess was that he wasn't just going to detransform or even speak in front of all of those people. "Should I go with you?" I asked, and he nodded.

Walker was absolutely baffled by this response. Though dogs can be extremely smart animals, nodding in such a human way must be very rare even for the most highly trained dogs.

"You should come with me, Sergeant," I said to Walker. He turned to see me in surprise.

"You want to follow this wolf?" he inquired.

"I'm sure you'd want to follow him too if you knew who he was," I said, not making things much clearer to Walker.

Apparently given up on understanding every single thing, Walker helped me stand up, which would be the first time I used my legs in hours. A slightly lighter blue and shades of orange were starting to bleed in the sky above us, marking the true beginning of the morning and indicating that I had, in fact, been sitting there for at least four hours.

Drake signaled me to ride him, which I did not dare reject with the pain I was still feeling on my shoulder. Though it was hard to hold on to Drake's back with my arm on a sling, Drake did not seem to be in a hurry, which calmed me, letting me know that the fighting was over and Foxworth's people were onto everything.

Drake walked from the woods to the cabin with Sgt. Walker right next to us. "So," started Walker. "What is this fellow's name?" he asked, not sure if to me or Drake himself. Either way, he was clearly expecting me to answer.

"Drake," I said. "He's the youngest of the wolves, and the one who protected me after I crashed against the tree." Walker seemed to be putting some pieces back together, but it would be impossible for him because he wasn't even aware of the three fourths of the puzzle he was missing.

"Does he know Peter Anderson as well?" asked Walker. It took me a second to remember that he was referring to Elijah.

"They all did," I said. "And they'll all vouch for his innocence, just like I did."

"I believe you, George," said Walker. And I knew he did, fortunately.

Gray, April 19th, early morning

Michael slowly opened his eyes, only to shut them at the sight of an intense radiant light straight into his face. As he regained consciousness, he identified the feeling of cold metal on his back and legs, and the familiar burn of closing wounds on his abdomen. Given the lack of movement around him, he figured he had already been operated on, and he was about to be transferred to a bed.

It shouldn't have taken too long for Michael to recover after the operation. Taking his inhuman regeneration into account, he assumed that by the next morning he would be perfectly fine, but the constant amount of trauma received to the same area over and over had made it hard for him to even breathe without feeling pain, something he had grown unaccustomed to decades prior. Still, not long after his awakening, he found himself laying down on a cold bed with no further instructions but to rest. Though physical rest would be more than welcome by him, peace of mind wasn't something he was counting on anytime soon.

Unable to sleep with all the commotion outside his room, Gray opted to at least use the noise as a sound wall for meditation, which he was almost able to achieve, until he heard the mention of George's name. Gray opened his meditating eyes and focused on the sound of Mr. Foxworth's voice as he spoke to the newly-arrived George, apparently being brought in by Drake, alongside another person Gray did not recognize.

George's voice sounded weak and fragile, and almost surprising in presence as Gray had almost completely forgotten about the boy's existence. But he couldn't say he wasn't glad to know he was alive. "This is Sergeant Terrence Walker," said the boy to Mr. Foxworth.

The old man and the sergeant exchanged greetings and introductions that Gray could not care for at the moment. He heard about a camp being set outside of town and first responders taking care of two of the captured hostages from the hospital. They had also taken in one of the missing kids, a girl called Monica.

"They found the other one a while ago," said Foxworth.

"Miles?!" asked George. "He's alive?"

"Under great care. He's very critical."

"If you don't mind, Mr. Foxworth," started Walker, "I would like to talk to you in private."

Moments of silence that probably included stares and head shakes that Gray couldn't possibly guess. Then he heard two people walking down the hallways and entering the room right next to his. The door opened and closed.

"With all due respect, sir," started Walker, "I need to ask you some questions about your operation."

"I was born prepared to answer anything you'd like to ask me, Mr. Walker," answered Foxworth, calm as ever. "I'd like to start by clarifying that every single person working inside this bunker is a trained professional who has been background-checked, tested, and is paid handsomely."

Foxworth's charming way of reading minds seemed to have worked on Walker, whose voice sounded friendly and approachable even with the unthinkable amount of questions he must have had. "I wouldn't doubt that coming into such a welcoming atmosphere, even in times like these."

The two men talked for about half an hour, clarifying logistic procedures about the transportation of the victims and their future care. Apparently, as Gray slept, Foxworth's team had already recovered every hostage and aligned them for treatment in the faux gas station on the other side of the street. None of the hostages had received fatal injuries, though a couple were in more severe conditions, including George's friend, Miles. Those who had received fatal injuries, however, were the contention team, including the two soldiers that Marcus had stabbed in front of Gray. At one point or another, the seven soldiers released to contain the possessed hostages had been killed, some in more gruesome ways than others. Alan Maffei, who had disappeared about a month prior and had been in a coma for days, did not survive the attack. But, as far as the

Adler Police Department were concerned, nobody had died the night before.

It was half an hour of recap and explanations about the hospital and Elijah's identity, how George had been saved and what had really happened with the kids that were kidnapped. Everything surrounding Earnest Erb – a name that ringed no bells to Gray – and the operation in the town of Foxworth, Minnesota. It seemed too easy for Walker to believe every word that Foxworth said, but his tone implied that he did, though Gray kept waiting for some kind of turn.

The plan agreed upon between Foxworth and Walker consisted of the police "finding" the hostages tied up in the woods not far from the cabin. They would arrange for somebody to recall the events as the media are to be told, and for no suspect to be linked to the case. "However," included Foxworth, "I must implore you to clean the name of my protégé."

"I will make sure it is arranged," guaranteed Walker. "I may not have known his real name, but Peter Anderson was a friend." And that was the last thing Gray needed to hear to know that everything would be fine, eventually.

George, April 19th, early morning

The moment Mr. Foxworth and Sgt. Walker left for a room, I walked to the tunnel in the kitchen. Drake, still a wolf, tried to stop me, but I wasn't stopping for anything. I needed to see what had happened as I was gone and Drake was protecting me. I dodged the dozens of people walking in and out of the tunnel and managed to take a peak inside, where I saw three or four people cleaning up the walls and ceiling of what looked like blood.

"Tell me everything," I said to Drake as he pulled on my pants with his mouth. "What happened?"

"You need to rest," he insisted.

"I am not moving until you tell me what happened." Drake's face filled with sadness, which served as a cushion for everything he was about to tell me.

I agreed to go to what still was assigned as my room and sit on the bed as Drake recalled everything he'd seen as soon as he got to the cabin. He told me about the fight that was going on, how he got there just in time to stop Andrea for doing even more damage. How Alex fell, and Gray killed Marcus. It was a lot to take, but I couldn't get myself to cry, because I felt I'd done it enough.

The knowledge of Alex's death would've hit me way harder in any other circumstances. We never liked each other very much, but I never wished him ill, much less death. He was an experienced man with a lot to give to the world, and I did feel sad for his loss, even though I doubted he would've felt sad for mine.

"Where's Andrea?" I asked, afraid of the answer.

"Resting under Ms. Rose" he answered. I put my head down and covered my face, not sure why. He put his paw on my knee, like he would put his hand on my shoulder if he were a man. "I saw her eyes, George. That wasn't her. She was a puppet, a tool."

I fell on my knees and hugged him without even thinking. He hugged me back, however he could as a wolf, and I felt his breathing steadying mine, slowly but surely, until I didn't feel like drowning anymore.

"Have you seen Miles?" I asked him.

"He's in care with the other hostages."

"Can I see him?"

Drake thought about his answer for a moment. He looked into my worried, guilty eyes, and nodded. We walked out of the room, down the hallway, and out of the bunker, where a cabin used to be and now there was the skeleton of a structure with no walls or ceiling. It had stopped raining a while back, and, to my surprise, it wasn't as cold as it had been when I first got back.

We walked across the street to the gas station near the cabin, but the door was shut and we were not allowed inside. There were no tables or sellable items, only people laying down in makeshift mattresses, being tended by six or seven different nurses, men and women. I counted fourteen people on the floor, all of them unconscious, but none of them Miles.

"He's in the back," clarified Drake. "He needed special attention."

We headed out the back and went in from the backdoor, which was open. Inside was a hospital bed with all of the fancy hospital things I would've expected to see in a room at Adler-Morrow General, including an IV cart. On the bed was Miles Goodman, shirtless, covered with a blanket. His left eyebrow looked like it had been cut off with a knife, his whole face was bruised and swollen, his neck and cheeks looked dangerously skinny. He seemed to have had a far worse time than Andrea.

"Mr. McKnight," said an elderly nurse sitting by Miles' side, who I had never met in my life. "You cannot be here. Please go back to the bunker." The nurse shooed us out before I could ask any questions or take a better look at the state of Miles' body.

I sat against the wall outside the backdoor, taking in the relatively warm air of the forest. The sky had finally taken in more blue. "I don't know what to do now," I said, not precisely to Drake, but there was nobody else there to hear it.

"I can take you to Taylor," he suggested. I felt really bad for Taylor after hearing about his eye. I wondered if their regeneration went as far as regrowing entire organs, at least one as small as an eye. I nodded, and so we went back down the stairs and into the bunker.

Taylor was in his assigned room from before the attack. Drake assured me he could hear him being awake, so I knocked on the door very softly. I heard a faint "Come in," and so I opened the door at a slow enough pace so that the light from the hallway didn't flood the entire room all at once.

The blonde wolf was bandaged all over his torso and around his neck. His right eye was also covered, and I didn't dare to ask if he was ever going to recover it or not. I just came in and smiled, and he smiled back. "I'm glad you're okay," I said.

"I will be," he replied. "Soon enough."

We all sat there in silence for another moment. I didn't really know what to say; if I had to apologize for keeping Drake from joining the fight, or give my condolences for Alex, or maybe thank them for everything they'd done for me. Yeah. Probably that.

"We should let him rest," chimed in Drake to break the silence. "You need to rest that throat."

"I-" I sloppily added, interrupted by Drake's comment. The two wolves – one an actual wolf and the other a resting, beat up man – turned to look at me, waiting for whatever I wanted to say. "I just wanted to thank you," I blurted out. They gave me a moment to breathe, then I continued. "I don't know when it was the last time I thanked both of you. For everything."

Taylor couldn't control his smile, which his face was clearly not in condition for. "Helping each other is part of being a team," said Drake, something I'm sure Taylor would've said too if it wasn't for his throat.

I hugged both of them however I could, with Drake half-climbing on the bed to meet our arms. I'm not sure how long of a hug it was, but it felt quite long, maybe because I had been longing for peace and quiet for such a long time, and so much stuff had happened in the last 3 days; more than everything that had happened the few days before.

There was a light knock on the door behind me. "Come in," said Taylor. In came Ms. Rose, who looked as exhausted as she probably felt.

"Excuse me, Mr. Kaminsky," said Ms. Rose. "I was asked to fetch Mr. McKnight."

"Is everything alright?" I asked, worried that, for some reason, something else had happened.

"Ms. Andrea has asked to see you."

Chapter 26
Reunions
Steph, April 19th, the small hours

The waiting was unbearable for every person in the Walker residence. Evelyn Kim had driven there in the middle of the night to be with her daughter as they all waited on updates from the house's patriarch. Supposedly, everything after that night would be fine, and finally over. It took way more time than they would've liked, but the call eventually came.

Mrs. Walker was dark and tall, just like her husband and son. Her eyes were baggy with stress and sorrow as she waited for her husband's report, and she jumped out of her chair when her phone started vibrating with his name on it. She answered immediately. "Terry?"

The sound of her husband's voice was instantly calming for the whole room, even for Stephanie and her mother, who were sitting on a couch to the other side and unable to hear what Sgt. Walker was telling his wife. She nodded and cried with relief, which let Stephanie breathe for what felt like the first time in a year.

"They found them," said Mrs. Walker as she hung up. "All of them. They're coming home."

"And my dad?" urged Stephanie.

"He's on his way to the hospital right now. He's the first one they found."

Steph and her mother hugged and sobbed against each other's shoulders. Scotch, ever proper and firm, looked as touched as ever, holding back a big smile.

"When this is over," whispered Evelyn to her daughter, "you'll tell me everything. Okay?" Steph nodded and hugged her mother harder.

Stephanie grabbed her phone and texted Roger and Stacy. That they had found everybody and it would all be fine. Given the time, none of them answered, but she expected them to explode with glee the next morning. Now they just had to wait for Walker to do his job and get everyone back safe. But as they waited, she kept thinking.

She thought about the nightmare that it would be for whoever's job it was to explain what had happened to these people. There was no way the real explanation of it all could be given, so she could not understand what was in stock for her father when he got back, or for her fellow classmates. Especially George.

What would be of him? He said he didn't want to go back, and he didn't look half as damaged as he described Andrea. Was he gonna be in trouble? Was he even going to appear along with the other missing kids? Would she ever see him again?

And so her moment of absolute joy was gone, replaced with hours of silent anguish.

Andrea, April 19th, early morning

Not many words could be thought by Andrea after she woke up for the third time that morning in the dark room. "Water." "Sore." "Head." And "George." IV in her wrist and legs feeling numb, she may have blurted out something to Ms. Rose as she woke up, because her eyes opened to find a glass of ice water and two small white pills right next to her bed.

Andrea straightened her back as much as possible so she could take her pills and refresh her throat and lips, which felt dry as a desert. "Be gentle with yourself," said Ms. Rose, standing in front of the bed, looking like she was about to collapse. "You don't wanna hurt your throat even more."

The auburn-haired girl thought carefully about her next action. Like a car engine warming up, she felt her throat vibrating before creating sounds, and spoke very softly at first. "Thank you," she whispered, not feeling any pain.

"My pleasure, miss," answered Ms. Rose with a smile. "Is there anything else you'd like right now? You need to rest a bit before you can eat properly."

"Could you," she started, giving space between words to test her voice as she raised the volume, "get George? Just so I can see him."

Ms. Rose looked on. "I'll bring him in if you promise not to get off your bed," she said.

Andrea nodded, and so Ms. Rose left the dark room. Alone on her bed, Andrea wondered what had happened ever since the last thing she remembered, which was holding onto the black wolfman and calling out for Marcus; after that, everything was a confusing blur. She couldn't remember fighting any more but she must've, she knew she must've done more.

The opening of the door brought her thoughts to a screeching halt as she got ready to see George. Ever since their capture, she hadn't known anything about him aside from his letter and the short story the blonde wolfman had told her. She hadn't seen him nor heard his voice, and although it had been a while since she stopped thinking of the possibility of being trapped in a government facility, seeing him would hit the last nail in that coffin. If only for that, he just had to show up.

Ms. Rose opened up slowly and entered the room. "Remember to stay in bed, please," she warned Andrea. "Mr. McKnight, please be very gentle."

"Don't worry," Andrea heard George say from the hallway. "I'm not in such great shape either."

Ms. Rose nodded softly and left the room, letting another, bigger shadow come in. He had never been much taller than her, but at the moment he looked towering, maybe a combination of the drugs, exhaustion, and the lighting. Still, the shape of George McKnight entering her room made Andrea very, very happy. He had one arm resting on a sling, his face looked tired and pained, slightly bruised. And he had a tattoo on his right shoulder, which wasn't covered by a sleeve.

"Hi," he said, shyly as ever, walking in and closing the door. The dark room was only illuminated by the candle Ms. Rose had turned on a while back. The light from the flame reflected on the metal bar from the IV, giving his face a bit more exposure. Still, Andrea's eyes were very accustomed to the dark, so she could see him almost clear as day.

"Hey," she said, not whispering but still low on volume, afraid of a sting. "You can sit," she pointed.

George sat slowly on the side of he bed, next to Andrea's numb legs. "I'm so glad that you're okay," said George, hesitating at his desire to gently touch her leg. She was glad he didn't do it, because it would've probably hurt a lot. "When we found you a couple days back, I only wanted to talk to you. But you were out."

"I'm sorry," she replied. "I wanted to talk to you as soon as I woke up, but you were off already."

"There's–" he started, holding a whimper. "There's nothing to apologize for. If anything, I should be sorry for all that you've gone through."

"Wh-why?" asked Andrea, the volume of her voice rising a bit without intention. "It's not like you've been safe and sound at home."

George couldn't resist anymore and let the tears out. From where she sat, Andrea could feel his desperation to hug her, and she felt the same. "It's so unfair," he muttered. "To see you like this. To know what you've gone through."

"Georgie," started Andrea, too low for him to hear in-between his cries.

"I spoke to Monica," he continued, making Andrea feel guilty as ever in the blink of an eye. Monica, her best friend and companion through all of this mess, and she hadn't even wondered about her. It felt as if George and the wolves had been on her mind for so long due to her mission, she had forgotten about everything else. Seeing George now felt almost like the fulfillment of her task, even though she was no longer under His control. "She told me what they did to you and how you were during that time. It's horrible."

And it had been horrible. But Andrea's desperation grew increasingly poignant because she wanted him to understand that it wasn't important at the moment. That she was safe, he was safe, and it was all over. She needed him – and herself – to see nothing more than that. That it was over. That nothing else was left to be done or fixed. Even though something told her it wasn't true.

"How is she?" asked Andrea after a moment of silence. "And Miles."

"She was taken to the hospital an hour ago," said George, rubbing his eyes. "Miles is still here. They're taking good care of him."

Silence again. Andrea was too busy thinking about her peers to say anything else. She didn't remember much of Miles during their capture, aside from him being dragged by Monica everywhere they had to go. Arabella was especially irritated by him, she recalled.

"What about the kind man I talked to when you left?" she asked, remembering the blonde wolfman who had been there when she awakened the night before. Something deep within her mind told her his name was Taylor.

"That sounds like Taylor. I doubt the other two were very kind to you." After this, George fell silent, like remembering a detail that had slipped his mind. "Taylor's fine," he continued, "under great care as well. Just spoke to him before coming here."

Andrea stared at George as he spoke. She had always felt fascinated by his ability to tell stories or anecdotes, and had missed sitting down with him to just talk for a while. Talking about something he knew or cared about was the one way Andrea knew George could let go of his worries and anxieties and just be himself. So she let him talk, asking him more questions about his time there and the people he had met, recalling the events at the hospital and so on, until somebody would come tell George that Andrea had to rest. But nobody came, so he kept talking, and she kept listening.

Gray, April 19th, noon

At a moment impossible for him to determine, Gray fell back to sleep for a few more hours. He woke up violently, feeling he had left something undone and had to run back to finish it, only to realize he had been in peace for quite a long time, and that his rest had done marvels for his body. The sudden thrust with which he straightened his back would've felt a lot worse a couple hours before, but now it was just a sting in what, judging by the looks of it, would be a very nasty scar across his abdomen.

Gray stood up from his bed feeling rejuvenated. His nostrils were passing air normally, his bones crackled on and on as he moved, his ears felt like they were attuning to all of the noise outside without the nauseating feeling of the completely unfiltered sounds of the world. Wearing nothing but his pijama pants, Michael opened the door to find the hallway completely empty, with most of the sounds coming from one end or the other.

He walked to the left, towards the main hall. Where the roundtable used to be was now filled with people on small mattresses being tended by a combination of Foxworth people and nurses from outside, being taken upstairs on stretchers by the two teams. These images almost forced Michael to walk up the stairs to the outside, to see what had become of the house and its surroundings. The wood cabin was completely gone, but so were many other things that he was used to: the isolation, the overcast that kept the world feeling grey, the cold breeze that would've ruptured his nose if he had come out outdoors the way he was dressed. Instead, the air felt relatively warm, and there were people walking on and about from the forest, taking the patients on stretchers. Some of these patients he recognized from the night before, remembering how some of those bruises were caused by his hands.

From a distance he identified Mr. Foxworth talking with a tall black man who he assumed must have been Walker. As he walked closer to them, their conversation continued, though Foxworth noticed his presence and clearly assumed he was listening in. "And so it will be done," said the old man to the sergeant. "I'm anxious to see the results soon."

"Is this one of your specialists?" asked Walker, referring to Gray, though obviously not aware that he could hear him.

"If you'd like to call him that. Yes," answered Foxworth. "He has healed well, apparently," he added, likely commenting to Gray more than to Walker.

"Glad to see everything going," started Gray as he got closer to the pair. He turned to Walker and stretched his hand, a sign of approachability that he knew would tell Foxworth he had many questions. "Michael Gray," he introduced himself, shaking Walkers hand.

"Sergeant Terrence Walker, at your service," answered the tall black man. The friendly and conversational tone of his voice matched perfectly with his face as he spoke, something that told Gray much of what he needed to know about this man's approach to his job. "We're just about done with the recovery of the people. Only missing those in critical condition."

"Where's Drake?" asked Gray to the old man, steps from blatantly ignoring Walker's comment.

"He's been around, here and there," answered Foxworth. "Right now I don't know where he is. Maybe accompanying Taylor. Or vice versa."

Taylor. He had been badly hurt and would probably lose an eye because of his wounds. "I'll go check on them," said Gray. "Great job," he nodded to Walker, leaving without waiting for a response.

#

His two companions were only a few doors down the hallway, but he hadn't payed attention to their sounds when he woke up. He went back into the bunker and knocked on the door, though he knew both of them were waiting for him. "Come in," called Taylor, and so Gray opened the door to find him sitting on bed against the wall, with Drake laying on the floor as a wolf, half asleep.

"Needed to check outside," started Gray. "There's a whole operation."

"We've been informed," yawned Drake. "We were using this time to relax for a bit."

"Sorry to interrupt," said Gray, without an ounce of sarcasm in his tone. This, naturally, surprised his team. "I wanted to check on Taylor's eye."

"Well, I still don't know about that," said Taylor. "They told me to wait patiently, who knows for how long. Maybe forever."

"We'll get through this," added Drake, yawning afterwards. "As soon as they finish upstairs."

But Gray wasn't sure what to expect after they'd finished upstairs. For one, several burials had to be arranged, including one for his mentor.

There was a knock on the door that they all heard coming. Judging by the smell, it was either Foxworth or Walker. "Come in," called Taylor, and in came Mr. Foxworth, cane in hand.

"They are finishing up now," said the old man. "Just wanted to let you know that it'll be okay to come out soon."

It was always okay for them to go out of the bunker, that they knew. What Foxworth probably meant was that the stress of the evacuation operation would be over and the wolves wouldn't be as overwhelmed with such movement of people. That'd be something Gray would surely appreciate.

"What about George?" asked Taylor, reminding Gray of that little detail he had forgotten.

"He said he wanted to travel back with his friends," said Foxworth, with a sort of hopeful look in his eyes. "He'll be back later today."

The boy wanted to travel back, but not stay. Gray felt a strange mix of thoughts as Foxworth said that, like a combination of relief and confusion. Relief because he thought George was leaving them, or because he was actually staying? He wasn't sure.

George, April 19th, noon

Sitting on what felt like a military briefing when you're 17 and not part of the military is really weird, especially when the briefing is held almost exclusively for you. At some point during my conversation with Andrea, Walker interrupted us to take us with a team of policemen who were in charge of taking all of those innocent people back to Adler, trying to spin the story of whatever had happened and what the conscious hostages were supposed to say. After about half an hour, the plan was set, and Andrea was to be taken in an ambulance back to society, this time to a fancy, huge hospital in Minneapolis. I insisted on going alongside her, even though I wasn't staying. My whole time there, I wondered if that had been the right decision.

Maybe I was wrong. Maybe staying with her until the very end was not the right thing to do, because it would hurt more after she had to leave. If we were to follow the plan that had been agreed by all parties involved, I *had* to leave her once we got to the hospital. And I wasn't going to ruin this plan.

I helped Ms. Rose take Andrea out of the bunker and into the ambulance where we were getting transported. Though I was focused mostly on her, I couldn't help but glance at all the people that was involved in this operation, including a very notable individual that I saw speaking with Mr. Foxworth and Sgt. Walker: Mayor Robbins, Antoine's grandfather. I saw him looking at me as I helped Andrea up the ambulance, but I was instructed by Walker to not say anything to anybody, so I kept quiet.

Ms. Rose and I put Andrea in the back of the ambulance. She had a bottle of water to drink but nothing else except for me. Ms. Rose left us both be as she said her goodbyes to Andrea. "Make sure to drink lots of water with your pills, okay?" she said, with almost no energy left on her body.

Not long later the engine was started and the ambulance drove away. I could see the cabin's skeleton blurring out as we drove off of Foxworth, Minnesota. I sat next to Andrea, who leaned her head against my shoulder and held my hand as the box vibrated with the feel of the wheels rolling on the road. I leaned my head over hers and took a deep breath. Moments later, we both fell asleep.

#

We were woken up by how the ambulance suddenly stopped in its tracks. The instinct I had developed the past couple weeks told me that something terrible was about to happen, but seeing Andrea next to me and feeling my arm resting on a sling reminded me that all of that was over for now.

It didn't miss me that where we were parked was completely dark. It wasn't until a paramedic opened the doors that I noticed we were inside a parking complex, with a direct entrance to the hospital. "Can you give us a second?" I asked the paramedic who was preparing to get her out.

"Thirty seconds, sir," said the paramedic, leaving us be. It was a strange response, which made me think that all these people may have been working for Mr. Foxworth.

"I'll make sure to monitor how you're feeling, okay?" I told Andrea hastily. "I can ask them for daily reports and stuff. I'm sure they'll be fine with that."

"You don't have to worry about me so much," said Andrea as loud and clear as her body allowed her too. "I want you to rest."

I ignored her. "Follow their instructions and everything will go smoothly, alright? I promise."

I felt like a giant clock was ticking as I spoke to her, and that she would be gone once the clock stopped. I wanted to say so much more, hug her and hold her hand for so much longer. I wanted to become invisible and follow her in, and be with her through the process. But I couldn't, and I had like 10 seconds left.

"Georgie," she said, grabbing my hand. "Please be safe out there. Worry about your wellbeing. Promise me."

I smiled at her as I saw the paramedic coming back to get her. "Okay," I said.

The paramedic said something I didn't hear and Andrea had to step down from the ambulance. Our fingers grasped for each other as she got further away from me and

I started tearing up. She was put on a wheelchair and gave me a faint smile as she was taken away, unable to turn her neck enough to see me.

I sat on the ambulance step as many other paramedics moved patients on stretchers into the hospital. The automatic doors opened to let everybody in, and I saw Andrea's auburn mane of hair go in and make more and more distance, until there wasn't anything else to see.

I had failed to notice the police cars that had parked besides all of the ambulances. As I sat down and sobbed, I heard heavy steps approaching me. I raised my head to see Sgt. Walker. "May I sit?" he asked. I scooted over to make space for him.

"I guess this was all a success," I muttered.

"I would say it was," he replied. "Generally speaking." Walker was about to put his hand over my shoulder, but decided against it. "It's all thanks to you, you know."

I scoffed. "Hardly. More like it was all *because* of me." I felt I was betraying what Andrea had just asked me to do, and what the vision of my mom told me. But I couldn't help it.

Walker sighed. "You called me, right? It is thanks to you that all these people got treated on time. Don't take that away from yourself."

"I really don't want to talk about this right now, sir. I'm sorry." I started standing up, but Walker didn't move.

"There's something else I'd like to talk to you about." As he said it, I sat back down, ready for more bad news. "It's about The Missing Four."

I had completely forgotten about that nickname. The clickbait, remarkable nickname the media gave us when we first disappeared. My intentional separation from the news helped me forget that my face was all over the state and probably the country, and now that Walker brought it up again, I couldn't help but feel worried about what Andrea would have to go through.

"You still have time to come back," continued Walker. "You know the plan. You know the story. You can come in and help maintain the—"

"I am not going back," I said, firmly. Not doubting myself for a second. "I have made my decision to return to Foxworth and that's it. You cannot change my mind."

"George," started Walker, with a tone that reminded me of Taylor's. Or Elijah's. "I'm asking you to think about it, alright? You're leaving behind so many things."

"I am leaving *nothing* behind," I blurted out, tears coming out again. "I didn't have a future then and I'm not even sure I have one now. But by staying in Foxworth at least I can try to make one for myself. I don't want to go back to my sad house and my asshole of a stepdad. And you can't make me."

I covered my face and cried uninterrupted. I could feel Walker's gaze on me and waited for him to say something, but he didn't. He let me get it out for a couple minutes before he spoke again. "I won't make you do anything, George," he said. "I'm asking you to think because I trust you're an adult who can make his own decisions. If you choose to disappear from this world, that is your choice alone. I won't stop you."

"Good," I said, not taking the moment Walker had given me to think of another response. "Because there's no changing my mind."

"Okay," sighed Walker. "There's one more thing I'd like to talk to you about.

Steph, April 19th, morning

Rejoice is a word not very commonly used, because it implies another level of intense happiness that is not usually felt on a daily basis, and not even on special occasions. However, rejoice is what filled Stephanie and her mother as they arrived to her father's room in the hospital to find him whole and breathing, though fast asleep. His right foot was covered in bandages and hanging from a pole next to his bed, a blood transfusion IV attached to his hand, and his face and arms were bloated and bruised. But he was fine.

In the room right next to Dr. Kim was Stephanie's other reason to rejoice. Mercedes Jackson was being treated for the same injuries as Dr. Kim, but was equally stable, which stabilized Steph's breathing for once. Mercedes' family, who Stephanie had never met, were also there, and they all hugged each other when the girl entered the room, as if it was all a big family reunion. Truly, there wasn't much in the way of Stephanie's calm.

noon

Stephanie had fallen asleep alongside her mother in her father's room. What woke her was the sound of activity outside the hallway, with dozens of paramedics entering at once, carrying with them people on stretchers. Stephanie took a glance at the group of people who entered, and instantly recognized the mane of auburn hair that sat on a wheelchair. "Andrea!" she called, but she couldn't hear her with all the commotion.

Steph found it strange not to see any member of the police alongside the paramedics, until she saw a couple of officers speaking with who looked like the Head Nurse at that hospital. Steph approached them. "Excuse me," she said. The officers continued their report to the Head Nurse and ignored her. "Hey," she called, louder.

The young female officer turned to see her. "Miss, we're on official police business." The woman took a quick look at the 'Visitor' sticker on Steph's blouse. "Please go back to the room you're visiting."

"I need to speak with Sgt. Walker, please," insisted Steph. The female officer continued her report with her partner and ignored Steph.

Frustrated, Steph went back to her father's room, where her mom was now awake as well, but he still wasn't. "What's wrong?" asked Evelyn.

"They just brought in the rest," she answered.

"Was George there?" she asked, enthusiastically. Enthusiasm that faded instantly once she saw how Steph's face changed.

"I don't know," she said, tearing up and hugging her mother.

As she sobbed on her mother's jacket, there was a knock on the door. "Come in," said Evelyn. In came the female officer that ignored Steph moments ago.

"Excuse me, Mrs. Kim," said the young officer. "Sgt. Walker would like a word with your daughter."

The two looked at each other as Steph wiped off her tears. "Is everything okay?" asked Evelyn, though Steph was thinking the same thing.

"I was only instructed to get your daughter, ma'am," responded the officer. "We need your verbal consent."

Evelyn looked into her daughter's eyes and saw how worried and hopeless she felt. "You may," said Evelyn. Steph hugged her mother again and left with the officer.

#

The female officer walked Steph down the hallway to the elevators, and pressed the button for the lowest parking level. "Is everything okay?" asked Steph, not sure why. She already knew the officer didn't know anything. But she needed something.

"You'll see soon, miss," she politely replied.

515

The elevator doors opened to an almost empty parking lot. Steph identified a police car in the distance, and a tall black officer leaning against it. The female officer escorted her to the sergeant. "Thanks, Collins. That'll be all," he said. And so she left.

"Good day, Mr. Walker," said Steph, shyly. "How did everything go?"

"Generally speaking, it all went very well," answered the sergeant. "There's something I'd like to show you, if you'd allow me." Walker gave her a moment to answer, and she nodded. "Please get in the back seat and I'll take you there."

Steph swallowed her nerves as Walker walked to the driver's seat and entered the car. Steph grabbed the handle and opened the door. She took a deep breath and went in, only to find that she wasn't alone.

Sitting in the backseat wearing an uncharacteristic tank top, with his right shoulder covered in bandages and right arm hanging on a sling, looking exhausted and beat up, was her best friend. The best friend she feared she'd never see again, that he would be taken in by the police after a huge misunderstanding, or that might have died under horrible circumstances. But he was there, alive and well, and there was not much else to worry anymore.

Epilogue

The quietest days Adler had ever experienced in its history took part between the loudest, marking the disappearance and subsequent recovery of 19 hostages from different backgrounds, ages and professions, including three out of the famous Missing Four of Adler, Minnesota. But it was the story that they carried with them that made everything more unbelievable.

Mayor Robbins reported on the afternoon of April 19th that an anonymous tip given to the Adler Police Department had guided them to the very place where most of the hostages were being kept; this was a small town not 50 miles away from Adler by the name of Foxworth. A place so small and remote and insignificant, it had slowly deteriorated into a ghost town without anybody noticing, except for members of a terrifying, sadistic cult. For lack of a better name, they are now referred to as The Foxworth Cult.

The town of Foxworth, Minnesota was the home of a group of very strange individuals that didn't seem to have a name of their own. It wasn't clear where they had come from nor exactly what they wanted, but it was clear that they were organized and efficient in their resolve, and this is where the first four victims came into the picture.

The official story told by Mayor Robbins, concluded after a long and arduous investigation and interviews with the survivors, told that these cultists planned to use the Adler Spring Festival as a distraction to abduct any passersby they could get their hands on. That is how they first captured the aforementioned Missing Four: Monica Lee, Andrea Clinton, Miles Goodman, and George McKnight.

The prime suspect at hand, a freelancer botanist named Peter Anderson, was first spotted near the scene less than an hour after the abduction, raising the suspicion of the police force, including Sergeant Terrence Walker, who actually knew Anderson in person. It was later revealed through investigative evidence that Anderson was not involved in any sense at first, and was later captured himself by the Foxworth Cult, making him the fifth victim.

The case of Earnest Erb was easily the hardest of them all to figure out. Theories flew in and out, including the possibility that Erb was also part of the cult. Ultimately, the conclusion agreed upon most was that the Erb family were also victims of being in the wrong place at the wrong time. Earnest Erb was likewise captured by the cultists, while his wife Irene and baby boy Jeffrey were likely murdered somewhere in the woods, though their remains have not yet been found. The Erb family are considered the sixth, seventh, and eighth victims.

The attack at the Adler-Morrow General Hospital is one that puzzled the Police Force and the FBI for quite a while, and some remain skeptical and unsure of every conclusion that has been drawn from the investigation. With all the information gathered from the site, surroundings, and later findings, it was concluded that the attack was also perpetrated by The Foxworth Cult, using a variety of makeshift explosives, stolen vehicles, and chaos caused by a lightning storm nearby. It is yet unknown how they managed to capture sixteen people with almost no signs of brute force, but the witnesses' lack of memory of the events imply that they were probably under the influences of chemicals like chloroform, which would fit the cult's low-end ways.

It is believed that the previously-captured victims were part of the attack at the hospital, probably being forced to perform actions against their will by their kidnappers. This helps explain the presence of DNA from two of the victims, George McKnight and Peter Anderson, and gives perspective on how the body of Earnest Erb ended up in the hospital grounds at the end of the night, most likely killed by the cultists after a failed attempt to bend his will.

The lead that brought the police to the town of Foxworth remains completely anonymous with no way of finding out any kind of details about it. Some believe it to be a member of the cult, others suggest it may have been an escaped hostage that managed to communicate with the outside world. Regardless, the timing for the discovery of the town was as fortunate as could be, since it was right before the members of the cult decided to flee the town and leave almost every hostage behind, possibly to die. Or possibly, their migration was caused because of the leak.

A very late spring arrived with the discovery of the hostages in Foxworth. First responders took in a total of 19 people, including every single one of those who disappeared from Adler-Morrow General. Monica Lee, first rescued out of the Missing Four, was also the first to give declarations to the press, asking for privacy and peace for her and her peers who had gone through unimaginable horrors that she, naturally, did not want to share. Later that same day, Andrea Clinton and Miles Goodman were rescued from Foxworth, the latter in critical condition from what is suspected to be a violent beating mere hours before his rescue. Sadly, it was reported that, though many DNA samples were present all over the scene, George McKnight was nowhere to be found in or around Foxworth. It is believed, though testimony and investigations have yet to prove this with certainty, that he was taken by the Foxworth Cult to wherever they settled after abandoning the town.

Though the remains of Peter Anderson were never found, it was concluded through matching witness accounts that he had been murdered by the cultists some three days prior to the rescue mission. Accounts from Andrea Clinton and Monica Lee recalled Anderson as a brave and kind soul who never stopped trying to save them until the very end, which provoked a very strong apology from the Adler Police Department.

Smaller parts of the case were resolved or figured out as time went by and the investigation came to an end. It was concluded that a small team of cultists were the ones who broke into the Police Department and stole their case's evidence, slowing down the operation even further. Officer Alan Maffei, who had disappeared a month prior, was believed to have been killed by the Foxworth Cult in an early attempt to start their operation, along with Barbara Hawkins, who disappeared shortly before Maffei with absolutely no traces of her remains. Maffei's remains, however, were found shortly after the recovery of the hostages, not far from Adler's limits. It is yet unknown how this turn of events occurred, especially considering the state of Maffei's body, which implied that he had been kept alive for about a month before his death. A new investigation has been opened regarding him.

Jefferson High School did not have much time to celebrate the return of their missing students, as they were compelled to lament the disappearance of George McKnight. Another, smaller investigation was opened for him, with key witnesses of the Missing Four, along with his best friend Stephanie Kim. The young man's stepfather, Robert Gil, was again found to be completely useless as an asset on the investigation, unable to give a concrete opinion on McKnight's attitude towards joining a cult.

Many more questions were still in the mind of the people of Adler during the days following the recovery of the hostages. But as the 19 people recovered physically from their horrible times, there was an incurable scar in the town of Adler, one that would haunt it for the remainder of its days.

#

Deep inside the woods is a boy. He wakes up every morning to run for an hour without stopping. Sometimes he runs without any direction, for exercise, but many times he runs forward, away from the past. Not all the time, but sometimes, many times. From his decisions, others' decisions, and no decisions alike. He runs, sometimes crawls, other times he walks, but he never stays down nor does he turn back. At times he forgets he is not alone, and relies solely on himself. But he works on fixing that every single day. He knows the day will come, and it will be the day he's stopped being a boy.
And become a hunter.

9 798838 745811